Praise for *Always Look Twice*

"This is a gripping romance and mystery that will keep readers turning pages."

Parkersburg News & Sentinel

"Elizabeth Goddard has done it again! So many spectacular lines and scenes throughout this book make it a can't-miss for romantic suspense readers."

Write-Read-Life

"Before opening this book, brace yourself. Elizabeth Goddard has a knack for leaving you breathless while stealing your heart at the same time."

The Suspense Zone

Praise for *Never Let Go*

"*Never Let Go* is a unique and intriguing romantic suspense that will have your heart racing. Goddard's fast-paced storytelling combined with emotional depth will keep you guessing until the very end."

Rachel Dylan, bestselling author
of the Atlanta Justice series

"From the riveting opening to the satisfying conclusion, *Never Let Go* is a stellar beginning to what promises to be a thrilling romantic suspense series."

Susan Sleeman, bestselling and award-winning
author of the White Knights series

"Fast-paced and suspenseful, *Never Let Go* lives up to its name. It grabs you by the throat from the first page, takes you through riveting twists and turns, and doesn't let go until a powerhouse ending. Goddard has a lethal way with words and characters. She's an author to watch—and love!"

Ronie Kendig, bestselling author of The Tox Files series

"A twenty-one-year-old cold case, arson, murder, romance . . . I couldn't put *Never Let Go* down until 'The End,' and then I wished for more."

Patricia Bradley, winner of the Inspirational Readers Choice Award

"Wow! *Never Let Go* has everything I want in a romantic suspense novel. Heart-pounding action, a second-chance romance, and a frightening cold case that won't let you put the book down until the very last page."

Lisa Harris, bestselling author

"With deception at every turn, danger behind every door, and a romance that was and could be again, Goddard has crafted an edge-of-your-seat experience with *Never Let Go* that hooks readers from the first page and holds them tight until the satisfying and surprising conclusion."

Lynn H. Blackburn, award-winning and bestselling author of the Dive Team Investigations series

DON'T KEEP
SILENT

Books by Elizabeth Goddard

Uncommon Justice Series

Never Let Go
Always Look Twice
Don't Keep Silent

UNCOMMON
JUSTICE
BOOK 3

DON'T KEEP SILENT

ELIZABETH GODDARD

Revell

a division of Baker Publishing Group
Grand Rapids, Michigan

© 2020 by Elizabeth Goddard

Published by Revell
a division of Baker Publishing Group
PO Box 6287, Grand Rapids, MI 49516-6287
www.revellbooks.com

Printed in the United States of America

Library of Congress Cataloging-in-Publication Data
Names: Goddard, Elizabeth, author.
Title: Don't keep silent / Elizabeth Goddard.
Other titles: Do not keep silent
Description: Grand Rapids, Michigan : Revell, a division of Baker Publishing
    Group, [2020] | Series: Uncommon justice; [book 3]
Identifiers: LCCN 2019041862 | ISBN 9780800729868 (paperback)
Subjects: GSAFD: Suspense fiction.
Classification: LCC PS3607.O324 D66 2020 | DDC 813/.6—dc23
LC record available at https://lccn.loc.gov/2019041862

ISBN: 978-0-8007-3862-4 (hardcover)

20 21 22 23 24 25 26   7 6 5 4 3 2

To Jonathan—

I adore how much you love the Lord, your devotion to him, and the way you answer his call to spread the good news, never fearing what others might think as you kneel to pray in the middle of a busy hospital or, when at the grocery store, ask a complete stranger if you can pray for him. You were born to do what others fear doing. Stand firm. God is with you.

Speak up for those who cannot speak for themselves,
    for the rights of all who are destitute.
Speak up and judge fairly;
    defend the rights of the poor and needy.

Proverbs 31:8–9

———————

Where there is much light, the shadows are deepest.

Johann Wolfgang von Goethe

PROLOGUE

Had we never met, you and I, then you never would have loved me. I never would have returned your love.

And now look at us. I've caused you trouble. Brought you pain. All I wanted to do was protect you. Please forgive me. Please know that I love you.

Loved you.

Her identification stripped, she signed her full name and added her address for good measure. She tucked the note into her jeans, her last words—if it came to that—meant to give him closure.

Her abductor thought that by hiding her here in the middle of nowhere, surrounded by this frozen world, she would be trapped.

For the average person, that was true.

With no internet or communication devices, she couldn't cause more trouble. In this rustic getaway cabin meant for the privileged, she'd been left with only what was required to sustain her life until

Don't Keep Silent

he arrived. He knew from experience her capabilities and vowed he wouldn't underestimate her again.

But all the same, he'd miscalculated.

Glancing through the small window, she took in the deep snow surrounding her and made her own calculations. He didn't understand that she would rather face certain death—woman versus nature, as it were—than face *him*. She wouldn't come out of that meeting alive, so her chances were better out there on the frozen lake surrounded by millions of acres of pristine, snow-blanketed mountain wilderness.

Considering how the cabin had been richly furnished, she was surprised that more work from local artists didn't grace the walls. The only art was the immaculate carving in the cedar logs—a surprisingly accurate depiction of a popular geothermal pool titled *Morning Glory Pool*—but she couldn't use that in her escape or for a weapon. Maybe the décor had been removed for her stay. Still, some things remained or had been overlooked—like the vintage snowshoes used as sconces—and that had given her hope.

All I need is an ounce.

After removing the snowshoes from the wall, she layered old newspapers underneath her clothes for added warmth. Then she grabbed some wool blankets from the closet and a Nordic-style comforter from the bed. Travel would be cumbersome and slow. The longer she could last out there, the better. Nonetheless, she would probably die from exposure.

But at least her death would be on her own terms.

She clenched her jaw. She couldn't—*wouldn't*—let him win.

Blowing out a long breath, she forced the tension from her muscles. Unfortunately, she'd had to wait until the two men who'd been tasked with guarding her had left on the snowmobiles—the only way to get in or out of this winter getaway. That meant darkness would drop on her world within the hour.

Her watchers had not considered her a "flight risk," as they called it. After all, without adequate protection, who would trek into the frozen mountain wilderness during the day, much less at night?

That had been the minions' first mistake. All she'd needed was one.

She drew in a quick breath and opened the door. Bitter cold whipped around her, sending snow into the small dwelling and stinging her cheeks.

Her throat constricted.

For a moment, she reconsidered her decision. But she had no real options. She repositioned the wool blanket to cover her face, all except for her eyes, and pulled the comforter tighter around the other blankets. The layers would keep her warm but slow her down.

The men had shoveled the snow away from the door so they could venture to their snowmobiles to fetch the man behind her abduction. Now she would use the cleared path for her escape, though no snowmobile waited to carry her away to safety. She'd have to depend on her own two legs.

She took a step. Then another. And another. The snowshoes held and, leaving the shoveled path, she hopped on top of the white crust and kept walking. The tears streaming from her eyes could be tears of joy or pure fear, she wasn't sure.

The wind pushed against her forward movement as if telling her to go back, whispering certain death in her ear.

Was she making a mistake?

No. Death waited for her at the cabin if she didn't leave. She eyed the frozen lake topped with many layers of white frosting. It was much quicker to cross here than to go all the way around. Nothing but mountain ranges were at her back. She wasn't going over those.

She wouldn't make it around the lake before dark, maybe not even across it. If she made it across at all, then she would face miles of wilderness.

The thought almost paralyzed her. Maybe she should go back. She glanced over her shoulder at the cabin.

No—her only hope was out there. Another dwelling. A hunter. A snowmobiler. A forest ranger. Even a forest road. Someone else was out there. Earlier in the day, she'd heard rifle fire. A snowmobile. *Another ounce of hope.*

Her kidnapper didn't realize her drive to live.

She took one step after another, willing herself to keep moving. Willing herself to survive. Unfortunately, with the deep snow she couldn't be sure what she was stepping on. March could warm the ice beneath the snow cover, creating treacherous breaks.

She plodded on, gasping for breath with each lumbering step. A half hour. An hour. Her movements kept her warm. If she stopped, she would die. She had to keep moving until she found shelter or help. The temperature dropped as night fell, but at least the moon lit her path so she could see the far shore that stretched before her.

There is still hope . . .

A crack resounded, and she stopped, feeling it to her bones.

The white powder covering the sheet of ice beneath her shifted.

And she knew how this would end a split second before the surface beneath her fell away.

CHAPTER ONE

TWO DAYS EARLIER
TUESDAY, 8:43 A.M.
DENVER, COLORADO

Dread warred with hope as Rae Burke shivered in the cold outside on the porch. The curtains remained drawn at the quaint home that her brother, Alan, shared with his wife, Zoey, and their adorable four-year-old daughter, Callie.

Rae knocked again, and a moment later the door cracked open enough for her to slip inside the dark house. Her brother remained in the shadows. She flipped on lights without asking permission. Better. Now the home had become warm and cozy. Nothing seemed amiss except for her brother, the consummate professional. She'd rarely seen him in sweats.

Rae dropped her purse on the foyer table and shrugged out of her coat. She paused to take a long look at him. Bloodshot eyes stared at her from an unshaven face.

"You couldn't sleep."

Pursing his lips, he shook his head. "Of course not. How could I?"

"Oh, Alan." She hugged him like only a sister could.

Keeping a hold on his arms, she took a step back. "I'm assuming you called the police."

He shook her off and rubbed his neck. "Yes, I called them. Of course, they wanted to know if we'd had an argument or if this was unusual behavior for her." He gave Rae a knowing look. Zoey had disappeared in the past, but that was before she had married Alan.

"How long has she been gone?" Maybe Zoey had needed respite. Caring for a child with special needs could be draining.

He glanced at his watch. "Long enough. Callie is Zoey's world. Callie is our world."

Rae nodded. "Zoey never would have left her. She never would have left *you*, Alan. Tell me what happened."

"Zoey dropped Callie off at behavioral therapy at nine in the morning. Her therapist called me at one. I brought Callie home, thinking I would find Zoey had fallen asleep. That she'd been taking a nap and slept through her alarm. I called her cell and texted, but she didn't respond." Alan paced the open living area. Shelves filled with early readers and books on raising children with autism lined the walls. "Her car wasn't here."

Deep frown lines carved into his ragged face. "Her last known cell location was here at home. But clearly, she's not here. So her battery died or she turned her cell off. I don't know. But I waited for her to come home or contact me. I hoped that she would return with a reasonable explanation. I called her friends. I called you. Finally, I called the police. I explained everything to them so they would understand that Zoey would never leave her daughter, but I had still given her time to get home."

Why hadn't Alan called Rae sooner? Hurt skated across her heart, but she shook it off. She could easily guess. Alan had hoped Zoey would return and Rae would never need to know—she'd warned him, after all. Zoey's disappearance could elicit an "I told you so."

"The only good news is that the police are taking me seriously now since she didn't come home last night. I wanted to call you before you saw something on the news."

"And you asked the neighbors what they saw?"

"Of course! What do you think?"

She hadn't meant to upset him. He was on edge, so she wouldn't react. Rae moved to the kitchen to make coffee. She doubted Alan had eaten. She looked in the refrigerator and found eggs. Bread for toast. Some jam. No bacon.

"What are you doing?"

"I'm cooking breakfast. You need to keep up your strength. Besides, Callie will be hungry when she—" Rae glanced around the house. "Is she at therapy or school?"

His face darkened. "I kept her home."

"Won't that mess with her routine?"

"I'll keep her routine the same as much as possible. This is why I can't do anything to find Zoey!" Alan whispered the emotion-filled words. Frustration and fear poured from him. "I can't drive around town looking for her. Callie needs me. She wants her mother. She asked for her constantly last night. Zoey was the one to read to her. I took up that honor, but Callie wasn't happy and tossed and turned all night."

Rae stirred together the eggs she'd cracked into a bowl. Zoey was a vegan—the eggs were for Alan—so Rae hadn't found milk to stir into the eggs. Not even soy or almond milk. The refrigerator should have been loaded with fruits and vegetables but was oddly sparse. Zoey had been distracted before she disappeared.

Alan continued to pace and vent and maybe even unravel completely. "She wants her mother, and I can't give her that."

A fist squeezed Rae's heart. "And you want your wife."

At some point, if Zoey didn't return or they didn't find her, or maybe even if they *did* find her—depending on *how* they found her—the police would look at Alan. They would suspect he was responsible for whatever happened to his wife.

That news story ran somewhere in this country just about every day of the week. Husband kills wife. Hides the truth. Rae kept that to herself. Alan didn't need one more thing to worry about.

She glanced at her still-pacing brother. He wasn't a killer.

Zoey wasn't dead.

She had to be alive. Rae wouldn't accept any other outcome—for her brother's sake. For Callie's sake.

The first seventy-two hours were critical in finding a missing person, the first forty-eight key before the clues and evidence started to go cold.

After putting the bread in the toaster, Rae scrambled the eggs. "Look, I know this is grasping at straws, but it's worth a try. Maybe she went home to see her mother. I know the police asked you if you two had argued and you told them no. But it's just me here. Did you fight?"

"No. We didn't fight." But the way Alan said the words, the slight nuance that edged his tone, gave her pause.

As an investigative journalist who interviewed those who often tried to hide the truth, she'd trained herself to watch for such distinctions. Still, Alan wasn't a liar. He wouldn't hurt Zoey even in a moment of anger. He was gentle. Those characteristics had drawn Zoey to him in the first place. If he was hiding something from Rae now, it had to be because any disagreement he'd had with his wife was a private matter.

"Okay, well, did you call her mom?" she asked.

"No."

Rae had never learned why Zoey didn't speak to her mom. But had Zoey shared her secrets with Alan?

Rae wasn't sure what to say next, so she busied herself with plating the eggs. Alan would have eventually cooked breakfast for Callie. He wouldn't forget to care for his daughter in the midst of this crisis, would he? She set a slice of toast on each plate along with the jam, then looked down the hallway.

Though Rae wasn't hungry, Alan might feel compelled to join her if she ate too. "Breakfast is ready. Should we wake Callie to eat?"

He glanced at the clock and quickly shook his head. "She ate earlier. Cheerios and the last of the almond milk. Then I put her in her room to play, but she fell asleep, so I put her in bed. I don't know if this will mess with her schedule too much, but since she didn't sleep well last night, she needs the rest. And I need the break. Callie has certain things she eats in certain ways." He eyed the eggs, then he glanced at Rae but said nothing more.

Had she made them wrong? Rae sagged. "I only meant to help. But you and I can eat. How about that?"

"How can I eat?"

"You have to stay strong for Callie, if not for Zoey." Rae slid into a chair at the table, hoping Alan would join her.

Frowning, he nodded. He approached the table and slowly sat, staring at the plate as if he looked right through it.

Rae played with the eggs on her plate and felt utterly ridiculous for thinking that either of them would eat. "Do you want me to stay here and help with Callie? I can do that." It wasn't like she had an actual paying job at the moment. Even if she did, she would drop everything to help her brother.

And Zoey. Her friend. *Oh, God, please* . . . There were no words to speak, even from her heart.

"No. Callie needs me if she can't have Zoey. At least for now. I want to make everything as normal for her as possible. I'm trying to keep up the pretense that her mother is gone to visit a friend."

"Do you think Callie knows something is wrong?"

"I'll keep her occupied so she doesn't have time to sense how seriously wrong things are. But that won't last. I don't know how she'll react. Kids like Callie are—"

"It's okay, Alan. You don't have to explain. This news would be hard on *any* child." Fear hollowed her out. "I want to help. What can I do? Anything. Name it."

Alan scooped eggs up with his fork. Like her, he pretended to eat, moving food around on his plate without ever actually taking a bite.

When he finally spoke, he choked on his words. "You warned me that she had secrets. That's what you said about the time she went missing for days when you were her roommate. Maybe her sudden disappearance now has something to do with then. I can't help but hope it does and that she'll come back to me. Come back to us."

That he'd connected the two incidents revealed Alan's desperation. When he lifted his eyes to her, Rae thought she could read his mind.

"You want *me* . . . You want me to search for her?"

"You investigate for a living. I know investigative reporting is different than, say, if you were a detective, but in some ways it's the same. You're like Dad was."

"Nothing like Dad." Their father had been an award-winning journalist, a foreign affairs correspondent. He'd stood up for the voiceless, exposing the evils of the world until those evils finally killed him, silencing his voice. She tried to follow in his steps—except for the dying part. Instead, she let everyone down.

"Yes. Yes, you are. The war zones, the battles you've faced are different, sure, but you find people, Rae. You find their stories."

Not anymore. She'd spent years writing exposés, only to be tossed aside after the "debacle," as her boss had called it. Well, that debacle might have produced a story that could have won her awards if things had taken a different turn. She focused back on the moment. "Did you tell the police about the time she disappeared before?"

"I've told them everything. I have nothing to hide."

Rae tapped the table.

"Rae, you never told me details about that time she disappeared in college."

"That's because I don't know anything." At least anything that would have made any difference then—or make any difference now. Rae forced herself to chew the eggs that had become cold and rubbery, and Alan followed suit. Good. At least her efforts to get him eating weren't for nothing.

And maybe she *could* investigate like he requested, and those efforts would make a difference too. "Mom. Does she know about this?"

"I've dreaded telling her."

"Call her. She'll come up and help with Callie." Mom lived in Texas now, working as a secretary for an oil and gas executive.

Rae glanced at the TV. Alan had the sound turned down. The news captioned a story about remains being identified. He normally enjoyed watching nature and science shows but was probably watching the news because of Zoey's disappearance. Rae knew one thing—if Zoey didn't come home soon, reporters would start to line the street. Detectives would be in Alan and Zoey's home asking questions and searching. His and Callie's lives would be turned upside down even more.

What was this going to do to Callie's regimen? Her gut churned.

"And Rae . . ."

She looked at Alan.

"Remember."

She'd never heard Alan sound so defeated. She forced confidence into her tone for his sake. "Remember what?"

"If you do this, remember that this isn't a story. This isn't for a Pulitzer Prize. This is our family. It's my wife—whatever secrets she has."

Regret squeezed her lungs. Rae understood. "No, it's not a story, Alan. I hope you know me better than that."

"I hope so too."

Rae also hoped Zoey would return on her own like she had the last time she'd disappeared. Zoey had survived an unspeakable trauma, and then she met Alan on the heels of that.

Rae suspected that Zoey had been the victim of abuse or a stalker before. Zoey never wanted to talk about her childhood home or her family, stating she would never go back. And now, though Rae tried to believe the best about Zoey's current disappearance, she feared the worst. Zoey was suffering, or she was already gone.

Alan pushed away his plate. "I think you should start by going to Jackson Hole and talking to her mother. Find her. She could have moved, for all I know. Zoey's father died a long time ago. That's all she shared about her life before. It's like she wanted to forget about her past. Hide from it. And after what she'd been through, I never questioned her about why she moved to Colorado. We put all our hopes in the present and future and put the past behind us. We even eloped so there was no pressure to invite the people from her past. And now, looking back, I realize that was a mistake. I should have pressed her for more information. Pressed her to include them."

"You can't think that you made a mistake when you married her. You can't."

"I love her. Love covers a multitude of sins, right? I didn't make a mistake. Callie isn't a mistake. I could have done things differently. So now, I'm going to do something. I think starting with her mother is a good place to begin. It's all I can think to do."

Rae's throat tightened. She should avoid being within a thousand miles of Jackson Hole. That valley was the current residence of the reason for her financial, emotional, and psychological woes. The source of the daily pain in her chest.

Alan watched her as if he sensed her hesitation and waited for confirmation. Was she willing to do this? The police would do everything in their power to find her sister-in-law, but Rae knew from experience that their efforts couldn't save the day every time. There was simply too much ground to cover. Too many criminals.

Rae closed her eyes and exhaled.

What should I do? What should I do? Am I the right person to take on such an enormous task? What if she let Alan down? Callie? Zoey.

"Why don't *you* call her mom, then?" Rae asked.

"And say what? This is your son-in-law? Your daughter is missing?"

"I see your point." Zoey's mom wouldn't know him from Adam. "Still, I think you should make that call."

Alan scraped his hands through his hair, then cracked a sob. Finally, he lifted his face, his eyes meeting hers. "I don't know how to reach her. Even if I did, I can't talk coherently at the moment. Rae, if you don't help me, who else will? I mean, besides the police. Besides the media that will eventually blast her face everywhere. I feel so helpless. I want to be out there looking, searching, but the truth is, that never was my thing. I'm not good at that even if I'm desperately looking for my wife. But it's *your* thing. You *are* good. If you don't do this—"

"All right. All right."

Rae stood and gathered their dishes to place in the sink.

"Just . . . let me think."

Alan approached. "It can't hurt to have one more person digging into things. In fact, if you need me to help you research, I'll do what I can. But remember, my time will be limited since I'm caring for Callie."

"You would have made Dad proud, Alan." She offered a tenuous smile. "You might not be an investigative journalist, but you do *think* like one."

"I'm no journalist. You got those genes. I'm a nerd. A computer geek. You know that."

Rae opened her mouth—

"Save it. I already searched her personal laptop. I know how to look, Rae. There's nothing there except research about autism and everything she can do to help her little girl grow up and live

21

a happy life. On her work computer, I confirmed nothing more than the part-time work she does for the cyber-security software company. I searched before I even called the police." He held Rae's gaze. "Not that I didn't trust her, but I had to look first."

Of course Alan had looked. Rae had often suspected one of the big reasons Zoey and Alan had hit it off so well was that they were both computer geeks.

"The police will want to look too. They'll look at all the calls she's made. Any digital trails she's left."

As much as Rae hoped that Zoey would walk through the front door any moment now, a sixth sense told her it wouldn't happen any time soon—if it *ever* did.

"There's one more thing you need to know before you search for her mother." Alan slid back into the chair at the kitchen table.

"What's that?"

"I've learned something about her past. The police told me there's no record of a Zoey Dumont who moved to Colorado from Wyoming. No Zoey Dumont who fits her description lived in Jackson Hole. Zoey Dumont isn't her birth name."

"Then who *is* your wife?"

He blew out a long breath. "I wish I knew."

CHAPTER TWO

Alan stared at the door his sister had exited. She was going to do what *he* should do—look for his wife. But he had other considerations.

His entire world felt as if it were folding in on itself. At the moment, he was so wiped out that he wasn't sure he could tell fact from fiction.

"Daddy?"

Ah—his most important consideration. Definitely fact.

Callie held on to a stuffed panda bear. She'd always preferred stuffed animals to dolls. She preferred the softness—a sensory thing—to the harder plastic from which dolls were made. Her room was painted pink and decorated with panda decals. Who knew one could purchase bedspreads and curtains covered in fat black-and-white bears. She crept toward him, rubbing her big blue eyes. Her long blonde curls had tangled during her nap. Even tangled, they were soft, so soft.

He loved hearing the way she called him Daddy and was grateful that she could at least speak. Some children with autism were nonverbal. He should have woken her earlier to better keep with her schedule, but he needed to make sure he and Rae had time to discuss Zoey without Callie overhearing their conversation.

She climbed onto his lap. She had her mother's eyes—no doubt there.

Zoey had finished college while they were married and she was pregnant with Callie. She'd only had a few credit hours left to earn her degree. When Callie was born, Zoey wanted to stay home with her and love and protect her as long as she could. With his tech job, they could afford that luxury. He loved being able to provide for them. Still, Zoey worked part-time, claiming it kept her mind sharp.

To hide the turmoil rolling inside, he smiled for Callie. Callie's eyes were bright and innocent. In that way, they were far different from Zoey's. He'd always sensed a murkiness in his wife that came with keeping the past behind her. He wanted to shield and protect her from the demons that haunted her.

He choked on the thought.

Protect them . . . Protect Zoey.

Right.

Zoey was gone.

For all any of them knew, Callie could be missing now too if she hadn't been in therapy. He hugged her again, grateful that she wasn't opposed to hugs. She was on the too-social end of the spectrum, easily warming to strangers, hugging them or even going along with them. Everyone was worthy of Callie's love. Everyone was welcomed into her world.

He kissed the top of her head and willed the surging tears back into place. He would protect her from *his* dark emotions as well.

After a while, the way her body went limp and comfortable against him made him think Callie had gone back to sleep. But then she lifted her face to stare at him. "Mommy. I want Mommy."

Emotional pain—much worse than anything he'd ever experienced—lanced through him. He couldn't take this. But he had no choice.

"I know, sweetheart." He snuggled her for a few moments, then tickled her, and she giggled, giving him the response he needed. Joyous laughter spilled from the small bundle—an amazing, miraculous creation.

But tickles and snuggles and excuses would only last so long.

If Zoey didn't return soon, he had no idea what he was going to do. He couldn't bear to think that something nefarious had happened to her. Deep inside, he somehow sensed she was still alive. Like the sense Mom always had that Dad was okay, until he wasn't. That day, she'd had a sense of loss. Then they heard that he'd been killed along with the soldiers he was traveling with.

Alan knew finding Zoey's vehicle would go a long way in learning where she had gone. Or if she'd been abducted.

He braced for the possibility that he might become a suspect in his wife's disappearance.

God, please don't let it come to that. For Callie's sake. She's so sweet and innocent. Just a child. She doesn't deserve to have her world rocked.

But what child ever deserved the loss of a parent? Yet that tragedy happened every day. His reporter sister had told him enough about the evils of this world—it boggled his mind. His father had exposed those truths too. A person would have to be completely unaware of the world around them not to understand the unimaginable evil waiting in the shadows.

If the police decided to invade Alan's life and arrest him, what would happen to Callie? He was innocent, but he'd heard those stories too—innocent men sent to prison. Dying at the hands of capital punishment. If the worst happened, Mom or Rae could take Callie, but Alan wanted to be the one to raise his daughter. He wanted to love his wife.

God, please let Zoey return safe and sound and unharmed.

And then when she did, then and only then, could Alan fall apart.

CHAPTER THREE

Liam McKade wasn't there for fun.

Skiers crowded into the Saddleback Mountain Café. They had their helmets and jackets off as they gulped down egg sandwiches and spicy hash browns—the breakfast of champions—to fuel their escapades on the mountain and power them through a morning of downhill delight.

Sure, he'd taken to the slopes early this morning—the first time in ten years. An ache that hadn't been there the last time he'd skied coursed through his entire body and throbbed most profoundly in his leg—that, from an on-the-job injury he'd received months ago. Full recovery would take time, he'd been told. The injury that haunted him was at least something he had in common with his brother Heath.

Still, too much time had passed between when he'd skied like a maniac when he was young and now. He'd have to work back up to his previous skill level. That is, if he lived a different life and had the time to focus on that endeavor. At thirty-one, he was still trying to figure out his place in this world. For the first time in a long time, he'd prayed for God to open doors and direct his path. It was a starting point.

Liam snagged a booth as patrons left. He was waiting for an old friend who wanted to catch up. Brad Whitfield was the man behind Saddleback Mountain Ski Resort. This had been his dream. Since coming back to the valley region of Jackson Hole last summer, Liam had put off his friend for as long as he could.

Brad was proud of his accomplishments, and Liam should wish him well and congratulate him. That would be easier if he were in the right frame of mind.

I'll get there.

He just needed time. It had already been months. How much time did someone need to come back from a near-death experience? Figuring out what he was going to be when he grew up would go a long way in his recovery—that and forgetting the face of the woman who'd blown his cover and filleted his heart.

When a man slid into the seat across from him, Liam almost protested. Recognition hit him slowly. It was in the eyes. Brad's face had filled out and grown wider. Was that due to his thick beard? Brad was the same age as Liam, but Brad's leathery skin made him look much older. He seemed to take in Liam's appearance too. Did Liam look different as well? If anything, the change would be in his eyes.

Brad's mouth spread into a wide grin. He reached across the table and shook Liam's hand. "It's been a long time, my friend." He caught a waitress's attention as she passed the booth. "Could you bring us coffee, Maggie?" Brad glanced at Liam. "What'll it be?"

"Strong."

"I'll have the same. Thanks, Maggie." Brad turned his attention back to Liam.

"Eh. Not that long. Thirteen years. Give or take." Liam returned the grin. To escape the drama of his home life with an alcoholic father and the perpetual state of grief he and his brothers lived in after their mother had died in a fire, Liam joined the marines. Then, somehow, he found himself waging war in a different battle and worked for the DEA—Drug Enforcement Administration.

He'd been in Jackson Hole for months. Why had he waited so long to get together with Brad?

A million memories of the two of them tearing up the slopes carved through his mind.

"I'm glad you could meet me." The skin around Brad's eyes crinkled. "As soon as I heard you were back in town, I knew I wanted you for this job. But the timing had to be right. Well, and I wanted to see you in person first. You know, just to make sure you're the same man you were. I see in your eyes that you are."

If you only knew. Liam chuckled. He must still be working undercover if Brad thought he was the same guy. He had definitely changed. But appearances could fool.

"Wait. What job?" Liam stiffened but leaned back to disguise his discomfort. He hadn't expected to walk into a job offer or . . . was this an interview?

Maggie returned quickly with two steaming coffees. "Here you go, gentlemen."

Brad winked at her, then smiled at Liam.

Liam sipped the black coffee and studied Brad as he talked. Liam couldn't help but watch him in that analytical sort of way that law enforcement studied people. They'd been best friends for most of Liam's life growing up here in the valley—at least that he could remember. He wished he didn't get a strange vibe from his longtime friend. He wished a lot of things.

He wished he'd taken a different path so he could shake the cloud that seemed to follow him everywhere.

"Liam?" Brad narrowed his eyes.

Liam suddenly realized that Brad had been explaining the job and he'd tuned the guy out.

"You seem a million miles away," Brad said.

Liam sucked in a breath. "Yeah, sorry."

"Is everything okay?" Brad asked.

Liam was blowing it already. "Sure."

Brad leveled his gaze. "You're staying at the ranch, right?"

"Yep."

"With Heath?"

"Yep."

"Emerald M has a nice reputation. Though this is our second ski season, it's our grand opening. We've gotten a few Emerald M guests here to ski."

"The ranch isn't open in the winter." Not yet.

"I meant referrals. Heath has been good to refer those looking to come back to the valley to ski. We'd love everyone to stay here at Saddleback, but I've been talking to Heath about opening up his place for the winter."

"So he told me." But not that it had been at Brad's urging.

"He's a good man. But if I remember correctly, you never got along with him that well before. Maybe that's what's eating at you."

"Nothing's eating at me. Heath and I are fine now. *I'm* fine." His smile was too big. Yep. He was still working undercover, settling into a persona. "Heath got married a few months back, by the way. And Austin's married."

Yep. It was time for Liam to move on. He'd come home hoping to forget what had gone wrong, but while trying to fit into Heath's idea of a good life, Liam realized he didn't know where home truly was for him.

Where is home? He didn't fit in anywhere anymore.

"How about you?" Liam asked.

"Married and divorced now. I have a daughter. Mom and Dad still live outside of Jackson." Brad chugged his coffee. "You married?"

"Never married. No kids." Liam was ready to move on to the next topic. "Thank you for asking me here. Let me hear more about the job."

Liam almost found himself hoping this would be a door God was opening for him.

Brad chuckled, giving Liam a look that said he hoped he listened this time. "Look, we're small now—thirty-five runs on two hundred acres—but we have plans to grow. The job is for security here at the resort." Brad leaned closer. "I know you have more experience than what's required of just a regular security guard."

Right. A high school diploma was all that had been required in the past, but Liam suspected much had changed. "Then what's this about?"

"You'd be head of security. Responsible for everything that goes on here—the policing and the investigations arm of the resort. I've learned a lot since opening this place—there are a lot of hoops to jump through. Business licenses. Forest service and backcountry leases and permits. Running a restaurant, rental shop, ski school, and ski patrol. I need someone with experience to run security. Someone who isn't a seasonal worker. You live here now. You know this valley, the mountains, the people, and how to keep them safe." He held Liam's gaze. "I want you in this with me. What do you say?"

Liam toyed with his cell. "I'm thinking . . ."

"Well, think hard and fast. This place is going to grow. I can feel it." Brad grinned. "Oh, and get this. Thanks to one of my investor's connections, someone who makes movies for YouTube contacted me earlier today and wants to make a movie about starting a ski resort. Can you believe it?"

Liam laughed with him and shook his head. He averted his gaze to look out the window. Skiers in brightly colored gear zigzagged down the white slopes.

Brad clasped his hands in front of him. "If you think you're interested, you'll need to meet a few of the people who've invested in this dream."

Liam wondered how Brad had pulled this off. "What have you told them about me, if anything?"

"While other resorts are going so far as using actual police to watch for drunk skiers, or people who venture farther than they should go in the backcountry, we don't want that here. Just so you know, resort security isn't a walk in the park." He took a sip of his coffee. "I told them I knew a guy."

"I appreciate the vote of confidence, Brad. I really do." Liam kept his smile in place. Brad's presentation definitely intrigued him. "But for one thing, I don't have hospitality experience."

"You'll be great. I want someone I know and trust. Look, we lost our guy last week—hence the right timing to approach you—but that means I need someone who can get up to speed, and fast. And if you'd been in the valley last year when we were hiring, you would have been my first pick then."

"Okay. Give me some time to think on it. Plus, I need to talk to Heath. He's counting on me to help with the ranch."

And Austin wanted Liam to work with him in private investigations.

Liam hadn't imagined he would have so many offers. But he didn't think he was cut out to drive a snow sleigh once Heath finally opened for the winter or guide guests at the ranch through the wilderness in the summer.

Nor was he inclined to return to his previous job facing criminals in the underworld of narcotics with the DEA. After the injury and blown cover, he had remained on medical leave, accepting his due of money from the government until he finally resigned.

Kelvin, his old friend in the DEA who'd been promoted to ASAC, Assistant Special Agent in Charge, had hoped Liam would change his mind and come back, so that door remained open. He suspected that's why Kelvin had called him. Liam hadn't returned that call.

Brad's cell rang, drawing his attention. Liam was relieved he was no longer the focus. Before Brad took the call, he smiled at Liam. "Listen, this would get you out of the ranch, if you'd prefer that. I don't mean to presume. But you could thrive in this environment. Think of the old days when we dreamed of running a ski resort."

It had only been a dream—one of many to take him away from his troubled home environment.

"I'll give you my answer soon."

Brad nodded. "Fair enough. Need to take this call. It's the You-Tube people again."

He slid from the booth as he took the call.

Liam finished his now tepid coffee but remained in the booth. The ski crowd had thinned out a little as skiers got back to the slopes they loved, but the lunch wave would hit soon. Another round of skiing might be just what Liam needed today to distract him from those who wanted him to make decisions. Skiing would require all his concentration. He could leave behind everything wrong with his world.

He glanced through the large doorway that opened up to the great room of the resort. Across the way, he spotted her.

His ribs caved in with a whoosh of air. His mind zoomed back to that moment when he'd woken up in a ditch and stared up at the overcast sky, drops of rain warning him of an impending storm that would threaten to drown him where he'd been left to die.

As life had slowly seeped out of him, only one question had haunted him . . .

That bullet he'd taken for her—had risking his life saved hers?

CHAPTER FOUR

A large panoramic window framed the cascading snowflakes and mountainous landscape of Saddleback Mountain Ski Resort. The perfect Christmas card. The scenery was breathtaking. In mid-March, with Christmas far behind, the serene picture did nothing to calm Rae's erratic heartbeat. After agreeing to Alan's request, she'd packed and arranged to get to Jackson Hole—that beautiful valley carved out of the Wyoming Rockies. Home to Grand Teton National Park and gateway to Yellowstone National Park.

She'd tried to stay at the ski resort—after all, it was the new resort in the valley, but they hadn't been able to accommodate her. Instead, after pitching that she was writing an article for *World Tour Magazine*, she secured a discounted rate at Jackson Hole Mountain Ski Lodge in between Jackson and Grayback.

Before Alan called with news about Zoey, Rae had been on a phone interview in which she'd assured the editor she would write a ski resort travel article for them as a test run. Like if she could write for them, then she could edit for them. Sure, she was grateful to be getting calls, but she couldn't seem to force herself into the mold. Editor for a travel publication group that included magazines depicting weddings and honeymoon destinations? Such banal happiness had never been Rae's thing. Making a difference in the world? That had been everything to her.

Using her time in Jackson Hole for dual purposes seemed strategic, but now that she was there, she knew she couldn't think about writing that article. Not until Zoey was home safe.

She gripped the resort brochure detailing the upscale rooms with terraces, chic dining as well as a burger-and-fries eatery, a spa and pool, many outdoor winter sports offerings, coffee kiosks, and on and on.

In her peripheral vision, she spotted the man she'd hoped to find. He wouldn't be happy to see her. In fact, at first, she'd recoiled at the idea of coming to Jackson Hole because she'd known he was there. Okay, well, maybe she'd been a bit of a stalker, but she'd wanted to make sure he was okay after the havoc her actions had caused.

Rae's palms slicked at the thought of approaching him. For the hundredth time she wondered what she was doing at this resort looking for Liam McKade. Because what if she actually found him?

No one had asked her to contact Liam. Alan merely begged Rae to find out what she could about Zoey's mysterious past and suggested Rae start in this valley—the place Zoey had left behind. Nothing could be discovered outside of physically coming here. Zoey didn't exist on social media because she didn't want to be found. Just like Liam McKade. No Facebook, Twitter, Instagram, or the latest, greatest social media platform for him.

As for looking into Zoey's past—well, sometimes a face-to-face conversation was required. Rae needed to have one with Zoey's mother.

Alan had been right to send Rae to this small valley situated between the Teton and Wind River ranges. All she'd ever wanted was to make a difference. She was accustomed to unearthing information. Following clues. Exposing sins. All in an effort to save lives.

This time—one life.

Did she need Liam to help her do that? Maybe she should just leave the resort and do this job all by her lonesome. She'd never needed help before.

Liam left the restaurant. Rae's pulse jumped at the sight of him.

He wore ski pants and a dark-blue ski jacket. With wheat-colored hair that hugged his collar, he looked like he belonged in the Swiss Alps. He looked good. Too good.

Her breath hitched. They'd had what could have been a good thing going until she'd blown it. She had believed she'd been doing the right thing. Why did seeing him still make her crazy? And how was she supposed to ask for his help when a thousand regrets and what-ifs swallowed her up?

Rae opened the brochure again and pretended to skim the contents while she tried to catch her breath.

I can't do this. I can't do this.

Zoey's life could depend on it.

I have to do this.

If she were working in her old role as an investigative reporter, she would walk right up to him and ask for his help. Then again, her boldness had gotten them both in trouble. She'd lost her job, and Liam had been forced to put himself in harm's way for her.

And that's exactly why she needed him now. If she could trust anyone, it was someone willing to put their life on the line for someone else. Still, she was prepared for his complete rejection. That is, if she could even work up the nerve to face him.

Rae moseyed around the corner. For now, she'd shadow the guy until she could find the right words of persuasion. Otherwise, there was no point in approaching him.

Her cell rang.

Reggie.

Dad's research editor was actually calling her back. She bit her lip. "Reggie, hi. It's so good to hear from you."

"You too, Rae. How are you? How's your mum these days?"

"Mom's great."

"Good, good. And you?"

"In general, I'm good."

He chuckled. "I heard the urgency in your voice, love, so I returned your call. Couldn't dispense with the pleasantries though. Tell me what's going on."

She sucked in a breath. Could she convince him? "When Dad was killed, you said to me, to all of us, that if we ever needed anything, you'd be there for us. If anyone else had said that, I would have taken it as nothing more than kind words. But you . . ."

"I was close to your father, Rae. Best man at his wedding. So I meant those words. I'm sorry I haven't been a big part of your life, so if there's anything I can do for you now, please tell me. I've struck out on my own and work for clients of my choosing, so I have no boss telling me what to do. I call my business the Information Depot."

Rae leaned against the wall and relaxed. "I need your help. I'm so glad you're willing to give it." Rae laid everything out for Reggie.

"What do you need from me?"

"I'll need your skills with databases and research," she said. "You have more access. I'll pay you, of course. Whatever the going rate is."

"My going rate for you is free. And it sounds like we need to get busy."

"Zoey Dumont isn't her birth name. Alan wasn't able to find a hard copy of her birth certificate. I found the digital copy on a genealogical website, but it reflects her legal name change, so I still don't know her birth name. But it did show that her mother's name is Samara Davidson and her deceased father's name is Mark Davidson. Please find out everything you can. Her real name. Her mother's address here, if it's the same or changed. Anything and everything I can look into while I'm here. We're running out of time."

"The first forty-eight hours are critical."

"Right."

"I'm on it, Rae. You've done good work already, but you need someone working alongside you. I'll let you know everything I find."

"Thanks." She ended the call, but she couldn't relax yet.

If he could help, she'd owe Reggie big-time. He was about to help her uncover the truth about Zoey and her past, whether or not it helped her find her missing sister-in-law. An ache coursed through her. The things Alan didn't know about his own wife had to be pure torture.

"You warned me," he'd said.

With his skill set, Alan could have found out more about her by digging on his own. Or hired a private investigator. Something. But Alan didn't want to know. Or had it been more that he feared knowing the past would somehow pierce their bubble of marital joy and happiness? He loved Zoey despite her secrets. His unconditional love for her was to be admired.

Except now they could all be paying the price.

She received a text. Reggie already?

Are you worried about stepping into an active police investigation?

She responded.

I'm helping the search for a missing person. My brother needs me to do this.

She left it at that and hoped Reggie would continue to help her. The police were only human. They made mistakes, and Rae couldn't afford the kind of mistakes they sometimes made. She was human too, and she'd made awful mistakes that sickened her if she thought about them. Though contrary to what some believed, Rae's drive had never been about the glory. Even now, she only wanted to find Zoey.

She read another text from Reggie.

Zoey Dumont's birth name is Tawny Davidson.

Startling her away from her cell, a face filled her vision. Handsome and rugged, but the eyes were cold and brown. And one thought gripped her heart—she would have died last spring if it hadn't been for Special Agent Liam McKade.

Rae fought to breathe.

"What are you doing here?"

Liam had never intimidated her.

Until now.

CHAPTER FIVE

Rae Burke. Meddlesome reporter and betrayer of hearts. "Why are you following me? I'm down and out for good. Don't you know that? There's no story here."

Her mouth hung open. A pretty mouth that he'd made the mistake of kissing before. That seemed like a lifetime ago. No. Another life entirely. He wasn't the same man anymore. The *incident* had to have affected her as well, so she couldn't be the same woman either.

"What? I . . ."

"Well?" Liam should just walk away and ignore her. He shouldn't have approached her to begin with. He didn't want any part of that life to come back and haunt him. Nor did he want the woman who had caused the massive dominoes to fall to enter his life again.

He needed to think with his head this time instead of his heart.

That she was speechless surprised him. *I never wanted to see you again.* He hadn't thought he could ever be that heartless. But she'd stirred up all the memories he was trying to forget. At least he hadn't said the words aloud. That would reveal entirely too much emotion. He didn't want her sudden appearance to affect him so much. It was *his* problem that it did. But she didn't have to know it.

39

As it was, he'd already overreacted. It's funny that this was his reaction to a woman he'd been willing to die for mere months ago. Hands on his hips, he released a shaky breath. Seeing her here had truly stunned him.

He'd try a different tactic. "Let's start over. You look good, Rae." She wore her blonde hair shoulder-length now. Soft and . . . pretty. Her blue-green eyes were definitely bluer today and filled with passion. He couldn't let the memories of her in his arms get to him.

Hadn't she caused enough trouble? Enough . . . heartache? "I don't know how you found me"—he forced gentleness into his tone—"but I just need to move on. Okay?"

Her brows slowly furrowed as she nodded.

Okay. They were clear. She understood. He could walk away now.

He turned and took a step, then another. Yes. He could do this. He *was* doing it. He was actually walking away. But she followed.

She caught up to him and kept pace. "I'm not stalking you, Liam. At least not like you think, but I did hope to find you."

He heard the hurt in her tone, as if he had meant something to her. She had used him in the worst possible way, and he'd shown himself to be the fool. He stopped and slowly turned to face her again. How could she even say his name like that, as though she was hurt and cared about him.

He tapped down the rising anger. "You found me. Now, what do you want? How *did* you find me anyway?" Oh yeah. Reporters were good at that. On the other hand, he thought the whole valley might be at this new resort for the grand opening.

"I saw your name on the Emerald M Guest Ranch website. I admit, I kept tabs on you just to make sure you were all right after everything. So I drove all the way out there looking for you and met this wonderful lady. Evelyn. She was happy to tell me I could find you here if I hurried."

Oh, I bet she was. Liam ground his molars. Evelyn had no idea what she'd just done. Nor would she ever find out. Evelyn kept after him to find a nice young woman. He'd gone out of his way to keep what happened to himself, but Evelyn had some sort of uncanny matchmaking radar about her. And that didn't bode well for Liam where Rae was concerned.

"Liam, I wouldn't be here if I didn't need your help. Someone's life is at stake. Several lives, actually."

Her striking eyes had snagged him before at the worst possible time. He couldn't let that happen again. "I think I've given you all I can give." Months of his life after throwing himself in front of a bullet. "But I'll bite. Whose life are you here to destroy besides mine?"

Okay. That was rude. Much too harsh. She hadn't destroyed his life. Not really. Maybe. Sort of. He squeezed the bridge of his nose and took a deep, calming breath. The last thing he needed was to make a scene in the very resort where he might become head of security. Or not. Plus, he represented Emerald M Guest Ranch wherever he went—how many times had Heath drilled that into his head?

Rae blinked a few times. Blinking back tears? Oh, so the woman had a heart.

Maybe she was playing him again. Regardless, he couldn't stand behind his attitude. "Look, I apologize if I sound rude. Rae, please, just go. I'm sure I can't help you."

There. He'd apologized, and now he would try again to walk away.

She touched his arm as if a simple touch would stop him in his tracks. But his legs slowed despite his best intentions. He angled his head at her, waiting for her explanation.

"For what it's worth, I lost my job, Liam." She fought the tears that welled in her eyes. Rae was strong and had seen more than most people—she'd been in the trenches just like Liam. They had that in common, and it had brought them closer.

He wanted to be surprised to see any emotion from her at all because he'd wanted to think of her as coldhearted; that way her betrayal wouldn't hurt nearly as much.

"I never meant for any of it to happen, and I'm truly sorry you think I destroyed your life."

Liam didn't want to see the sincerity in her eyes. His chest contracted. He nodded, letting her know he'd heard her and that was the end of this conversation. He turned to walk away *again*, and this time she didn't follow. The truth was, she hadn't destroyed his life. He'd wanted a reason to get out, and she had given him that. But the cost had been high. Maybe too high.

He walked through the resort and forced his mind back to Brad's offer of head of security. Austin's offer to work with him in private investigating. Heath's offer to remain on Emerald M Guest Ranch and help run the place and expand.

But his thoughts drifted back to Rae in spite of his efforts to stay on track. Rae. He loathed the sound of her whispered name in his head.

At the exit, he pushed through the revolving door as he zipped his coat, then tromped outside where huge flakes of snow landed on him. Brad had done well for himself, but he'd come from a wealthy family with the kinds of connections to pull something like this off—all the legalities and paperwork and expensive real estate. Liam never doubted that Brad would do something big, though his friend had never had anything to prove.

Liam turned around to take in the posh resort—just what this valley needed, another ski resort. With four stories, it almost looked like an apartment building. Liam considered Brad's plans for expansion—at least what he'd read in the resort brochure—including adding private cabins and heli-ski tours. Brad could never expand unless he owned the land or made use of a forest service lease.

Liam let his gaze slide down the roof and to the window, where he had the misfortune of spotting Rae sitting at a booth next to a panoramic window. She stared at her cell, then lifted it to her ear while she typed on a tablet.

Whatever story she was after now—oh, wait, she said she'd lost her job. Hmm. Whoever she was trying to save now, he hoped she wasn't digging into the dark underworld Liam had tried to protect her from before.

She wasn't good at that part of her job. Hadn't she figured that out yet? He'd heard all about her father's career going into war zones. What Rae didn't seem to comprehend was that her father had also had a photographer along, as well as a few soldiers surrounding him. Rae might not have been on foreign soil, but she'd gone into war zones all the same—without trained soldiers to protect her.

Who would save her this time? She was going to get caught. Liam just hoped this guy wasn't as bad as those he'd had to protect her from before.

Liam turned and looked at his truck sitting across the parking lot. All he had to do was keep walking. He shook his head at his rotten bad luck that she'd shown up. Then he turned around and walked back through the revolving door of the ski resort.

He strolled into the café to find a seat, taking the same booth he'd shared with Brad. He hadn't intended to follow her, and this would be the end of it. Still, he was curious about her next victim.

A text came through. Liam glanced at his cell and his gut tightened.

Heath.

Are you still at the resort?

Liam wished he knew how to dodge that question.

Why?

Oh, never mind.

Confused by Heath's question and reply, Liam started to ask his own questions. He glanced up when a foursome entered and headed straight for his booth.

Heath grinned and slid in next to Liam, forcing him over. His new wife, Harper, squeezed in and sat entirely too close to Heath, red hair spilling over her white vest jacket. Liam was crushed against the wall. He grinned for their benefit. He could do this.

Austin and Willow sat across from them. "Hey, bro," Austin said. "Looks like we're not interrupting anything. You're not waiting for anyone, are you?"

Liam kept his focus on Austin so he wouldn't telegraph that he was there to shadow someone. "Nope."

"Good." Austin smiled and pecked Willow on the cheek. The two had married early last spring, and Austin still couldn't take his eyes off his new wife.

"I hope it's okay if we join you," she said. "I know these guys can be overwhelming."

"I'm used to it."

Liam admitted she was beautiful, with her dark eyes and long dark hair. Her name totally fit. She was a forensic genealogist. He still wasn't sure he understood everything that entailed, but apparently Austin's new private investigation business worked well with her consulting business. He hoped the honeymoon phase lasted on both fronts—business and personal.

They were leaving tomorrow morning to head home to Seattle.

Heath and Harper were headed out too, only on their honeymoon. They married a few months ago in late fall but waited for the winter months when Emerald M Guest Ranch was free of guests before going on their official honeymoon in Hawaii—the exact opposite of the Wyoming mountains in the winter. After getting engaged, Harper moved back to Grayback and began working for Bridger County as a forensic photographer.

Liam had never seen his brothers this blissful, like they both walked around in some sort of radiant heaven Liam had no way of entering. He couldn't be happier for them, but their contentment only magnified the despair that hovered around him, so he'd tried to get away from them, if only for a few hours.

He laughed inside. There was no escape. All the love, joy, and happiness he thought he'd fled earlier today had followed him here. While he certainly didn't want the gloom to follow either, why was he struggling with how happy both of his brothers were? Jealousy had never been an issue for him before, but he had no idea how to get such happiness for himself.

Still, there was good news. With both happy couples leaving tomorrow, he would have a few days of peace and quiet at the ranch. Heath had tasked him with running the place in his absence. It was winter. The guest ranch was closed. What could happen?

A waitress came by and took their orders. Liam ordered coffee but no food. He tried to pay attention to his family while he kept his sights on Rae, who was focused on her tablet.

Heath leaned forward and clasped his hands. "Well, I've got the news we've all been waiting for."

All eyes riveted on Heath.

"What news would that be?" Liam asked.

"I heard from the sheriff this morning. I'm glad he caught me before we left." He squeezed Harper's hand.

Liam leaned in. "And?"

"It has taken months, but we finally know that Dad wasn't drunk when he was in the collision that killed the senator and his family. The medical examiner who signed the report had moved on, and it took time to track him down. By the time Detective Moffett found him, he was gone. Cancer. But she was able to talk to his sister, who told her that he'd carried a secret, a weight that had burdened him."

Heath paused and hung his head as if in pain. "Said he'd been paid to doctor the report to make it look like our alcoholic father was responsible. That the senator's blood alcohol concentration showed he was the intoxicated one." He looked back up at them. "Too many glasses of wine with dinner? We all know who paid for that report to be doctored—the same man who told me Dad hadn't been drunk and the accident wasn't his fault, right after he shot me. He was connected to the senator and his family, and he shifted the blame to Dad. And now, all involved parties are dead."

"And that means we can let go of the past and move on," Austin added. "Good work making sure the department kept searching for answers. I know it wasn't a priority for them."

"But it was a priority for us," Heath said. "I had to know."

"Me too. I feel like a weight's been lifted," Austin said. "For years, I blamed myself."

"I think we all carried some of the blame," Heath said. He and Austin looked at Liam.

He lifted his hands as if in surrender. "I wasn't even there when it happened."

"And maybe you can blame yourself for staying away for so long." Heath grinned as he squeezed Liam's shoulder. He hadn't meant anything by the comment, but as the saying went, there was truth in jest.

"Even though life was kind of hard, we made it. We took care of each other." Austin put his arm across Willow's shoulders.

"Yeah, do you remember the code?" Liam asked.

Heath snorted. "You mean, 'How's the fishing?'" He angled his head as he explained to Willow and Harper. "We had a code in place. Our way of watching one another's backs. When Dad was on a bender, the fishing wasn't good, and that meant to stay away."

"Only problem was, the fishing was hardly ever good," Austin said.

"But you built that fort." Willow smiled. "You could go there."

Austin winked. "Yes. Yes, we could. I'm glad that's all behind us now and we survived."

The waitress delivered their food, and the conversation moved on.

One thing Liam knew was that his family could move on and leave the past behind, but Liam eyed the woman in the booth by the far window. His recent past had followed him here, and he couldn't leave it behind just yet.

While his family dug into their jalapeño burgers, sweet potato fries, and chicken fingers, they laughed together. Snuggled. Teased each other. Shared a few quick kisses.

Liam listened to the two happy couples and let himself become invisible.

He sipped his black coffee and watched Rae exit the café in a manner that let him know she was hard on a trail. Unfortunately, he had a bad feeling about her endeavor, which had required her to muster the courage to ask him, of all people, for his help. That should tell him something.

And maybe Rae interrupting his day was Providence shining down on him, because he needed an excuse to get away from his syrupy family and the reminders of everything he was missing. His past had followed him here, and he couldn't let it out of his sight.

CHAPTER SIX

Liam had excused himself, and he didn't think anyone noticed. He'd been invisible just like he'd wanted. Though maybe he was lying to himself.

He reached for the door of his new four-wheel-drive truck with a plow on the front.

"Liam!"

The shout came from across the parking lot. He opened the door and turned to see Heath practically jogging toward him. Liam chuckled at the sight.

"You're going to slip and fall!" he called.

Gasping for breath, Heath caught up to him. The parking lot wasn't small. "When you excused yourself, I thought you were coming back. Then I spotted you through the window. Where are you going?"

"I have something I need to take care of."

Heath frowned. "Okay. Fair enough. But why do I get the feeling it's more that you're trying to avoid us?"

"It's not that, Heath." Liam climbed into the cab and started the engine to get the heat going. The diesel's rumble had the added benefit of drowning out most of Heath's words, but Liam might as well hear him out. Heath would keep at him if he didn't, so

Liam killed the idling truck and turned his focus back to Heath. "I'm listening."

"I've kept my peace and given you the space you've needed since you came home last summer. I was glad to have you back. I know we haven't seen eye to eye and we still have our issues, but are you ever going to tell me what happened to you? Because something's eating at you, and it's only getting worse. I'm leaving in the morning. I didn't want to leave without asking you about it."

Did Heath just want to confirm that Liam would be responsible for the ranch in Heath's absence? Nah. That wasn't fair. Heath truly cared about him. Not everyone was all about themselves or had a secret agenda. Liam would keep reminding himself of that until he finally believed it. He caught a glimpse of Rae getting into a vehicle.

"There's not much to tell. I was working undercover. I made a mistake. I got too close to someone, and in the end, she was only using me. She blew my cover, or rather, forced *me* to blow it. We both almost died."

Heath hung his head. "I'm sorry. But you both survived. And where is she now? You said that you got close to her."

"I also said she used me."

"Are you sure about that?" Heath knew Liam had trouble trusting.

"One hundred percent."

"That's too bad."

Rae steered from the parking lot. Liam needed to go if he was going to follow her—some kind of insanity getting the best of him. "She showed up here today."

Heath's eyes widened. "Interesting."

"She asked for my help, and I turned her away."

"So, are you upset because she showed up or because you rejected her?"

"A little of both." A lot of both. "If it's all the same to you,

Heath, I don't need your advice." Liam's gaze followed the vehicle. He glanced at Heath. "But you're going to give it anyway, aren't you?"

Liam grinned to take some of the sting out of his words. Even if he hadn't, Heath was his brother. Nothing would ever change that.

Heath studied him. "No, little brother. Not this time. I already know you'll do the right thing."

Liam hadn't decided if that was a good thing or a bad thing. He'd spent so many years trying to disconnect himself from his dysfunctional family that fitting back in and trying to make it work seemed out of reach, though he'd tried over the last several months. Granted, living with Heath and his new wife wasn't anything like the past they shared with their troubled parents.

"Will you be home for dinner tonight?" Heath crossed his arms. "We're all heading out tomorrow early. I know Austin will want to say goodbye before he goes."

"But not you?" Liam teased.

"I don't like to say goodbye. Besides, I'll only be gone a week."

Liam needed to talk to Heath about their living arrangements. Since Harper had moved in, the house seemed to grow smaller for Liam every day. But he could do that later. "I'll see you tonight, then."

Liam shut the door and started the truck. He steered from the parking lot to follow the woman he wished had stayed in his past and far from this valley.

CHAPTER SEVEN

Rae followed the instructions the female GPS voice delivered and steered toward her destination. She'd entered the address Reggie had texted while she was still at the resort. Though mostly plowed, the road had spots that were slippery. Why, oh, why had she thought to approach Liam?

He certainly hadn't needed an apology from her. For months now her conscience had eaten at her about everything that had happened. It hadn't ended well. Somehow, Liam seemed to have misunderstood everything. For certain, Rae's motivations. Never mind that she'd failed to make it right. But no time to think about that now. She needed to prepare for her next surprise visit.

This time of day, she might have better luck if she tried Zoey's mom—Samara Davidson—at her place of business. Rae had learned that she owned Mountain Valley Adventures, a heli-skiing company that was founded years ago. Rae struggled to picture the Zoey she'd known working alongside her family in this kind of endeavor. Nothing about Zoey ever said she enjoyed skiing. But heli-skiing—helicopters delivering tourists to fresh, undisturbed powder on mountain peaks no one could otherwise reach?

Zoey was tough but brainy and bookish. Had that been part of the new persona she'd put on when she'd escaped her life here? Now *that*, Rae could believe.

Why so many secrets, Zoey?

Rae came up behind a snowplow and slowed. Another car behind her honked, then passed them both. Rae would stay behind the plow for now, thank you very much. Even though she'd rented a four-wheel-drive SUV, it was on the smallish side and she wouldn't press her luck. Considering her treacherous drive to Emerald M Guest Ranch earlier to find Liam, she was glad she'd opted for this model. Still, she could appreciate cleared roads.

She turned onto another road, then it hit her—would Zoey's mother be distraught over her missing daughter? She might not be working today. Rae should have thought of that to begin with. But some people preferred working through a crisis. Rae would start there and then head to the home address if Mrs. Davidson wasn't at work.

On the one hand, Rae hated the thought of intruding. Then again, searching for Zoey was better than sitting at home. Giving her absolute best to find her sister-in-law had been behind her reasons for eliciting help from both Reggie and Liam. In Liam's case, she'd hoped to open the doors to a conversation. To mend what had been broken. But that was a no go. She'd just do this on her own since he had rejected her in a much more spectacular display than she could have imagined.

He obviously thought she deserved his reaction.

The GPS interrupted her thoughts, letting her know she was now at her destination. She was relieved.

Rae steered into the parking lot of an upscale log-cabin lodge and took in the majestic and peaceful scenery—mountains and snow-covered peaks all around her. A wide rushing river curled around the base of the mountains.

She spotted a helipad but not helicopters—the guides had taken the tourists out. She didn't know much about how it worked. Did the helicopters drop them off and return later? She would assume, but maybe it involved a tour of the area before taking to the slopes. How long were the tours? A day? Half a day?

Rae turned off the vehicle and composed herself. This one conversation could mean everything, and Rae needed to be calm, collected, and confident before she came face-to-face with Mrs. Davidson. She had to remember to use Zoey's real name—Tawny—with Mrs. Davidson, though Rae could only think of her as Zoey.

Shouldering her bag holding her tablet, paper, pen, and cell, she left the vehicle and hiked across the plowed parking lot, maneuvering around a few expensive-model cars. She should expect heli-skiing was a sport for the well-to-do sorts. Or thrill seekers, at the very least, who spent every last dime on extreme sports. Was heli-skiing an extreme sport? She would have to find out. She could use the information in the travel article she hoped would land her that job when this was over. Pushing through the doors of Mountain Valley Adventures, Rae found a reception counter.

A young woman wearing a beautiful cream sweater stood behind the counter and smiled. "Welcome to Mountain Valley Adventures. How can I help you?"

Her name tag read "Kelly."

"Hi, Kelly. My name is Rae Burke. I'm here to see Samara Davidson."

"Do you have an appointment?"

"I'm here to talk to her about a private matter."

The statement didn't move Kelly.

Rae lowered her voice. "It's about her daughter."

Kelly's eyes widened slightly. Was her reaction simply from surprise, or did she know that Tawny, aka Zoey, was missing? She must know. Surely the police had figured out Zoey Dumont was Tawny Davidson. They would have beaten Rae here, wouldn't they have?

"One second." Kelly left her post and headed down a hallway. Rae was surprised that someone who ran a heli-skiing business would be locked in an office, but then again, business owners often got stuck with the daily grind that had nothing at all to do with the fun or the very reason they got into the business to begin with.

"Sam, someone's here about Tawny." Kelly kept her voice low, but it still echoed enough for Rae to hear.

She emerged from the hallway and smiled again. "She'll see you now."

At the entrance to Samara Davidson's office, Kelly pushed the door open wide and gestured for Rae to enter.

A woman stood with her back to Rae, arms crossed, in front of a striking window view of the mountains.

Tension rolled off the woman and slammed into Rae. She was definitely intruding. Shoving past the awkward moment, Rae fully entered the office and waited for Kelly to shut the door behind her. Zoey's mother didn't turn to greet her. Rae would give Mrs. Davidson time to compose herself.

Seconds ticked by. Had she forgotten someone was in her office?

Finally, Rae spoke up. "Mrs. Davidson, my name is Rae Burke. I'm sorry for my intrusion. I'm here . . . I'm trying to find Zoey . . . um . . . your daughter, Tawny."

This was all kinds of awkward—Zoey and her mother had been estranged, or so Zoey had told her. Did Mrs. Davidson even know Zoey had married? Did she know she had a grandchild? Rae was wholly unprepared for this exchange.

Zoey's mother turned to face Rae with red-rimmed eyes. "The police were already here to inform me she was missing and to ask their questions. Who are you, exactly? Another detective?"

"No. I'm . . ."—*Steady your voice*—"I'm Tawny's sister-in-law. I was her roommate in college."

Mrs. Davidson stared at her with her unusual blue eyes—contacts, for certain. Rae wasn't sure what she'd expected, but now that she'd met Zoey's mother, it all made sense. This woman ran a business for the well-to-do and managed heli-skiing back-country guides, mostly people with medical emergency certifications and a long list of skills and education in everything about snow science—glaciology, avalanche forecasting, and explosives. They were thrill seekers. Tough. Rugged.

This woman supervised *that* crew.

She was tall and regal like a castle, striking like her daughter. And somehow she managed to make the backcountry ski garb she wore seem elegant and like she was ready to take to the slopes all at the same time. A chill crawled over Rae as she had a sudden vision of Zoey standing in front of her—twenty or so years into the future.

Mrs. Davidson crossed her arms. "And?"

Oh boy. She wasn't going to make this easy. "Mind if I sit down?"

"Go ahead."

Rae had hoped sitting would allow the tension to ease from her body, but the chair made no difference. Regardless, it was show-time.

Mrs. Davidson took a seat behind her enormous desk, the picturesque mountain scene behind her, seeming to frame her—another postcard moment.

"It must be hard to work in this office with such beauty at your back." Rae hoped light conversation would bring Mrs. Davidson around. If the woman was like this all the time, she had no problem seeing why Zoey had left or why they were estranged. Zoey's mother clearly had high expectations of everyone around her.

The woman huffed and smirked at the same time. "Small talk doesn't suit you."

"No, I suppose it doesn't." She'd found common ground at least. The woman liked to get right to the point.

"Does anyone know you're here?" Mrs. Davidson asked as she tapped her laptop keyboard to bring the screen to life.

Rae had wanted her full attention, and given the topic, she would expect no less. "Yes. My brother, Tawny's husband, Alan, knows. He asked me to come, in fact."

"I assume he's looking for her as well."

This woman could be a wealth of information. How deeply had the police probed? Still, Rae sensed that she wasn't going to give Rae too much. She seemed cautious. Wary. Downright cold as stone.

"He's done everything he can, but they have a daughter." Again, Rae was reminded how unprepared she'd been for this side of things—Zoey's mother might not even know. But what daughter would keep so much of her life from her mother?

By the shift in the woman's demeanor, Rae could tell she knew about Callie. Interesting. Zoey had kept private. Away from social media. Had she kept in touch with her mother, after all?

"Alan has to stay with Callie." Rae had to direct the conversation to find out as much as she could in the shortest amount of time. "Is there anything you can tell me that might help?"

"I haven't seen or talked to Tawny in years."

"Mrs. Davidson. Zoey—"

"Who?"

Oops. "Zoey . . . It's what Tawny changed her name to when she moved to Colorado. I was friends with your daughter for a few years before she met my brother. As I already mentioned, we were college roommates. During that time, she disappeared for a week, and when she came back to the dorm, she'd been beaten and traumatized. I've always suspected a stalker. That may have been the reason she fled to Colorado. I'm sorry if this hurts you, but I have to know—why did she leave Jackson Hole and change her name? Was she running from someone?"

That Zoey had *fled* her home seemed painfully obvious. But from whom, wasn't clear. Maybe she'd left this seemingly cold, demanding woman behind and met her abductor in Colorado.

ELIZABETH GODDARD

Maybe no one had followed her from Wyoming. Would Zoey's mother even know?

Mrs. Davidson's whole demeanor changed. Softened. She appeared to decide. "Please . . . call me Sam. It's short for Samara. Everyone here calls me that."

Sam had suddenly dropped the castle fortifications. "Okay, Sam, then."

"I'll answer your questions, but first I have a few of my own. Do you have special skills?" Sam asked. "What makes you think you can find my daughter? The police are already looking for her. Why not allow them to do their own work? I've contacted the FBI as well to see if they'll look into her abduction."

Which one of those should Rae tackle first? Sam's questioning Rae's private investigation made sense. Who was she and what could she do? Now, see, this was why Liam could help her. She could hire him as a private investigator. She could use his intimidating demeanor at times and more personable, lovable-guy persona at other times. Like now. But . . . using him. Using him was what he blamed her for to begin with.

Time for Rae to make her case. "I'm a journalist. I write exposés. I spend months finding people and digging into their backgrounds. Usually that's to expose the travesties and atrocities done to them. That's my skill, if you will." If she shared her father's name and his legacy, would that matter? "As I said, my brother asked for my help. I knew Zoey. But not nearly well enough. She wanted her privacy, her secrets. I never pressed her." Rae hadn't even known Zoey's birth name. "But now's the time for me to invade her privacy and uncover her secrets. Knowing more could help me find her. "

Her explanation appeared to satisfy Sam. The woman blew out a breath and suddenly appeared more human. More approachable. More rocks tumbled from the castle walls. "Tawny was . . . is . . . beautiful. She's more than beautiful. But she always seemed to attract the wrong sorts. Could never seem to lose them."

"My brother was smitten when he met her," Rae said, "and she married him. He's not the wrong sort, so I hope you can find comfort in knowing that."

"But she's gone now. The husband is usually a suspect."

"I don't believe for a moment he's involved, but if he is, the police will know soon enough. That said, I've seen enough victims who never got justice. Enough unsolved crimes to know that law enforcement can't be everywhere. Police detectives, investigators, special agents, the lot of them, they can't solve every crime. Millions of crimes happen every year, many of them violent. So, here I am. I'm doing what I can to help. It can't hurt, can it? Zoey could be running out of time."

"All right. Okay. I'm convinced you have the right skills. You definitely sound like a reporter. I was already considering hiring a private investigator for all the reasons you mentioned. Tawny needs all the help she can get." Sam swiveled the chair to the side so she could turn her head to the view. She gazed at the expanse for a few moments, then said, "Tawny grew up in this business. She learned everything, including how to guide tourists as well as how to keep the books. For some reason I will never understand, she was more drawn to computers than the scenery. I put her on the payroll in high school to manage the finances and develop our website. She attended a community college for a year here before . . ."

Sam frowned as if emotion would get the best of her, then she quickly composed herself. "She was the smartest among us. She takes after her father in that regard, except he loved the outdoors and had no interest in technology. He founded the business thirty-five years ago. He was a thrill seeker. Loved the adventure of it all and wanted to share that with the world. He died in an avalanche before she was born."

"I'm so sorry."

Sam shrugged. "She was surrounded by father figures. And I

won't lie, a couple of stepfathers too. But a man became obsessed with her. He was one of our clients, actually. She couldn't get him to leave her alone."

"And did you tell the police?"

"Of course. What could they do? Nothing, really. Not until he actually hurt her, and then a spoiled wealthy type would lawyer up and make it all go away. Tawny left with my blessing. I had hoped that she wouldn't be gone long. That she would come back. That we would keep in touch." Sam's eyes teared up. "Sometimes I've regretted telling her to disappear. Sometimes I wish . . . I wish I would have hired a hit man to get rid of him. It just isn't right that she should have to lose so much. That I should have to lose her because he wanted something, someone he couldn't have."

The woman's passion and emotion washed over Rae in waves. She felt her pain to her core. There was a story there too. A way to make a difference.

Sam's eyes took on a distant look.

"What's the stalker's name?" Rae asked.

"Simon Astor."

Rae committed that name to memory. She could find him after she left Sam. Find him and also find out if the police were looking at him—he could have taken Zoey.

Was it a stretch to think that Zoey had been taken by this Simon guy five years ago when she disappeared the first time? She'd left her home because of a stalker. Changed her name, the works. What if he'd found her again? After all, it had been easy enough to find Sam's name on Zoey's birth certificate. Astor could've had a resource like Reggie at his fingertips and found her if he'd wanted. Then, because he was obsessed, he abducted her.

"Is there anything else you can tell me?" she asked.

"I've told you everything." Sam rose from the chair and moved to stare out her window again.

Rae empathized with her. She could understand the woman

drew strength from the scenery. But she also sensed that Sam was lying—she hadn't told Rae everything and was intentionally holding back.

Rae grabbed a pen and paper from her bag. She had everything except a business card inside, of course! "If you think of something else, please call me." She wrote down her personal cell number for Sam.

Sam moved from the window and reached over her desk to take the paper with Rae's number. She stared at it, tapping one edge with a short but manicured nail. She glanced up at Rae, startling her again with the brilliant blue eyes. "Why should I call you instead of the police?"

Rae arched a brow. "I didn't say you should call me instead. You should tell the police everything. Offer up anything that can help them. I'm sure you understand why you should tell me as well."

Sam nodded, a knowing look in her eyes.

"Like you," Rae said, "I have a personal stake in this—she's my sister-in-law and mother to my niece. My brother's wife. My task lies in finding Zoey."

"What's she like?" Samara set the paper on her desk.

"Who?"

"My granddaughter?"

Sorrow squeezed Rae. The ache of unshed tears rose in her throat. "Callie is beautiful and wonderful. She's special."

I'm so sorry you've been denied that relationship.

"Special. The way you say it . . . how so?"

"Callie is, well, she's autistic. But not in the way people usually think. She isn't afraid to look people in the eyes or to have anyone touch her. She's too friendly." But rigid and inflexible in other ways. "She has the most amazing, beautiful blonde curls. Big blue eyes like her mother's and . . . her grandmother's."

Tears shimmered again in Sam's eyes as she nodded, a deep, painful frown lining her features. Maybe Sam had long ago prepared for the possibility she would one day hear news her daughter had met a tragic end. Rae was only beginning to understand Zoey's escape from her past. She had reinvented herself to protect herself as well as her mother. All because of a dangerous stalker? Rae had a feeling much more was going on.

"I hope you find my daughter. I hope someone finds her. And when they do, enough of this. I'm going to see her and be part of her life again. I can't believe we've let Simon ruin our lives like this. But now it can finally be over if only Tawny is found alive."

"Do you think he could be involved in her disappearance?" Rae asked.

Sam pinned Rae with her gaze. "Simon Astor is dead. The story made the news this week when his remains were discovered."

CHAPTER EIGHT

From her vehicle, Rae watched the Mountain Valley Adventures facilities. What should she do now? Where should she go? She'd seen on the news the story about remains being identified and had all but forgotten about it. Those remains belonged to Zoey's stalker, and now Rae's theory had fallen apart. He couldn't have been the one who took her two days ago, though admittedly that had been a loose theory.

And now they had reached the forty-eight-hours mark.

Oh, Zoey.

How was Alan holding up? She should call him, but not yet. She needed something to give him hope. She needed to stay focused and keep working before she made that call, because she was sure that she would be down and out for the day after talking to him.

Rae grabbed her camera and took a few snapshots of the place. The wide, flowing river, skirting patches of ice. The lofty mountains, their jagged peaks frosted in thick white icing.

She heard the rotors long before she saw the helicopter swoop in and land on the helipad. A guy hopped out, then assisted others out of the helicopter and piled gear high on the helipad. Skiers sorted and grabbed their skis, bags, helmets, and more. The man she assumed was the guide left them and jogged toward the lodge. Rae took more pictures. She zoomed in on the guy before he disappeared inside the building.

Then she put Sam's home address into her GPS. Was it the same home where Zoey had grown up? A look at public records might give her that information, though she wasn't sure it would be vital in her search for Zoey. She could wait and see what else Reggie came up with.

Rae drove slowly down a winding path for a half mile, then found a large luxury log cabin tucked away deep in the woods. Samara Davidson must make a nice living from the heli-skiing business.

Rae examined the GPS map to find what was public land versus what was private and steered along the narrow road until she found a shoulder to park on. She got out of the vehicle and took a few pictures of the home and the surrounding area. However, if she was going to hike in those woods, she'd need snowshoes. Good thing she'd thought ahead. A good camera and sturdy snowshoes were a must in the Rockies during the winter. She knew that much from living in Colorado. She got the snowshoes from the back of the car, strapped them onto her boots, and then slung her camera over her shoulder.

Rae hiked into the forest to take pictures of the home from various angles. She didn't expect to find Zoey at the home, but neither would she discount the possibility—she'd seen too much in her experience to be surprised.

Just . . . be alive, Zoey. Somewhere.

Rae took other pictures as well so anyone looking on would think she was a nature lover out for a walk. According to her GPS, the national forest surrounded Sam's home. Public lands.

When she was about fifty yards from the road, the sound of a vehicle drew her attention. Through the trees, she spotted a new

Jeep driving up to the Davidson home. Zooming in on her camera, she caught the model—Grand Cherokee Trackhawk.

The vehicle stopped on the circular drive in front of the house.

Crouching behind a tree, she positioned herself with the camera. Okay, so she didn't look like a nature lover out for a hike if anyone spotted her at this moment. Sam got out of the vehicle, followed by the guide from the last group. They entered the home.

She'd mentioned that after Zoey's father died, Zoey had a couple of stepfathers, and then the male guides served as her father figures. Perhaps the two female guides Rae had seen in the brochure were like sisters or friends. Just one big happy family.

Rae might need to schedule a heli-ski tour and see what she could learn from the guides, specifically this one who was close to Sam. Taking photographs of them wasn't the best journalistic technique. But the code of conduct included situations where this kind of activity was justified. She wasn't working for anyone and wasn't officially an investigative reporter, and she promised her brother this wasn't a story. Then why did she care about the code?

She zoomed in. The curtains remained pulled back from the large windows. Sam stood near one window and stared out—just like she had at her office—only she was on her cell. While she spoke, her features contorted, and she lowered the mini blinds and probably pulled the curtains shut, too, for good measure.

Who would she call after a visit from someone like Rae? Maybe it had nothing to do with Zoey's disappearance. But Sam wanted to find her daughter. Rae had to believe that about the woman and that her story about their so-called estrangement involving a stalker was true. A story that Zoey hadn't told Rae. Footfalls crunched in the deep snow behind her. If she kept perfectly still, maybe whoever was in the woods wouldn't spot her.

Oh. Right. Her big footprints would give her away. Plan B, then.

She could stand up and resume taking pictures of the woods, but she sensed it was too late.

Her pulse skyrocketed. She reached for the pepper spray and prepared to defend herself as she spotted the blue jeans bursting from the deep snow.

CHAPTER NINE

Rae aimed a can of pepper spray at him. He held up his palms in surrender, catching himself before he reacted according to his training and was much too aggressive. "What do you think you're doing?"

Her shoulders drooped. He was relieved she hadn't sprayed him in the face.

A full ten seconds passed as she regained her composure, pressing her hand against her rapidly rising and falling chest. "You scared me to death. You *followed* me?"

"*You're* outraged that I followed *you*? Look, didn't you learn anything?"

"I'm not facing off with drug dealers or human traffickers. This isn't like that. It's personal."

He looked forward to hearing about that. Not really. It could only mean trouble. "Let's get out of here before whoever you're watching sees us and calls the police."

He offered his hand and she took it. He practically pulled her to her feet. "Since when are you the kind of reporter who tries to see inside someone's home?"

"I know what you think about my methods."

"That I think this is a questionable endeavor? Well, then you're right. Are you done taking pictures?"

"Now that you're here, sure, I'm done."

"Then let's go." Liam turned to walk back to the road, and Rae followed. He hoped their voices hadn't carried. He didn't want to draw attention to their proximity to the home in the woods.

He almost smiled. He had to hand it to her—she was the most determined person he'd ever met.

As they approached her rental, Rae hiked past him and stood next to the hatch at the back. She said nothing as she worked to remove her snowshoes, taking out her frustration on the equipment. Finally, she tossed the snowshoes in the back and slammed the hatch shut. "Okay, now you can tell me why you followed me."

"Because I had a feeling you were putting yourself in harm's way again."

"I know I came looking for you earlier today, but I don't need you to take a bullet for me this time."

No one ever planned for that. "I don't know what you're doing here, but I don't want to see you get hurt."

Again.

"You didn't seem interested in hearing my story earlier." Rae stomped around to the door and opened it as if to get in and leave him standing there, but she leaned against the vehicle instead. "I don't intend to get hurt. Now, if you'll excuse me, I have work to do. I don't need your help, after all."

"So you say now. You came to me and asked for my help." This . . . this contentious exchange between them had never been their way before. Liam blamed himself—he didn't want to let her get under his skin. He'd set the tone earlier and now Rae was continuing it.

"And you told me in no uncertain terms to go away." She blew out a breath, then a bird caught her gaze as it fluttered away in the branches above.

Liam took in her blue-green eyes. As always, the shift in their color amazed him. They appeared greener now as the forest closed in and wrapped around her, framing her face. Her long neck stretched as she watched the bird. There was a time when he thought he couldn't get enough of looking at Rae's eyes. Of being with her. Even as they were both caught in the middle of a tough and dangerous investigation, he'd somehow fallen for her.

That was then.

This was now.

"You're right. I told you that," said Liam. "But you're not going away, are you? You're here in my neck of the woods and you might not know this, but I'm not that big of a jerk." Her eyes softened, and he felt that familiar kink in his heart. "I only *act* like I'm a big jerk."

That elicited a smile she so obviously fought, but then a chuckle escaped too. She straightened and composed herself before squinting and angling her head as if considering his words. "Okay. I didn't mean to give you a hard time. But you gave me one earlier. I don't have time to play games or act like I don't need your help, because I do." She shivered. "I'm freezing. Let's go somewhere warm and I'll tell you everything. Snow is beautiful on a postcard but not much fun to sit in while you're on a stakeout."

"Is that what you call what you were doing?"

"I hadn't intended to stay long, so call it what you want, but you were right before."

"What are you talking about?"

"I should've been a private investigator. Except, well, I want to help the public, not individuals." She got into her car. "I'll follow you."

"Okay. I know the perfect place."

"Um . . . unless it's on the road heading back to the Jackson Hole Mountain Ski Lodge where I'm staying, I might need to say no. I don't want to get caught somewhere far from the lodge if it gets dark. I'm not that great at driving in this stuff at night."

"How did you get a room? The place would have been booked months out."

"I told the lodge I was going to write a story for *World Tour*. The marketing and publicity person there seemed impressed. As it turns out, they need extra publicity with the latest, greatest resort's grand opening this season. I got a discounted rate. Go me."

"Wait. You work for *World Tour*?" Her deception hit him all wrong, but he had no right to throw stones. "The reporter extraordinaire, Rae Burke, daughter of Buckner Burke, working for something as lighthearted as a travel magazine?"

"Don't look at me like that, Liam. I *am* going to write that article for the magazine. I'm interviewing with them, and since I don't have a lot of samples to give them on travel, they wanted to see this from me first." She flashed a grin. "If I can dig up dirt, write exposés to take down organizations or just plain evil people any day of the week, surely I can write about"—she waved her hand around in the air—"something as frivolous as skiing in Jackson Hole. No problem."

He couldn't wait to read it. "Okay. You convinced me. Now follow me back to your place."

A good half hour later, he parked his truck and Rae pulled in next to him. The red Suburban that had followed her into the parking lot slowed, and the driver watched her.

The hair on the back of Liam's neck prickled. Rae got out of her vehicle, and Liam climbed from his truck. He stepped in front of her, instinctively shielding her, and the vehicle sped away.

"I think someone might have followed you."

An image from the past flashed through his mind. Rae tied to that chair. Gagged. Her eyes wide with fear as Liam tried to free her, though he knew it was a trap set for him.

He had gained access to a far-reaching trafficking organization. They suspected that an undercover cop had infiltrated, but no one in the organization knew he was the cop. Not until that moment when someone walked in to find Liam setting Rae free. Still, they didn't know his true identity. They knew him as Liam Mercer.

He took that dive then to catch the bullet meant for her.

Rae sucked in a breath, drawing him back to the present.

He had never wanted to see this woman again.

So help him, God, he wanted to walk away from her now. But he'd experienced what could happen when it came to Rae's determination. He knew he wouldn't walk away.

He'd prayed one simple prayer—that God would open a door for him to walk through, and look what happened.

God, please don't let this be a repeat.

And it wouldn't. He couldn't let it be. Because what were the chances that he'd have to take another bullet for her when there were so many other ways to die?

CHAPTER TEN

Rae's pulse jumped. She searched the parking lot but didn't see what had spooked Liam. "Please don't scare me like that."

"I wouldn't make it up."

Liam stood tall and intimidating. His shoulders were broad, and he sported a Jason Statham five-o'clock shadow even in the early afternoon. Wariness lingered in his eyes—only this time, he was suspicious not of *her* but of whoever he thought had followed them.

"Nobody could know I'm here. No one." She shook her head in disbelief. "No one except Alan, but he wouldn't have told anyone."

"*World Tour*? They don't know?"

"I didn't tell them what I was writing about specifically. Or where I would go for research. So, you might want to consider that someone could be following *you*."

He scoffed. "Not hardly."

Liam had gone to great lengths to hide his true identity. No social media presence whatsoever. Rae knew him because they'd been more than close. To look at them now, that was hard to believe. Regardless, she would never share his true identity with anyone.

"You say no one knows you're here. Where did you go right before you stalked that house in the woods?"

That heli-skiing place. "You're right."

"The number of people who know you're here and why you've come will grow exponentially with each person you talk to."

A few snowflakes danced across her cheeks, and she wiped them away. In the distance, beyond Grand Teton, the sky was finally clearing with the promise of a beautiful day. Memories of her time with Liam suddenly flooded her heart. Good memories that knocked into her at the absolute wrong moment. She wrinkled her forehead as she shoved them away. They were not welcome. Not now.

She shrugged off the melancholy. Rae had to remain focused on her mission to find Zoey, help her brother, and be the resourceful aunt Callie needed. What did her career in journalism mean if she failed the most important people in her life? She certainly wouldn't be living up to the standards her father had set.

She grabbed her purse and camera before locking the car and pushing past Liam to head to the resort. Liam caught up with her and walked beside her. She still wasn't sure he intended to help. But if she laid it all out for him, how could he say no? And if someone followed her, she definitely wanted him at her side. He was here with her now and that gave her hope.

"Why did you agree to write a travel article?"

"I'm using it as my cover while I'm here. You know about covers."

"That, I do. But the way covers work is that you're putting on a persona. You're not in any way yourself. You're someone else. You're not hiding that you're a reporter, even if you're pretending to write a travel article. So I'm not sure this is an undercover operation."

"I *am* writing the article." They neared the door and she stopped. "I guess I'm not really working undercover, then. But if anyone asks, I'm here writing a travel article. Only people I'm questioning will know my true purpose here. Does that work for you?"

A dimple emerged in his left cheek. How did he do that without truly smiling? But his eyes—oh, they were smiling. And her heart was tripping over itself.

"Doesn't matter about me. I just hope it works for *you*, Rae." She heard the caring tone in his voice.

I do too, Liam. I do too.

As they approached the entrance to the resort, she took one last glance over her shoulder, hoping she'd see who had followed her. Hoping she would see no one.

Together they pushed through the doors. Warm lighting and caramel-colored wood welcomed them deeper into the rustic facility bursting with western décor, fabulous art, and a homey, comfy feel. She had no idea how they accomplished meshing the styles together, but it was meant to accommodate patrons from all backgrounds and reminded her a bit of Samara Davidson.

Zoey.

"Let's grab something warm to drink at the kiosk and then we can head up to my room. I don't want anyone overhearing what I have to tell you."

With a caramel macchiato and a black coffee in to-go cups, they headed up to her room. At her door when she went to use the key card, he took it from her. "Excuse me," she said.

"Someone followed you. I hope I'm being paranoid. But a little caution can't hurt, especially since I don't know what you've gotten yourself into this time."

"Nobody can get into my room without a key. Even if they could, there are cameras everywhere."

Liam ignored her and removed a weapon from a holster beneath his jacket. Rae hadn't realized he was carrying, but she should have suspected. More like expected. He pressed the card against the key reader and held the weapon as if he anticipated a threat waiting for them inside.

Memories rushed back to her. Setting up that meeting with a known human trafficker, pretending to be someone else to find out about Dina. Being taken to be trafficked herself. Her heart pounded. The images and crushing emotions flashed before her in milliseconds.

She shook them off to concentrate on the muscles in Liam's back. His coat lay at the entrance, where he'd dropped it.

He flipped on the lights.

"Really, Liam." Rae shook her head. He could be over the top at times.

"Really, Rae. See for yourself." He peered into the bathroom to make sure it was clear.

Rae entered to find her room ransacked. A few heartbeats ticked by, then she gasped. "Wha-what were they searching for?"

"They weren't very discreet. Maybe it's a warning. Nobody knows you're here, though, remember?"

"No need to be sarcastic. You already made your point earlier."

Alan knows I'm here. Sam knows. Why would she have me followed? Why would she have my room ransacked? Or was this a random break-in, after all?

Liam pulled out his cell phone. Rae pressed her palms against her temples. What was she going to do now? She needed to focus on finding Zoey. She didn't have time for this.

"Who are you calling?"

"The resort security."

She tried to grab his cell. "Wait. Let me think about this."

"Think about it? What's to think about?"

Rae didn't want to make a big deal or take the time to mess with it—if a life was on the line. Still, this *could* somehow be related to Zoey. "I guess you're right. Okay. Go ahead and call them. But I'm not telling them everything. I don't want the wrong people to know what I'm up to."

Still on his cell, Liam gave her a funny look. Yeah, she understood him loud and clear. Looked like the wrong people already knew. She wasn't sure how that was even possible.

And the question racing through her thoughts right now? Who *were* the wrong people? Did this break-in mean she was on the *right* track?

Rae started to gather her items and put them back in the drawers. Liam was right. This wasn't a theft as much as a warning. Someone wanted her to know they were watching, and they could get to her. Chills crawled over her.

He pressed his hand against her shoulder. "Don't touch anything. We want security to see this. They'll be here in a few minutes."

Rae stopped putting items away. She should have known not to mess with things. For five minutes she and Liam stood in place in the room. With Liam there too, the room seemed to grow smaller with each passing moment. On her cell, she searched through her emails, hoping to find something from Reggie, or even Alan.

"I need fresh air, even if it's cold. Can we at least open a window?" She moved in that direction, but he caught her and shook his head. A knock came at the door.

Liam looked through the peephole, then quickly opened the door to a tall man wearing a resort security jacket. "I'm Greg. You called for security. What's happened?"

"See for yourself." Liam opened the door wide and waved the man in.

"Someone broke into my room and ransacked it," Rae said.

Greg frowned. "I'm sorry to hear that. Was anyone hurt?"

Rae shook her head. "No. I wasn't here at the time."

"Is anything missing?" Greg asked.

Her gaze shot to the desk and her heart skipped a beat. She rushed to where she'd left her laptop. Then she searched the room. "Oh no!"

"What is it?" Liam asked, concern in his eyes.

"My laptop. It's gone!" Rae covered her mouth. She eased onto the edge of the bed. "My life was on that. Everything. My contacts. My articles." Information she'd kept about Zoey. She hadn't noticed it was gone because . . . because . . .

She looked to Liam. That he could distract her so completely infuriated her.

Rae quickly got on her cell. "I'm going to find it with the locator app. Find, lock, and . . . no. I'd better not erase."

She waited for the app to show her laptop's location. "Nothing. How can it show nothing at all?"

"Depends on what software you're using," Greg said as his gaze roamed the room. "Or if you only have software and not a tracker on your actual hard drive."

Greg. Security guy. Make that security tech guy.

Her pulse felt as shaky as her limbs. "I should just erase everything."

She had stored some of her files on the cloud but had kept more sensitive data only on her laptop. Like her bank information, passwords, and . . . a few articles.

Secrets.

Okay, so erase, then. "It's not letting me hit the erase button."

"Your software could require that your laptop be turned on," Greg said.

"Calm down, Rae." Liam now. "There are ways we can track your laptop if someone gets past your log-in and into your files. Like if they access your email account, for one thing, but I don't have the expertise for all this. You need someone else."

"Reggie!" He'd know exactly what to do. She called him, but it went to voicemail. She left him a message with all the information she could regarding locating her laptop. Why didn't he answer? Maybe he had a life outside of his business as a research editor.

Deflated, she dropped her cell to her side. *My laptop. My notes.*

Liam stared at her, but he looked right through her. What was he thinking? "The entire reason they broke in could have been to get your laptop. Maybe they ransacked the place in a quick search for anything else that could be useful—or for drugs."

"What?" Rae stiffened. "I don't do . . . oh, you mean like prescription opioids?"

Liam nodded, a contemplative frown growing between his brows.

"Well I don't use those either."

"As for retrieving information, the thief could know exactly what he's doing," Greg said. "By now, he could have removed the hard drive to retrieve your data and ditched the shell of your laptop, in which case you won't recover anything."

"Oh, that's just great." Rae squeezed her fists. "You guys make it sound like my laptop might have been brutally murdered." She plopped onto the bed and tugged her tablet from her bag. "I'm going to change all the passwords I can."

"That would be wise," Greg said.

She glanced at him. "Any chance your security people can dust for prints?"

"We work with the local authorities. A report will be filed about the break-in and stolen computer. I'll give them a call now."

If they had to go through the local police anyway, what was the point of calling in the resort security? But she didn't pose that question to Greg. He seemed like a good guy and was just doing his job. Resorts needed security for a thousand reasons that didn't have to do with her predicament.

She met Liam's gaze. "I'm going to need a new computer. I don't have time for all this. Zoey . . ." She caught herself. She hadn't even had a chance to tell Liam what was going on.

Liam knitted his brows, but the look he gave said he understood her need for privacy about the investigation. "Let's say this was intentional and not random. What would be on your computer that would make it worth their while to risk security cameras and break into your room?"

"Why does anyone take a computer?" she asked. "To find out more about the owner. Get bank accounts, though they are in for a big surprise there." She was barraged by worry that they'd targeted her and taken her computer to find out about much more. "What else could it be?"

"I think you know, Rae. Let's go with this thought. Let's say they want to know more about what you're investigating. What's on your computer about this investigation so far?"

"Whoa. Wait. Who are you two?" Greg tucked his cell away. "The police are on their way. But seriously, what investigation? What am I missing?"

She'd come here looking into her sister-in-law's background, hoping *that* alone would give her an idea as to what had happened in the past and what was happening now. She didn't want the security guy to know all her secrets and wished he would leave now. Could someone have stolen her laptop because they'd taken Zoey? Or maybe they were looking for her too. Rae's head was beginning to throb. She was overthinking this. She hadn't answered Greg and wasn't sure what to say. Fortunately, someone called him, and he got on his cell again.

Liam moved to watch out the window. She joined him.

Her room afforded a spectacular view of the mountain and ski slopes.

"You're not staying here tonight." A statement. No question in there. "You can stay at the Emerald M Ranch. You'll be safe there."

"I want to stay here. I have to experience the resort and the area to write an article. Staying here gives me more opportunity. I don't want to end up with a giant bill for this room if they think I'm a fraud." She sounded so crass, given that Zoey was still missing.

"It gives you more opportunity for trouble." Liam crossed his arms.

"I haven't even told you what's going on."

"Knowing more won't change my mind."

At least his true thoughts were out in the open.

CHAPTER ELEVEN

He knew the instant Rae turned her blue-green eyes on him. "Hey. Don't talk to me like I don't have a choice. It's my decision where I stay."

"So make your decision to stay at Emerald M, where it's safe." Fueled by remnants of their past, he turned to her and inched closer. "Don't be stubborn about this and put both our lives in danger."

Hurt flashed across her features. He backed off. He hadn't meant to hurt her. Only to put a little fear in her.

"Let me think about it," she said, her voice softening, "but thank you for your offer to stay at the ranch."

He couldn't press her, so he prayed she would see reason and come to his way of thinking on her own.

She glanced over her shoulder at Greg, who was still on the phone. "I should just file a report about the laptop and be done with it. This is taking too long." Her eyes glistened with unshed tears. "I need to find my sister-in-law. She's missing." She rubbed her eyes, exhaustion clearly setting in on top of everything else.

Evidence was quickly growing cold. "I hear you. Normally I would agree that we should just file a report, but in this case, the person who took your laptop could lead us to your sister-in-law.

There's a risk, too, that it's not related. Let me find out more from Greg and see if we can at least get a detective in here."

Rae had been about to tell him everything, and then he would understand why she'd found him today and asked for his help. He already saw that she needed protection, as well as help with her reporter-style private investigation.

Liam waited for Greg to finally end his call, but by the sound of the conversation, he knew the security guard was speaking with local authorities again.

Greg ended the call and tucked his cell away. "The police should be here any moment now. Or, rather, the sheriff's department. Technically, we're in the county. I tried to make it sound urgent so you wouldn't have to wait. The resort's reputation is important as well, so we want to keep this low key for now. I apologize if that sounds insensitive."

"That's understandable," Rae said. "I'm in the middle of something and need to hurry. I appreciate you making this happen as fast as possible."

How much of her investigation would she share with the deputy who would show up? Could they even help if she told them?

"Can your security cameras show us who entered this room?" Liam said.

Greg nodded. "Yes. We'll show those to the police."

"We'd like to see if Rae recognizes the burglar."

"That makes sense. We'll wait for whoever they're sending."

If Liam took the job Brad had offered, he could one day work a break-in like this himself. "How often do break-ins happen at resorts?"

"I've been working here for three years. Before this, I was over at Teton Village closer to Jackson. Honestly, this is the first time I've seen it. Like you said, we'll see who entered the premises. People know about security cameras, and they serve as a deterrent. I'm surprised this happened."

Liam almost snorted. Greg had never dealt with someone like Rae. Determined to find the answers. Expose the truth. And save those in desperate situations.

Besides being Rae's sister-in-law, who exactly was this missing woman?

A knock sounded at the door. Greg opened it, and after a quick exchange, a sheriff's department deputy entered the room—Deputy Randall Cook. Liam had met the guy after working as a consultant for Bridger County last summer. Though Liam himself didn't work for the sheriff, Heath did. Liam would use that and any other connection he had to his advantage if that would help Rae find her sister-in-law so she could then leave the valley.

Liam thrust his hand out to shake the deputy's.

Deputy Cook glanced around the room. He pulled out a paper tablet and a pencil, and Rae told him about the break-in.

Cook tapped his pad with the pencil. "Let's have a look at the security cameras now."

Rae, Liam, and Deputy Cook followed Greg to the elevator, took it down to the resort's basement, and crowded around a computer screen behind Greg. He quickly found the footage they needed.

A bouncer-sized man wearing black skiwear and a mask carried skis over his shoulders from the elevator and down the hallway and stopped at Rae's room. He flashed a key card in front of the reader and entered.

Rae gasped. "How did he get a key to my room? That's ridiculous."

"I apologize for what's happened, Ms. Burke," Greg said. "We want your experience to be the best." Greg kept his face neutral, but Liam could tell this disturbed the guy too. Why wouldn't it?

"Unfortunately, master key cards are fairly easy to come by if someone is determined. I'll recommend that we ramp up protecting the master cards. In the meantime, I can question all the staff

ELIZABETH GODDARD

to find out whose card is missing and go at it from that angle. Our policies require housekeeping to keep those cards with them at all times—not sitting on the carts where they can be taken and inappropriately used by an unauthorized person."

Rae blew out a breath. "It's okay, Greg. Not your fault."

A few minutes later, the masked intruder exited, still carrying the skis.

"Look closely there," Cook said. "I can't tell for sure, but it looks like he's hugging your laptop under his jacket to the left while he carries the skis over his shoulder."

"Let's see." Greg fast-forwarded the footage until Rae and Liam entered with their coffees, then they reviewed it again. No one else had entered. "He's the guy who took it. Give me a minute here."

Greg reviewed cameras on the other floors during the same time period. The masked man had only entered Rae's room.

Deputy Cook stepped back from the computer and studied Rae. "Looks like you had something in your room or on your laptop that he wanted. Any idea what he wanted or who he is?"

"No. I don't recognize him, at least what I can make of him with a mask on, if that's what you're asking."

"That's only half of what I'm asking." Cook continued to stare at her.

Rae glanced at all three men watching her. "I'm looking into a missing woman. Zoey Dumont."

"Who?" Cook asked.

"I'm sorry, Tawny Davidson. She changed her name to Zoey Dumont."

Cook frowned. "Are you saying you believe this break-in has to do with her?"

"I'm not sure what to believe," she said.

"Let's see if there are any identifiers on this guy," the deputy said. "We can't see any tattoos because he's covered head to toe."

"Even if he wasn't covered, the footage is too grainy," Rae said.

"Looks like he's wearing a sports watch," Greg pointed out.

"Great," Cook said. "That, to go with his black attire and mask. That doesn't help us."

"But look closer. The watch face is green. That's unusual. And it's on his right wrist," Liam said. "That could mean he's left-handed. It could help us narrow things down."

"Have you learned anything about Zoey?" Rae shifted her full attention to the deputy. "Are you actively looking for her?"

"I'm not working on that, but others are. I'll let them know what's happened here." To Greg, he said, "Can you move her to another room? I'd like the sheriff in on this. We need to get evidence techs in here in case this is related to the missing woman's disappearance."

"Sure, but can I ask a favor?" Greg handed off a USB drive presumably holding a copy of the footage. "Please don't string yellow crime scene tape across her door. We don't want to scare the guests."

"Fine by me. Don't let housekeeping in, then. But doesn't seem like you have much control over who is getting into the rooms. I'll get someone to guard this room until it's processed in case our visitor decides to return." Cook called for assistance on his cell.

Liam could hardly believe the turn of events.

"I'll assist you in moving to a new room," Greg said.

"That won't be necessary," Liam said. "She's checking out."

"I'm not checking out." She stared Liam down. "I need to keep a room here, Liam."

Fine.

"I just need to make sure we have one available." Greg waited on his cell.

Liam secretly hoped they didn't have an extra room. That their last vacant room was now a crime scene.

"I'm writing an article, so I need to be close."

"I'm so sorry for what's happened." Greg spoke to her though he was on hold. "But sounds like you're working double duty, Ms. Burke. Writing an article and also looking for a missing person." He frowned and addressed the person on the phone. "Okay. Not good." He ended the call, then peered at her. "There's nothing available until tomorrow."

Liam turned to her. "It's okay, Rae. You have a safe place to stay. And it won't change the potential for your article."

It looked like he was getting in deep. *What am I doing?*

An hour later, Deputy Cook allowed Rae to take her luggage from her ransacked room. The deputy had waited there to make sure no one entered until others had arrived to process it.

Greg stayed with Rae and Liam and escorted them all the way to the exit. "Again, I'm so sorry about what's happened. I hope it doesn't reflect on us in that article you're writing."

Rae shrugged and offered a small smile. "It's nothing to do with you, so don't worry."

"Are you going to be all right?" Greg had that look in his eyes like he might want to ask Rae out. She seemed alone and vulnerable, but not needy. Never needy. Misplaced jealousy crawled through Liam. Or rather, slithered.

"Yes, thanks, Greg."

"You're welcome. Call me if you need anything." He handed her his card. "Anything at all."

She nodded. "I will."

Greg left them at the exit. *I can't believe this guy.* But Rae hadn't caught on to Greg's interest in her. Liam obviously hadn't given off any possessive vibes, and why should he? He'd gone to a lot of trouble to avoid feeling emotional connections.

Liam had been watching to make sure Greg left for good, then realized Rae was watching *him*.

"You can step away from this if that's what you're thinking," she said.

Where had that come from? Rae was scared about everything that was happening. Liam could easily see that. He sensed, too, that she was still hesitant about staying at the Emerald M.

"You want to know what I'm thinking?"

"I'm not so sure anymore." She arched a brow.

"Too bad. I'm thinking that I'm glad there wasn't another room for you here," he said. "You need to be somewhere safe. Emerald M has plenty of room for you this time of year. As for your room here, I want to know how the masked man knew where you were staying to begin with. He knew the exact room, Rae. You need to stay somewhere safe while we work on finding answers."

"We?"

"Yes. We."

"You haven't even heard the details yet. Once you hear them, you might decide to take off."

"Do you really think I'm going to leave you when you're looking for your missing sister-in-law?"

She sucked in a breath. His words seemed to bolster her. It stung that she had doubted he would stick it out.

"I looked for you because I had hoped you would help. But your initial reaction gave me reason to doubt." A tenuous grin lifted one corner of her lips. "But I'm glad to hear that you're in this with me. As for asking more of you, I think I'm safe now. He got my laptop. There's nothing else I have that anyone could want."

"You, Rae. They could want you. Even if you check in at another place in town, then they could get to you."

She stared at him and chewed on her lip. He hadn't meant to scare her more. Okay, yeah, he'd meant to scare some *sense* into her.

"The safest place for you right now is with me. Will you stay at the Emerald M? It's been a long day and looks to be an even longer night. We'll get some dinner, and you can tell me everything. We'll put our heads together and then, Rae, we'll find her." Liam almost cringed at his own words. He was sounding more like Heath. He hardly recognized himself.

She angled her head, her silent question clear. Who *are* you?

CHAPTER TWELVE

Rae had the eerie sensation that her life had been hijacked as Liam steered them along the two-lane highway that wound through Bridger-Teton National Forest. Reporting the stolen laptop and looking at video footage had taken entirely too long. Now they were headed to Emerald M Guest Ranch in Liam's truck. She hadn't wanted to make that drive at night, even following him.

Rae had agreed to go with Liam, and until she knew more about what was going on, she didn't want to stay anywhere else. Especially after learning that someone could easily come and go in any hotel room if they got their hands on a master key. Even if Greg had found her another room at the lodge, she wouldn't have slept a wink. The break-in had left her feeling violated.

Would the masked man be able to access her information? If so, and he took the time to read Rae's writings and the articles her father had written, he would know more about Rae than even her family knew.

Nausea stirred in the pit of her stomach.

She focused ahead, the driving snow in the headlights all she could see as she remembered the scenery from her early morning venture out to the ranch along this same treacherous road.

If she hadn't spent the time tracking Liam down, would she be closer to finding Zoey?

"Okay, Rae," the patient man next to her finally said. "I've been waiting for you to open up for miles. I know you mean well. You're not some nosy reporter looking for a story. What happened in the past aside, if I'm going to help you, beyond being an obviously needed bodyguard, you have to talk."

"Thank you for that, Liam."

She wasn't sure he was being completely honest, especially after his initial reaction to seeing her earlier. But his tone gave away the pain in his words. He still believed she'd used him, but did he fully understand she was motivated by the need to help others? Compelled to tell their stories no matter the cost?

Her last run-in with him had erupted in disaster that left him injured. She'd hurt him physically, and she would expect emotionally as well. Psychologically? Maybe. But he appeared to have picked up the pieces and moved on. Except what was he doing here in Jackson Hole instead of working an undercover case in a drug-laden location?

Regardless, now was that moment they would talk. The moment she'd been waiting for all day, and still she dreaded it. She blew out another breath and hesitated.

"You came to me today, Rae. I'm here because I don't want to see you hurt or dead. Now, tell me what's going on."

"It's complicated."

"If you remember, I do complicated well."

She snuck a glance his direction and found him grinning. His grin had always gotten to her.

"Look, I'm already in this. You owe it to me to tell me what's going on. Why are you here in Jackson Hole trying to find your sister-in-law?"

After what had already happened today, she was rethinking her initial decision to ask for his help. She could hire a private investigator. Someone else. She'd only thought of Liam because he'd been willing to die to protect her. That was someone she could trust. But that didn't mean she wanted to put him in that kind of danger again—he'd already sacrificed so much.

Exhaustion weighed on her, and she rubbed her eyes. "I'm not sure where to start."

"We have a ways to go on this drive, so you can start at the beginning."

Rae blew out a breath. "Before Zoey was Alan's wife, she was my college roommate. That's how she met Alan, in fact. One night, Zoey didn't come back to our dorm room. We had planned to see a movie that night, so I was worried when she didn't show up. I was about to go to the campus police when Zoey texted me to cover for her. Said she needed a break from classes. She gave me no other explanation. It was just weird, and I was still worried. A few days later I came home and found Zoey soaking in the tub. Dark circles under her eyes and bruises on her body. I wanted to rush her to the emergency room or call the police, but she made me promise not to tell another soul. Zoey warned me that if I told anyone, she would disappear again and for good this time."

Rae rubbed her eyes again. She needed to remember everything. "So, I kept Zoey even closer. I took her home to meet my family a few weeks later. She met Mom and Alan. Dad had died a couple of years before. I didn't tell anyone about what happened to Zoey, except for Alan. He was falling for her and needed to be warned about what he was getting into. But by the time I got to that conversation, Alan was already smitten. He proposed, and they married three weeks later."

"Your brother's actions remind me of you, Rae. You're the hero of basket cases and underdogs. You don't wield a gun. Your weapon is the mighty pen or, these days, laptop. How about word? That's it. You use the written word as a weapon."

She tossed him a weary smile.

"Sorry. I'll shut up now. Tell me the rest."

Rae shared the rest of the story about Zoey's current disappearance. Her voice shook. Just thinking about the incident in college stirred disturbing memories.

"You think the two disappearances are related or else you wouldn't have brought up what happened in college. How could they be related?"

"The billion-dollar question. I suspected she had a stalker back then. Anyway, Alan asked me to find her and suggested I talk to her mother and look into her past."

"Wait a minute. He asked you to do this? Why can't he do it?"

"They have a four-year-old daughter, Callie. Alan is the one who called the police, and he knows they're looking at him closely. The husband is the first person on their radar. Beyond that, Callie is autistic. He needs to be there for her. But I found out today from Samara Davidson, Zoey's mother, that Zoey did have a stalker and that was the reason she fled Jackson Hole and changed her name. She had hoped to escape him. Maybe that was even part of the reason she married Alan. Regardless, I know she loves him. I know she loves Callie and would never willingly leave. But I had theorized that her stalker had found her again and took her."

"And now you've decided that's not the case?"

"I learned that authorities recently found and identified his remains. So he can't be the person who took her. I'm grasping at straws."

"Hold your next words. I need to concentrate on this drive. It's tricky when it's dark." He stopped the truck and engaged the plow. "You actually drove on this road today?"

"Yes. I rented a four-wheel drive because I didn't know where my search would take me." She let him concentrate on the drive, the truck pushing snow out of the way.

Finally, he steered the truck under the Emerald M Ranch archway, then kept going until he parked next to three vehicles in front of the huge log cabin with a wraparound porch.

"If we're lucky, my family might already be in bed since they have to get up in the middle of the night if they want to make their early morning flights."

Rae's eyes pooled with tears, and she was grateful he couldn't see them in the dark. "Before we go in, I need to ask you something. First, though, thank you. Thank you for being here with me. You didn't have to, you know. After the trouble I caused you. You're here in Wyoming instead of working as an undercover agent—that's because of me, isn't it?"

"If anything, I should thank you for giving me a reason to get out. Anything else?"

Rae wanted to dig deeper into his comment, but now wasn't the time. He'd been generous enough and she didn't want to push him. "Yes. There's something else. I want to make it official. I want to hire you."

"Hire me for what?"

"To help me investigate. Are you available?"

"I'll have to check my calendar." He grinned. "Obviously my schedule has a few openings." Liam shifted to hold her gaze. "I'm not sure you should get involved any deeper in this. I know you want to find Zoey, but I'm worried about you. This isn't safe. You've been here a day and look what's happened."

She keenly felt his scrutiny. "Then I can hire you for double duty. Bodyguard and investigator."

"Why can't I simply help you?"

"I think it would be better if I made it official by hiring you."

"Oh, I get it. You think I might get frustrated and leave you holding the bag, so to speak."

Something like that. "Let's just say that this way there won't be any question about what's happening. Plus, if anyone asks, you can say you're working as a PI. I looked it up. In Wyoming, all you need is—"

"A business card. Meaning, you don't need a license or certificate. And that's why you sought me out?"

His gaze was pensive, as if he didn't want to let her in again. She didn't blame him. Even though his words sounded stern, the familiar small dimple emerged in his cheek. He couldn't possibly be happy about her reappearance in his life, could he?

"I couldn't trust anyone else with this."

She wanted to say more but was afraid she would shut him down. Liam knew full well why she trusted him. He'd saved her life once already, but what she was sure Liam still didn't understand . . . *I didn't use you to get a story.*

She'd used him to save a life.

His expression hardened.

Yeah. His mind was going back to their dark past.

And so was hers.

CHAPTER THIRTEEN

Liam didn't want to go there with her. Talking about what happened before wouldn't fix anything. Rehashing it wouldn't remove the pain in his leg or the numbness in his heart. She might trust him with her life, but he certainly had trust issues when it came to her. Still, he was tired, and it was late, and someone was missing.

He shoved open his door and hopped from his truck, glad Pete or Leroy had shoveled the area so Rae could easily get out on her side. He said nothing. He needed to let it go. It's why he'd stayed here for months. And now he found himself with her. A cruel joke.

Just move on, Liam. He'd made the decision to help her, and he couldn't be much help if he carried resentment around on his shoulders. Even if she'd used him, he needed to forgive her. What he didn't know was if she'd ever truly felt anything for him.

He hiked around the truck to help her. "Please keep your voice down. We don't want to wake my brothers and their wives if they've already gone to bed." Even though it was only around ten o'clock, he hoped they'd made an early night of it.

He'd missed dinner, though he'd assured Heath he would be there. So he'd missed saying goodbye. But they wouldn't be disappointed in him for staying true to character. Regret kicked him in the gut. When he'd come back, he'd wanted to be different.

Liam led Rae to the porch, and they treaded lightly up the steps. He unlocked the door. Years ago, they never locked it. Out here in middle-of-nowhere Wyoming, the only creatures in this edge of the forest that edged the Gros Ventre Wilderness were the wildlife. But recent dangerous incidents that encroached on their quiet ranch had changed their definition of security.

Inside the spacious log home, Liam flipped on a small lamp near the door. The faded aroma of elk burgers still lingered in the air. The dogs, Timber and Rufus, were probably sleeping with their respective owners. The dogs were on the old side and good about not barking unless they sensed danger.

He glanced at Rae. "I can show you to a guest room. But honestly, I'm famished. If you're exhausted, you can go to sleep, or you're welcome to join me in the kitchen for leftovers."

"I'm hungry too." She dropped the bag holding a few belongings on the floor next to the door.

Liam led her into the kitchen and flipped on the lights.

"I'm exhausted, but I don't think I can sleep." She kept her voice low as she climbed onto a stool and ran her hand over the butcher-block countertop. "This place is beautiful. So what's your story, Liam? How do you go from ranch life in Jackson Hole to working undercover for the DEA?"

Liam retrieved plastic containers of leftovers from the fridge. He'd hoped to avoid that particular conversation and would make it as succinct as possible.

"My parents fought a lot. Mom died in a fire when I was a kid. Dad drank and wasn't fun to be around. The ranch was run-down and falling apart. Nothing like what you see now. So when I turned eighteen, I joined the marines. I figured nobody would ever push me around again if I was a marine. I joined law enforcement after that, and the next thing you know I was working undercover to take down drug-trafficking rings. They said I had a knack for it." His only failure, his last operation. But . . . *Let it go, Liam*. No need to rehash their past. He cleared his throat. "After I got out of the hospital and still wasn't approved to go back to work, I ended up coming back here. I was impressed to see what Heath had done. He'd expanded the home and the ranch. Built cabins for guests. Created a glowing reputation. Added horses and a guided offsite tour. I've been working with him since I got here." At least he was trying to work, though oddly enough he found it uninspiring. He tried to find peace. Tried to make Heath happy too.

He dished up plates and stuck one in the microwave to heat. "While that's warming, I'm going to get my laptop."

His room was on the first floor, just down from Evelyn's attached cabin. Heath had added that because she'd wanted her own separate entrance to the home after Heath and Harper were married. Back in the kitchen he found Rae warming up the next plate. She'd set utensils on the counter. A memory startled him.

Rae had been arranging plates on a table for a quiet meal for them. A romantic meal. She had smiled up at him, bashful, when he'd walked into the room and noticed what she was doing. His heart had pinged around inside then.

It pinged around inside now at the memory.

He'd been foolish to work with a reporter, but she was a different breed. Plus, she'd wanted to make the world a better place, though they had gone about that task from different angles. She'd already discovered information he could use in his own investigation, so their liaison had formed naturally and out of a desperate need to find a missing trafficked woman, to find the hidden person behind the drug and human-trafficking ring. Their partnership had been unofficial and off the record. But he'd grown attached to her.

And it had been because of Rae that he'd known he'd wanted to escape his life working with the DEA. She represented goodness, or at least he'd thought so. Admittedly, he'd been blinded by his feelings for her, then blind*sided* when it all came crashing down.

The microwave dinged and brought him back to the present. She glanced up at him, only then noticing he'd returned with his laptop, and she smiled. Yep. That same smile that had caught his attention to begin with and stolen his heart.

He shook off the sudden melancholy and slid his laptop onto the counter. Booted it up.

"What are you doing? Aren't you going to eat?" She climbed onto a stool next to him as she slid a plate for each of them onto the counter.

"I'm sure you've heard of multitasking." He sent her a half grin. "I want to see what we can find out about the man you mentioned who had stalked Zoey. What was his name again?"

"Simon Astor."

Liam typed in the name, and instantly the headlines regarding remains popped up. "When did you say that Zoey went missing the first time?"

"Five years ago."

"It says here that Simon Astor has been missing for five years."

Rae stared at him, those big blue eyes blinking rapidly as her face paled. "You don't think . . . You don't think that Zoey killed him, do you?"

"It might explain why she made you swear not to tell anyone that she'd turned up bruised and beaten after she'd been gone for a week."

Rae's frown deepened. "Maybe she was afraid of being arrested, even though she would only have killed him in self-defense. Still, I can't believe it. There has to be another explanation."

"Or maybe she was afraid of being linked to his murder for

entirely different reasons. Depending on who this guy was connected to, she could have been afraid for her life."

Liam took a few bites of the juicy elk burger as he stared at the
news story. That pasty face, along with the thinning, dirty-blond
hair—the guy seemed familiar. Just like the name. *Where do I
know him from?*

Rae played with her food. The idea that Zoey could have killed
this Astor guy disturbed her. He understood that. He also understood that neither of them would sleep tonight. "Tell me the rest.
I want to know everything," he said. "Like, what do the police in
Denver know?"

"We told them everything. My brother told them what happened to Zoey while she was in college—her disappearance and
how she'd been violently assaulted. Alan wondered if her disappearance was connected to what happened back then. I did too.
At the time, I didn't have Simon's name. My brother has done
everything he can to find her, but he has Callie to think about.
He wants to keep her in a stable environment for as long as possible."

"So, if the police know about all this, then why aren't you letting them do their job?"

She skewered him. "Really, Liam. You have to ask me that? You
of all people should understand. Atrocities happen every day that
police aren't aware of. There simply aren't enough law enforcement entities to cover all the evil in the world. If there were, then
bad guys wouldn't get away with murder. This is my brother's
wife. My friend. If the worst happened and I didn't do anything
at all, if I didn't at least use some of my skills, then I would never
forgive myself."

Liam understood that exact motivation—it was what motivated
him now.

Rae took a bite of her burger. He was glad to see her eating.

"Samara Davidson said the police had delivered the news and

asked a few questions," she said. "More than that, I'm not sure if they're even looking for her here in the valley where she grew up."

"We'll talk to the county sheriff, an almost-friend of mine. At least get the lines of communication going in addition to what we've already explained to Deputy Cook. He's more of a patrol guy, and I don't want anything to fall through the cracks of misinformation."

They finished up their meal in silence. Liam gathered their dishes.

"I don't want to approach the sheriff only to have him tell me to go away," Rae said. "You don't think he'll try to stand in our way?"

"We're not going to do anything illegal, so why should he?"

She nodded. "The more people on this, the better. We'll talk to your sheriff tomorrow. But let's get started early. In fact, I don't know why we don't just work through the night. Zoey could be suffering while we take our sweet time eating leftover elk burgers."

She always had a way of making irrefutable points. That, along with her determination, was probably part of what made her a brilliant journalist. He worried about her. Dark circles were beginning to emerge under her eyes. As if undeterred by exhaustion, she shoved her blonde hair behind her ears, revealing small topaz earrings, and leaned in to look at his laptop screen. She lifted her fingers toward the keyboard.

He gently took her hands in his, ignoring her soft skin. "Sometimes you need to rest to think clearly. Tomorrow is almost here. A few hours of sleep will go a long way in helping us find Zoey."

"You're right. In the meantime, I can let Reggie know what I've discovered."

"Reggie?"

"I have my resources." Rae explained about her father's research editor. "I have my own skills with databases, but they're limited in comparison. Reggie has his own business to help reporters and journalists with information. It's called the Information Depot. It helps speed up the process. You must have the same kind of people in law enforcement. Your computer geeks and white hat hackers."

Rae texted a message on her cell. He assumed it was to this Reggie person.

She swiped at her eyes. "So, I'd rather let's stay on focus."

Her cell buzzed. She glanced at the screen. "Speaking of which, this is Reggie." She answered the call. "Reggie, hi. I'm here with Liam McKade, who I've hired to protect me and help me investigate. I'm putting you on speakerphone. What do you have for me?"

"Nice to meet you, Liam."

Liam noticed the distinctive British accent. "You as well."

"I'll get right to it, then. It took me longer than I thought today. Had to put out a few fires, as it were." Reggie tapped on a keyboard. "Here goes. Tawny Davidson, also known as Zoey Dumont Burke. Tawny Davidson was born to Samara and Mark Davidson and attended school in Jackson. She worked with the heli-skiing business founded by her parents, managing all the financials and billing."

"Wait," Liam said. "How do you find this stuff out?"

Reggie chuckled. "I have a lot of practice at searching efficiently. I know which archives to look into, and I feed that into a custom knowledge base. Why don't we skip to the fun parts, shall we? I've fed into the knowledge base all the information from Tawny's life in Jackson Hole and her life as Zoey Dumont and then Zoey Burke up until her disappearance. There's been no credit card or phone activity since her disappearance, by the way. Cross-referenced that with news or anomalies to find any possible correlations."

Impressive. "And?"

"You told me of her disappearance five years ago, Rae. Using an algorithm, I cross-referenced disappearances that occurred around that time to find any possible connections. One in particular was flagged. Simon Astor. He hails from Arizona, but his family owned second homes in the Jackson Hole region where Zoey grew up.

I also noted that his remains were recovered this week, the very week that Zoey disappeared again. Could be coincidental. Or there could be a link."

"There is. He stalked her," Rae said. "He's the reason she moved. But he's dead, so he couldn't be responsible for her current disappearance. But the fact that he disappeared five years ago, too, and didn't resurface until his remains were discovered recently raises a lot of questions."

"Indeed, it does. And there's more. Simon Astor's brother is Enzo Astor, the wealthy son of a real estate mogul, now the mogul himself. Enzo Astor owns multiple properties in Jackson Hole, Colorado, and Utah—mainly hotels and ski resorts. What do you think now?"

"Wait," Liam said. "What about the newly opened Saddleback Mountain Ski Resort?"

"Yes. That's one of his investments."

Interesting. Brad had mentioned there was more than one investor. Who else?

Rae stared into space, probably lost in thought, then her eyes brightened. "Okay. What if Simon the stalker found Zoey in Denver while she was in college, and he took her. She killed him. Then five years later his remains are discovered, and Enzo believed Zoey was responsible, so *he* abducted her. There's no hard evidence, but we have to start somewhere. I'm just trying to figure it all out."

"There could be a possible connection there, but as you say, you have no hard evidence, just conjecture," Reggie said. "In journalism, we know to follow the paper trails, the digital trails, as well as the facts. Our mantra is 'follow the money.' I'm working on that end of it. I'll continue to funnel the information your way."

"You've done so much already, Reggie. I can't begin to thank you," she said. "Please keep working. We're already past the forty-eight-hour mark." Rae explained about the rest of her day and that, using her tablet, she'd already changed all her passwords.

"In an effort to find your laptop," Reggie said, "I'll be monitoring all possible access to your social media or emails, anything that could give me an IP address or something to follow, in case they were accessed before you changed your passwords. In the meantime, I'll email a copy of what we discussed tonight so you can refer to the data, and we'll be in touch tomorrow. And Rae?"

"Yes?"

"I'm glad you've hired Liam. Liam, please keep her safe at any cost."

"I'll protect her with my life." He shrugged. He'd already proven that, hadn't he?

"That's fair. *Sayonara*." Reggie ended the call.

Liam had to laugh. "That's *fair*?"

Rae chuckled too. "He's a character."

"If your father had access to this guy, I can see why he won awards, though probably it had more to do with going into the field in the middle of conflicts."

Rae nodded, a distant and somber look in her eyes. Thinking about her dad and how he died? Liam wished he hadn't brought it up.

"So, Reggie will follow the money, and maybe tomorrow we'll know something more about Simon's brother," she said.

"It's no different in the DEA."

"The love of money's the root of all evil," she said.

"You got that right. If there's one thing I learned working in the DEA, money has a close relationship with drugs. In the end, all crimes are usually related to drugs, including trafficking of arms or humans." He and Rae had already found that out, up close and personal. If they didn't find Zoey soon, they might need to work the drug angle and see where that led them.

Footfalls drew his attention. Heath stood there with bed hair and frowned, then smiled at Rae. "Hi. I heard voices, so thought I'd check."

Timber had followed him downstairs. Heath scratched the dog's head and studied them.

Liam made the introductions quietly. He hadn't thought about how much information he would share with Heath, who was also a Bridger County reserve deputy. For a while, Liam had experienced that feeling that his past would follow him, and here Rae sat, but it was more than that. The uncanny awareness that the evil he'd escaped hadn't let go of him or Rae. He couldn't shake the sense it was all related—maybe it was some form of paranoia or PTSD. Regardless, he didn't want his brothers to pay the price.

"She's going to need a room in the house tonight. I'm giving her Evelyn's old room."

Heath raked his fingers through his hair as if just realizing it was askew. "I'd suggest getting some sleep before you wake up the whole house."

Heath—that *look* in his eyes—glanced at Rae again and then at Liam. He reminded Liam of Evelyn, who was determined to win at her matchmaking games. His brother approached him and gave him a bear hug. He whispered, "You be careful while I'm gone, you hear?"

When his older brother released him, Liam nodded and held Heath's gaze for a few seconds. Heath had always been protective, especially after their father failed them so miserably.

"You have fun on your honeymoon, and don't worry about me." The words felt good to say.

Appreciation swarmed in Heath's gaze.

He took Rae's hand and held it between both of his larger ones. "It was good to meet you, Rae. I hope I get the chance to get to know you better in the future."

Then his brother left them.

What in the world had he meant with those last words? Liam didn't want to think about it. He couldn't afford the time, so he focused back on the task before them. His mind went to his experience with the DEA and his conversation with Rae before Heath appeared.

Money. Drugs. Trafficking.

Liam got the distinct impression that darkness had indeed followed him here.

Maybe it was time to shine a little light into the shadows.

CHAPTER FOURTEEN

Alan sat in the chair in Callie's room. His heart ached, and he moved in a constant state of nausea.

He'd called Rae, but she hadn't answered. He hoped Rae had learned something from Zoey's mother, but the more he thought about it, the more he realized his mistake. He couldn't lose Rae too. He never should have asked for her help. He pressed his hand over his eyes.

The detective informed him they had talked to Zoey's mother—Samara Davidson—and told her about her missing daughter.

They'd shared her real name.

Tawny.

Alan could have unearthed her past if he'd chosen to dig. But he'd allowed Zoey to keep her demons far from them, where they should have stayed so they wouldn't come between them.

Except they'd come between them anyway.

He dropped his hand from his eyes to watch his daughter. His beautiful, sweet daughter. She didn't deserve any of what was happening. He hoped he could protect her forever. Callie's face was so sweet and innocent. How would he prevent evil from reaching into her world? He could keep the news that her mother was missing from her for only so long.

God, how do I tell her? Please . . . Please don't let it come to that.

He held back quiet sobs. If the police found some reason to arrest him for Zoey's disappearance, it would only be a matter of time before they learned the truth.

His cell buzzed in his pocket, so he eased from the chair and crept out of Callie's room. The bogeyman wasn't going to get her as long as her father was there. That's what he'd told her, so he'd stayed close until she fell asleep.

But he hadn't kept the bogeyman from snatching her mother.

He quickly answered the cell.

"Rae," he whispered as he moved farther down the hallway and into his study. "You scared me when you didn't call me back. I've changed my mind. I asked you to help, but please just come home."

"I can't come home. I don't trust the police will follow this lead. They won't look at this the same way I will. But don't worry. I've hired someone to help."

"I don't want you to do this, after all. I can't lose you too."

"You won't. I promise. Any news from the police there? What do they know so far?"

A knot lodged in his throat. "They found her car."

Rae gasped. "Oh, Alan."

"I don't know what I was expecting, or even hoping. If they never found it, I could hope that she'd taken off on her own for some important reason that I would somehow and someday understand. It was parked at a local grocery store. The police are looking at the security cameras in that area."

He stood up to look out the window at the dimly lit street. A few cars were parked at the curb in front of neighboring homes. Alan's remained in the drive. At some point he expected reporters would camp out waiting to catch a glimpse of them in the windows or question him if and when he had to leave. He dropped the mini blinds to cover the window now.

"They set up a hotline, you know," he said.

"Oh? Good, I'm glad to hear it. Any leads?"

"Too many leads, and none of them legitimate."

"We'll find her, Alan. Don't worry." Rae sounded as if she believed her own words, but he knew she only meant to encourage him.

"There's something I need to tell you." *Oh, how do I tell her?* "Something you don't know."

The connection crackled, then she asked, "What is it?"

"In case things go from bad to worse and I'm charged for whatever happened to Zoey, someone's bound to find this out and I don't want you to be blindsided. I'm not Callie's biological father."

"Alan, I—"

"Save it. I knew that when I married her. It was the real reason we married so quickly. I loved her and didn't care. Maybe it was the real reason I didn't care about her past—I was afraid to find out. All I know is that I can't let them take Callie away. I'm the only father she's ever known. I want you to know, because, well, that's what you do. Like Dad, you're . . ." Emotion choked him. He couldn't say the words. *You speak for those who can't speak for themselves.*

"Who could take her away from you? Your name is listed as the father on her birth certificate, right? Please don't worry. It's not going to happen. You're exhausted and not thinking clearly."

"If her real father knows—whoever he is—if he knows, he could come for her."

"Alan, please. Stop this. One thing at a time. You focus on keeping yourself together. Pray. Take care of Callie. Hold her close and love her. With the private investigator I've hired and Reggie, the same resource Dad used, together, we're going to find Zoey."

One way or another. Dead or alive. She didn't say it, but they were both thinking it.

CHAPTER FIFTEEN

After ending the call with Alan, Rae moved to the window. Liam had settled her into a cozy western-styled bedroom on the first floor of his family's sprawling ranch home. Comforting scents of cedar and vanilla wrapped around her. She put her face close enough to the glass that she could feel the cold seeping through. The sky had cleared again, belying the forecasted blizzard that would be on them within a day or two. In the meantime, she would enjoy the stars that shined bright in the deepest part of winter's night. The snow gave off a blue-gray sheen that sparkled as it blanketed the ground and laced the evergreens.

Breathtaking. Another postcard moment.

Eerie and silent except for the creak of the house shifting now and again. A tuft of snow falling from the roof. A tree branch scraping the window.

While she'd never been a big fan of silence—keeping quiet about wrongdoing was the worst kind of evil in her opinion—she could allow herself this moment of peace. This was a different

108

kind of silence, and it had a sound of its own. As she listened, she took in the scenery. In the distance, the jagged edge of a mountain peak clawed at the sky above the trees.

Her breath caught in her throat. "It's truly beautiful here," she whispered.

God, you're here in this place. In the stars above. In the mountains and the woods, smiling down at me from heaven and here with me now, closer than I can understand.

She knew that. Would hold on to it. But sometimes it seemed that God's silence—even when he was near—could be deafening.

Rae didn't understand why any of this was happening to her brother. Had happened to Zoey. Just like she never understood why such horrific crimes had been committed against people whom she interviewed for her stories. Why humans committed such heinous acts against fellow humans.

Who could ever understand why life unraveled beneath them? No one. She wouldn't ask the creator of the universe why, because there would be no way to comprehend his answer. All she could do was trust him to make a way for her. To hold her in the palm of his hand. And Zoey too.

God, please protect Zoey.

She'd wanted to say so much more to Alan, but she doubted he could handle more. From the beginning, she'd wondered if Zoey's child belonged to Alan. Zoey and Alan had married quickly, and when Callie was born weeks early but with the development of a full-term baby, Rae had her answer. But Alan had all the same facts she had, and as he said, he went into the relationship with his eyes wide open. He was Callie's father, and she would continue to think of him that way. He hadn't cared that Zoey was already pregnant when he met her, and he'd loved her unconditionally.

Rae sighed. To be loved so deeply.

She wasn't sure how long she gazed at the stars before more

snow clouds drifted in. If Zoey was still alive out there somewhere, where could she be?

"What do I do when I have so little to go on and no time left?"

Lord, am I following the wrong lead here? I've never felt so lost.

CHAPTER SIXTEEN

12:47 A.M.

Liam stood outside, his warm breath billowing into the cold, lonely night. He crept to the far corner of the wraparound porch and leaned against a pine post. He didn't want to disturb anyone while making his call. Maybe he should sit in his truck instead.

A pang of guilt stabbed him. He'd missed the family dinner with his brothers and new sisters-in-law. He wanted to fit in. He really did. But now wasn't the time to figure out how he could. Besides, Heath was too enamored with his new bride to worry about Liam too much. Austin too.

Good for them.

Liam trusted Heath to understand that Liam had missed dinner because he'd gotten involved with helping Rae. After all, Heath had stated that he knew Liam would do the right thing. Doing the right thing had dragged Liam even deeper into the situation, and now he was fully enmeshed in the search for Rae's missing sister-in-law. Protecting Rae was beginning to look like an enormous task. From experience, Liam knew this woman and the trouble she could stir up. In less than twenty-four hours, he'd been proven right.

He stared at his cell and retrieved an image of Enzo Astor. Liam's gut tensed. He thought he'd recognized Simon, the brother who was dead, but it was actually his older brother, Enzo, who looked familiar. Where had he seen this guy before? He wasn't getting the kind of déjà vu feeling that gave him warm fuzzies. He scrolled through the numbers on his cell, which he'd gotten when he'd come home on medical leave.

He'd kept only one number from his old cell. Kelvin. That might have been a mistake, considering the guy had called him a few times to check on him. The same guy who had ordered Liam to remain on medical leave until Liam had recovered psychologically. Then and only then, Kelvin said, could he return to work. So Liam resigned.

Liam hadn't been ready for that conversation and had no desire to see a psychologist. He told himself he was never going back. Kelvin wanted him back, and Liam was stringing Kelvin along with the possibility. Why was Liam still hanging on to the small possibility that he would return to work for the DEA and the world of shadows?

After they both got out of the academy, Liam and Kelvin became special agents in the Denver Field Division. While Liam's cover was blown when he saved Rae's life, Kelvin was promoted to ASAC and became Liam's boss.

Liam called the number.

A groggy voice replied. "McKade. Do you know what time it is?"

"Sorry about that."

"You finally decide to return my call and you wait until one a.m.?"

"I thought it was earlier. I'm in mountain time."

"Funny. So am I."

Liam didn't cringe that he'd been inconsiderate though. After all, Kelvin had pestered him on his leave and then after he'd resigned too.

"I get it. This is payback."

"Maybe."

"So, are you ready to come back? Getting bored yet out there in the sticks?"

Liam scratched his whiskers, then thrust his cold hand into his pocket. "That's not why I'm calling."

"Do tell." Liam could hear Kelvin rustling something on the other end. A voice in the background asked who was calling. Kelvin's wife.

Oh boy. Now he was kind of sorry. "I apologize for calling so late, but this couldn't wait."

"Well, *I* can't wait."

"I'm sending you a picture. Tell me where I've seen this guy."

"What's this about?"

"It's a long story. I need to know who he is and why his face is familiar."

"You could have texted me," Kelvin growled.

"And miss the sound of your pleasant voice?"

"Send me the image. I'll see what I can find. But it sounds to me like you're ready to come back to work." Kelvin ended the call.

Nice try.

He wouldn't be able to sleep until he knew who this guy was. Rae could have gotten entangled with a dangerous group—something for which she had a knack. While he waited to hear back from Kelvin, Liam would do his own research to find out what he could about Enzo Astor.

He knew Kelvin would bug him about work again. Liam was supposed to get back to Brad about his job offer soon too. Opportunity for failure seemed to be opening up everywhere. With Rae's sudden reappearance in his life, he had the oddest sensation that he was being sucked into a lethal vortex from which neither of them could escape.

A wolf howled in the distance as snow clouds blew in and blanketed the sky in utter darkness as though nature were warning him.

CHAPTER SEVENTEEN

5:28 A.M.

Rae opened her eyes and shut off the alarm on her phone two minutes before it was set to go off. No early light bled through the blinds to nudge her awake. Just her internal alarm. She wanted to roll over and sleep some more, but she'd save that for a day when she wasn't searching for a missing person. She'd needed the rest. That she'd even fallen asleep at all surprised her. At the moment she needed good, strong coffee to fuel her, and now that she thought about it—she could smell coffee brewing. Maybe that was what had woken her before the alarm.

After dressing, she found her way to the kitchen. Liam sat at the counter staring at his laptop. His jaw even more scruffy, he wore the same clothes he'd had on last night when she left him.

"Good morning." She slipped by him and headed straight for the coffeepot. A mug sat on the counter next to the pot, along with creamer and sugar packets.

"That's for you." He lifted his mug as if to toast. "I'm already drinking mine."

"Thanks." She poured the coffee and fixed it the way she liked, then breathed in the rich aroma. Strong. Definitely the way she needed it.

Rae slid onto a stool next to Liam. "Did you even sleep?"

"I tried." He viewed the screen with intense interest but offered her a quick glance. "I'm just trying to piece this together without enough information. But I'll give it a rest and make you some breakfast."

"You insisted I go to bed. What happened to 'We can't think without rest'?"

"Okay, so you can think, and I'll try to keep up." He winked. "Relax. I slept a little bit. I need to shower and get ready. I'll fix breakfast and then get dressed while you eat."

"What about your family? Are they still here?"

He shook his head. "Early morning for them. I can't believe you slept through the ruckus."

"And I can't believe you let me. I could have met them at least. I only got to meet Heath."

He paused as if considering her words, then shook his head. "I thought you needed the rest. Sorry." Liam slid from the stool and approached the cabinets, where he pulled out a frying pan.

She rushed over and took it from him. "No. I'll cook us both breakfast while you get ready. Zoey needs us."

"No, I'll cook breakfast." Evelyn stepped into the kitchen and took the pan from Rae. "I have one job around here, and you'd better let me do it." The woman chuckled. She was too happy for this early hour.

She eyed Rae. "I see you found Liam. Either that or he found you."

Evelyn sent Liam a look. What was that about?

"Yes, I found him at the resort, just like you told me."

"Morning, Evelyn," Liam said. "I'd never dream of taking your job from you. I didn't want to wake you."

"Pfft. I've been in my room reading my devotionals." She retrieved eggs, bacon, butter, and bread. "Now, what will it be? How do you like your eggs, dear?"

Rae wasn't usually one for breakfast this early either. Her stomach always wanted to sleep in whether or not Rae was up, but today would be long. "However Liam's having them is fine."

"Scrambled." He drank from his mug. "Thanks, Evelyn. Do you mind if I shower? I promise to be here before you plate the eggs."

"Get to it." She whisked the eggs, a look of satisfaction on her face.

"I'll be back." Liam stared at Rae.

For a moment, she thought he might have been going to give her a peck on the cheek. Then he left her sitting there and headed for his room. Something about standing in the kitchen with him had seemed warm and cozy and homey, as if Rae belonged here and they were a couple. She shook off the thought.

And chased after Liam.

She caught him at the hallway. "Did you learn anything last night?"

He rubbed his chin, fatigue evident on his face. "Yes. Simon's brother, Enzo—his face seems familiar. So I called my old boss. I'm waiting for him to tell me if this is a guy that's on the DEA's radar."

Rae let his words soak in. "Wait. You called your old *boss* because this Astor guy seemed familiar? Are you saying that he's not just a guy you've seen around Jackson Hole?"

Liam frowned. "I'm not sure. Let's just say that seeing his face jarred me in an unpleasant way. It can't hurt to find out if he's someone I should be worried about."

"Okay. Well. That's something. Now, go get ready. We have work to do."

"I like a take-charge kind of woman." He turned his back on her and walked to his room.

She knew he'd only meant to tease.

She returned to the kitchen. "Is there anything I can do to help?"

Evelyn smiled. "Nothing at all. But if I think of something, I'll let you know. Go ahead and enjoy another cup of coffee. I've poured some for myself, and now I need to make another pot."

"Let me do it." Rae poured the last drop into her mug and made more. "I'm sure you're surprised to see me here." Rae explained to Evelyn some of what had transpired that led her to stay at the ranch last night. She wouldn't want Evelyn to get the wrong idea about her and Liam. Had it been only yesterday morning when she'd driven out here to search for him? She was grateful for Evelyn's willingness to help her.

The bacon sizzling in one pan, Evelyn scrambled the eggs in another. "I wasn't surprised at all. I had a feeling I would see you again." The woman winked, then focused on her breakfast preparations.

Rae went to the counter and climbed onto the stool where Liam had left his laptop open. She eyed the keys, her fingers itching to wake up the screen. He wouldn't mind, would he?

She drank more coffee and resisted, wanting to ask permission first, not wanting to add to her already destroyed reputation where Liam was concerned. She wouldn't give him the impression she was using him.

Still, she could be working while he got ready. He wouldn't be much longer. Evelyn was about to plate those eggs. Rae touched the keyboard.

"Just what do you think you're doing?" Liam's voice came from behind.

Evelyn slid two plates onto the counter. Eggs, bacon, and toast.

Wow, he cleaned up fast. Rae slid his laptop over to him and grabbed her plate. She glanced at Evelyn to avoid looking at Liam. "Thank you for this. I'll do the dishes."

"All you have to do is stick them in the dishwasher. Now, I have some chores to do and then I'll be gone most of the day, Liam. Leroy is taking me out to run errands. Do you need anything?"

Liam's hair hung wet at his shoulders. He smelled like soap. He'd also shaven in record time. Rae wasn't sure which look she liked better.

"No," he said. "I hope Leroy takes you out for a nice lunch too. Thanks, Evelyn."

She smiled and left them to eat breakfast. He eased onto a stool.

"I wasn't going to look at your laptop," she said. "At first. I want to research. I should have grabbed my tablet, but I need to get a new laptop today and get my information from the cloud."

"We'll grab one when we're in town." He seasoned his eggs with Tabasco sauce. "You're in charge here. This is your investigation. I'm only assisting as needed. I'll type up an official document, short and sweet, that we can sign if it makes you feel better." He held her gaze as he chewed a piece of bacon. "I'm your hired hand, though you know I'd be here with you even if you hadn't offered to hire me, don't you?"

"Maybe. Regardless, thank you for agreeing to help me." She toyed with her cup. "I talked to Alan last night."

"And?"

"Police found Zoey's car at a grocery store parking lot. So they're talking to people there and looking at video footage."

He paused midchew. "You're concerned that your trip here is a waste."

She nodded.

Liam finished chewing, frowned, and pushed the eggs around on his plate. "Let's give it more time, okay? Working multiple angles is the right thing. We'll see what Sheriff Taggart says too."

"Okay. You're right. While the police are busy there, I can stay here."

"What do you want to do next, then?"

"Let's stake out this Enzo Astor guy's home and look for signs of Zoey."

"If he abducted her to get revenge because, like you're theorizing,

119

he believes she killed his brother, his own home or one of his main properties could be the last place he would take her."

"Think again. Abducted women are often kept in the homes of their abductors, hidden in basements or secret closets." Dead or alive. Rae shivered.

"Let's see if we can talk to Sheriff Taggart first. I want to keep in close contact with the sheriff's department. Plus, we can learn about other potential leads if he's willing to share." Liam finished the food on his plate and looked around as if he wished there were more. "I'd like to get a sense of whether they're actually pursuing a search for Zoey in Jackson Hole or if the search is contained to Denver."

"I'd like to know that too, but I don't want that to throw me off. Still, what if we have this all wrong? What if we're following the wrong guy? I'm in the wrong place? What if Zoey is on the other side of the country? Or even still in Colorado. What if she's already gone?" Dead. Rae couldn't bear to think of it.

She grabbed their dishes, took them to the sink to rinse, and then put them in the dishwasher. Liam followed and assisted.

Then . . . he stepped closer and gently gripped her arms. "Coming here to question her mother was the right way to go. You've learned a lot since being here. You know what you're doing, Rae. Just keep those nosy investigative reporter skills going and stop second-guessing yourself." He smiled, revealing those dimples and letting her know he meant to reassure rather than insult her.

It took a lot for him to encourage her, considering what she'd put him through.

His smile flattened. "Listen. I've worked in law enforcement long enough to know that law officers can't always be there in time to save those in trouble. People die. Cases go unsolved. Bad guys get away. You came here to ask questions and search for answers and look what happened—your laptop was stolen. Someone followed you. We can only assume those things could be related to

Zoey's disappearance, and I'd say that's as good a reason as any to stay in the valley and keep searching."

She nodded. "That and I've pursued leads in the past that have been ignored by law enforcement—and that sometimes pays off."

"I'm going to start my truck and let it warm up. Scrape the snow off. Please be ready to leave in a few minutes. Gear up, layer up to be out in the elements. Wear snow pants. Be prepared for anything." He stirred his laptop awake and turned it toward her. "When you're done, you can work while you wait for me."

He bounded out of the kitchen, leaving Rae in the enormous vacuum his departure had created.

CHAPTER EIGHTEEN

Rae had called Reggie while Liam drove to the address listed for Enzo Astor's home, located up a winding road in a mountainous community. Since it was still early, they hadn't yet made it into town, where they could get her another laptop and see the sheriff.

But one thing at a time.

Holding the cell to her ear, she hoped she wouldn't lose the signal. "A shell company?"

"Wyoming has been home to thousands of shell companies created by people all over the world, and, in fact, one address held over two thousand companies—some of which were involved in criminal activities," Reggie said.

"You mean like the Cayman Islands?"

"Yes, only a much smaller operation. The address is for a place called WCS Incorporated. The laws have changed things up, but there are loopholes. Think a dummy corporation."

"Like a front organization."

"Yes. They've been used to keep anonymity and to hide identities in the case of tax evasion."

"Or money laundering."

"Right. There are still ways around the laws to keep anonymity. All that said, I'm following Astor's trail, though I'm not sure how much help this will be in finding Zoey if he's connected to her disappearance."

"I understand. It's the only lead we have at the moment. We don't know if this man's a criminal." She glanced at Liam, remembering that he thought he'd seen the guy somewhere and called his DEA contact.

"All possibilities are on the table until we find your Zoey," Reggie told her.

"I can't tell you how much I appreciate you. There are no words."

"Even for a journalist?"

"Nope. No words."

"I'll keep searching, but I wanted you to know where some trails have led me. I have another client I need to attend to this morning, but then I should be back on this case in full force. And in the meantime, Rae, I hope and pray that Zoey turns up safe and unharmed."

"Me too, Reggie. We all hope that."

She ended the call.

"I think this is it," Liam said. "The GPS took us the wrong way. If I had followed those instructions, I would have driven off a ridge. But there's a long drive, and just through the trees you can see a home that could be a resort all by itself."

"Reggie said it's valued at seventeen million dollars."

"And it's smack in the middle of this neighborhood with other luxury homes but spread out enough that each house has privacy. I wouldn't expect anything less from a real estate mogul," he said.

"I would have expected Astor to have a ranch somewhere. In fact, he probably has one. This is likely his home closer to town."

Liam steered his truck along the neighborhood road and made a U-turn while Rae shared what Reggie had told her. Several other cars were parked at the curb to a neighboring home, so Liam's truck wouldn't stand out too much. Still, he parked next to a boulder, but not so close that they couldn't see the comings and goings at the house.

"We can sit here and wait for a bit," he said. "Don't worry. Nothing about this will be time wasted. While we're making phone calls or trying to figure things out, we can watch Astor's home in case there's movement. The point is that all possible venues are being tapped. I'll contact the sheriff to see what's cooking there. You can ask the detective if there's any news on your stolen laptop and segue into questions from there."

"Sounds like a plan, except for the part where I really need to replace my laptop."

"And it sounds to me like you already have a computer at work for you. His name is Reggie."

Rae laughed. "I'm sure you're right. What could I learn that he hasn't already figured out or will find out? But you know the old adage 'Two heads are better than one.' In the meantime, we can brainstorm a few things. At least I have my tablet until I can replace my laptop."

"What's on your mind, then?"

"I can't figure out Samara Davidson. She seems well-to-do. Why couldn't she have somehow paid for Zoey's protection when she was stalked here years ago or used her influence to get Simon to leave her daughter alone?"

"Maybe the business wasn't doing that well until recently, and even so, Simon had access to more money. In comparison, he had nearly unlimited resources."

"And now that Zoey's missing, why didn't Sam also hire a private investigator?"

"How do you know she didn't?"

"I don't. She said she'd been thinking about hiring one. She also claimed to have contacted the FBI to request help. It's not that I suspect her involvement, but her reaction was off. As though she was hiding something."

"You can never tell how people are going to react in certain situations."

"True. But her response was to leave immediately after my visit. She left with a guy I assumed was one of the guides. He exited the helicopter with a tour group. They went to her home and she made a call. I can't help but think it was related."

"I'll look into the guides she has working for her. Can you send an image to me? I know you took his picture."

"Sure, I'll send it. It's loaded on the cloud now from my camera." The ache that had started when she heard about Zoey's disappearance throbbed harder and deeper. "I feel like we're not any closer to finding her. Investigating is excruciating when you have a personal stake in it."

A few moments of silence ticked by, then Liam said, "I completely understand. I have a personal stake in this too."

"You—" She glanced at him.

His brown eyes had darkened, but warmth emanated from them.

"You don't mean me," she said.

"I do."

She had the strongest sense that he'd planned to say more, and she wanted to hear what he would have said, didn't she? Rae pushed away the sudden longing. She couldn't let her thoughts dwell on the what-ifs of their past relationship.

He shifted in his seat. "We're spreading the net wide, Rae. Doing our best. If Zoey can be found, you're the one to do it."

"I'm glad you think so."

"You believe that too or you wouldn't be here. So put that confidence into this search and stop worrying so much."

He's right. "How do we get into Astor's house? How do we get up close and personal to see if he really did take revenge and abduct Zoey—or worse?"

As a journalist, she might need to approach and ask him the hard question, to pull that card. But she needed facts, something other than circumstantial evidence, which she didn't have yet. All she had was conjecture. Inwardly, she growled at herself. Outwardly, she squeezed her fists and wished she could crumple something.

"Let me call the sheriff while we wait. You get on your tablet and do what you do."

The more she thought about it, the more she itched to face the man. "I don't think I'm patient enough for a stakeout. We need to do more. Like knock on his door."

Liam reached for something in the door pocket.

"Binoculars? I didn't see those before."

He peered through them. "They're stashed in my door. Always in the truck. And . . . there's movement."

CHAPTER NINETEEN

8:30 A.M.

Liam made sure to wait until a couple of cars passed them as he followed Astor out of the neighborhood. Another man rode in the truck with Astor as they took the state highway and headed toward town.

Liam had left a message for Sheriff Taggart, whom he'd gotten to know well enough over the last few months, especially when he assisted in solving a crime when he first returned to Wyoming. Heath and Harper also worked for the sheriff's department. He hoped that Taggart was looking into Zoey's disappearance, though she'd gone missing in Colorado. With the stolen laptop and the man who had followed Rae, it seemed plausible that the events here in Wyoming were connected to Zoey's disappearance.

He stole a glance at Rae now and then. She typed on her tablet. An article? A text to Reggie or someone else? She was in deep thought, so he wouldn't break her concentration.

His greatest fear had suddenly shifted from not being able to find his way to not being able to keep her safe. And where would his teaming up with her again leave them on the other side of this? Alive?

Or dead?

Again, the images of her abduction, the wide-eyed terror on her bruised face, grated through his mind.

"You okay?" she asked softly as she kept typing.

"I'm fine." When he fully reined in his emotions about the whole ordeal, he would like to hear her side of what happened—if she had a side that could possibly make sense to him. But dredging that up now wouldn't help Zoey. Liam struggled to keep thoughts of those black days locked in a box in the corner of his mind for now.

He turned down the road that was becoming all too familiar. Rae put away her tablet. "The Saddleback Resort?"

"Looks like it. It makes sense. It's a posh, new luxury resort."

"And Astor has invested in it."

"So the question is, what is he doing there today? Checking out his investment? Or taking advantage of it?"

"What do you mean by taking advantage?"

"Taking to the slopes. I mean, come on, this guy must invest in resorts for a reason. He wants to be in on the action and ski the new slopes." He thought about Brad's offer. He still hadn't gotten back to him. Would Brad call Liam before he moved on to another candidate?

He steered into the parking lot, found a spot at the far end, and shifted into park but left his truck running. What should he do? Work for Brad? If he did, he'd need to put him off until Zoey was found. If he took the job, Heath would be upset. His brother wanted the best for him, Liam believed that, but he also knew that Heath thought the best for Liam was working at the ranch. Home. Family.

Deep inside, Liam wanted all that and more. But it consistently seemed out of his reach. Finally, he turned off the ignition.

"What are we going to do?" Rae asked.

"We'll go inside and hang out. Follow him around. Watch and wait."

"As for waiting, I don't like this sitting around business."

"You've already made that clear. And as I've said before, have some patience." *Listen to your own advice.* Liam didn't like it either. He was more practiced at infiltrating drug-trafficking gangs and power players. What was the best way to help Rae?

"They're going in," she said. "I'd like to know who he's with."

"Let's go, then."

Astor followed a group of resort patrons through the doors. "If he skis," Liam whispered, "then we'll ski too."

Her beautiful eyes narrowed. "Wha-what?"

At the look in her eyes, he chuckled. "You said you were tired of sitting and waiting."

"I did, didn't I? Honestly, I never pictured you on skis."

He arched a brow. "Then you don't know me that well."

"No, I guess I don't."

They got out of the truck, and she walked next to him through the front doors and the expansive great room with the massive fireplace. "I don't see him. We should have followed more closely. Again, I'd rather just talk to him."

"You were never patient, Rae."

He led her through the resort. A couple rose from their chairs, and Liam quickly grabbed their spot by the corner near the windows. Rae plopped into a chair and turned her attention to the ski lifts. The elevators were behind them. Liam focused on those.

"From here," he said, "we can see him coming or going or even getting on the ski lift there. But if he's here to ski, I have to ask why this guy doesn't use the heli-skiing. He can certainly afford it. Why go where everyone else goes?"

"Wouldn't you want to check out your investment?" she asked.

"Yes. But I wouldn't have to ski to do it," Liam said. "I can grab us coffee while we wait. Act normal."

"No. I see him." Rae peered around Liam. "He's with his sidekick. They're heading into the café."

"It's crowded but not so bad that we can't get a table. Crowded serves our purpose. We won't be so easily noticed." But it would be more difficult to glean information from the two men's conversation.

Liam accompanied her inside the café, where patrons were asked to seat themselves. Three college-aged women left a booth as Liam and Rae passed, and they grabbed it. The men they'd followed were two booths away.

Rae and Liam ordered coffee.

Coffee, coffee, coffee. Liam was already too wired. This was what he hated about stakeouts. He could relate to Rae's impatience and agreed that at some point they might need to bump this up. Correction. *He* might need to bump things up. He didn't want Rae going even deeper into this dangerous situation.

"You make a great private investigator," she said. "But don't you get bored?"

"Not with you as company."

She glanced up at him from her tablet.

He averted his gaze. Flirting with her was playing with fire. "If I did this for a living, yes, I would probably get bored. I prefer getting in the middle of it. Or at least I used to." Part of him missed the action, but another part of him struggled with what was considered the means justifying the end. He'd seen a few undercover agents lose their identity because they'd played their role so well for too long.

Was that what was happening to him? Had he lost his true identity? Because right now, he didn't know where he belonged.

Again, he wondered, *Where is home?*

Astor slipped from his perch and appeared to head toward the restroom.

"Excuse me." Liam exited the booth and pulled out his cell as he walked. He entered the room after Astor, who was on his cell phone too.

"You'd better be there," Astor growled: "The black diamond. I don't know the name. It's the one near Bear Claw Café."

He turned as if suddenly realizing he wasn't alone in the restroom. Liam ignored him and tucked away his cell to wash his hands. His cell buzzed at that moment. He dried his hands and pulled it out to see who had called. He hoped Astor paid him no attention. Another guy walked in as Liam exited.

Good.

On the way back to the table, Liam listened to the voicemail Sheriff Taggart had left him. It was likely Sheriff Taggart had been the man to deliver the news to Astor about his brother's remains. The sheriff would be interested to know that the timeline of what had happened involving Zoey's disappearance five years ago coincided with her stalker's disappearance, and that his remains had recently been discovered.

But the timeline meant nothing without evidence. The sheriff must have hung up because he didn't say anything in the message. Liam slid into the booth across from Rae and thought about the words he'd overheard. He and Rae had already villainized the guy in their minds as someone who would want to take Zoey. So even the most innocent sounding words carried a menacing tone. Still, Liam didn't think he had misunderstood Astor's antagonism on the call.

"Liam, did you hear me?" Rae asked.

"What?"

"They're leaving."

"Okay, sure. We'll wait a few seconds. We don't want to be seen following them out immediately." Even though Astor's face was familiar to Liam, the man hadn't seemed to recognize him.

He considered what to do next. Bear Claw Café would require a ride up the gondola. Astor had said the black diamond near the café, so Liam could only assume he planned to ski the trail. It made some kind of weird sense to arrange a clandestine meeting on a black diamond—the steepest and most difficult ski trails on the mountain except for the double black diamonds. Acid boiled in his stomach.

"Are you okay? You seem a million miles away."

"Sure. I was running through all the possible scenarios." He didn't want to leave Rae behind for this, but he didn't want to take her with him either.

He left enough cash on the table to cover their drinks and a tip and slid from the booth.

She eyed the money. "I'll get it next time."

They exited the café in time to see Astor and his sidekick take the elevators.

"What now?" she asked.

"How would a journalist handle this?"

"I would approach him and introduce myself. Identify myself as a journalist. Give my condolences. I would try to get him to talk. See what he thinks about his brother's death. I'd go from there." She angled her head in thought. "I could get a sense of him. I can read people."

Liam wasn't sure Rae approaching the man was a good idea. Then again, that might be their only choice.

"You might get your chance, but right now we're getting ready to play in the snow."

She swung her head to face him. "What?"

"Looks like at least one of us gets to slay the pow." Liam grinned.

Her beautiful eyes widened. "Why?"

"I overheard him." Liam shared what he'd learned about the meeting at black diamond near the Bear Claw Café. "Unless you don't think it's a good idea."

"Smart thinking having us dress for the occasion. Such a furtive meeting deserves good shadowing. But I'm going too."

"I'm not sure it's safe. I don't know if it's even worth it. Can you ski a black diamond?"

She looked at him long and hard. "I bet you're the kind of guy who can ski that and crush it."

Liam shrugged. He was out of practice, but she didn't have to know that.

"Hold on." Rae pulled up the ski map on her tablet and together they perused it. "I admit that I'm more of a cross-country skier. Looks like I could take this blue slope here and meet you at the trail where it intersects with that black diamond. The trails run sort of parallel until they intersect. That's where the black diamond ends. There's a restaurant there too—Crosspoint Restaurant— and a gondola."

"I don't want to leave you on your own. Maybe this isn't a good idea."

"Remember Zoey, Liam. We're wasting time discussing it. I'm going. I'm not going to sit here and wait around."

Liam nodded. Astor was up to something, but whether that would lead them to Zoey, he wished he knew. "We'll gear up at the shop, then get the ski passes. Come on. Let's hurry."

Liam was eager to learn who Astor planned to meet on the black diamond trail, where absolutely no one was likely to follow him.

After they'd geared up and stored their belongings in lockers, they waited in line for the gondola to return to drop off passengers and load the next group. They'd lost sight of Astor while getting ready to hit the slopes, but they would stick to the plan and ride the gondola to the drop-off at Bear Claw Café, where they hoped to find him again.

Rae leaned close and whispered. "Have you ever gone skiing while working undercover?"

He chuckled. "No. This will be a first. But you'd be surprised what lengths I've gone to in order to keep my cover."

She frowned and glanced away. She didn't want to be reminded that she was the reason his cover had been blown.

CHAPTER TWENTY

On the crowded gondola ride to the Bear Claw Café, Rae stared down at the tall, white-laced evergreens below the hanging box of people.

I'm looking down on the trees!

"Are you okay?" Liam grabbed her gloved hand and squeezed. "You look a little pale. A few minutes on the slopes will bring the color back."

Liam tried to make small talk and act natural, considering Enzo Astor was on the same gondola ride to the top. Fortunately, Liam and Rae had beaten him to stand in the line, so if he noticed them, it wouldn't appear they'd been following him. He was alone now.

Liam acted as though he was seriously into Rae and wasn't aware of the man they were watching—he put on a good show. She could almost believe it was real.

The concern in his pensive gaze rolled through her. Standing so near him, feeling him so close as they rode the gondola reminded her of the past when she'd been in his arms. Two investigators

134

whose paths had crossed, who'd shared a passion for helping others and were compelled to find the truth at all costs. For Rae, finding Dina had been worth the cost of losing Liam's trust—but why had she had to choose between the two?

She longed to make him understand. Liam tried to act relaxed, but he didn't fool her. She felt the tension coming off him in waves. Though he appeared focused on her, he was well aware of everything and everyone around him, as he was trained, but no one would ever know, except Rae.

"Yes. I'm okay." *Just breathe.* Rae's palms began to sweat in her gloves.

She had never liked this part of skiing—the sheer drops on the lifts with her legs dangling over the edge of a flimsy chair that rocked or the boxed-in feeling of a gondola or tram ride to the top.

Not to mention that in her boots and suit, she felt more like an astronaut in a space suit than a skier. At least when she arrived at the top and exited the gondola, she'd be on the ground and not tethered to the international space station floating in the fathomless vacuum of space.

Think about something else.

She'd rather focus on Liam's clean-shaven face, his intense gaze that studied her as if he saw right through her. Better that than the fact that the gondola took them higher and higher up the mountain. Rae tucked her scarf around the helmet. Her actions gave her something else to focus on.

"You ready? We're almost there."

"As I'll ever be." Definitely ready to get out of the box and onto solid ground.

They exited the gondola and moved along the path, then stopped to take in the breathtaking vistas from the top of the mountain. Others headed to the café while some skiers went straight for the slopes.

Liam pulled her aside and adjusted her helmet and goggles,

waiting to see what Astor would do, she assumed. Their helmets included headphones so they could communicate.

"When I was a kid," he said, "I had a friend whose family took me skiing with them all the time. It was my getaway. My way to clear my head."

"Are you clearing your head now?"

"If only it was that easy. I think skiing could help us both, except for the fact that we're not here for fun." His reflective goggles made it almost impossible for her to see his eyes, but she knew he was staring at her, waiting for her response.

"He's heading for the slopes, Liam."

He dropped his skis and positioned his booted feet in place. "I have to follow, Rae. You going to be okay?"

"Yeah. I'll take that blue slope. I'll be fine. I'll meet you at the Crosspoint Restaurant where the slopes intersect."

"Remember"—he knocked on his helmet—"you can still talk to me. We need to find something solid to connect Zoey's abduction to someone here in Jackson Hole. We're going to do that today." He skated over to the edge.

Rae watched him shove off after Enzo Astor. Rae made her way to the jump-off point for the blue slope. She pulled in a few breaths and then eased off the edge. *What am I doing here? What am I doing here?*

Zoey is not on this mountain.

But you're on the mountain, God.

"Rae? You okay?" Liam's voice came through her headphones loud and clear.

"Yes. I'm fine. You just focus on watching Astor and that difficult trail. Don't worry about me."

She could hear his increased breaths over the comm. A few grunts. Maybe even a groan. She was glad she wasn't the one skiing such a difficult trail.

She'd forgotten how spectacular the view could be from a slope like this. In the distance, huge snow-covered peaks stretched as far as she could see and opened up enough for a glimpse of the valley beyond.

This. This was why people skied.

To get closer to you, God, whether they know it or not.

White stretched before her. The sound of skis carving the snow met her ears from all directions. From her own skis. Those she passed. Those passing her. She took her time, traversing the slope slowly, one side to another. Liam had mentioned that skiing cleared his mind. While he followed Enzo Astor, Rae tried to let the mountain air clear her mind and allow her to think of something she might have missed. Some way they could find Zoey—if her sister-in-law was even here. Or if she was somewhere far away.

She focused on veering to the left so she wouldn't miss the restaurant where she was to meet Liam, who would quickly ski down that black diamond. A skier in a black suit whizzed by her, his skis cutting into the snow next to her. Her heart jumped to her throat.

"What's happening, Rae? You still doing okay?"

"Yes. What do you have on Astor?"

"Nothing."

"Then you'd better focus on skiing."

"Right." He gasped for breath. "Let me know if you need me."

Rae kept her leisurely and safe pace. She noticed the man who'd skied too close had stopped to adjust his goggles right in front of her. She swerved far from him and tried to avoid other skiers. She kept her emotions and outbursts to herself so she wouldn't distract Liam.

A skier came much too close again. The black-suited guy. He veered straight toward her this time.

Rae swerved away to avoid him but lost control. She tried to regain her balance but instead flailed toward the trees lining the slope. Trees. Every skier's nemesis. The whole reason for wearing a helmet.

Her efforts to correct her course failed. She rose with unintended flight into the air but landed on her skis in the ungroomed part of the mountain. She tried to avoid trees as she slowed down. An abrupt stop would send her tumbling.

"Rae? What's happening? You don't sound good." Liam's frantic voice sounded in her helmet.

A quick glance over her shoulder let her know the black-suited guy was trailing her, bringing his bad intentions with him. Her pulse spiked. She had no doubt he'd forced her from the groomed slope intentionally. No slowing down for her. Rae had to keep skiing if she had any hope of getting away from him.

"Someone's after me." She gasped. "He forced me from the groomed slope. I'm in the wooded area . . ." Rae, moving too fast for comfort, ducked under a branch. "The area that separates the blue slope and the black diamond."

Heart pounding, she tucked her body to pick up speed while avoiding trees on an ungroomed strip of mountain.

Behind her, the swish of skis in the snow grew louder. He was faster.

Any hope of escape fled.

CHAPTER TWENTY-ONE

Hold on! I'm coming for you."

Liam stopped to get his bearings. He was farther down the mountain than she was. Liam started toward the trees between the two slopes, searching as he traversed the dangerous slope.

Come on, come on. Where are you, Rae?

As he entered the ungroomed area, he caught a glimpse of turquoise. There. Rae skied back and forth between the trees and toward Liam—and a man followed her.

God, please help her! Let me get to her in time!

Dense evergreens blocked his view. He hit a drift and leapt into the air. "Rae! I'm behind you."

She didn't respond—probably skiing for her life as she moved farther and deeper into the woods. He caught flashes of her turquoise ski jacket. Close behind her, moving in, was a man in black. Panic swelled in his chest.

Why did I leave her? How could I have let this happen?

She disappeared. No more flashes of Rae between the trees. He pushed himself, evergreen branches and needles scraping him. His injury from the past stabbing through him.

A swath of color caught him off guard. He wedged his skis to slow and almost hit her. Liam sucked in a breath. Rae was on the ground, facedown. She groaned.

His heart tumbled over and over. *No, no, no.* "Rae, I'm here." Liam broke away from his skis and dropped to the ground. "Are you okay?"

She turned her head, then rolled halfway. "Yes. But he's getting away. Go after him!"

"No. I need to make sure you're all right."

"I'm fine. I just need a minute." She removed her skis, got to her knees, and he helped her the rest of the way to stand. "Now, go. You could go after him."

Liam glanced around to make sure she was safe. The skier who'd trailed her was nowhere in sight.

"I'm not leaving you. I wouldn't leave you to go after him." He gritted his teeth. "What happened?"

"He forced me off the slope, then he came up on me fast. I crashed. If that was his goal, he succeeded. Then he stopped next to me. I don't know if he was going to do something or speak to me, but I heard you shout my name and he left. So, I owe you. Again."

"I shouldn't have left you to go after Astor. I'm so sorry, Rae. I had no idea that someone would go this far and attack you on the slopes in the middle of the day where everyone could see." Though anyone who witnessed it might have thought it was an accident.

Liam hugged her to him until his racing heart calmed. "Are you sure you're okay?"

"Yes. I'm just a little shaken. I can't believe any of this."

His limbs quaked, so he understood how she felt. Liam released her to look at her face. "Who knew you were coming to Jackson Hole?"

"We already talked about this. Alan. The police. Zoey's mom."

"And whoever she told." The snow picked up and skewed his view of the resort below.

The sense of being watched skittered over his back.

He pursed his lips. "Let's get off this mountain before something else happens. We'll hike over to the café and take the gondola down."

"Are you that worried?"

"Aren't you?"

She didn't respond as she lifted her skis over her shoulder. The cold air and mountain view had given him a fresh perspective, after all, but he would have preferred more time to wrap his mind around the scenario unfolding.

Liam studied her, looking for signs of trauma. Was she afraid? "Did he say anything to you?"

"No."

Liam took her in—the way her turquoise suit complemented her striking blue-green eyes. Her silky blonde strands escaping her helmet. He didn't know if he could go through this again. Seeing her put herself in danger, her life on the line, while she searched for someone. His biggest fear—would he be there in case the worst happened? He'd barely made it in time today.

Liam turned to hike, and Rae kept pace with him as they traversed the mountain. "Just a little farther and we can catch the gondola down the rest of the way."

"Good, because my legs are shaking."

He remained alert to their surroundings.

Who was the man who'd forced her from the slope? Was he the same man who broke into her room and took her laptop? Had he wanted to warn her? Or harm her? There were certainly easier ways to go about both those things. Then again, she was on a ski slope, so he could have meant to take an easy opportunity to hurt her when he saw it.

They continued their hike through the trees, heading toward the gondola. Evergreens separated the runs—green and blue, and a few black—that ran parallel to them as they hiked.

"Liam, look," she said. "It's him."

He turned to see where she pointed. Through the trees far from the slope were Astor and a man in a black ski suit deep in conversation. The man who chased Rae? Or just another skier wearing black? He couldn't be sure, though this guy was big too. He had a similar build to the man who'd stolen her laptop.

Was this the man Astor planned to meet? Anger boiled inside, ready to erupt. He wanted to approach them and find out what was going on. But Liam wouldn't put Rae in more danger by leaving her while he moved in to confront the two men.

Rae tugged her cell phone out and took pictures.

"We're getting out of here." He gripped her arm and urged her onward.

Liam never liked to be in this position. This went beyond theft—someone had tried to harm her. He could hardly believe he was in this kind of situation with Rae again. She lifted her face and offered a tenuous smile as if she were thinking the same thing.

He shouldn't be surprised.

They made it to the café just as the gondola arrived. He stepped in the line with Rae, who peered at the images she had taken. "I wasn't sure if I'd imagined it," she said, leaning in to whisper, "but these pictures confirm it. He's wearing that funky green-faced watch on his right wrist. It's him, Liam. It's the same guy who took my laptop."

CHAPTER TWENTY-TWO

Inside the resort, they returned the ski rental equipment and gathered their items from the lockers.

Liam pressed his hand into the small of Rae's back and urged her toward the exit.

"We're going to see the sheriff. No more phone tag. He needs to know that the laptop thief tried to harm you today, and that he's somehow connected to Enzo Astor. It wouldn't surprise me that Enzo was behind it."

"What about the resort security?"

"They'll need to know, but this is bigger than what they handle."

"Definitely bigger." Maybe bigger than she could have imagined. Rae tried to steady her breathing. She hadn't stopped shaking since being forced from the groomed slope. The sound of those skis racing toward her from behind skittered across her nerves.

Rae needed to get to the bottom of this and fast. Seeing the man meet with Enzo Astor only raised more questions. The next opportunity she got, she needed to kick into reporter mode and ask Astor the hard questions. She wouldn't bring that idea up now. With that scowl on his face, Liam was in no mood to hear it. He had other ideas about what their next step should be. She agreed that going to the sheriff was a good idea.

Rae was moving to step through the revolving doors that emptied into the parking lot when she spotted Astor. She stopped in her tracks, resisting Liam's efforts to urge her forward. She was done playing games.

Liam's frown deepened. "What are you doing?"

"You'll see." She turned and walked toward the man and stood in front of him. Smiled.

He made to move beyond her. "Excuse me."

Rae walked with him. "Mr. Astor?"

"Yes." That she'd known his name must have stopped him.

"My name's Rae Burke. I'm a journalist. I was so sorry to hear about your brother's death. Would you say that after five years, this brings closure for you?"

Rae knew how to do this, and she was good at it. But this time her nerves were on edge, her heart in her throat. She struggled to hide her anxiety. As for Astor, she couldn't read his reaction, which was unusual for her. If she had to guess his true emotions, she'd say displeasure. Rather than blasting her for the intrusion, though, he acted as if it was important to maintain a good appearance.

Rae became aware of bystanders interested in their exchange.

"Miss . . . What was it again?" he asked.

"Rae Burke. You can call me Rae."

"Rae. I'd be happy to discuss this with you." He lowered his voice. "Without anyone looking on or listening in."

"I'd like that too." She ignored the shiver trailing up her spine.

Astor's eyes flicked beyond her. "And this is—"

Rae felt the warmth emanating from the man who stood much too close. She didn't have to look to know Liam was standing behind her. And his presence made her feel safe.

"Liam McKade." Liam, his demeanor sincere and friendly,

thrust out his hand to shake Astor's. Liam projected the required personality. He'd joined her in this mission.

"Liam's an old friend I'm visiting while I'm here to work on a story."

Astor's demeanor changed. Was it Liam? He had bumped into Astor in the restroom earlier and Astor could realize they'd been following him.

The man pushed past her. "If you'll excuse me, I'm busy at the moment. Maybe some other time."

He kept walking. Rae shooed Liam away to catch up to Astor and walked with him again.

"I could meet you somewhere." She leaned closer. "Without Liam, that is. I need to talk to you."

Astor seemed to consider her request, then tugged a card from his jacket and slipped it to her. "My private number. Call me anytime. People don't usually want to talk to reporters, but if a story about my brother's death can help find his killer, then I'll do anything."

He strode away.

Rae stared after him.

Truth echoed in his words. She watched until he disappeared through the exit, then glanced down at the card.

"Are you done?" Liam asked. She sensed his tension and anger.

"I am." She focused on the exit. Time to see the sheriff.

"Let's go," he said.

She followed him out to his truck and climbed in.

"Are you crazy? I can't believe you approached him without talking it through with me first."

"I told you I would. I don't need a committee and focus group to tell me when to step out."

The furrow between his brows deepened. "What did he say to you?"

"He gave me his card with his private number and said to call anytime."

"What's with you and all these guys who give you their phone numbers and tell you to call?"

That drew a blank—oh, right. Greg had done the same thing. "I'm a reporter. More than that, I'm approachable. But Liam, Enzo Astor has no idea who I am. He couldn't be behind my stolen laptop or what happened on the slopes today."

"What makes you think that?"

"He wants to talk to me because he thinks getting the news out about his brother's death could help him find out who killed him."

"You're kidding me."

"No. That's what he said. And . . . I think he was telling the truth."

"You got that from all of three minutes with him?"

"I think he's disturbed about Simon's remains being identified and wants to know who's behind his death."

"That doesn't mean he doesn't know who you are or that he didn't hire the masked man." Liam's somber expression seemed permanent as he shrugged out of his jacket and shifted the truck into gear. "This is a dangerous game you're playing. We now know Astor is connected to the masked man. You shouldn't have approached him. He played dumb with you, acting like he didn't know who you are and why you're here. He knows something, Rae. He must somehow be involved with Zoey's disappearance like we suspected. And in a way, that's good news. It means we're on the right trail."

"Given Astor's reaction to my question, I'm not sure about that."

"If he's involved in an abduction," Liam said, his pitch increasing, "he's practiced at hiding the truth. In fact, what better way to deflect than to agree to an interview with you? Because this is dangerous, I want you to talk to me first about who you're approaching. You hired me to protect you, remember?"

"I warned you I would talk to him, and the opportunity presented itself. This is what real journalists do. I'm done following him around. We aren't getting any information like this. Besides, I want to get into his home."

He steered toward the parking lot exit. "Not alone, you don't."

"I could meet him somewhere else, but I need to at least follow through and get an interview." She could get answers that police sometimes failed to find. But given the amount of time that had already passed without finding answers to Zoey's disappearance, the feeling that any cold, hard evidence was slipping through her fingers left her desperate. Compelled her forward.

"Somehow, we need to get inside Astor's home. I mean, just to make sure Zoey's not there."

Liam's cell buzzed, and he swerved away from the exit and into a parking spot. "I need to take this call. Wait here."

He climbed out and sent her a killer glare as he did.

Her adrenaline still surged after the encounter with Astor. Though she felt more like she was clawing her way to answers, this was what she was born to do.

She was never going to make it as a travel magazine editor.

CHAPTER TWENTY-THREE

While Rae waited in his truck, Liam stood outside to return Kelvin's call. He'd failed to answer in time. He hadn't *wanted* to answer in front of Rae, so he'd quickly parked and escaped the vehicle. She might question him about the call, but he needed to process the information before he relayed it to her, if he even needed to tell her.

He wished he could have gone after that skier who'd forced her off the slope so he could find out who he was and why he'd targeted Rae. But Liam didn't dare leave her alone after what happened.

Now he wasn't sure that he ever could. At least not until this ended.

He called Kelvin back and hoped he didn't get voicemail. As he waited for the call to connect, his mind remained on the investigation. Their next stop was to see Sheriff Taggart. The Bridger County sheriff's responsibilities had grown in the small county, considering that the ski resort had recently opened. With the increase in tourism and population stretching Sheriff Taggart's department, Liam might see a shift in the man's attitude and the time he could give Liam.

Jackson Hole had changed a lot since Liam had lived here as a kid. More tourists and, though Jackson and Grayback remained western towns, one couldn't escape the sense of over-commercialization. Then again, catering to the tourists passing through and the wealthy who remained kept the region alive. He could well expect Heath to bump up his game when it came to Emerald M. Those were changes Liam didn't much like.

But before he even attempted to track down Sheriff Taggart, he needed to speak to Kelvin. Maybe Kelvin had learned something about Enzo Astor that Liam could potentially use if necessary when talking to Taggart.

Liam leaned against his truck. He glanced at Rae sitting in the cab, staring at her cell.

Kelvin answered.

Liam jumped right in. "So, Enzo Astor. Is he someone you're watching? What did you find out?"

"We're working it, but I don't have all the particulars. And when I do have them, you're not cleared to know them. Not yet."

"Well then, what *can* you tell me?" *Why did you call?* Liam ground his molars.

"I get that you're concerned you might have seen him before in a not-so-above-the-board dealing. He's a face you can't place, and the two of you are there in the same valley. I'd be concerned, too, except this guy owns property in Wyoming, Montana, and Colorado. Has a home there in Jackson Hole. So he appears to be there for legitimate reasons, at least on the surface."

"Tell me something I don't already know."

"Again, I don't have anything else for you."

"You mean you don't have anything else you're willing to share? Or that you really don't know anything?"

"Be patient, Liam. I don't know anything yet. You and I go way back. I wouldn't leave you in the dark, especially after what you went through in getting the goods on Malcom Fox."

"That's good to know." Liam's undercover work had been instrumental in putting away Malcom Fox, a man who trafficked drugs and humans. He was believed to have blackmailed more than one senator, as well as other high-ranking officials who would not come forward with information. Fox's operation was the reason Liam had run into Rae in the first place. Liam had given two years of his life working undercover, climbing his way up in the organization until he identified Fox as the man behind it all. And then—*bam!*—enter Rae Burke, who stole his heart and the covert intel he'd gained to go with it.

Sometimes repercussions came with taking bad guys down. Big men could exact revenge even from prison, though Malcom was only waiting for his trial in prison without bail, for which Liam was grateful. Fox was considered a flight risk. Now Liam found himself in Jackson Hole and no longer working for the DEA. So why had seeing Enzo Astor's face left him disturbed?

Liam measured his next words. Should he tell Kelvin? "There's another aspect you don't know about."

"Yeah? What's that?"

He sucked in the cold air and blew out a big white cloud. How did he begin to explain this to Kelvin? "Enzo Astor is the brother of Simon Astor, who disappeared five years ago. Before he disappeared, he'd stalked a woman named Tawny Davidson who moved to Colorado to start a new life, changing her name to Zoey Dumont. Five years ago—around the time Simon disappeared—she returned home to her college dorm room bruised, beaten, and unwilling to tell the police. Simon's remains were recently found and identified. Zoey disappeared again recently, around the same time. This, mere days ago."

"How do you know this?"

"Because Zoey's former college roommate and current sister-in-law is Rae Burke."

A few breaths escaped before Kelvin responded. "You've got to be kidding me."

"Unfortunately, I'm not." Life could be a series of unexpected events all tangled together.

"And she's there, in Jackson Hole."

"Yes. Looking for Zoey."

"Because?"

"Rae came to town to talk to Zoey's mother and learned about Simon. Now she wonders if Enzo Astor took Zoey to exact revenge." Liam might be telling his old friend and boss too much, but then again, someone besides Liam and Rae needed to know—in case the worst happened.

"What are you going to do?"

"We're shadowing Astor. We need to find Zoey. He's our strongest lead."

"I'm going to have to ask you to stand down, at least until I learn if he's someone we have an interest in. You haven't been cleared for this. That is, unless you want to come in and we'll get that process going."

Coming in would take too long. Zoey's life could depend on it. Most certainly Rae's could.

"No can do."

"McKade, stand down."

"Are you forgetting? I don't work for you. I don't have to stand down."

This was one moment when he wished he was still an agent in the field so he would have access to intel and backup and also have the power behind the badge, but it would take much too long to go back. They would put him on another case anyway. "Look, I'm sorry. I'm helping Rae, and she needs my protection. Don't worry, I only have eyes on Astor. I'm hanging out at the same ski resort."

Kelvin sighed. "This doesn't feel right to me. You should be working for us. You're a good agent."

"I appreciate the words, Kelvin. If you learn something more about Astor, then I'd at least like to know if you already have an agent in place."

"That depends on if I'm at liberty to tell you."

"I love working with the government," Liam drawled.

"I look forward to the moment you actually work for us." Kelvin ended the call.

A resort minivan steered from the circular drop-off beneath the awning and exposed a man leaning against the building. Black clothes. Binoculars? He ducked behind a building.

Liam held back his need to get his hands on that man. He glanced at Rae. With the additional pictures she took on the slopes today, maybe they could identify him, though it was doubtful.

Funny that he'd returned to Jackson Hole to mentally recuperate, regroup, and maybe find himself again, find where he belonged. But working with Heath at the ranch for months had him floundering without a goal or a vision.

Now it seemed that his goal and vision were crystal clear. Rae Burke.

That it was about her all over again—the reason he'd come back to Jackson Hole in the first place—was hard to wrap his mind around. That's what he got for thinking he was done with her.

CHAPTER TWENTY-FOUR

Rae downloaded files from the cloud onto her newly purchased laptop, thanks to a quick stop on the way to the sheriff's office, and watched Liam pace in the small office while they waited on the sheriff.

"He'll listen, Rae. He has to," Liam said.

She had the feeling Liam was trying to convince himself.

"Besides, we have to report what happened today. I'd prefer Taggart himself hears about it rather than just filing a report, and he has to agree that it's part of his larger investigation."

Now Rae waited on the downloads, so she tried to reach Reggie. She hoped he had more information for her. Reggie was truly a godsend, and she was grateful he'd been more than willing to get on board with helping her. In journalism, knowledge was power. She knew approaching people and asking them questions point-blank were important parts of the investigative process, and she'd done that with Enzo Astor today. But she needed additional information on him. If she knew more about the man, she would have

153

ammunition when she met with him. Still, she couldn't shake the sense that she'd yet to truly find Zoey's trail. At least she wasn't in this alone, and many well-trained agencies were searching for her friend and sister-in-law.

Oh, Zoey . . .

Reggie didn't answer, and she ended the call without leaving a voicemail. He knew what she needed. She tapped the edge of the desk. "We need to pick up the pace, but how?"

Was it possible that she could have gotten more done without Liam at her side?

"No. We need to take our time and rethink our strategy. You're in someone's crosshairs, Rae. I'm pretty sure it's Enzo Astor's. That changes everything."

"Just so we're clear, Zoey is the one in immediate danger."

Uncertainty surged in Liam's gaze. What was that about?

The door whipped open and Sheriff Taggart rushed in, his expression almost warming when he spotted Liam. Almost. Taggart was in his forties, and his deeply furrowed brows appeared hooked together permanently. He seemed to have more than his fair share of troubles.

"Thanks for giving me a few minutes, Sheriff. This is Rae Burke," Liam said. "There's a situation going on."

"By all means, fill me in." Sheriff Taggart took his seat. He shook two pain relievers into his hand and popped them into his mouth, followed by a long swig of water from a glass that had been sitting on his desk.

Liam appeared to wait for the sheriff's full attention, and when he got it, he succinctly explained Simon's death and Zoey's disappearance, their search, the stolen laptop, and the incident on the slopes. Rae couldn't be sure if the sheriff had been aware of the possible connections. She offered the images from her cell phone, which he studied, then returned.

The sheriff nodded as if he'd heard the story before. "I got a call from the Denver Police and had the unfortunate task of delivering the news to Mr. Astor about his brother's remains. I also spoke with Samara Davidson about her missing daughter." He rubbed his jaw. "This county has seen better days. I'll pass this information on to one of my detectives. It sounds like a stretch, but we'll see if there's anything to learn."

"No," Liam and Rae said at the same time.

Taggart frowned. "Excuse me?"

"Sheriff," Liam said as he leaned forward. "Enzo Astor was seen meeting with the same man who stole Rae's laptop and ran her off the slope."

"You're positive it was the same man?" Sheriff Taggart studied Liam.

"I didn't see his face, but he was wearing the same green-faced watch as the man who stole the laptop—and on his right wrist."

Rae scooted to the edge of her seat. "Sheriff, if I may, Zoey's life is in danger. We want to save her life, not hear about her death in the news. Or have a police officer knock on my brother's door to tell him his wife is dead."

"Those are a lot of accusations with nothing to go on. I don't have a reason to search Mr. Astor's home. I'll give this to one of my detectives to see if we can get probable cause for a search warrant. I have two detectives at the moment." He flashed two fingers. "Two."

"Wouldn't you agree that human life is more important than, say, ticketing horse abusers and managing road closures?" A typical day for the county sheriff's offices. Liam's tone didn't go unnoticed by the sheriff.

Anger flashed in the sheriff's eyes. Maybe even a little hurt.

Interesting.

"Look, Sheriff. That wasn't called for," Liam said. "I'm sorry. I just want you to know what's happening. I had hoped you would understand the urgency."

Sheriff Taggart appeared to consider his words carefully. "I appreciate that, Liam. Go ahead and file a report on the incident at the resort involving the jerk who bumped Ms. Burke off the trail. Beyond me passing this to a detective, why don't you tell me what you want me to do."

Rae didn't for a minute believe he was asking for their directive. "We just want you to be aware there's a possible connection. I want to find Zoey, and right now I don't know what else we can do."

Liam leaned back. "Do you have any new information about Simon's death, Sheriff? Maybe your detective could deliver that and use it as an excuse. I could come along."

"You're not in my employ."

"You used my assistance before." Liam crossed his arms.

"I don't need it now."

"We're looking into this with or without your help, Sheriff," Rae said.

Sheriff Taggart squeezed the bridge of his nose.

"I've hired Liam as a private investigator to find Zoey. To save her. To save my brother and their four-year-old daughter. We can do this together. Or not."

"Someone followed Rae and then broke into her room and stole her laptop. Someone forced her off the slope and maybe wanted to kill her today. Someone doesn't want her to find Zoey, Sheriff. Good enough?"

"You two aren't going to stop digging, are you?"

"No. My sister-in-law's life is at stake. I'm a reporter, and Liam is a brilliant investigator. I've worked with him before." Maybe Liam didn't want the sheriff to know about their shared past, but it was too late.

Sheriff Taggart pinned his gaze on her. "You're positive your brother isn't responsible for her disappearance?"

Anger burned her cheeks. She kept her words steady. "I'm 100 percent sure."

"No one can be that sure." He tucked his chin, his eyes flooding with compassion. "Even if it's someone you think you know and trust. Even if it's a loved one."

Okay. Well. Sheriff Taggart spoke like a man who'd experienced betrayal.

"As a journalist," he said, "you already know that more often than not, husbands are responsible. Or that someone she knew took her."

Rae could work with that. "Exactly. That's why I was betting on the previous stalker. I thought Simon had found her and abducted her, but then I learned he's dead. Now, see, it could be the ex-stalker's brother exacting revenge after he learned of his brother's death and put two and two together."

"Even if everything you said is true, we can't charge anyone. We can't arrest anyone without evidence."

"The only evidence we care about is Zoey, Sheriff." Desperation edged her voice.

"I don't advise you get into the middle of an investigation and muddy the waters, but right now I don't have an actual investigation going. Not enough facts to say that Zoey is here. But this is what I *will* do. I'll call Denver PD and connect with their investigator. Find out what I can. Then I'll go to Enzo Astor's house with a deputy and tell him what we've learned. We'll see if we can get an invitation inside, or at the very least look around outside."

"If Zoey is being kept there, though, we could tip them off. She could get hurt. So please be careful."

"True enough, but the way I see it, it's better to get a reaction than to leave things as they are." The sheriff swiped his hand over his tired face. "I don't have to tell you that evidence is growing colder by the hour. The chances of finding her alive are growing slimmer."

"No. You don't have to tell me." *I know. God, I know that, please.* Rae pushed back the nausea.

Liam rose as the sheriff did, and they shook hands. They were familiar with each other. Not quite close friends, but their natural camaraderie said there was trust between them.

She followed Liam out of the county offices and climbed into his truck.

"What's the matter?" he asked.

"The clock is ticking and we're getting nowhere. That's because I only know how to get information and write stories."

"What are you talking about? Remember when I said you would make a great private investigator? Well, you *are* making a great private investigator. Using your skills to find your sister-in-law. What should we do next?"

She angled to look at him. "Are you trying to mentor me? Or just asking because I've hired you and I'm the lead on this?"

He shrugged. "Take your pick."

His eyes held hers as if he wouldn't let go. As if he peered inside her soul, then his dimples emerged again. Warm sensations skated across her heart. *Don't get attached. When this is over, Liam and I will go back to being less than comfortable with each other. I'll leave this valley and Liam McKade far behind.*

He shuttered away whatever emotions had surfaced in his eyes, then started the truck.

Rae wanted to talk to Samara Davidson again, but she had to follow this lead through. "We need to be at that house after the sheriff makes contact. We're going to stake it out to find out where else Astor's been going besides the resort."

"Don't forget, you have a masked man after you," Liam said.

"And that's why I have you, Liam, to keep me safe from the monsters and bad guys."

"Let's be sure to keep a safe distance from whatever monster emerges after the sheriff's visit. That's bound to set off Astor's alarms—that is, if he has something to hide." Liam glanced her way. "And you and I are going to be waiting for what he does next."

"Then if nothing comes of that, I'm going to call him on his private number and arrange an interview."

Rae ignored the warning in Liam's eyes. Astor could be behind Rae's stolen laptop. With the information he found on it, he could learn what she knew about Zoey. He could have hired the masked man to scare her or injure her or force her to discontinue her search. With those thoughts, she now leaned toward Liam being right about Astor, after all. Despite Astor's response when she'd approached him, he'd known exactly who she was, and he was the reason behind Zoey's disappearance. He'd gotten revenge for his brother's death.

An eye for an eye.

A death for a death.

CHAPTER TWENTY-FIVE

Callie sat at the counter eating Goldfish crackers and drinking strawberry almond milk, thanks to the local grocery delivery service. Alan imbibed black coffee. A knock came at the front door. Callie's eyes widened. He suspected she hoped it was her mother who, for some reason, had knocked on the front door instead of waltzing in, filling the room with love and joy.

He glanced through the peephole. Detective Beverly Mansfield again. Thirty-something. Small but fierce. Eyes that held little warmth.

Fear and hope jumped around in his chest. He glanced over at Callie, whose eyes remained riveted on the door. He hated that she would soon be disappointed, and he wished she didn't have to be here to see the detective or hear her accusing words. He'd have to remedy that.

He opened the door and leaned against it, blocking Callie's view as much as possible. "Detective."

Alan didn't exactly want to invite the woman into his home. Was he required to show manners? She seemed to lean strongly toward suspecting him in Zoey's disappearance. However, the detective and her search could bring Zoey back to him. It was a double-edged sword.

"Please tell me you've found her," Despair echoed in every word.

By the look in her eyes, good news wasn't the reason the detective had come.

"I'm sorry. Not yet. You'll certainly be the first to know when we do." Her response sounded slightly threatening.

Or maybe he was paranoid.

"Would you mind if I came inside so we can talk in private?"

He glanced beyond her. As expected, a few reporters had gathered at the curb. He had no choice, really. Alan opened the door and let her step inside. "Let me situate Callie in her room with some toys. I don't—"

"Understood." Detective Mansfield's chin bounced up and down.

Hands in her pockets, she started strolling the room. Taking in the bookshelves. Looking for clues. Evidence. Alan should be glad Mansfield took her job seriously and would leave no stone unturned, as the saying went. He simply feared she would find some reason to arrest him. Innocent men had been sentenced to death before. He feared not for his own life but for Zoey's and Callie's lives. Zoey would want him focusing on Callie. He wished he weren't so torn up inside so he could function better through this ordeal, for his daughter's sake.

"Come on, sweetie. Let's move the Goldfish and milk into your room. I'll set them up on your table. You can play with your dollhouse while you eat."

She scrunched her face. "But you said no eating in my room."

"I know what I said. I also said unless it's a special time."

"Is this a special time?"

"It is. I need to speak with Detective Mansfield."

Callie's face scrunched again, only this time painfully. "Is she here to talk about Mommy?"

Alan shot the detective a look. He had wanted to spare Callie the pain. He'd hoped that she would keep believing his lies that her mother was visiting a friend. Still, he wasn't about to admit the truth to his little girl. He would fiercely protect her to the end. "It's grown-up talk, Callie. Nothing for you to worry about."

Alan grabbed the snacks, but Callie rushed over to the detective and hugged her legs.

Mansfield angled her head, then gave Alan a strange look. He thought he'd explained that Callie was on the other end of the spectrum. Overly friendly with strangers. She wanted to hug them all and bring them into her world of joy. Alan would do whatever it took to keep her world from collapsing.

"Callie, please come with me." He offered his hand.

"Listen to your father. Go with your dad." Detective Mansfield appeared so uncomfortable that Alan wanted to let her "suffer" a bit longer.

He inwardly chuckled, but it was a sick sound to his heart.

"Callie, please."

She lifted her face. "Do you know where my mommy is?"

Alan's broken heart could have shattered into a million more pieces right then. He set the snacks on a side table and crouched to eye level. Alan pulled Callie toward him. "Mommy's visiting a friend, Callie. I told you."

She stuck her lips out in a huge pout and hung her head. Alan gathered her into his arms and sent Detective Mansfield a glare. He couldn't help himself. "I'll be right back."

He picked up Callie with one arm and gathered the Goldfish in his other hand. Callie held her glass of milk. Concentrating on keeping the milk from spilling seemed to distract her for the moment.

Once Callie was settled in her room and appeared happy eating and moving furniture around in the Barbie dollhouse, Alan returned to find the detective flipping through a book she'd lifted from a shelf. She snapped the book shut and set it back in place.

162

The detective tried to present herself as unbiased and like someone who was only interested in the facts. But she did a poor job hiding that she strongly suspected Alan had killed Zoey and stuffed her body in a freezer in some warehouse across town.

"What's happening with the investigation?" he asked.

Mansfield held out a photograph. "Do you know this man?"

Alan's heart jackhammered. He took a good, long look. A big guy, but beyond that, nothing particularly notable. Could have been anyone on the street. "No, why?"

"In reviewing security footage from the area where her car was discovered, we found these images of your wife with this man."

Mansfield showed him the rest of the photographs. Zoey seemed to be speaking with the man as if she knew him. She stood entirely too close to him. Blood rushed to Alan's head. He couldn't control his increased breaths and was sure the detective watched with great interest. Headlines flashed in his mind.

Husband Kills Cheating Wife.

Focus. You must focus for Callie!

God, how do I stop my pounding heart? The questions? The suspicions ramping up the hurt inside?

Zoey would never cheat on him. Alan believed that. He had to hold on to that belief.

"So, you think this man abducted her?"

"No. She left with him."

The detective's words hung in the air. His pulse pounded in his ears. Mansfield watched his pupils for a reaction.

"Not voluntarily." Alan's words sounded much too loud, and he softened them. He glanced at the hallway, hoping Callie hadn't heard his distress. "He must have forced her to go with him."

"And why would he force her? Do you know something you're not telling me?"

"No! Of course not! Detective, I want you to find my wife. It's clear this man abducted her. Now, who is he?"

"We were hoping you could tell us."

"How can I tell you when I've never seen him in my life?" But Zoey clearly knew the man. From where? How often had she met with him? Alan wasn't sure he could hold his world together much longer. "Please make me copies. I can ask if anyone knows him."

"Daddy?" Callie crept from the hallway.

Alan turned on the detective. "I'm going to have to ask you to leave now."

Detective Mansfield kept trying to turn this around on Alan. He hoped Rae was having better luck with her own investigation, especially now that she'd employed a private investigator's assistance.

After Detective Mansfield left, he was able to distract Callie with her toys again. He took the milk glass and bowl to the kitchen. The anger and hurt that boiled to the surface could break him.

When he looked in on Callie, she'd fallen asleep on the floor. Normally he would have lifted her and tucked her into bed, but he couldn't risk facing her. He couldn't let her see him like this. He quietly shut the door and headed to his own room. He wanted to punch the wall, but that would wake Callie. Instead, he punched his pillow repeatedly until it burst open and down feathers accosted him.

Then he fell to his knees and sobbed.

CHAPTER TWENTY-SIX

Liam sat with Rae in his truck. Again. The heater pushed out hot air to keep them warm on a colder-than-usual winter day.

Seemed like all he ever did anymore was wait. Now he was waiting for the sheriff to follow through. Liam hoped that would happen within the next hour, considering a life was on the line. Sheriff Taggart was a good man and a good sheriff, so Liam would give him the benefit of the doubt.

"I know we have a plan, but it's not good enough. There has to be something else we can do. Something we're missing," Rae said. "I thought you were a hotshot agent who took chances."

"That was then. This is now. I only took risks that were deemed necessary and approved by my supervisor."

"And now you're your own boss."

"No. I'm working for you. Besides that, I don't want to get arrested."

"You're playing it safe when Zoey's life is in danger."

Liam understood her frustration and the fact that she was

becoming physically and emotionally exhausted, especially considering she was close to the missing woman. He had to hand it to Rae, she was as strong a person as he'd ever met. "If there was something to go on, then the sheriff would barge into that house. These things take time."

"Time she might not have."

"You're letting your emotions rule you. Time doesn't have to be wasted. Put your mind to finding something we can use. Have you looked at this guy's Twitter feed or something? His social media?"

She blew out a long breath. "You're right. I'll put in search parameters to track his movements. You know, like geolocated posts on social media that would potentially put him in Denver the day she was taken."

"That sounds like a plan." He let Rae work. Astor had resorts in Colorado, so his being there didn't mean he abducted Zoey, but Liam wouldn't be any more of a downer than he already had been. Rae needed her creative juices to flow.

"I've discovered that if you start digging," she said, "you usually find dirt. All we need is some dirt that will give us the ability to thoroughly shake him down. I have a feeling about this."

"Gut feelings have their value, I'll give you that."

"When Zoey disappeared in college, she begged me to keep it to myself. I shouldn't have agreed. Zoey didn't leave me much choice then. If I hadn't, maybe none of this would be happening now. Instead, I've regretted that decision. Why didn't I do more? Why didn't I say something?"

Rae's words resonated with Liam, and he reached over and squeezed her hand. "You couldn't have known that your decision to keep her secret would impact her future. Don't beat yourself up. Sometimes we shouldn't keep silent. Other times we need to keep secrets."

"And sometimes we need to speak up. Become a voice for the

voiceless. That's all I ever wanted and why I became an investigative reporter. To follow in Dad's footsteps, but Zoey was a big part of it too."

Rae pressed her head against the seatback and released a remorseful-sounding sigh. "She never told me what happened that week. But seeing her like that compelled the journalist in me to expose the truth about what happened to trafficked and abused women and led me down the road to interview women in prison who were being trafficked, being hunted while still in prison. Prisons have become a lucrative recruiting ground for sex buyers. People don't know about this. The women are promised somewhere safe to go when they're released, because where else are they going to go? They're outcasts. These sex buyers, these recruiters, send money to them for their basic needs while in prison. They become a lifeline for the women, and once they get out of prison, the women go into another prison of sorts when they're trafficked. It's a never-ending nightmare for them."

She sat up, her gaze fixed on Liam. "In fact, I think Zoey was the one to bring up the women trafficked out of prison. Her comment was one of many ideas I put into a file to explore later."

"I get it. The prison trafficking story wouldn't let you go."

She cleared her throat as if clearing tears. "No. It wouldn't. And the next thing I knew, I had spent months interviewing Dina in prison. I gained her trust and she depended on me, Liam."

He hated hearing the pain, but he knew he couldn't stop her from sharing this even if he wanted to.

"In the end, I let her down, because then she was trafficked again. I was so scared that she would suffer for talking to me at all!"

He vaguely remembered her telling him this when he was in a drugged-up haze in the hospital recovering from the gunshot he'd taken while saving her life. But when he woke up fully, Rae was already gone, and he was angry and in pain. She'd had her reasons for using him, but he hadn't wanted to see her.

"That last night," she said. "That last time we saw each other before everything exploded in our faces. That night before you were shot because of me and your cover was blown, I had overheard your conversation. I heard the name Malcom Fox, and I made the connection."

Rae wiped her cheeks. "I knew I finally had a name for the man behind the group responsible for taking Dina and so many others for that prison-trafficking scheme. I also knew that if I told you what I had planned, you'd prevent me from going after her because it was too dangerous."

She huffed a laugh and surveyed her hands. "I'm not good at asking permission. I'm sorry. Again, I didn't work closely with you, get to know you, just to use what information I could secretly glean from you."

He'd shifted to watch her as she spoke, and as she said those last words, her face colored. Her cheeks grew even more rosy than they were from the cold. Rae hung her head, and he had no doubt what she was thinking about. Every conversation, every thought seemed to come back to their previous investigation—the two of them together a volatile mixture that had reached the flashing point and ignited.

"I'm sorry about everything, Liam. I didn't mean to use you."

"You don't need to keep apologizing. I'm over it." And her. At least that's what he would keep telling himself.

She had come into the field office wanting an interview and had somehow ended up talking to Liam, who'd also been tasked with looking into the drug and human trafficking ring. She claimed to be gathering research for an article. Something about her—her deep-seated passion as well as her optimism—drew him to her that first day. They were on the same page in some respects, reaching into the dangerous shadows to pull people out. He saw a passion in her that he once had when he'd first started, but his job had lost its luster. Rae inspired him. Though he was working undercover, they shared information. But going after Malcom Fox—that was his mission, his task. Not Rae's.

He could still hear the terror in her frantic voice when she called him about Dina's disappearance. Rae feared she'd been trafficked again.

Then Rae disappeared, leaving Liam feeling helpless. Until he saw Rae bound and gagged—then he hadn't been helpless. It had all been an elaborate setup to flush out the undercover cop in Fox's organization. Liam did everything he could to save her, including giving up his cover. In the end, Fox was charged, so all was not lost.

A car sped down the street going much too fast, drawing him back to the present moment.

He said nothing more regarding her apology and explanation. Being here with her almost felt like they had come full circle. Except he'd prefer not to be betrayed and used, but maybe it was more that he reaped what he sowed. Working undercover required him to get close to people, befriend them and gain their trust, all so he could use them for information to catch bigger fish. Rae had been doing her job like he had. That was all. She'd saved a life. He could applaud her for that. Dina had been found.

But had Rae ever *cared* about him? Some part of him wanted to believe that she had. Or maybe part of him wanted to believe that she hadn't—so he wouldn't so easily give his heart up again.

Her eyes shimmered. "She escaped because I followed through."

"I hear what you're saying—you're going to follow this through and hope for the same results. But remember that Dina escaped as you were caught and could have died."

"I know you risked everything to save me. Please tell me that you know I never meant to hurt you. I never lied to you about—"

"Movement. The sheriff is exiting the building with a detective." Liam was glad for the break. Their conversation about the past was circular. It could go nowhere.

Rae said nothing for a few moments, then, "He isn't going to be happy that we're following him."

"Nah. He'll see us and know what we're up to. I just wish Heath were here. He could make this a lot easier. He would convince the sheriff to let me assist. Or Heath could be the one to go to the house with him."

"I don't get it," she said. "Why don't you just work for the county, then? You could do a lot of good."

"Yeah, well, there's considerably more freedom involved in what I'm doing now."

"Freedom that's limiting you. You could just as easily interrogate this guy if you were officially a detective. Detective Liam McKade."

Hmm. Different from his old title, Special Agent Liam McKade. It did have a nice ring to it. "Well I'm not a detective, and I don't want to interfere with the sheriff's investigation. Let's see if he uncovers something with his visit to Astor."

He steered onto the road, following the sheriff but not too close. His cell rang. The display read Bridger County. He answered.

"You're following me—why?" Sheriff Taggart asked.

"I thought that would be obvious and you would understand."

"I don't like being followed, McKade."

"We're headed in the same direction, Sheriff. That's all. We could have just driven to the house and waited for you."

"I don't recall inviting you. But let's cut to the chase. What are you planning?"

"After you leave, we want to see if there's a reaction."

"I want to hear from you later today." Sheriff Taggart ended the call.

Except I don't work for you, as you keep reminding me, Liam thought. Still, everyone would benefit if they worked together. Liam had seen firsthand what happened when team members didn't play well together.

Liam followed the sheriff on the straight road out of the valley and then onto a curvy, winding mountain road that swept past houses hidden on steep inclines in a densely wooded neighborhood. Finally, near Enzo Astor's home—the same house they had watched earlier—Liam parked along the road. "I'd like to hike in and watch."

If nothing happened today, maybe he would surveil the home tonight.

Rae continued to work on her laptop. This was more what stakeouts were like—sitting and waiting and nothing at all like action movies. But the hunt stirred him. This felt right.

"I got an email from Reggie."

Rae's super geek resource guy. "And?"

"Reggie says he might have something for us on the shell companies, but he's having trouble tying Astor to it, which is what makes him think he's onto something."

"I get it. In the DEA, we could find the drugs coming in and watch the cash flowing out, but where it went, nobody knew. Usually it went to an anonymous shell company incorporated in Delaware. Just one big dead end."

Rae lifted a finger. "He says it isn't out of the ordinary for real estate investment funds to own multiple properties, and for those properties in turn, for example income-producing commercial properties, to also own companies that own more properties. That said, E.S.A. Holdings is unusually convoluted. He has a friend in the US Treasury's FinCEN—Financial Crimes Enforcement Network—who's looking into it for him to see if there are any anomalies."

"Oh boy. As in officially looking into it?"

Rae shrugged. "He didn't say."

"Why doesn't Reggie work for the feds? They need him."

"He's British." She chuckled. "In the meantime, he attached some documents for me to look through, though I feel wholly incompetent compared to him. I'm just glad I have him. He can save us a lot of time. When I'm working on a story, it can take months. Sometimes years. That's what has me concerned—we don't have that kind of time."

He understood. Infiltrating trafficking rings and building trust took time. "What else?"

"Sam mentioned a client had stalked Zoey, so we know Simon frequented their heli-skiing business. Maybe once was all it took for him to become obsessed with her. That brings me to this. I'd like to talk to Zoey's mother again."

"What about our stakeout?"

"We could split up. Time is running out for Zoey."

"Not a good idea. The guy in the mask? He's been watching us too."

A vise squeezed his chest, cinching tighter with each day, each hour—he feared time could be running out for Rae too.

CHAPTER TWENTY-SEVEN

"What?" Rae gasped. "When were you going to tell me?"

"I'm telling you now."

Rae looked in the mirror to check behind them.

"Don't worry. I don't think he's following us now. All that to say, I'd prefer it if we stick together."

Because he couldn't let her get hurt? It seemed the two of them working together was inevitable. The chemistry between them remained, despite issues that needed to be worked through. He seemed to have let go of his resentment regarding her previous actions, and she hoped it was more that he finally understood she'd had no choice. Maybe he'd been hurt that she hadn't let him in on her plans, but what was done was done.

As Providence would have it, they were here now working together as though they were being given a second chance to make things right.

Her cell phone rang. A fist gripped her heart.

"It's my brother." She answered. "Alan. How are you?" Stupid question. But what else could she say?

"Rae . . ." His voice croaked.

Oh no, what . . . "Alan?" Tears choked her throat. She imagined the worst kind of news. "Please tell me what's going on."

"Oh . . ." He blew out a shaky breath. "They have pictures of Zoey meeting someone at the place where they found her car. She left with a guy. It looked as if she left willingly."

Oh. Man. What could Rae say to that? "What do the police think?"

"The detective on the case asked me if I knew the man in the picture, and she kept pressing that point. I think she's formulating a theory that I'm a jealous husband and I knew Zoey was having an affair. That I killed her."

Rae bent forward as if she felt the proverbial punch to her own gut. A moment passed before she could gather her composure enough to speak again. "And what do you believe? Do you think Zoey was having an affair?"

Please, let it not be so.

"I don't want to believe it. I can't believe it, yet the images show her talking to him like she knew him well."

"But she wouldn't leave Callie. Even if—and I'm sorry to say this—even if she left you, she wouldn't leave her little girl. I know this to my core, and you know it too. Something else is going on here. He must have been able to coerce her. To threaten her. Send me the pictures."

"I'm still waiting to get them. As soon as I do, I'll send them."

Rae glanced at Liam, who watched her. "Can you at least describe him?"

"He wore a ball cap, but he had light brown hair. Was kind of stocky. The complete opposite of me."

"Alan, listen to me. Get ahold of yourself. I don't believe for a minute she was having an affair. So we're going to go with the supposition that she was forced to leave."

"How could he force her?"

"By threatening you and Callie—the most important people in her life."

Callie's soft voice sounded in the background.

"I have to go," Alan said. "I'll send you the picture if I ever get it."

The call ended.

Rae stared at the screen as tears dropped to her phone.

"Hey." Liam's gentle voice comforted her. He took her hand in his. She continued to glare at her phone. Then she sniffled and wiped the moisture from her eyes. Rae lifted her gaze to meet the concern in Liam's. "Did you catch any of that?"

"I got the gist of it."

Rae shared everything Alan had said.

Liam shook his head. "That's rough. You said you don't believe she was cheating. How sure are you, Rae?"

"She loved him. I just know, okay?" She huffed and stared out the window. "Look, Zoey was super smart. She had amazing job offers. If she didn't love him, then she didn't have to stay with him. But she chose to stay home with her little girl. She wanted to be there with her."

Rae said nothing more, and silence filled the cab for a few moments.

"Okay, then," Liam said. "We already know she's missing, and now it appears that she was probably abducted. Now we know more. Still, there could be more to it. Could be the man was taking her to show her something. Maybe she was going to purchase a surprise for Alan. I don't know. This man could have abducted her that way. The point is, we stick to our plan while we wait for more information—like the name of the man she was last seen with."

Rae nodded. Liam made sense. She glanced up in time to see the sheriff's vehicle exiting the long drive. Time to focus her thoughts on the current situation and, like Liam said, stick to the trail they were following.

"Here he comes. I wish we could have been there to see and hear Enzo's words, his response to whatever news the sheriff delivered," Rae said.

"The big question is, what will happen next?"

"I hope it doesn't involve more skiing."

Liam chuckled. She liked the sound of it, and they needed levity. A breather from the heaviness. Poor Alan. How was he handling the weight of this and caring for Callie? Wasn't Mom coming to help? When was she supposed to get there? Rae never remembered to ask. Still, the focus required to care for Callie could be exactly what Alan needed right now.

The sheriff's vehicle steered onto the street and passed them, then made a U-turn to park behind Liam's truck on the shoulder. Sheriff Taggart got out and hiked over to Liam as if he would give him a ticket for a traffic violation. Liam lowered his window.

"Well?" he asked.

"I delivered the news."

"What news would that be?"

"Let's make this official." Sheriff Taggart leaned closer. "I'll read you in on this case since you're working as a private investigator and protecting Rae."

Rae's heart jumped. This was good news. The sheriff was taking them seriously.

Liam nodded. "Sounds good to me."

"I informed Mr. Astor of the news we received this afternoon. That an anthropologist evaluated Simon Astor's remains. His skull was fractured, and that's believed to be the cause of death."

"Fractured?" Liam said. "As in . . ."

"Murdered." The sheriff adjusted his hat. "Since we now have that evidence, it takes our search for Tawny Davidson into new territory." He peered past Liam to Rae. "What you've told me about your sister-in-law could be part of this, as you've already suggested. But she's missing now, and our priority is to find her.

176

We don't have enough to necessarily draw the conclusion that Enzo Astor abducted or instructed others to harm her, but neither can we dismiss it since we have a possible motive."

"Thanks, Sheriff," Rae said.

"How did Astor take the news about his brother?" Liam asked.

"He was pensive when he answered the door. Angry when I told him. Said he was going to head to Colorado to look into his brother's murder."

"Do you believe he'll do that?"

"I guess we'll find out. What are you going to do now? Follow me back?"

"No. We'll stick to our plan and see what he does next. We'll follow him."

This mode of investigation might get them nowhere fast, and Rae needed to convince Liam they should split up. They could accomplish much more. This wouldn't be the first time she'd been in dangerous situations when investigating.

"Be careful." Sheriff Taggart tipped his hat, then headed back to his vehicle.

Rae gasped. "Liam, when I approached Enzo earlier today, he said he would agree to talk to me. His exact words were, 'If a story about my brother's death can help find his *killer,* then I'll do anything.' We've speculated all along that Simon was killed and possibly by Zoey—in self-defense, of course. It's been our rationale for following Enzo and now . . ."

"And now, we could have our confirmation that Astor knew his brother had been murdered before the sheriff delivered the news."

CHAPTER TWENTY-EIGHT

Liam rolled his neck to ease the tension. He would have to text the sheriff regarding Rae's earlier conversation with Enzo Astor, building the case for storming his home, little by little. Often that's all they could do. Chip away until they uncovered the truth.

A truck exited the driveway. Liam lifted his binoculars to check the passengers.

The truck stopped where the drive intersected with the road and then pulled out and turned north, towing a trailer loaded with two snowmobiles. This wasn't what Liam had expected.

"Is he in that truck?" Rae said.

"Yes. Along with his usual sidekick."

"Aren't we here to see if he responds to the sheriff's news?" she asked.

"And this is his reaction. Strange, but there it is."

"Since he left his house, this might be a good time to hike the woods and get closer to the house. Look through binoculars. Take pictures with a zoom lens."

"Or now might be a good time to follow him and see where he goes after learning his brother was murdered five years ago, though he's known that for a while, it would seem. I'm not convinced he doesn't know *who* killed his brother either."

"You mean Zoey."

"We can't know that she killed him."

"The timeline works. If you had seen her when she came back—"

"I hear you. But something seems off. I don't know what it is yet."

"Let me know when you figure it out."

"You'll be the first to know," he said as he continued to follow Astor's truck.

Liam hung back as far as he could and ended up stuck behind a snowplow and two additional cars. He didn't dare pass them on the bridge. The truck turned onto a road and left the snowplow behind. By the time Liam's vehicle approached the turn, he could no longer see the truck. But he'd seen it turn, so he followed. A "Road Closed" sign sat off to the side.

He kept going. "This is where following them gets tricky. The road hasn't been plowed, and the snow is getting deeper. I'm not worried right now. My truck has four-wheel drive and a plow on the front. But at some point, Astor's truck will have to stop. I suspect that's what the snowmobiles are for."

"What are they doing? Having fun? Why would they be out having fun after the news of his brother's murder?"

"Good question." Liam slowed the truck. "We don't want to follow too closely. Let's wait here."

"We could get out and hike up the road."

"I'll give them time to get on their snowmobiles and leave. Then we'll drive in."

They waited a good fifteen minutes—enough time for them to unload and get on the road. In the distance, he heard the whine of the snowmobiles. Good enough. He steered along the forest road, the woods thickening along with the snow, but he kept to the tracks the other truck had created until finally he spotted the empty truck and trailer ahead. He stopped about ten yards from Enzo Astor's truck.

Beyond Astor's vehicle, the snow was several feet deep.

"Let's look around." He climbed out and met Rae at the grill. She hiked next to him, stepping in the truck tracks to both walk easier and try to hide their own presence there, until they stood in front of Astor's truck. The snowmobile tracks were visible and disappeared a quarter of a mile farther as the road wound deeper into the forest. Liam listened. He could barely hear them. A clump of snow dropped from a nearby low-hanging branch, startling Rae.

"I wonder why they didn't just take the snowmobiles from the house. Why drive out here, then take them?" Rae said.

"People ride them for miles, sometimes hundreds of miles. But there's a ridge they couldn't get over. We crossed the bridge back there."

"Do we keep walking?"

With his binoculars, he peered through the trees at the trail left by the snowmobiles. "I don't think we should hike any farther in." He didn't want to be caught in a precarious situation.

Rae's face had turned red with cold. "Where does this road go?"

"It's a forest service road. I'd need to look at a map." They should head back.

But the silence gave him pause. "Do you hear that?"

Rae angled her head. "No. What am I listening for?"

"The sound of the snowmobiles. They stopped."

"What does that mean?"

"They got stuck. Took a break. Or maybe they made it to their destination." Liam listened to hear if the snowmobiles started up again. After a minute, he turned around. "We should head back."

At Astor's vehicle, they peered inside the darkened windows, which mostly reflected the trees. Yep. Nice leather interior. He wouldn't expect any less on this kind of truck.

"Nothing. Not even a strip of paper with a scribbled name or cell phone number that could lead us to Zoey." Liam smirked.

"Nothing but a paperback novel stuck between the console and seat," she said.

He continued walking and paused at the tailgate to wait for Rae to catch up. Then they quickened their pace as they hiked to Liam's truck. He sighed as they closed the distance. It was easier to do a stakeout in the city. No doubt about it.

As he climbed back into his vehicle, his cell rang. Taggart.

"Yeah." Liam answered. "Glad you called. I need to know who Enzo Astor's associates are. Who's this guy always tagging along with him?"

"Where are you?"

"Um . . . why do you ask?"

"No reason. First, if I learn about his associates, I'll share with you, but it seems like this is more up your alley. You and the reporter's. Let me get to the reason I called. Listen, I'm not going to be able to pressure Astor or look too hard at him, at least on the record."

"What are you talking about?"

"The mayor is friends with Enzo Astor. She called me. I'm not sure exactly why since all I did was deliver news to him." He cleared his throat. "Maybe I asked an overstepping question or two. Whatever the reason, she got a phone call. I suspect Astor spotted you following and thinks I sent you."

"Interesting. At least we got a reaction."

"That, we did."

Astor's phone call to the mayor seemed like a knee-jerk reaction at that. Like he was overreacting. "What do you make of it?"

"I don't know, but I've been instructed to steer clear."

"You don't report to the mayor."

"No. I report to the constituents of the county, and the mayor just happens to run the county seat of Grayback. That's all I'm going to say."

"Don't tell me that politics is going to win the day again. This guy has a motive, like you said already."

"It's not going to win. You're on it, McKade. There's a reason for everything. There's a reason you're not working for me."

CHAPTER TWENTY-NINE

Rae watched Enzo Astor's truck and trailer as Liam backed his vehicle along the forest service road. The road was too narrow to turn around, especially with the big kind of dual-wheeled truck Liam drove. She considered what Liam had shared of his conversation with Taggart. Was there a story there regarding the mayor's connection to this real estate mogul? A connection worth looking into? Or was her journalistic mind kicking into overdrive?

At the very least, she would put another possible story aside until Zoey's whereabouts were discovered.

Liam turned onto the road heading who knew where. Rae was totally lost in this scenic mountain wilderness. She might like to come back and visit sometime. She never got out of the city much. There was something about this place—maybe it was the serious lack of population, but the peace and solitude could calm a quaking heart.

But not her quaking heart. Not yet.

If only she would allow the scenery to slow her racing heart and calm her mind, maybe with that calmness, she'd gain some clarity. Liam seemed more at home here than he ever had when she'd known him in Denver. And really, how well could you know someone after only three months? Some people fell in love and got engaged in that time. Others, less than a few days. She couldn't save what she and Liam might have had, but she could possibly save what Alan and Zoey had.

Rae shook off her melancholy. "I guess this means we're not going to sit and wait on them to see where they go next."

"We can."

"I need to see Samara Davidson. I think there's something more there." Again, she wished they could split up. "If we could get our hands on some proof, then the sheriff would have no choice but to barge into that home. Oh, except the mayor told him to back off. I can't believe this. Maybe we should visit the mayor ourselves. I have no qualms about facing off with this woman who might be standing in the way of Zoey's safety."

"Let's stick with going to see Samara Davidson."

Realization dawned. "Oh, I get it. We're not going to follow Astor all the way in because you're in protective mode. If I wasn't with you, then you'd go all the way in on your own and see where they headed."

He half smiled and shook his head.

"That's it, isn't it?"

"That's partially it. Remember when I said there is a time to expose the truth and a time to keep secrets? Well, there's a time to pull back. Even without the sheriff being instructed to back off, I'd had the feeling that we were closing in on him too fast. We need to give him some space to make mistakes."

"I take it you've learned that through experience."

"Yeah. I'm going off a sense of things. The rhythm of the hunt."

Rae studied him as he drove. She wished she could look at his face and see the expression in his eyes. He had a gift, and she'd be a fool to ignore him. "So it's like you have your fingers on the pulse of my investigation."

"Something like that."

She grabbed her notepad and pen while Liam drove. "While

you're monitoring the pulse, I feel like there's something we've missed. I'm going to run through what we know so far."

"I'm listening." The timbre of his voice reassured her. She hadn't known she needed it.

"One. Astor doesn't seem overly concerned about his brother's death. The news came out this week. He said he was going to look into his brother's *killer*. But then he gets on a snowmobile for what . . . fun? I don't get it."

"None of us really knows how we'll respond under certain circumstances. None of us grieves the same. Enzo apparently suspected Simon had been murdered and possibly even knows who murdered him, so this news wasn't a shock to him. Regardless of whether he knew or not, his brother has been missing for five years. He's had time to come to certain terms with that. Five years is a long time, and Enzo Astor probably suspected his brother was dead because he knew Simon wouldn't willingly leave an inheritance or access to millions on the table."

"Next. He told the sheriff he was going to Colorado. Then he calls the mayor to get the sheriff off his back."

Her cell rang, and she glanced at the screen. "It's the Mountain Valley Adventures number. Maybe it's Sam." She answered the cell. "This is Rae."

Silence met her on the line.

"Hello? Hello?" Rae looked at the cell. "The call disconnected."

Should she wait for Sam to call her back or should she try calling? Rae glanced in the passenger-side mirror.

"Liam, I think there's a truck coming up on us way too fast. Is it me, or is there a problem?"

"I see it."

Liam accelerated.

Rae's pulse skyrocketed with the increased speed on the treacherous road. In some places, huge snow berms blocked them in on both sides, but in other places the berms had fallen away. Spilling down the mountain? Those spots terrified her. Rae pressed her feet to the floorboard as if she could slow them down or prevent them from descending the jagged-edged drop on the side of the mountain.

Please let me be wrong. Please let me be wrong.

The plow attached to the grill of the enormous vehicle grew large in the mirror. She braced herself and with the impact, a scream erupted.

CHAPTER THIRTY

Liam's truck lurched forward.

This could not be happening.

His heart hammered.

Instinct took over, and he pressed the accelerator. His laser focus zeroed in on the curvy mountain road ahead of him.

Could he make those turns at this speed? Reason warred with instinct. Liam gripped the wheel, tension cording his neck.

The curvy, two-lane mountain road was treacherous on a good day, even without a thin layer of ice beneath the snow.

The Hummer sped up. It could have a more powerful engine. Liam's one advantage—the Hummer was a slower, heavier vehicle. With the current road conditions, that advantage might not matter.

Liam skidded over into the wrong lane, then swerved back into the right lane. The driver's intention was clear—to cause death.

Liam couldn't let that happen.

"That thing is big, Liam. You can't fight that. What are we going to do?"

"It's slower. We're coming up on a rise. I can pick up speed and put more distance between us."

Maybe he could beat them at their own game. He floored it. Except he had to slow down on that switchback coming up or he'd never make it. Forcing Liam to increase speed and then lose control could be the pursuer's strategy.

He ground his molars and slowed the truck. Speed limit signs warned to take the curve at fifteen miles per hour.

In the rearview mirror, he watched the Hummer close the distance. Much too soon it would catch up to them. As he slowed to take the curve, he mentally willed his tires to grip the snow and ice and stay on the road. As he steered into the curve, he leaned to the right with the momentum.

Come on, come on, come on.

The vehicle straightened out and he punched it again.

"*Phew.* We made it." Rae's voice shook.

"We're not out of the woods yet. Call 911. Tell them what's happening."

"I'm on it!"

While Rae made the emergency call, Liam sped up and almost left the Hummer behind.

"Hello? Yes. I have an emergency. Someone is trying to push us off the road. Please help!"

Rae sighed, then sat silently. "Wait. Could you repeat that? You faded out . . . Uh-huh? I don't know where we are. Just a second. I'm putting the phone on speaker. Liam . . ."

Liam relayed their general location along the highway.

The connection went silent.

Eyes wide with fear, Rae glanced at him. "Hello? Hello? I think I lost the call. Can you believe it? Maybe they got what they needed to help us. I'll try to call them back when I get a signal again."

But law enforcement—Wyoming Highway Patrol or the county—would never make it in time to save them. That burden was on Liam's shoulders alone.

He wished he could stop, get out, and face off with whoever pursued them. Who was behind them? The man in the black ski mask? But he had no good options.

"I think you're coming up on the curve too fast," she said.

"I don't need a back-seat driver."

"I'm in the passenger seat."

"Whatever."

But she was right. The road had been carved out of the mountain—rock on one side and a gorge on the other. He pumped the brakes to slow them. He had to gain control—accelerate enough to escape their pursuer but not too fast or he'd propel the truck right over the mountainside.

If he could just make it to the valley.

"Liam. Let's just pull over. Just stop, and let's face this guy. "You have a gun, don't you?"

Whoever was chasing them probably also had a weapon. Liam didn't need to get into a shootout with Rae caught in the middle. Only she wasn't in the middle—she was the center of the conflict. *She* was the target. Stopping to face off would give their pursuer the advantage.

Besides . . . "And where would you like me to do that? I have a snow berm on the right masking the rock wall behind it. And a mountain cliff on the left where the berms have fallen away, leaving only a guardrail. I'm doing my best here, okay?" Oh yeah . . . and a bridge coming up.

Liam accelerated.

The driver behind them was equally determined.

Whipping around another switchback, Liam again increased speed on the snow-packed road. "Although I might consider stopping right in the middle of the road and facing off with him if you weren't in the vehicle with me."

He pursed his lips as tension built in his neck and his knuckles turned white from squeezing the steering wheel.

"There's another forest road up ahead. If we can make it to that, I can turn off. We'll go as far as we can, but then when I stop, I want you to get out and hide in the woods."

"Would hiding in the woods be less dangerous?"

"For your sake, I hope so."

After that, he wasn't sure what he would do.

He'd grown up driving in the mountains on icy, snow-covered roads. This ridge, part of the gorge, was a steep, rocky wall with an ice-covered river at the bottom. It never once occurred to him that he might fall victim to these treacherous roads one day. The thought of plunging down a mountainside had never scared him.

Until now.

Other cars passed him going in the opposite direction. Behind his pursuer, a few other vehicles followed. Maybe the Hummer's driver would back off to avoid witnesses.

"What if we don't make it to the forest road? What are we going to do?" she asked. "How do we lose them?"

"I'm trying. See if you can get the license plate while I focus on the road."

"I don't see one on the front."

He slowed again. The next part of the road would involve several twists and turns that could prevent him from keeping the distance between his truck and the Hummer.

"I'm sorry this is happening." His vision tunneled at the absolute worst time. He felt helpless again.

Helpless to save her.

He shoved the barrage of emotions out of his way.

"Don't apologize. Just focus on the road. You can do this, Liam. I'll call the sheriff's office since I can't be sure that dispatch got the necessary information. The cell coverage isn't the best."

Rae sounded calmer than she should. Maybe she trusted him far too much. She didn't understand that he was about to fail them both. Liam shifted into four-wheel drive as he made the turn on a steep switchback.

The Hummer cut across at an angle and rammed them in the side.

Liam felt the instant his truck had been captured in the monster's jaw. The Hummer's plow pushed against the door on the passenger side.

With the impact, Rae screamed and dropped the cell.

Time shifted into slow motion.

Nothing Liam could do would save them. He tried to dislodge his truck from the Hummer's snowplow as it continued to shove them across the road toward the edge. Liam's truck tires spun out on the ice.

The Hummer must have studded tires with imbedded metal to grip the ice like tiny ice picks, because it kept pushing.

Pushing.

Pushing.

Liam's truck was fully loaded—except for studded snow tires.

"How do we get out of here?" Rae's voice shook.

With the plow against the passenger side, they weren't getting out that way. He glanced through the driver's-side window, and fear gripped him as he looked down into the gorge.

Through the passenger-side window, above the top edge of the plow, he could barely see the driver, whose face was hidden behind the visor pulled low, sunglasses, and a ball cap. Then the man suddenly lifted his sunglasses and looked Liam in the eyes. A murderer wanting the thrill of seeing terror on his victim's face?

Liam wished he could somehow climb out of the truck and stop the man, but he had lost control of the situation and there was no getting it back. He wanted to reach for Rae. Hold her like he would never get to hold her again. He'd failed to protect her.

A helplessness he'd never known gripped him as the guardrail gave way.

CHAPTER THIRTY-ONE

This can't be it. I don't want to die, God!

Rae squeezed her eyes shut as if she could block the sheer terror gripping her. She felt queasy as she sent a thousand prayers for help. Metal crunched as the truck leaned. Were they going to roll? Instinctively, she put her palms against the top of the cab and prayed the seat belt would hold her in place and the cab wouldn't be crushed. A pathetic cry escaped her throat.

Too many ways to die in this scenario flashed through her mind all at once. She feared a free fall. Then the sudden impact.

Death.

Palms sweating and heart racing, she tried to focus on praying. On trusting God.

Tires spun out and the engine roared as Liam accelerated, trying to gain control. She couldn't look. Her breaths came faster. Suddenly . . .

The truck bounced and jarred her. Rae shrieked and opened her eyes. The truck lurched forward.

Oh, thank God . . .

"Yes!" Liam shouted. "We have traction."

She had a strong feeling they weren't out of danger yet. "This is good?" She squeezed the armrest as the truck cleared a copse of trees.

"We're at a steep grade, but it's maneuverable. This snowy slope is better for a controlled descent than the straight, rocky drop. If I can just make it . . ."

Her head hit the top of the cab. This was far from controlled. But she saw now what had happened. Liam had maneuvered the truck so it caught a slope, barely missing a hundred-foot drop.

"Hang on. We're not out of this yet."

"Have you done this before?"

"What? Drive down the side of a mountain? No." Terror twisted with the exhilaration edging his words. "Right now, I need to prevent us from hitting that river at the bottom."

An explosive pop resounded, and Liam lost control. The truck swerved to the right, then toppled onto the driver's side—all of it happening within a few seconds. Leaning toward her, he held on to her. The truck rocked back and forth. Would it roll all the way?

When it stopped rocking and settled, Rae blew out a breath. "Is it over?"

"I hope so." Liam slowly released her, and gravity pulled her toward him, though her seat belt fought to keep her in place. She sucked in a few breaths, trying to grasp the events.

"What just happened?" she whispered.

"I think a tire blew. We're lucky the truck didn't keep rolling, but it looks like we're up against a snowbank. It could give way, so we're still in a precarious position. I don't want to tip the truck and start rolling or end up plunging to the bottom." His brown eyes were dark and in them she understood what he didn't say.

And that would kill us both.

"We're alive." He said the words as if he struggled to believe them.

Rae got that. She couldn't believe they'd actually survived either.

The way breath whooshed from him concerned her. "Are you okay? You're all right. Please tell me you're all right."

"Yeah. Sure." He unbuckled. "Are *you* all right?"

"My chest hurts from the seat belt. I feel jarred." And bruised. "But I'm alive. Thanks to you and your driving. That was incredible. You're incredible." The buckle kept her in the seat, so she left it on for the moment.

"I don't know about that. Listen, we need to get out of here. Whoever ran us off the road might come down to finish the job."

"You don't need to say more."

He positioned himself against the door and dug around in the console.

"What are you doing?"

"Your door isn't going to open. I have to shoot out the windshield. Cover your head." He tossed her his coat.

"What about the airbags? Will they deploy?"

"I don't think so, but be prepared for that too."

"What about you?"

"Don't worry about me. You ready?"

Rae buried her head in his coat as she covered her ears. She might have screamed with the first blast—definitely with the second. She started to drop the jacket but pulled it back over her head as cold air rushed through the front of the cab.

"Stay there."

She felt him shift around. Heard glass breaking.

"I'm kicking out the rest. We don't want to get shredded climbing out and then bleed to death."

A few more moments, then she dropped the coat to look. Liam had cleared much of the windshield away. He looked cold but determined.

"Here, Liam. You need your coat."

He dropped back into his seat. "Thanks."

He dug around in the back seat, then yanked a blanket forward. I'll cover the glass for our great escape with this."

"Are you sure we shouldn't just stay in the truck?"

He leveled his gaze at her. "I'm not sure about anything right now."

Rae nodded and tried to unbuckle. "It's stuck. It won't unlock."

Liam stretched his legs and jammed his hand into his pocket. He pulled out a knife and flicked it open. "I've got it. And I've got you. You'll fall toward me once I cut you out."

She braced herself. "Is it a cowboy thing to carry a knife in your pocket?"

"Nah. Just a practical thing." Liam quickly sliced through the belt.

The full weight of her body fell toward him. He caught her against him, his face inches from hers. "It's okay. I've got you." With those words, emotion and a deeper meaning lingered in his eyes.

Warmth surged through her. "What next?"

"I'm going to climb out and make sure it's safe. I'll need you to use the console and the dash, maybe support yourself up while I maneuver out. I knew I should have waited to cut your seat belt." He winked. He wasn't insinuating that he'd wanted her to fall into his arms, was he? She just had an overactive imagination that was taking her to crazy places in the worst of circumstances.

"Once I'm out," he said, "make yourself comfortable in my seat. Then I'll help you. Unfortunately, most of the broken windshield glass is scattered on the ground where we need to exit, so it's going to be tricky, even with the blanket covering the glass."

Using the steering wheel for support, she positioned her knees at the topside of the console and pushed away from Liam, giving him room.

He grabbed yet another blanket and handed it to her. "Extra blankets can save your life."

Using the other blanket to protect him against stray shards, he scrambled over the steering wheel and climbed through the open windshield. She slowly lowered herself into the driver's side. She sat against the door in an awkward position, her legs across the seat and over the console. But it was the best she could do unless she wanted to keep holding herself up. She watched him place the blanket over the ground.

He peered into the truck. "Wait here. I have to make sure it's safe."

Then he disappeared.

"Liam."

Minutes ticked by.

"Liam? Where are you? You can't leave me in here."

He wouldn't leave her. She knew he wouldn't.

But her heart rate kicked up. She gasped for air. The cab suddenly felt like a box closing in on her, even with the wide-open snowy mountain range blasting arctic air at her.

Rae shoved down the panic. It made no rational sense. And yet she still couldn't control it.

Whatever. She was getting out of there.

CHAPTER *THIRTY-TWO*

Palming his gun, Liam looked up at the evidence of their descent from the highway above. His heart still raced, and his hands still shook.

From here, Liam could make out a lone figure standing on the ledge, leaning over to look. The guy wore common enough attire—a ball cap and sunglasses—but Liam hesitated to call out for help. That was likely the man who'd tried to kill them. Still, other vehicles were on the road and had witnessed the whole thing. If their attacker was smart, he would have already fled the scene. He'd need to ditch the Hummer too. But if he was as bold as he'd been up to this point, he could put a bullet in Liam right now and then come after Rae.

A siren rang out in the distance, echoing through the narrow gorge. About time. But it sounded much too far away. The man disappeared. Liam guessed their attacker had wanted to see for himself if his handiwork had killed them as expected. But Liam was very much alive. It would be a stretch to hope the man believed Rae had died and would stop his attacks.

Liam eyed the ledge above him, wishing he could scramble up the rocky incline in time to find out who was behind this. *Come down here and face me so I can put a fist in your face. Maybe some lead too*, he thought. But confronting their attacker now was just too dangerous.

While acid boiled in his gut, he continued to squeeze the grip of his weapon. The rev of a big engine let Liam know the man was fleeing the scene. Liam kicked a rock.

"Liam!" Rae's voice sounded distant and muffled.

He scrambled down to her. She was halfway through the windshield, but her foot had somehow caught in the steering column.

"What took you so long?" she asked.

"I told you I wanted to make sure it's safe."

"Safe or not, I need to get out of here," she huffed.

"Hold still. I'll get you out." He leaned against the hood, reached through the windshield, and freed her foot. In that position, she couldn't control her fall and slid right into his arms again.

He peered into her frightened yet determined eyes. This was becoming a habit. A bad one for him. Instead of lowering her to the blanket, he carried her.

"Put me down. What are you doing?"

"Just hold your horses. I'll let you down when we're out of the danger zone. You know, the windshield. My boots are better than yours, okay?"

"Now, wait a minute." But she grinned.

The last thing they needed was to add a bloody injury to this critical situation. They'd been fortunate so far. At the front of his truck, he set her down. She shifted on her feet as if savoring the feel of solid ground.

Liam glanced up at the ledge. A small crowd appeared above.

Then, finally, the sight of a brown uniform worn by Bridger County deputies sent relief whooshing through him. A plain-clothed figure stepped close to the deputy and crouched.

"You okay down there?" Detective Moffett shouted.

"We're alive," Liam called. "But we're going to need help getting up."

"I'm calling for help. Anyone need medical attention?"

Again, he shouted, "I think we're good. No medical emergencies, that is. But watch your back up there."

"Come again?"

"Watch your back. Someone ran us off the road."

"So I heard. WSP is already on it. It's going to take a while to get to you." The investigator turned her attention to her radio. She wasn't patrol, but she'd come all the same. The squawk echoed all the way down to him, but he couldn't make out any words.

"That's just great," Rae said.

The tension that had coiled in his gut finally eased, if only slightly. Yes, they were alive, but it had been a long day and promised to be even longer.

Liam wrapped his arms around her thick coat. "I'll keep you warm, Rae. It'll be okay. You'll see."

His words sounded like a desperate attempt to convince himself.

Together they studied his vehicle, resting on its side like an abused horse that had lain down to die. It had partially wedged against the snow, and that had prevented it from rolling all the way over.

"Good thing you had us dress to be prepared for anything. I bet you hadn't thought of this."

"No. I never imagined it."

He and Rae might need to start climbing instead of waiting for help. This place was majestic, but rocky ledges with breathtaking vistas and snow-covered mountains could often exact a terrible price when a traveler made a misstep. Or in this case, was shoved from the road.

Still, they'd been fortunate.

Rae stumbled against him. He was about to let her go and then he hesitated, getting caught up in the emotion dancing in her blue-green eyes. A heartbeat or two and then he could actually breathe, and he released her.

She took a step away from him and glanced at his truck again. "Did this really happen?" she asked, her entire body shuddering.

He regretted releasing her so soon and tugged her back to him. Things could have ended so much worse. "It's okay. It's going to be okay." *God, please let it be okay. Let it end.*

Liam soaked in the reassurance acquired only through human touch. And maybe even only this particular human's touch. Because holding Rae against him, holding on for dear life, was more than simple human touch. At this moment, it was everything. "You said it already, Rae. We made it."

"Was it the masked man again?" she asked.

"I don't know *who* he is, but I know *what* he is."

"Dangerous. You don't have to tell me."

Liam held out no hope for Zoey. Did Rae truly believe her sister-in-law was still alive? One thing was clear, someone didn't want Rae to continue digging into Zoey's case and had wanted to finish them both off today.

Why would someone try to kill the two of them in this way and leave themselves so exposed? Regardless of the price their attacker was willing to pay to see them dead, the man's attempt to kill Liam and Rae had backfired. Perhaps a witness had videoed the murder attempt. That thought gave him hope. If they had footage of the event, they could get a close-up of the person behind the steering wheel of the Hummer.

A ruckus from above broke their connection, and Liam let go of Rae. "Looks like help has arrived."

"Liam!" Sheriff Taggart stood on the ledge along with a team with climbing gear.

"Mountain climbers. My favorite," he mumbled.

"Someone will come down to you," Taggart shouted. "Get you hooked up and then we'll lift you out of there."

That was the easy part. "What about my truck?"

Getting his truck off this mountainside was going to be a nightmare for someone. But that wasn't his problem.

"Special equipment will have to be brought in for that. I hope you have good insurance. You can make the arrangements."

Or maybe it *was* his problem. He turned his focus to Rae, and she tucked a blanket around the both of them. Their combined body heat would keep them warmer. Fulfilling Rae's request to keep her safe and help her find Zoey was already costing them both.

And the price was still rising.

CHAPTER THIRTY-THREE

Rae sat in front of the huge fire, covered in a blanket, watching the flames and letting them mesmerize her. After the day she'd had, her body was bruised, her brain was fried, and she felt dazed. So she stared.

For a few moments she could pretend all was well with the world. That Zoey was home safe and sound and nothing out of the ordinary had taken place a few days ago. That Rae's sitting in this ranch home belonging to Liam McKade's family is also perfectly normal.

Evelyn approached and set a cup of hot tea on the coffee table. "Are you all right?"

Rae pulled her gaze from the flames. "I'm going to be." She was a writer, but she couldn't form the right words. "I wish I could thank you enough and express my gratitude."

The older woman's warm smile edged on incredulous. "I've done nothing anyone else wouldn't do, hon. But if there's nothing more I can do, I need to get ready for my date."

"Date?" Rae perked up. She leaned forward and grabbed the tea.

"Well, don't act so surprised. Besides, my son, Leroy, is going too."

Rae almost choked on her tea. "On your date with you?"

Evelyn laughed. "Well, it's a group outing, really. We're going on a moonlit park ranger–guided snowshoeing hike. That's a mouthful."

"Don't worry. I caught it. So, you're going snowshoeing at night?"

"Yes. It should be beautiful." Evelyn puffed a pillow and repositioned it on another chair. "Please let me know if I can do anything else."

She headed for the door leading to her attached private cabin.

Evelyn was such a sweet lady. Liam had explained that Heath had hired her several years ago to work for him, but she and Leroy were more like family to the McKades. Meeting the woman, she totally got that. From what Rae knew of their childhood growing up, the brothers probably needed the extra encouragement a sweet-souled, grandmotherly person like Evelyn brought them.

Rae was exhausted and should have gone to bed, but her mind wouldn't shut down. She and Liam had given their statements and shared everything they knew about what had happened on that treacherous mountain road today. She shuddered as she remembered.

Because of the twisted angle of the switchback and the danger, only one person had caught sufficient video of the Hummer from behind. But no image of the driver. Add to that, muddy snow had covered the bumper and concealed the license plate.

She shook her head.

Rae thought back to her and Liam's conversation with Sheriff Taggart as he sat across from them—both of them still traumatized after their near-death battle in the gorge. The sheriff had directed his words at Rae. She could still feel his anger—not at her, but at the situation—washing over her as he spoke.

"Right now, we have questions and no answers. We have theories. Astor could have a motive for kidnapping or harming a woman who might have killed his brother. But we have no evidence." The sheriff rubbed his face. "Quite frankly, you're too close to this to see anything clearly. I'd suggest you go home, but I won't waste my breath."

"Obviously, Sheriff, someone thinks I'm on the right track. How do you explain what's happened to me?"

"Exactly the reason you should go home and leave this to law enforcement agencies."

"You told me the mayor shut you down, Sheriff," Liam said. "You encouraged me. Knew that I was going to keep digging."

"I know what I said, but things keep changing by the hour, it seems." He got up and paced behind his desk. "The state's involvement has escalated with the incident this afternoon. The mayor wouldn't expect me to stand down at this point."

"If we can figure out who the masked man is, that would help since he's tied to Astor." Liam tapped his fingers on the sheriff's desk. "We can go after Astor from that angle. Even if we can't, you can still question him about the pictures of him with the same man who forced Rae off that ski slope. Who stole her laptop."

"Detective Moffett is holding off on paying Astor a visit. His being seen with a man dressed in black skiwear, even with the green-faced wristwatch, is not enough. And you can't be sure it was that same man in the Hummer."

"We just have to find the Hummer," Liam said. "How many could there be in this valley? I could start searching there."

Liam reached for her hand and squeezed, reassuring her they would keep searching for answers.

With an arched brow, the sheriff glanced from Rae to Liam. The look on his face made it clear he thought the two of them had an interest in each other that went deeper than a collaboration to find Zoey.

A log rolled from the fire and brought Rae back to the present. Back to her tea and the warm blanket on the comfy sofa at the Emerald M.

She shut her eyes and tried to once again capture that earlier moment when the crackling fire and warmth lulled her frazzled heart and mind away from the drama.

Footfalls let her know she wasn't alone, and she opened her eyes.

Liam sat on the sofa—the other end. He joined her in staring at the fire. Neither of them spoke, but it was a good, comfortable silence. It seemed like they were forever doomed to share traumatic, life-threatening experiences together.

Nothing more.

From the first intake of his breath, signaling to her that he would speak, she dreaded his words.

"The authorities know everything we know now." He kept his voice low, his tone stern. "They're tracking with you."

She shifted on the sofa to look at him. "You're not quitting on me, are you?"

Liam moved closer. "Never. But I think you should stop. You're putting yourself in danger. You know how that can end. Do like the sheriff said and . . . and go home."

"You know I can't. I didn't stop searching for Dina, no matter the danger. No matter the cost. I won't stop searching for Zoey. Someone close to me and dearly loved by my brother and Callie. And by me." Tears fought for an escape. She refused them freedom. "This is far more than a story this time. The authorities will do their absolute best, but you know as well as I do that it's not always enough. More often than not, their efforts aren't enough. So, no. I won't quit. I won't go home. Can you blame me?"

Standing, he dragged a hand down his haggard face. "No. But you can't save everyone, Rae."

"I don't need to save everyone. I just need to save Zoey."

"She was your friend first, before your brother met her. I know how you are—you hold yourself responsible for her, and for your brother meeting her, and for their child. You can't carry the world on your shoulders."

Okay. So the tears escaped after all. "I don't need to carry the world. I only need to find Zoey. I came to you because I knew you would understand. I knew you could help. So please don't quit on me now."

He sat close to her. Her breath hitched at his nearness.

With his thumb, he gently wiped the tears from her cheeks. "If I could tell you to leave and trust that you would, I'd take that path. But I've seen you in action. You're willing to risk everything for someone else. I can't let you do this alone. And I know you won't stop. So I'm here with you every step of the way."

She'd dreaded bringing him into this, but Rae wouldn't have anyone else in it with her.

A myriad of emotions warred in his expression, poured from his eyes. *What are you thinking, Liam McKade? Why am I so drawn to you?* Protection emanated from him and concealed any agitation or bitterness he might have still harbored toward Rae. She'd been in his arms before, and unfortunately, she wanted to be in them again now. Her heart pounded with longing and questions—would he hold her?

As if sensing her unspoken question, he rose from the sofa and moved toward the flames—a much safer place for him.

"I see no reason why we can't also look into things while the police do their own thing. Maybe if someone finds enough evidence, the feds will get involved too. The more people searching, the better."

Sam had mentioned contacting the FBI, but Rae had no knowledge of their interest in Zoey's case or if they planned to get involved. "You were once a fed."

He rubbed the whiskers on his chin and slid his hand up around his cheek and then down to his neck. "That's why I can't be sure there's not more going on here."

"What do you mean?" He'd mentioned contacting his former DEA boss about Enzo . . . had he learned something?

"I don't know. Just a feeling."

"A gut feeling? You once told me to listen to that."

"I'm listening. I'm not exactly sure what my gut is telling me."

Rae got up to move closer to the hearth as the fire died. The flames reflected in Liam's eyes, and shadows danced across his somber features. Except for her father, Liam was the most intense man she'd ever known.

Evelyn stepped into the living room, drawing their attention. She'd donned an adorable Nordic sweater. Her cheeks were rosy red to match her lips—not too much, but just right—and she wore snowmen earrings. "Well? What do you think?"

"You look great!" Rae smiled.

"Where are you going at this hour, young lady?" Liam asked.

A knock came at the door. "Oh, that would be my date."

Liam's surprise almost made Rae laugh.

"Are you sure Leroy is okay with that?" he asked.

Evelyn opened the door. "Leroy, what are you doing here?"

"I'm going to wait here with you. We're all riding together."

"I thought you were meeting us."

"Why meet you when we can ride together? Mom, dating at your age. Really."

"If you want to tag along with us, that's fine, Leroy, but please don't be such a fun sucker." Evelyn laughed. She wasn't truly miffed at her son.

Leroy stepped into the house.

"Watch the boots."

"Okay, Mom." He kissed her on the cheek, then smiled at Rae and Liam. He must have noticed the questioning look on Liam's face. "We're going on a moonlit snowshoeing adventure."

"Is that safe?" Liam asked.

"A park ranger guides it. You should try it sometime."

"Oh, there's Tom now, pulling up to the house. Let's go." Evelyn gave them a small wave, then she and Leroy exited. She closed the door behind them.

Tom was going out of his way to impress Evelyn if he drove all the way out to this ranch and up that road in the winter.

Deep in thought, Liam peered off into space. Then he slowly turned his gaze on Rae, and she knew that look.

He'd gotten an idea.

Rae had a feeling she wasn't going to like it.

CHAPTER THIRTY-FOUR

If he had his way, he would wait until Rae fell asleep. Then he'd take off on his own for this particular reconnaissance. If it worked, it would save them some time and possibly give them answers. But he couldn't leave her alone since Evelyn and Leroy were gone. Pete's cabin was too far from the main house. Liam had believed she was safe here, but after today, he should expect the unexpected.

Maybe he should forget about his harebrained idea. But it wasn't that crazy—just different. Rae had perked up and looked lively since Evelyn had announced her date. Plus, Liam had brewed a pot of strong coffee. He was going to need it.

He'd been worried about her going to a mental and emotional place from which she might not return. Then he reminded himself what she'd already been through. If anything, Rae was strong. She'd be all right. Still, he was glad to see that glow of color in her face, along with the familiar spark of curiosity—every reporter's superpower.

"What are we doing?" Rae had a blanket wrapped around her shoulders as she sat at the kitchen table.

"You'll see." Liam spread out a map and searched the forest

roads—one in particular. "As for what's happened to you since you arrived in Jackson Hole, I figure there are only a few possibilities. One is that someone knows you've come here to find Zoey, and they're trying to stop you or sidetrack you. We've theorized *that* someone is Enzo Astor—and the masked man works for him."

"The other possibilities?"

"My past. Your past. Our past. All or any of it involving trafficking. Drugs. Money laundering."

"I get what you're saying, but I can't get caught up in anything that leads me away from finding Zoey."

"I hear you. All I'm saying is that every possibility should be on the table."

Rae frowned. "Because you've seen Enzo Astor somewhere, you think he could somehow be tied to both Zoey and your past dealings."

"Again. Everything's on the table until we take it off." Liam shrugged. "You were interviewing Dina for the article about women taken from prison for trafficking, then Dina suddenly disappeared. What were you working on when Zoey disappeared?"

"I had gotten a few phone interviews. Landed the possible job with *World Tour*."

"Was that it?"

"I mean, I was looking into possible story ideas for writing an exposé. I figured I'd write it on my own, without the backing of a newsgroup or editor. Freelance. At my last real job for a newsgroup, I was working on the prison trafficking article that ended up exposing the man behind the ring."

"Right. Malcom Fox. His organization was doing what every savvy drug trafficking organization is doing these days—diversifying to include human trafficking, both labor and sex. But again, linking the people behind the trafficking has always been the hard part. Let's hope Reggie can come up with a link."

"Do you really think any of this has to do with what happened before?"

"We can't ignore the possibility." Liam struggled to wrap his mind around the likelihood. But if there was a connection, they needed to find it—and fast.

He had to figure this out, even if he couldn't figure his own life out. Sheriff Taggart had told him there was a reason for everything. Before her untimely death, his mother had often said that everything happened for a reason. When she died, Liam closed himself off from the pain. He thought that if everything happened for a reason, then considering all he'd been through, he had no hope of figuring life out. So he never tried.

But Rae—she made him *want* to try.

He waited for her gaze to find him again.

There. Her blue-green eyes focused on him. He swallowed against the tightness in his throat. Liam had thought he hadn't wanted to see this woman again, but she was here now in his home, and he knew this moment was meant to be—proof that things happened for a reason, after all. Their interactions in this life weren't over.

Could they resurrect what they'd shared before?

Rae covered her face, then quickly dropped her hands. "What can we do about any of it tonight?"

"Snowmobiles."

"Snowmobiles?"

Liam grinned. "Heath has six of them. We're trying to gear up for opening in the winter."

Rae arched a brow.

"That forest road where we saw Astor and his buddy go—I want to see if I can get up there from another angle instead of taking that road—because after we were there, someone tried to kill us."

"The sheriff said the state was also looking into it."

"Of course they are, but as far as what Astor was doing on

the forest service road today, Taggart might have called a ranger about it. I'm doubtful the ranger will even go in and check it out. Even if they do, that doesn't mean they're going to look at things the way we are." Funny that he was now trying to persuade her to cooperate in the investigation for which she'd asked for his help. "Sheriff Taggart knows we're on this, and that frees me up to look deeper. Plus, I have you, Rae. Nobody is going to dig as deep as you will to find Zoey. Are you with me?"

"Did you have any doubt?" Her eyes brightened with hope.

That Liam had put that sparkle there both thrilled him *and* scared him to death. He didn't want to let her down. But he had hope too. Maybe they made a good team, after all. But this was far from over.

"When are we going to do this?" She studied him. "Wait. You're not saying we're snowmobiling *tonight*, are you?"

He nodded. "Evelyn is snowshoeing tonight. People ski at night, and they snowmobile too. We just have to take precautions. Be careful."

"Won't we tip someone off? Won't they hear us?"

He stuck his finger on the map. "That's a popular snowmobile spot. It's a few miles up from the forest service road."

"Well, that's probably where these guys were going."

"Maybe. But I think if they had planned to snowmobile for fun, they would have taken a different road. We can get to that road from this snowmobiling spot without raising too much suspicion. We're just out having fun."

She snorted a laugh.

"What's so funny?"

"We're going to pretend we're having fun as we approach a potential danger zone. For some reason that made me think about my father and the lengths he went to in order to get into war zones."

Rae studied the map, then continued. "He loved us, we knew

that, but even when he was back home, his mind was always somewhere else. In some war zone on the other side of the planet. He suffered from severe PTSD but didn't let that stop him. I laughed because he was never in situations where he could just pretend he was out having fun." She blew out a breath. "In the end, he got trapped in a small town under siege. It was being bombed. Civilians getting bombed. There was literally no reason for it other than the powers that be wanted to exert authority. Children died. People had no access to food or water or electricity. Dad was right there in the middle of it, suffering with them. Reporting so he could ask the world when they would send help."

Liam was mesmerized as Rae shared the story, admiration for her father glowing on her face. "He called in. Did a phone interview to tell the world. Mom suspected that he somehow had a feeling he wasn't going to make it out that time. So he'd arranged for that interview. I remember watching the news, listening along with her and Alan. Listening to his voice as images played across the screen. We were all crying as we watched." Rae hung her head for a few moments and then lifted it, her eyes closed. "Sure enough, a bomb hit the house where he and some other journalists were staying, killing three of them. Dad included."

Liam said nothing. He waited to see if she would say more.

She drew in a long breath, then opened her eyes.

"So . . . I see nothing wrong with following Enzo Astor's movements tonight in our search for Zoey. This operation is nothing in comparison."

Rae somehow wanted to fill her father's big shoes, but she'd chosen a different, and thankless, path. Liam had a feeling that her perspective was the catalyst that often put her in harm's way. He'd have to take extra precautions with her, a tough gig. "I'm sorry, Rae."

"Don't be." She sipped on her coffee. "What are we looking for specifically?"

"Someone could be using a cabin accessible only by snowmobile this time of year. It's not uncommon, but we're looking for suspicious usages."

"Our chances of seeing that activity might be better at night, too, since it might actually increase once it's dark out. Plus, we can watch from the shadows and more easily see inside. I like it."

"Good." For some unknown reason, he reached across the counter and took her hand.

"But you don't have a truck."

"No, but Heath does. I have the keys. I'll use his until the insurance replaces mine." He relaxed, now that she was on board. "I can't sit around the house and do nothing. Even researching gets tedious. If we were in the city, we wouldn't think twice about doing a drive-by in the evening. So think outside the box a little bit."

"I think you and I are in sync. I won't sleep tonight anyway. This keeps us working, and it'll just be another stakeout."

"I'll say it again, you'd make a good private investigator."

"And you'd make a good journalist."

CHAPTER THIRTY-FIVE

Alan wanted to collapse on his bed, but Mom had come to help and was staying in the house. Providing encouragement and support. At this moment, she was still fiddling in the kitchen, making herself tea like she did every night, and he felt obligated to sit with her for a few moments.

Barefoot, he strolled into the kitchen and grabbed a glass of milk—the real stuff, compliments of Mom.

He did everything by rote now.

His Zoey. He'd lost his Zoey.

He'd been a fool to love her and marry her, but if he could go back, he'd do it all over again. Because he could never give her up. And Callie. She was all he had left.

"Alan." His mother's soft words couldn't pull him out of his daze.

Oh. Right. Time to sit and talk while she drank tea. More like listen. He could only listen. He had nothing more to say to anyone, especially to the police who were eyeing him closer than ever now. He and Zoey had argued the day she disappeared. The police knew about that now. A neighbor had shared. Alan hadn't thought of it as an argument. Just a disagreement. Didn't every married couple have disagreements?

He slouched in the chair at the table and chugged his glass of milk. "Yeah?"

He looked at Mom, then just as quickly looked away. He couldn't bear to see the agonizing emotions in her gaze. Sympathy and pity, regret and sorrow. She hadn't thought Zoey was good enough for him, though she never said so. He knew. No one would ever be good enough for him. Mom had been there, of course, when Rae brought her college roommate home for spring break, the purple bruises still visible. No one had said anything. They'd all welcomed Zoey, fully knowing she needed comfort, safety, security, and most of all . . . love.

Alan had fallen, and he had never looked back.

"Alan, I took the liberty of going through the mail you haven't looked at since . . ."

He pressed his head into his folded arms on the table.

"Alan, pay attention."

"I'm here."

"Sit up. You need to see this."

He lifted his head. "What could be so important?"

Mom shoved an envelope toward him. "This came for Zoey. It has no return address. The postmark date says it was sent the day she disappeared—and from a post office in Wyoming."

Hope surged at first, then died just as quickly.

He eyed the yellow padded envelope. A million possibilities raced through his mind, none of them good.

CHAPTER THIRTY-SIX

Geared up in a snowmobile suit, Rae assisted Liam in getting the snowmobiles off the trailer.

This is what I would call an extreme stakeout.

But given DEA agent/cowboy Liam McKade, she shouldn't expect anything less. And in truth, she hadn't been surprised when he'd laid out his plan.

In fact, his idea had confirmed she'd made the right decision in coming to him in the first place. He was fully invested in finding Zoey. Her friend's disappearance had many tangled layers. Now, if Rae could somehow separate those layers. She had a feeling about tonight. Her reporter's instinct? Dad had nudged her to pay attention to that. But even if they found nothing, that would tell her to move to another lead.

She couldn't recall participating in anything so adventurous before. Liam had made her practice riding the snowmobile in front of the house at Emerald M, and they'd left tracks all through the snow. The main concern was to keep from getting stuck in the deepest snow.

After the traumatic experiences of the day, she needed this midnight ride to draw her thoughts away from that terror, and so far it was working. Adrenaline pulsed through her.

He put on his helmet and paused. "Don't worry, Rae."

"Do I look worried? I'm not worried."

"Listen. Do you hear that? Other snowmobilers are out. The moon is out, and the sky is clear. Groomers like to clean up the trails at night to avoid higher snowmobiling traffic, but there are pockets of snowmobilers here and there. I knew someone would be out here tonight."

"Is there a thrill-seekers anonymous group they can attend?"

"Ha. Funny. Seriously, are you sure you're up for this?"

"If you're going, I'm going. End of story."

"I hope you're right and this is the end of the story. I hope we find answers."

She pulled on her helmet and secured it, then hopped on the snowmobile and turned it on. Piece of cake. She was glad she'd practiced riding the snowmobile at his ranch before they tackled the ungroomed areas.

Liam positioned his snowmobile on the road in front of her. The snow was packed down a bit from activity earlier in the day. His snowmobile lurched forward, and Rae's full concentration remained on the red lights at the back of his machine. Her goal was to keep him a few yards ahead of her, but not too close.

On a treeless, snow-covered hill in the distance, snowmobile lights buzzed around. Fireflies in a synchronized dancing light show.

They continued along the road, passing the hill as Liam led them deeper into the woods. He slowed his machine a bit as the forest grew denser and the road narrowed, and they traveled at a slower pace until he stopped in the middle of the road. When Liam got off, she did too. He gestured at the wall of snow up ahead. "I think it's too risky. I don't want to get stuck. I just want to get in and out."

"In and out? Where are we going?"

"Time to put on the snowshoes."

"We're hiking the rest of the way?" Though her tone sounded incredulous, the scenery at night—the brilliant moon creating an entirely different kind of snowy landscape—captivated her. This was some kind of crazy beautiful that she'd never experienced.

Plus, she was in this with Liam, of all people.

She focused on donning her snowshoes. He finished putting his on and waited for her. Finally, she was ready to go. Her heart drummed as she hiked behind him.

"The snow's deep enough that most of the forest floor—tree trunks, branches, and shrubs—are covered. But you could still trip."

Liam paused and held up his hand. "Let's keep it down from here on out. I just want to see what's in these woods, if anything. Find a cabin while staying on public lands. See what's what."

They continued hiking. Exhaustion contended with the adrenaline that had gotten her this far. Up ahead, faint light from windows drew them closer. Liam kept to the shadows in the trees, and Rae followed his example. "Whose house is this?" she whispered.

Liam pressed a finger against his lips.

Several snowmobiles were parked around the house. A man with a gun lingered outside the sprawling cabin.

Liam crouched behind a tree. Rae did the same.

A man with a gun. What could that mean? Wealthy people often had bodyguards and security.

Liam tugged his ever-ready binoculars from his coat pocket and peered at the home. No blinds or heavy drapes hid what was going on inside. They apparently didn't expect anyone to be out in this part of the woods at night in the dead of winter.

Rae was dying to look through Liam's binoculars. She wanted to know what he saw. She held out her hand, and he ducked and slid close enough to hand them off. In the distance, the whir of snowmobiles approached, coming from the opposite direction from which they'd hiked. Liam had been right to take this route. But if it didn't snow tonight, their tracks would give them away, and they would not be able to do this again.

Peering through the binoculars, she saw a couple of older men and much younger women in the house. While she looked, Liam took a few pictures with his cell phone—not optimal, but better than nothing.

One young woman appeared to be sleeping, her head tilted against the sofa back.

"Zoey . . ." Rae said. Had she spoken out loud?

The woman lifted her head. It wasn't Zoey. Hope whooshed from Rae.

CHAPTER THIRTY-SEVEN

The guy with the gun tossed his cigarette and perked up. Had he heard Rae?

Liam doubted it. Even from here, he could hear voices and music from inside the house, which would have covered the sound of Rae's voice.

Was this simply a private party? It was an inconvenient place to have one, but they were guaranteed to remain undisturbed. So why the security detail? He'd seen a lot of different setups while working with the DEA, and just about any scenario was possible and would be used for criminal purposes.

He had a bad feeling about what was going on in that house.

Drugs? Or . . . human trafficking? While looking through the binoculars, he'd spotted Astor's sidekick inside, but not the man himself. So this must be where they'd been headed to earlier in the day.

Rae had pressed herself into the shadow of the tree trunk, so Liam did the same. If the guy decided to explore beyond the near perimeter of the house, he and Rae were in trouble. Their tracks were visible. They couldn't simply hide.

This was unfolding much differently than he'd imagined. He

peered around the tree. The guy had become interested in the woods and was starting forward.

Liam's heart pounded. How was he going to get them out of this?

A shout resounded.

"Let's go!" he whispered.

Rae shook her head and gestured toward the house. Liam looked at the house again. Someone inside had called to the guy standing guard. He headed toward a side door, probably welcoming the relief from the cold.

Liam shoved from the tree and grabbed Rae's hand. "Time to go." While they had the chance.

He led her back through the woods along the path they'd already taken. He wanted to sag with relief when they made it to their snowmobiles. Adrenaline pumped through him. Rae took off her snowshoes and stored them, then straddled her machine like an old pro.

He couldn't help but smile. She would go to any lengths to save another human. Take crazy risks because sitting at home nice and comfy when others were suffering didn't suit her. He liked that about her. It was how he felt once, and he realized that he'd lost himself. Rae was helping him find himself again.

He started up his machine and worked it around, then led her past the hill that had grown quiet. Crazy snowmobilers had called it a night. Once they made it to Heath's truck, they loaded up the snowmobiles and climbed into the cab. He started the engine and cranked the heat as she pulled off her gloves. When she glanced at him, she was breathless and her cheeks were rosy, but she said nothing.

Rae was probably thinking it through like he was.

"Let's get out of here." He backed out as far as he could, then turned the truck around to head home.

He wished he was working DEA again. He wished he could

somehow go in undercover and figure this out. And in the process find Zoey for Rae.

"I thought . . . I thought it was Zoey. I guess I want to see her so badly that I thought that girl was her."

"It's okay. Don't beat yourself up."

"But I almost got us caught. If that guy hadn't been called back inside . . ."

"He wasn't a great security guard, which worked out for us," Liam said. "But I have to wonder why they need a man with a big gun to stand around outside." He'd let Sheriff Taggart know. They'd agreed to keep each other informed.

"To keep people out?" Rae asked.

"Or to keep them in." Even though the threat of a family member being killed or harmed was often enough to keep trafficked people enslaved, a deadly weapon could work just as well.

CHAPTER THIRTY-EIGHT

As Liam drove, Rae peered out the window at the stunning night. The beauty could almost make her forget her search for Zoey. Adrenaline seemed to drain out of her as warmth filled the cab and the smooth hum of the truck threatened to lull her to sleep. But those women at that house—were they there against their will? Trafficked, as Liam suggested with his comment? How could they find out?

"I think my next step should be to call Astor. He told me he would talk to me. We could get the sheriff involved. I could go in wired."

"I don't think that's a good idea."

"I could meet him at a public place. You could be nearby. Set up surveillance or record it. Asking the hard questions, facing off with the right people, is what I need to do." It's what her father had done. She wouldn't say that out loud because she knew exactly how Liam would respond—her father had been killed for his efforts.

Was Rae ready to die? To risk her life?

"Not saying it's a good idea, but let's talk about it in the morn-

224

ing. I'll let Taggart know what we've come across. He might need to communicate with any trafficking task forces he belongs to."

There. She had her next step. She would speak to Enzo Astor. If she got her chance, she needed to make the most of it. What would she ask him? How would she learn if he had anything to do with Zoey's disappearance? She had experience and skills, but right now she felt so helpless and like none of it would make a difference. She closed her eyes.

"Rae . . ." His voice was soft.

Hands gently squeezed her shoulders.

Rae opened her eyes. Liam was standing next to the opened passenger-side door. "You fell asleep."

"Oh."

His face was close to hers. He studied her, his gaze roaming over her features. "Are you okay?"

"Yes." Her voice cracked with exhaustion. "But with the door opened, I'm cold."

He lingered, and she wasn't sure why. Rae lifted her hand and cupped his cheek, feeling the stubble there. "Thank you for this."

"For what?"

"For . . . for tonight. For helping me."

"You're welcome." He eased away from her—not that she'd wanted him to, which should disturb her. Rae slid from her seat and dropped to the ground, putting her even closer to Liam. He didn't budge an inch.

She pulled her gaze from his intense stare to look up. The stars lit up the deeply black sky, and the moon that had shined so bright earlier was nowhere to be seen. "This place is magical."

"It is."

She could hear his breaths. Feel the warmth from his body as he pinned her in. She felt the draw of him and could no longer ignore her insane attraction to the man. Rae's heart rate jumped.

Liam must have been drawn to her as well, otherwise, why did he stand so close? Maybe their thrilling escapade in the woods had knocked away all their barriers.

She hoped not.

Then again . . .

Would he kiss her here under the stars? After everything they'd been through, she couldn't want that from him. That was her head talking. But her heart wanted that kiss. Her senses were already reeling.

Liam ducked his chin and inched forward but then hesitated. A grin tugged at his lips. An invitation. Rae ignored the warning signals in her head and met him the rest of the way. His lips pressed against hers. His hand came up to cup her chin as his lips explored. Pleasant sensations flooded her. All she wanted was to melt into him. All she wanted was his arms around her.

What am I doing?

She ended the kiss and pulled away before she wound up in his arms, because once she found herself there, she wouldn't want to leave. Rae's breath caught.

She shouldn't be surprised that they would take this kind of risk. They were both risk-takers in almost every way.

He peered at her as though dazed and lost and missing her lips.

"I'm . . . I need to go," she whispered.

He moved out of her way. She headed to the house, leaving him behind and feeling ridiculously awkward as she clomped up the porch. *I sure hope Evelyn is back from her date.* At this hour, she'd have to be.

At the door, she turned around. "Oh, I forgot. Do you want me to help you unload those?"

"No," he called. "We'll tackle that in the morning. You're good to go."

"What are you going to do?"

"Check on the horses."

Cowboy code for "I need time alone to think."

226

"See you in the morning." She quietly opened the door and stepped inside. Evelyn had left the door unlocked for them. Rae was relieved. She didn't have a key, and she wanted to avoid another close encounter with Liam.

Rae shut the door and sagged against it. Despite their hours of work, she felt no closer to finding Zoey. The pressure, the burden of Zoey's life weighed on Rae. She shouldn't be wasting time kissing Liam.

Her father would have done much more in this situation. He'd pushed so hard in his work that he'd gotten himself killed. She'd chosen to think of him as a hero. A martyr even, for the sake of all that was unjust in the world.

Was it time for Rae to step up to the task?

The fire in the fireplace had been stoked since they'd left. Rae paused at the fire and took in the flames, the glowing red embers morphing and crackling and popping, and yet dying at the same time.

"Tomorrow, Enzo Astor. Tomorrow, I'm going to ask you about Zoey."

CHAPTER THIRTY-NINE

Callie slept soundly.

For the first time since Mom's arrival, Alan was grateful for her presence. Initially, he assumed her presence would require energy he didn't think he had. But now that she was here, he realized how grateful he was. She could help with Callie in ways he hadn't known he needed.

And Mom had forced him to look at the package that had arrived.

His throat narrowing, Alan could hardly swallow as he eyed the old paperback—a Zane Williams adventure novel. A cryptic message? Had Zoey been stalked? How long had someone been stalking her? Why hadn't she ever told him?

Except he should have known. He'd guess that her disappearance before, the bruises, had to do with a stalker who'd finally gotten his hands on her. Alan had guessed that was what had happened, but he'd never known for sure. He'd been a coward not to ask her when he thought he was simply loving her the only way he knew how.

But this strange package—this could mean something. It could mean everything. Or it could mean nothing.

What do I do with this?

His better judgment told him to give it to the police. This was new evidence. Or was it? Would they see it the same way and ultimately block his efforts to learn more? He had to work while he had the opportunity.

He'd have to do more research. Maybe she'd requested the book. Bought it used online, for all he knew. He had no idea, and he was jumping to conclusions. He couldn't present this to the police until he knew more, otherwise he could end up looking the fool.

A husband who didn't know enough about his wife.

Detective Mansfield already thought Alan had something to do with Zoey's disappearance, or he was a clueless husband.

But this book. He recognized it. He'd seen a box of books by the same author in her belongings they'd cleared out of the room she'd shared with Rae in college. He could swear Zoey had gotten rid of those books. How strange that the day Zoey disappeared again, one of the same thriller novels had been mailed to her.

All he could think about was her stalker. But if he was dead—then who was stalking her now? Was this the first book, or had that person mailed others?

Alan stared at the packed bookshelves.

CHAPTER FORTY

Liam cornered Sheriff Taggart at the county office. He was exhausted after his and Rae's middle-of-the night exploration. Who was he kidding? More than their brief stakeout had kept him up all night. He hadn't been able to shut his mind down after that kiss. His heart either. What had compelled him to invite a kiss? Rae had been caught up in the moment as well, or else why had she responded to him? She'd said nothing about it this morning, and that was just as well. He had better shake it off and put his energy and thoughts into their discovery. He needed to inform the sheriff as soon as possible about what they'd seen at the house. Rae waited in his truck so she could make phone calls. She'd left a voicemail for Astor but had not received a call back yet. Liam was relieved. He didn't feel comfortable with what she considered the next logical step.

The sheriff went through a stack of phone messages. "I'm listening, Liam. Go ahead."

"I need your full attention."

"And you have it."

Okay, then. "Yesterday, after you informed Astor of his brother's murder, Astor and his associate transported snowmobiles by truck to a closed forest road, where they snowmobiled into the woods. We followed them as far as the truck, but we couldn't go all the way. So last night, we snowmobiled into the woods along the same road coming from the east. We found a cabin with a lot of activity involving young women. I saw Astor's associate there but not Astor himself. He could have been there but out of sight."

"Is that it?" Sheriff Taggart asked.

"There's something going on at that house. An armed guard was outside. The point is that I'm concerned those girls were being held against their will. Take a look at these pictures." Liam held out his cell with the images he'd taken.

"You took pictures?" Taggart ran his hand down his face. "You're stepping way over the line."

"Am I? Look at these girls. This guy could be trafficking humans and drugs and who knows what else. They look too young. They're at least underage to be drinking, if that's all that's going on." What more did Taggart need?

A deep frown developed on Taggart's face as he adjusted his glasses and looked closer at the photographs. "I can't just go knock on the door. I have to have a good reason."

"And these pictures aren't reason enough?"

Squeezing his eyes shut, Sheriff Taggart rubbed his left temple. He dropped his hand, opened his eyes, and blew out a long breath. "You should know better, McKade. In the absence of a criminal background or arrest, or proof that a crime is being committed, I can't get a warrant. These girls could be there for a slumber party. I'll let Detective Moffett know. She's digging into info on Astor for me. She'll find out who owns the property, to start. We get a connection to a crime, then we can try for a warrant. But right now it looks like at least one of those girls in this picture could be his daughter. I need more. Like I said. Slumber party."

"You have a connection to a crime. He's connected to the masked man."

Sheriff Taggart sighed. "It's circumstantial. We're not certain it's the same person. I know you don't do this kind of sloppy work in the DEA. Not if you want your charges to stick."

Liam backed off. Fisted his hands. "Right. Okay, you're right. Maybe I'm going after this too hard, but it's more that I got a bad feeling. Seeing that armed guard—he was far from friendly. Something wasn't right at that house, okay? And it isn't easy to get in and out of there. Snowmobiles only."

"Sounds inconvenient but not criminal."

"Or . . . it's exclusive."

The sheriff looked at him long and hard. "I've spent a lifetime here in this county, so I have to say you've probably seen more of this kind of thing in your line of work."

"Unfortunately. I want to be wrong. Please . . . just prove me wrong."

"We don't have a lot of human trafficking in this state, but it does exist. Traffickers prefer the bigger cities. More clients that way."

"Maybe." Liam couldn't help but think about resorts and hotels for tourists—common places for all kinds of trafficking. Was there something going on with that angle? What they saw was just a cabin in the woods, but Enzo Astor owned resorts. Was there a connection? "Well, I've given you everything I know. I hope you can do something with it."

Liam wished he could do something himself. He wished he were carrying a badge and could wield it to enforce the law. But at the moment, he appreciated the fact that he had the freedom to protect Rae.

"You would be an asset to my team. You sure you won't—"

Liam held up his hand. "Thanks for the offer."

He could only imagine what working with Heath for the county would be like in addition to working for him at the ranch. No thank you. "Rae and I are actively looking for Zoey. And we already know someone doesn't want us to find her."

"That's the theory you're going with?"

"For now, yes. Why? You have another theory?"

"Not yet. We came up empty on the search for the Hummer. After the incident on the road, they must have parked it somewhere. Hid it away. Or hightailed it out of state. I have someone looking into witnesses and everyone who owns and drives a Hummer here as well as in neighboring states. There can't be that many."

"It all takes time," Liam said.

"Too much time."

A text came through on Liam's phone.

Two texts. One from Brad, who wanted an answer about the job offer. Another from Kelvin with an image. "I'll talk to you later." Liam exited Sheriff Taggart's office. He was beginning to appreciate Rae's sense of wasting time. His visit with Taggart felt more like that, but then again, if the sheriff could do something with the information, he would.

Liam, his heart in his throat, stopped to read Kelvin's text.

An image—Enzo Astor on the steps of a business complex with Malcom Fox not too far behind. Liam stared long and hard at the image. The text also said, "Taken a year ago."

A year ago. This must be why Liam recognized Enzo. The image didn't show the two men interacting, but what about the pictures taken before or after? Did Kelvin only have this one?

This could possibly give the sheriff probable cause—Enzo in the vicinity of a known drug and human trafficker. Their intuition about the man had been right on. Liam turned to catch Sheriff Taggart. Except there was a disturbance rippling through the office.

Someone had found a body.

Liam pressed himself into the wall as deputies geared up and filed out, followed by Sheriff Taggart. The sheriff eyed him on the way out. "A young woman's body was just discovered."

Liam's heart lurched.

Please, let it not be Zoey.

"Watch your back." Sheriff Taggart left him standing there.

"Always." Liam wanted to go with him, but despite what he'd discovered last night and any possibility that the body was somehow connected, this was a law enforcement matter. He forwarded Kelvin's text to the sheriff.

How did he tell Rae about the body when he was still reeling from the news himself? And the picture of Enzo Astor and Malcom Fox. After taking a few long breaths to compose himself, he exited the county offices, stepped out into the cold, and found Heath's truck empty in the parking lot.

Rae was gone. Frowning, he glanced at his cell and saw the text message she'd sent. He'd just missed it.

Meeting Enzo Astor at airport before he leaves.
My only chance to catch him.

CHAPTER *FORTY-ONE*

Liam would absolutely kill her. She knew it. The cab driver drove her out of Grayback and toward Jackson Hole Airport.

If she had gone into the sheriff's office and announced her plan, then the deal would have been off. There was no time for deliberation. She shouldn't have waited until this morning to call Astor for that interview, but Liam had wanted to talk it through. And now here they were in this situation. Astor was leaving, and she didn't want to miss her chance.

He'd agreed to talk to her for a few minutes before his flight left. So she'd made this decision on her own. They had to pick up the pace.

The cab stopped at a drop-off area. After paying the driver, she hurried into the terminal. She wasn't wired like they had discussed. She would have to ask if she could record the interview. She had a feeling that would be a resounding no. But she wasn't writing an article, and all she needed was to find out what he'd done with Zoey. Like he was going to tell her if she asked.

Come on, Rae, if you've ever done anything good in your life, you can do this. You can learn something that will make a difference.

One way or another.

Astor had agreed to meet her at a coffee kiosk, so she hurried through the terminal in search of one this side of security. Someone grabbed her arm and she whirled around.

The man released her arm. "You're here for Mr. Astor."

She nodded. "Yes. I'm Rae Burke."

"Follow me."

This was a safe place. Security everywhere. Cameras everywhere. She should be perfectly fine. She ignored the cell buzzing in her pocket. Liam would make his way here when he read her text. Honestly, she hoped that was soon.

The man led her down a sterile, empty hallway—away from others. "Where are we going? I thought I was supposed to meet him at a kiosk."

"A conference room the airport makes available for meetings, privacy, whatever's needed. For a price, of course." He grinned, then opened a door to a room with a long table and comfortable-looking chairs. Windows served as a wall on the far side, allowing her to see outdoors. She pushed the panic down and entered the room.

At the end of the table, Astor, his cell to his ear, sat with his sidekick who was at the "party" last night. The guy must be a personal assistant of some sort. Rae hoped to get an introduction.

Enzo ended his call and looked at her.

She approached and offered a journalist's smile—warm and friendly but serious—and a handshake. "Mr. Astor. Thank you for agreeing to see me."

After shaking hands with Enzo, Rae thrust her hand forward to the man sitting next to him. "Rae Burke."

He glanced at Enzo. "Jack Anders."

Rae dropped her hand and turned to Astor. "I appreciate you giving me even a few moments of your time."

"I had hoped to have a more extended visit with you, but something's come up."

"We could postpone and meet later this week. Will you be back?"

Without answering, he gestured for her to take a seat. "I don't have much time, so let's get right to it. You had questions about my brother's death."

Rae set her cell phone on the table. "Yes. May I record our conversation?"

"I'd prefer that you didn't." He adjusted his round glasses. "I'm upset about some news I recently received. I can't be sure that I won't misspeak. You understand?"

"Oh, of course." She cleared her throat, feeling ill-prepared for this interview and certainly not presenting herself like the experienced professional she was. So much was at stake. She pulled a paper and pen from her bag. "Then I'll just take notes."

He clasped his hands. "When you first approached me, you asked me . . . five years after my brother went missing, if the discovery of his remains would bring closure for me. No. I learned that my brother was murdered. So there can be no closure until his murderer is brought to justice."

Rae scribbled notes and mentally prepared her next question, hoping the conversation would flow naturally. She put aside her questions about the timeline. "Do you have any idea who committed this murder?"

"Yes."

At the resort, he claimed he didn't know. She sat back. "Who do you suspect?"

Enzo leaned closer, his jaw working, the vibes coming from him suddenly terrifying.

"Ms. Burke."

"Rae, please."

"Do you think I'm so lacking in intelligence that I don't know that you're not currently working for any reputable journalistic newsgroup?"

"I'm freelancing." Projecting confidence, she held his gaze.

His smile almost disarmed her as he leaned back. "You're a journalist with a purpose. You wouldn't be questioning me if you didn't see me as a means to an end. So, what's the endgame here?"

Her mouth dried up. She swallowed. *Here it goes.* "I'm looking for Zoey Dumont, also known as Tawny Davidson."

She left off Zoey's married name to sidestep Rae's connection to her.

He smiled but failed to hide the sudden widening of his pupils. "I have no idea why you would think I know where she is. I'm sorry to disappoint you, but I can't help you find her. I don't know her."

Her pulse inched even higher. *He knows something.*

She couldn't let him leave. She had to go for the jugular, or at least any exposed place she could find. "Your brother did. He stalked her. Followed her all the way from Jackson Hole, Wyoming, to Denver, Colorado."

He clasped his hands and leaned closer. "So, your purpose in meeting with me was to speak ill of the dead. This interview is over. I have a flight to catch."

Astor stood and exited the conference room, Jack Anders following him out.

"You knew your brother had been murdered before the anthropologist made that discovery," she shouted after him.

Feeling both bolstered and desperate, Rae followed them out of the room. She caught up to Anders and walked next to him. "You work for Mr. Astor as a personal assistant?"

"Bodyguard." He gave her a cold, intimidating look and moved beyond her to walk next to his boss.

Rae slowed her pace and watched them go.

Astor had definitely reacted to her question, but not in the way she'd expected. But just what *had* she expected? She hadn't really believed that he would tell her that he had something to do with Zoey's disappearance, but she'd had to try. Any journalist worth their weight would have tried.

Still, he'd reacted to Zoey's name—the emotional response was evident in his eyes.

Rae headed down the corridor and found a seat near a window, where she wrote furiously on her notepad—her impressions, what she thought she'd learned from the interview. Enzo Astor believed he needed a bodyguard. He also believed he knew who had killed his brother, but he stated he'd learned the news of the murder recently. How recently? He wasn't specific.

Frustration boiled through her, and she fought back angry tears. She wanted to scream or rail at someone.

Where are you, Zoey? Are you even still alive?

"Rae!" Liam rushed forward. "Rae. Don't ever do that again. What were you thinking?"

"Doesn't matter. I failed, and he's gone. He's getting on a plane."

Liam whipped out his cell and moved far enough away that she couldn't hear him.

Something had happened. What had happened?

Rae found the strength to get up, and she made her way to Liam, who spoke in hushed tones. He ended the call and whirled around, almost stumbling into her. He hadn't known she'd followed him.

His eyes widened as he dropped his cell into his pocket. "How long were you standing there?"

"What's going on?"

He gripped her arms gently and guided her to the seats next to the window. "Why don't you sit down?"

"No. Tell me what's going on. Is it Zoey? Or my brother? What?"

"They found a woman's body."

Rae gasped and held her breath.

"We don't know if it's Zoey, Rae. We don't know."

CHAPTER FORTY-TWO

As Liam watched her, he felt like his gut would turn inside out. Rae dropped into the seat and kept her eyes focused straight ahead. No tears. She appeared stunned by the news, though after what they had both been through, it shouldn't come as a surprise. Still, this was her friend, her sister-in-law, she feared for.

He crouched to eye level. "We can't know if it's her. In the meantime, we have work to do."

Her blue-green eyes had shifted to a dark, stormy blue. "What work? If the woman is Zoey, our work is over."

"Let's keep at this, believing that Zoey is still out there, okay? Are you with me?"

She hesitated, then finally nodded. "Yes. Okay . . . so Astor has left. The sheriff didn't stop him. He was right, we've got nothing on the guy. So what if he has a bodyguard?"

"A bodyguard?"

"The guy we always see with him is a bodyguard."

Liam scratched his jaw. "Interesting to know. Give me his name, and I can let Taggart know. Why does a real estate mogul need a bodyguard? Could be something. Could be nothing."

Considering the image he'd received from Kelvin—Enzo Astor and Malcom Fox in the same picture—Liam leaned toward his having a bodyguard meaning something. Astor was involved in illegal activities. Somewhere. Somehow.

"His name is Jack Anders."

Liam texted the information to Sheriff Taggart, who already had his plate full, but at least he would have the information and could forward it to one of his detectives.

"I can get Reggie on it too. But right now I want to go to where they found the body. We're looking for a missing woman, Liam. We need to be there to see if it's her." She rubbed her arms and looked away, tears welling in her eyes but not spilling over. "What am I going to tell Alan?"

"Nothing. Not yet. Let me talk to Taggart first. He's going to call me as soon as he learns more." Liam had to keep her away from the recovery scene. He moved to sit by her. He wanted to take her hand, but tension rolled off her. He knew when to keep his distance. "It all takes time. Investigations take time."

"Time Zoey doesn't have." She exhaled slowly as if all the fight had gone out of her. "So, what do you want to do next?"

"I want you to pull yourself together and be the truth finder I know you to be. You and I are going back to the resort." He thought about the image Kelvin had sent. "I learned something earlier today. Enzo Astor and Malcom Fox could be connected."

She sat up taller. "What?" She asked the question as if confirming she'd heard him right.

He slowly nodded. "This gets more complex by the day."

She rubbed her forehead. "I hope you're wrong about that connection."

"Me too. But unfortunately I don't think I am." Liam showed her the image Kelvin had texted him.

"Why do you want to go back to the resort?"

"We're chipping away at this, hoping it will lead to Zoey. Astor had his clandestine meeting with the masked man at the resort. He's invested in it. Maybe we'll spot some other kind of *activity* there. Maybe we'll run into the masked man or find him following us again." And this time, Liam would face the man and get answers.

"Activity. You mean trafficking?"

"Yes. That's one possibility. Let's stake out the resort while Astor's gone. In the meantime, we can hope Detective Moffett finds something. We can work all angles while at the resort too. You can contact Reggie, and I'll work things on my end while watching the goings-on." Liam remembered Brad's text. He needed to give him an answer. "I didn't tell you this before, but a longtime friend is running the place, and he offered me a job as head of security."

Her eyes widened. "What are you going to do?"

"If it's not too late, I think I'm going to take the job."

She frowned. "You're quitting on me?"

"Whoa. I never said that. Let's call it working undercover. I could freely get into suspicious areas and look around. It's an idea. Unless you have a better one."

Rae hesitated, appearing to measure her next words. "Liam, I hate to bring this up, but you don't suspect your friend is part of a trafficking ring, do you? I mean, why would he hire you, an ex-cop, if he was?"

"Believe me, I've considered that possibility, but I don't think so. I've known Brad for a long time. Sure, people change. But he approached me, knowing my background. I'm sure he wants to make sure it never happens. I can do that for him while we look for Zoey and at the same time clear the possible link between Enzo Astor and the resort involving money laundering or trafficking."

"Or confirm it."

"Yes."

"Don't you think you should talk to him about what's going on?" Rae held his gaze.

Right. His first thought had been to use the job opportunity to work undercover. Brad *couldn't* be involved, and Liam should be up front with him. "Thanks for that."

"For what?"

"For suggesting that I should try trusting for a change." He and Brad had been best friends, and the guy had found a way to fulfill his dream. Brad wasn't the type to get involved in illegal matters, and that was one reason why he wanted someone like Liam on board. Liam would hold on to that thought.

"You're welcome." A small smile lifted her lips. "If you're going to work for him, then get me a job there too."

"Wait, so *you* can work undercover? What about your ethics as a journalist?" Liam arched a brow. "That aside, I have no intention of leaving you unprotected."

"As for my ethics, as Astor pointed out to me this morning, I'm not actually employed by a news organization."

"Let me talk to Brad and maybe we can work something out, so we can accomplish all our tasks."

"Are you going to call him?" she asked.

"We'll go there in person."

She narrowed her eyes. "Are you going to tell him the truth?"

"Yes. I think I want this job, Rae. After this is over and you've gone home, I still have to figure out what I want to be when I grow up." He grinned, hoping to lighten things up.

"You can't get it out of your blood, can you?"

He knew exactly what she meant. Though Kelvin had reminded him that the door was open for him to return to the DEA, Liam couldn't see going back. But he obviously hadn't given up the idea, and now he finally understood why not. He couldn't let law enforcement go completely. He couldn't wrap his mind around being the guy at the ranch to drive the horse-drawn sleigh or take guests out for a hike in the woods. He would feel like he was failing someone somewhere else in the world who was suffering. This security position could fill the void for a while.

Where do I belong, God?

For now, his priority was helping Rae. He'd wanted to escape the shadowy world he'd left behind. But he found himself drawn back to it all over again, if only to shine a light.

CHAPTER FORTY-THREE

Liam was moving through the revolving doors at the resort, Rae too, when his cell rang. He stood off to the side of the entrance to take the call. Rae stood with him and watched, fear still clinging to her features.

Sheriff Taggart. "We've identified the woman. I'm not releasing her identification until I've notified the family, but at least I can let you know she isn't Zoey Burke."

Liam released a breath. Though relief swelled inside, at the same time, his gut twisted. "I appreciate you letting me know. Do you have any idea what happened?"

"It's too soon to say. I need to go."

"Thanks again." Liam ended the call.

Rae's wide eyes pinned him. "What did he say?"

He tugged her over into a corner away from others.

"It isn't Zoey," he whispered.

She steepled her hands over her nose as she closed her eyes. He knew what she was thinking. As grateful as she was to hear the news, they couldn't rejoice over that kind of loss. Someone had

246

lost a daughter, a sister, maybe even a mother. He thought about embracing her, but then he spotted Brad.

"I see my friend. I need to catch him." He waited until she opened her eyes and blew out a breath.

She nodded. "Okay. Let's go."

Liam grabbed her hand and led her as he weaved his way through resort patrons and furniture until he was right behind his friend. "Brad."

Brad turned around and his face brightened. "Liam, it's great to see you. Since you didn't reply to my text, I wasn't expecting you." He tucked his chin. "I hope you showing up here means what I think it means."

Liam nodded with a half-smile. "Let's talk first."

His brows furrowed slightly as he angled his head. "Of course." Brad's gaze shifted to Rae. "And who's this?"

"This is Rae Burke. She's an old friend. I'd like her to join us, if that's okay."

Brad's gaze lingered on Rae as he smiled. "Let's find a booth and get coffee."

Liam hoped he was doing the right thing in sharing about their investigation with Brad. This being the grand opening season of Saddleback, Brad might cut all ties with Liam because he didn't want bad press. However, that might be the precise reason he would work with Liam—to prevent the possibility of illegal activities. Still, Brad wouldn't be happy to hear the news, so Liam would leave out their investigation into Astor specifically.

After coffee arrived, Brad clasped his hands and waited.

Liam blew out a breath. "Where do I begin?"

"Liam, it's me. We're friends. Just say what's on your mind."

"First, I'm very interested in the position. I want you to know that. But Rae has hired me to work with her on a time-sensitive investigation."

Brad's gaze remained intense. "I see. To tell you the truth, I really need someone in place within the next couple of days. I was hoping I could impress the investors by having you in place as head of security."

"And you still can, Brad. But let me tell you everything. Understand this information involves an active police investigation, so please don't repeat this to anyone, even someone you believe you can trust."

Brad nodded and managed to slip in a wink at Rae.

Really?

"Rae's sister-in-law is missing, and we've been doing everything we can to find her. In the meantime, someone has targeted Rae, stolen her laptop, and run her off a ski slope." Liam believed the same man had also pushed his truck off a cliff.

"Wait—you mean here at Saddleback?"

Liam realized they'd never reported that incident to security here. "The ski slope incident, yes."

Anger flashed in Brad's eyes. "And the sheriff's department knows?"

"They know, and we're working together."

He hung his head and shook it.

"I know you don't need this happening during your grand opening," Liam said. "But I have an idea."

When Brad lifted his face, he appeared distraught. "Let's hear it."

"Working as head of security would give me access so I could find the culprit. I could start working for you—but it would be a soft start, if you will. I'll learn the system and the people, but my priority will be Rae. I'm helping her investigate, and I need to keep her safe."

"When do you expect to complete your commitment to her?"

Liam shared a look with Rae. The question held nuances of meaning for him, and he suspected for her as well.

"I believe the investigation into Zoey's disappearance is coming to a head," she said. "We should know something soon."

Liam had mixed feelings about that. From experience, he'd learned that pieces of the puzzle could make you feel like you were closing in but then lead you nowhere. He hoped for both their sakes that they found Zoey soon.

"Well, what do you say, Brad? I know it's a lot to think about," Liam said. "I wanted to find a way that we could make this work."

A spark ignited in his eyes. "I think this is a brilliant idea. I want this man taken down. Who better to do that than you? If working security here helps you do it, all the better." He leaned forward with a conspiratorial grin. "It would be almost like working undercover, wouldn't it?"

Liam felt uncomfortable with Brad's comment, but he kept his composure and nodded. "Maybe. So you're okay with this?"

"Look, I was about to beg, okay? I thought I was going to lose you. I want you working here with me, Liam. This is a small price to pay."

"I'm glad to hear it."

Brad glanced at his watch. "Do you have time to get started this morning?"

Liam again looked to Rae, and she gave a nod. "Let's do this," he said.

Brad was all too happy to give them a guided tour of the resort. He beamed with pride, and Liam hoped his resort wasn't involved in illegal activities like trafficking—drugs or human. Although those activities could happen without management's knowledge, Liam wished they had a different lead to follow.

Brad escorted them to the business offices, glancing often at Rae. "So as head of security, you'll be responsible for the entire security department. It's like you're the chief of police of the resort. You keep our people safe from fires, industrial hazards, and everything to do with keeping people secure twenty-four hours a day. Work with the local law enforcement on all investigations. We have state-of-the-art security cameras, radios, and technology. Everything you would need to go with a salaried position."

Liam smiled. This was an opportunity for him to work in a pseudo law enforcement capacity, though it was completely different from his previous experiences. He was grateful to Brad for being so receptive to his needs. And to Rae for suggesting he simply be up front with Brad.

Rae cleared her throat. Brad's smile beamed at her. He seemed to be interested in Rae. Liam had to refrain from acting possessive. Rae hadn't signaled to Liam that she wanted that from *him*. Though they'd shared a kiss last night, she'd ended it and rushed away from him. That was for the best. The kiss had been a moment of weakness on both their parts.

He shoved thoughts of it away.

"I'll need to protect Rae, and I need her to stick close."

"What do you have in mind? You want her to work security with you? You're both in training?"

"I think I could do more if I worked somewhere else in the resort." Rae held Liam's gaze. "The sooner we end this, the better. I'd still be close, Liam."

She made a good point. "We can give it a try. If I don't think it's working, then you're with me."

"And Brad, you understand this is only temporary for me," she said. "I'm not going to stay on, like Liam. I'm only here to search for my sister-in-law."

"Did you work with Liam in the DEA?"

"Not exactly. I'm an investigative reporter."

Brad hesitated as if he would ask her more. "Understood. For Liam, we'll make this work. I'm sure we can find something for you to do. When Liam is filling out his paperwork, you can talk to our human resources manager, Natalie Ramirez."

"Thanks."

The tension eased from Liam's shoulders. This had gone better than he'd expected.

"Then let's get going," Brad said. "I'd appreciate it if you'd let me know where you are, or at least stay in contact, so I'm able to get ahold of you if needed. Why don't you fill out your paperwork today and stay as long as you like to get familiar with what's going on." Brad slapped Liam on the back. "I couldn't be happier that we're going to be working together."

Liam smiled at his friend.

Brad grabbed Rae's hand and held on to it longer than necessary. "It was so nice to meet you."

Enough already. It was time to let Brad know how Liam really felt, despite his better judgement. He took Rae's hand from Brad's grip and weaved his fingers with hers, then gave Brad a look.

Brad laughed. "I see how it is."

But Rae also gave Liam a look, one that stabbed him.

CHAPTER FORTY-FOUR

While Liam was with Brad getting to know the resort security systems and protocols, Rae sat out in the hallway in a plush chair next to a bushy plant. Liam claimed he was protecting her when he led Brad to believe they were together. All well and good, but she didn't want to pretend they were together, even for this "undercover" work. Ridiculous though it was, the thought hurt too much. Would that mean kisses that weren't real? What about last night? He hadn't exactly kissed her first. Instead, he'd leaned in close enough that she knew he *wanted* to kiss her. He'd ultimately left the decision up to her. And what had she done? She'd closed the distance. For a few sweet moments, she'd kissed him, and she hadn't held back. Not one iota. She hadn't had the strength to resist him. For a split second, she closed her eyes and remembered the sensations—heart-pounding, dangerous sensations.

Even now at the memory, her heart thumped erratically.

She couldn't do this.

Not now. Not . . . ever . . .

Though it was a struggle, Rae forced the memories and emotions from her mind. Then she opened her eyes and looked at the employment paperwork she was required to fill out, though the arrangement was only temporary—for her, at least. All it had taken was a word from Brad. She concentrated on finishing. She would be a "floater" until Natalie decided where she would best fit.

Were they going about this all wrong?

Her reporter instincts were working like a broken compass and spinning in all directions. She had no gut feeling for this course.

God, I need a direction in this. It seemed like every possible lead she chased down gave her very little return on her investment.

Maybe Zoey's disappearance had nothing at all to do with the trail they were following.

Instead, Rae's being here had somehow caught the wrong attention. Astor and Fox could be connected. If they could just track down the Hummer driver or whoever stole her laptop or knocked her off that slope, they would get some answers. So in that way, Liam was onto something. Hanging out here at the resort and actually working could let them see who was coming and going.

Rae's cell rang. Her heart jumped, and she answered. "Hi, Alan."

"A package arrived yesterday. I searched through Zoey's things and found other similar packages. I think she has a stalker— obviously this stalker isn't Simon."

"What?" Oh my . . . "Did you tell the police?"

"I will tell them. I thought you should know. Be careful, Rae."

"Give me details. Tell me about the package."

"It was one of those tan book mailers. Inside was a used paper-back thriller novel."

Rae scrunched her face. "How is that from a stalker?"

"She had a stash of these books in her room in college."

"I think I remember, but I'm still not sure it means anything."

"Think about it, Rae. She got rid of those books. Why has she suddenly been receiving one a week for the last month? And get this, they're coming from Wyoming. The last book was mailed the day she disappeared."

Rae sat up. So someone from Zoey's past had kept up with her? "This person didn't know she was missing when the book was mailed."

"Maybe it was the guy the video captured her leaving with. Maybe she confronted him. He'd already mailed the book before they decided to meet. The detectives are trying to identify him."

"Why don't you tell the police?"

"I want to do some research first. The books could be nothing at all. I don't know what to think, Rae. I'm so desperate, I could be grasping at straws."

Rae understood that sentiment. She felt the same way. She had an idea though. "Okay. Let me know if you find anything else that can help. I need to go. I'll be in touch."

Wyoming, huh? Samara Davidson had tried to call Rae, but she'd been distracted with all that had happened. She could ask her about Zoey and those thriller novels she'd had in college. Did they mean anything? Who had Zoey kept in contact with since leaving Wyoming and changing her name?

Liam was with Brad, and now wasn't a good time to ask him to leave. Besides, she had a feeling this job could really work out for him. Brad was willing to allow them to conduct their investigation while working at the resort—seeming to get a thrill out of his role.

The last thing Rae wanted to do was be the reason Liam lost a job. He hadn't even gotten a good hour into his job here. She'd give him that, at least.

Rae turned in the paperwork and didn't wait for an assignment. Going to see Sam wouldn't take long. She could be back before Liam even missed her.

CHAPTER FORTY-FIVE

Rae had called a cab for a ride to the hotel, where she'd left her rental car. Now she stood at the front door of Sam's expansive home. She'd already stopped by the heli-ski facilities and learned Sam wasn't in.

She held her cell and would call if necessary, but she preferred catching people in the moment. Or rather, off guard. Sam wanted to find her daughter, that much Rae believed. Other than Rae and Alan, no one knew Zoey better than her mother, even though she claimed she hadn't seen her daughter in years.

The door swung open, and Sam's smile was forced. "Ms. Burke. I wasn't expecting you." Then she gave a smirk. "And *that's* your journalistic tactic."

"I missed a call from you. I figured I'd come see you in person, that's all. And, oh, remember, you can call me Rae." She thought they'd already gotten to first names. "I thought we were on the same team. Team Zoey. We have to find her. I shouldn't need to use *any* tactics."

255

Sam nodded and opened the door wider. "Fair enough. Come in."

She led Rae to the kitchen. "After three decades of building a business that serves many people with unlimited resources, I just . . ."

"You have an image. A reputation. You're always on." Rae set her bag on the counter. "I get it. But your daughter's life could be at stake."

Sam's hands trembled, and she cupped them around a big coffee mug. "I was just about to have some tea. Would you care for some?"

"No thank you." Sam seemed like the kind of woman who would be out there in the helicopters or somehow more hands-on. Not drinking tea. But given the situation, she was probably off her game. Still, she'd been living like this for years—not truly knowing how her daughter was doing or what she was up to.

She poured the tea into the mug. "You know, I'm sure you're well aware that with each passing hour, the chances that Zoey is still alive . . ." She tossed back the tea.

Rae watched her—there was more than tea in that mug. No wonder Sam wasn't at work. She couldn't afford for her clients to see her intoxicated or uninhibited.

"While I would agree that's normally the case, this happened before. Zoey disappeared for a week during our college years. She came back. That gives me hope."

Rae wished it were more than that.

Sam's eyes widened, and once again, Rae saw Zoey in her mother. The resemblance was uncanny.

"Let's go somewhere comfortable." Sam led her into a sitting area and plopped onto a comfy sofa. Rae eased onto a plush chair opposite the sofa. Bookshelves lined the walls behind Sam.

"Tell me more about that time," Sam said.

Rae shared about the incident and how she took Zoey home

with her, then Alan met and fell in love with her. "And the rest is history, as they say."

"Did Tawny love your brother?"

"At first I think Alan offered stability. Kindness. He was safe. I know Zoey loves him deeply now. And their precious—" Callie. Tears choked back her next words. She had to focus. "Callie. I'm sorry, I didn't mean to get choked up. I came here to ask more questions."

"If it will help find Tawny, then ask away."

"You've made it clear that you and Zoey were deliberately estranged. You kept your distance. But you know about your grandchild you've never met. When was the last time you communicated with Zoey?"

Sam's face paled. "I . . . uh . . . Tawny contacted me a few weeks ago." Sam set her spiked mug of tea on a coaster and moved to the window. She peered out as if fearing someone was watching, then partially shut the mini blinds.

"Before that, we didn't communicate. It was too painful. She had to get a life of her own and live it, so she claimed. I had the distinct impression she wanted to protect *me*. But who do *I* need protection from? She claimed that any communication could . . ."

"Any communication could what?"

"Tip off her stalker. He had resources. I know it's hard to understand from the outside looking in, but I finally came to believe that her decision was for the best. The only way. Or rather, I accepted it."

"But he's dead now."

"I only just learned that. And Zoey was already missing."

"Do you think her disappearance is related to Simon Astor, or his death?" Rae asked.

"I had hoped not."

What else could Sam know that she was not sharing? "How *could* they be related?"

"I don't know. I honestly don't know."

It was Rae's turn to get up. She peeked out the mini blinds. A small credenza edged the window. Pictures. Sam and Zoey as a teenager. Smiling with the group of heli-ski guides. One guide in particular stood with Sam and Zoey. Rae could look into that later. She walked the room, browsing the photographs. Those not of family were of the thrill-seeking skier nature—pristine snow-covered mountains. Rae stopped at the bookshelf.

She found what she'd been searching for and tugged a Zane Williams novel, one of several, from the shelf.

"Why were you sending these books to Zoey?"

Apprehension surfaced in Sam's eyes. Before she could reply, the front door opened and slammed.

"Sam?" A man's voice boomed through the house.

The woman eyed Rae and gave a subtle shake of her head. She wouldn't discuss the books in front of him? "In here."

The man in the picture with Sam and Zoey entered the sitting room. He spotted Rae. His frown was quickly replaced with a smile.

Rae extended her hand and introduced herself but was careful, given Sam's subtle warning.

"Ivan Anatole." His grip was strong. "Sam tells me you're looking for Tawny."

"Yes."

"You're a reporter and you think you can help the police?" His brows furrowed.

Rae shrugged. "My brother asked me to help, but even if he hadn't, I would be here now."

"Why do you think she's in Jackson Hole?"

"It's complicated." Still, she explained in general terms why she was there, but she left out that she had also been targeted. "I see you're in photographs with Zoey. I mean . . . Tawny."

"I've been in her life since she was born, that is, until she left.

Her father died, so I tried to be there as much as I could. Others on our team helped as well." He winked at Sam.

"Ivan taught Zoey how to ski," Sam said. "He mentored her in guiding our clients on the slopes where we'd drop them."

Devotion glimmered in his eyes. "She was an expert skier. I always thought she should have gone for the Olympics. But she had other interests."

"And skiing with our clients, one of them, took her away from us." Sam stared off into the distance.

Rae had never known this side of Zoey. "I wish I could somehow know and understand her better. Maybe I could take one of those heli-skiing tours. Ski the same places." Was Rae trying too hard? Truly understanding another was often vital in her search for the truth. But could it make a difference this time?

"I wish you could too, but we're booked for months out." Ivan frowned. "Tawny will be found, and when she is, make her take you and show you her life before . . ."

Rae suspected he didn't want to mention Simon's name. "I'll do that. You're right, we're going to find her."

Rae appreciated the hope Ivan expressed, though maybe he was forcing it.

Ivan watched Sam, adoration along with concern in his expression. Then he turned his attention to Rae. "What else do you want to know?"

"Anything that can help me figure out what happened."

He sat next to Sam and put his beefy arm around her. "Sam and I have called friends. We've called everyone we know to find out if they have seen Tawny. I have a friend who has access to facial recognition software, and he's been searching too."

"That's good to know."

"I'm glad you're looking into this." He frowned and checked his watch. "But I have to get back now." He kissed the side of Sam's head, concern for her almost hiding the pain in his eyes. "Got to go, babe. Just wanted to see how you're holding up. I'm glad you have company."

He popped up from the sofa and eyed Rae.

"Thanks for what you're doing. It's good to know that someone like you is out there looking for Tawny." He shook Rae's hand again, a message in his eyes. *Take care of Sam* . . . After Ivan left, Rae looked to Sam, who seemed oblivious. Dazed, with droopy lids. How much had she had to drink already? Or had she taken something with the drink?

"Ivan can't sit still. He's running everything for me. I had to leave today. I can't focus until we know something. I don't know what I would do without him." Sam positioned herself against a pillow, legs curled under her, and closed her eyes. "I've held it together all these years, and now I'm falling apart."

Sam had kept it together because she'd known exactly where Zoey was, but now that Zoey was missing, Sam was crashing.

Rae held up the book and thumbed through it. She didn't want to leave without knowing more about the thriller novels—if there was something behind Sam's mailing them to Zoey.

A quiet snore rose from Sam.

Rae grabbed a soft throw and covered the sleeping woman.

CHAPTER FORTY-SIX

Liam shoved through the front door of the Emerald M and found it warm and inviting as always. He shrugged off his coat and hung it on the coatrack. He removed his gloves, hat, and boots too. Evelyn didn't want boots leaving a trail of melted snow. He did all this while holding back his anger. Pushing down his temper.

When he'd left the meeting with the security guys he would be supervising, he couldn't find Rae, who was supposed to stick around and complete whatever task Natalie gave her, anywhere at the resort. Liam panicked. Then Natalie reported that Rae insisted she had to leave and that if she wasn't back by the time Liam returned, to reassure him that she was all right.

That hadn't been their agreement. Liam texted her. She was about to head back to the resort, but Liam instructed her to go on to the ranch—she was closer, and he wanted to head that way as well. She shouldn't have *left* the resort to begin with.

Berating her would get him nowhere. He wasn't in charge. Only a hired hand—Rae's PI guy and supposed protector. But he couldn't protect her if she ran off to chase a lead while he was working at the resort. Going to work for Brad had been a mistake, after all, even if they'd meant to use that time to further their investigation.

He and Rae had a lot to think about.

And a lot to talk about.

Add to that, Heath had called him. The guy was *on his honeymoon*—and he hadn't trusted Liam enough to run the ranch in his absence. Liam tried not to let that upset him. Heath needed time to focus on his new bride. He deserved happiness, so Liam had reassured his brother everything was fine.

As for love and happiness, Liam doubted he could ever have that with anyone. Rae had been the only person he'd pictured himself with, but that image had been destroyed before.

Rae emerged from the hallway, pulling him from his exasperation. A soft smile was on her lips as she approached. "I'm sorry, Liam. Please don't be upset. Let me explain."

His anger bled out. "I hope you know how worried I was."

"It was a lead I needed to follow, and you were working. I didn't want to mess that up for you."

"You're my priority. I shouldn't have taken the job—it was a distraction. I thought it could help us."

"I understand. I think we're both tired, and there are no clear paths here." She gestured to the living area, and he sat in a plush chair. She eased onto the sofa at the corner near him. So close, but he'd felt the distance between them today when she disappeared to explore a lead on her own. How did he hold her close, but not too close?

Liam listened as she explained everything that had happened.

"This Ivan. Are you sure he's not the guy in the black mask?"

"Yes. He truly cares about Sam, and it seemed like he thought of himself as a father figure in Zoey's life. I'm not suspicious of him. Sam is fragile right now, worried sick about her daughter. Ivan is covering for her, and he's overwhelmed."

Rae angled her head to look at him. "I thought she was much stronger than what I saw today. Seeing her like that left me hollowed out. But like any mother would be, Sam is grieving." Rae shut her eyes. "God, please let someone find her, preferably alive and well."

He watched Rae. Beautiful, ambitious, determined, and fearless. He lifted a hand, wanting to reach across the short distance to touch her cheek, her hand, anything, but he dropped it before he made contact. Someone important to her was out there.

Alive?

Dead?

He didn't know. But the deeper they got into this, the stranger it became. Fear shot through him—the fear that he wouldn't be there to save her this time.

"We need to stick together," he said. "If you're thinking of pursuing other leads without me like you did today, maybe I should call Brad and tell him it's off for now."

"I'll be careful, Liam. This isn't my first . . . um . . . rodeo. You know?"

"I do know." Her last "rodeo" nearly killed them both. If none of that had happened, where would both of them be now? Would he still be working for the DEA? Doubtful. Would she still be unearthing injustices to prove she was worthy to a father who was no longer in this world?

Would Liam and Rae be together? He had no business thinking about that. None.

Rae stared at her phone. "I texted my brother to tell him I found those same books at Sam's home. I hope he can figure out why they were so important to Zoey and if they mean anything in all this."

Liam wasn't sure the books had any significance. "My mom read a lot of novels. The shelves were stuffed with old paperbacks. They all burned in the fire."

"What are you saying, Liam?"

"She shared them with friends. Got them at yard sales. But I would never say they were important to her. So what if Zoey liked that author and his books? So what if her mother had some too? Getting that novel in the mail might not mean anything." He closed his eyes and sighed. "Listen, I don't know, but I don't want you to hold out hope that this is the clue to save the day." He opened his eyes to find her staring at him. He hadn't meant to strip her of her hope that she would find answers in the novels.

Liam swiped a hand down his face.

"I'll be back," she said. "Evelyn said dinner will be ready soon. I'll see you then."

"Fine."

Rae headed for her room, and Liam got up and peered through the front window. For once he could be grateful for the treacherous roads leading to the ranch, more so in the winter. Heath had made progress on improving the drive up because he wanted to open the ranch for business next winter, but he hadn't made *that* much progress. Rae wouldn't be in danger here. He didn't believe anyone would want to hassle with that drive. No one would make the hike through the deep snow of the Gros Ventre Wilderness to get to her. He was relieved that no one had tried anything this afternoon.

Maybe Astor had left and taken the danger to Rae with him. At least Liam could relax for a few moments.

He made his way to the kitchen, following the heavenly aroma that filled the house. Evelyn must have been cooking a stew. She stepped from the walk-in pantry. "Liam. Thought I heard you come in. I hope you're hungry."

"Sure am."

Evelyn smiled.

"How was your date last night?" he asked.

She chuckled and waved him off. "Let's just say I won't be taking Leroy with me next week when we go to dinner in town."

264

"Oh, that smells amazing." Rae entered the kitchen.

"You have a seat." Evelyn gestured to the counter. She seemed happy in the kitchen, and Liam was glad for it.

Hands thrust into his pockets, he leaned near Rae. "Get some grub while I find Pete and Leroy to see how everything is going here. I'm supposed to supervise while Heath is gone." He hadn't exactly had a lot to report when Heath had called because he'd been preoccupied with Rae and left the ranch to run itself—with Pete's and Leroy's help, of course.

Rae's eyes were a soft blue tonight and pinned him. "And you took two other jobs? Helping me investigate and working security at the resort? Liam, what are you thinking?" Her smile twisted.

His gaze stayed on her lips longer than it should have, but he liked her smile. The way she'd teased him. "I'm some kind of crazy."

Hadn't he prayed for doors to open? The trouble was that he'd had no idea which was the right one to walk through. But he'd fixed that and walked through three of them.

He left Rae and Evelyn, grabbed his coat and boots, and tromped down to the barn to check on the horses in their stables. The cold air slapped him in the face. As much as he struggled with feeling at home—anywhere—he could never get this place out of his blood.

When he'd needed to flee from what had happened, Emerald M and Heath had been waiting for him, and he couldn't have been happier to stay.

For a while.

Admittedly, he could think a lot clearer here in Wyoming, and even more so on this ranch. That was, without Heath around. They loved each other, but their personalities clashed too much for comfort. Liam had hoped they could find a way to get along.

Maybe the security job would work out and he could move closer to town or the resort. But all that would have to come after Zoey's disappearance had been resolved.

God, please let her still be alive somewhere.

While he would want that for anyone—life over death—he had a personal stake in this disappearance because of how it would affect Rae. He couldn't bear to see her lose her sister-in-law.

If Zoey was still alive, he could think of a few terrible reasons why she would have disappeared, and he wasn't sure they were better alternatives to death. Still, after what she'd already been through, Zoey sounded like a true survivor.

Like Rae.

As he approached the barn, he heard raised voices. Now he understood the real reason Heath valued Liam's supervision. He wouldn't bother eavesdropping. He pushed the door open and walked in on Leroy and Pete exchanging heated words.

"Hey," he said. "What's this about?"

They stopped and stared at Liam. Hands on his hips, Pete looked away. Neither of them appeared willing to tell him what was going on.

"In case you weren't aware, Heath left me in charge while he's gone." He wished he hadn't said that. He could sense resentment from both men. He could understand their perspectives. Liam showed up just a few months ago and now was suddenly in charge? What did he know? How would Heath want him to handle this? He held out his palms. "Look, I know I'm the new guy, and you both know more about the inner workings of this place than I do, but we're not exactly guest-ranching at the moment. I'm happy to help resolve any issues if you want to share them."

"All due respect, Liam," Pete said, "you're not around enough to help."

CHAPTER FORTY-SEVEN

5:56 P.M.

Evelyn encouraged Rae to go ahead and eat because the stew was best eaten hot, and Liam could be a while. So Rae sat at the table with the older woman and enjoyed the most amazing venison stew. It warmed her up inside.

"Any news on your missing sister-in-law?"

"We still don't know where she is." Rae lifted a spoonful of stew to her mouth.

"I'm so sorry. The only thing I know to do is pray, so I'll keep praying for her and for your family."

"Thank you." Rae took another bite of stew, though her appetite was quickly disappearing. After her visit with Sam and learning that she had been in contact with Zoey recently and also had a stash of those thriller novels, Rae had the strong sense that she was closing in on the truth.

God, where is Zoey? Help me find her.

The front door slammed. Rae heard Liam removing his coat and boots. Then he entered the kitchen, his expression hard. He approached the counter and his eyes grew wide. "You didn't wait for me?"

"You told me to eat," Rae said. "Evelyn did too."

He laughed. "I did. You're right. I'm just surprised, that's all."

Oh, now he was just teasing. But behind his smile, he seemed upset.

Evelyn had gotten up from the table to ladle stew into a bowl for Liam. "There's corn bread too."

She set the stew and corn bread in front of Liam. He started in immediately.

He finally slowed long enough to notice she was watching him. "What?"

"Is everything okay?" she asked.

"Sure. Just peachy." He focused on his meal.

Was he still upset with her for leaving the resort? Nothing she could do about that now.

"I can see something's on your mind, Rae," he said. "Why don't you tell me?"

Rae had not gotten an answer about the Zane Williams books, but she'd known by the look in Sam's eyes that Sam had in fact sent them to Zoey. "Don't so quickly discount the books, Liam. Hear me out. Alan told me that Zoey had received one book per week for a month. Sam had sent them one at a time. Why? I'm thinking Zoey suspected something was going to happen to her," Rae said. "The books. They were there before in college. They're here now, and Zoey's gone again. What do the books have to do with anything? Why did Sam send them? What does she know that she's not telling me?"

Liam chewed on a piece of corn bread. "So how can we find out more?" he asked.

Good. At least he was willing to listen to her about the books. Rae hopped off the stool, moved to the coatrack, and then tugged the novel from her oversized pocket. She made her way back to the kitchen and held up the book. The cover featured a scuba diver in a bright blue sea. "I just happen to have gotten my hands on one. *Lost Gold* by Zane Williams."

"Did you buy it?"

"No. I snagged it from Sam's bookshelf. She shut down on me before I could ask. I'll return it, but if she isn't willing to be forthcoming, then I feel like it's okay that I borrowed the book from her."

"What about fingerprints? You're getting yours all over it."

"Sam has more on her shelf. I need to see what this is about. And I'd like to talk to Ivan more too."

"When are you going to do all this? You have a job at the resort to see if you can find any suspicious activity there, remember?"

"Right. I'm only working part-time, *remember*?" She skimmed through a few pages of *Lost Gold*.

Liam swallowed a spoonful of stew. "Okay. I admit that I may have been wrong about the books, and you could be onto something. Why does Sam have the books that Zoey kept in college? Why did Zoey suddenly want the books sent back to her?"

"And why *these* books? I mean, why Zane Williams? Is there some significance to the author, the titles, or the series?"

Liam had that uncertain look in his eyes again.

"What are you thinking?" she asked.

He frowned. "While there could be something to find here, I'd like to have something real to go on. This feels like we're sticking our hands in a sandbox, lifting them out only to have the sand pouring through our fingers because everything is circumstantial. Loose connections that slide through our fingers because there's nothing hard to grab on to. And your thoughts on the books seem very loose, if you ask me."

Why couldn't he see what she saw? She tamped down her disappointment. Rae wouldn't be deterred. "We keep digging in that sandbox then until we grab on to something solid." She turned her attention to her laptop and did a web search for Zane Williams.

Once she found him, she said, "He writes thriller novels mostly about underwater shipwrecks. Treasure. That sort of thing."

Liam's cell rang. He glanced at the screen and frowned. "Excuse me." He rose from the table and left her there with Evelyn.

"He's such an intense man," Evelyn said. "But he has a heart of gold."

Rae had seen that heart of gold. She'd shattered it all by herself. Did Evelyn know that story? Rae didn't feel like revealing too much of the past.

Evelyn got up and started clearing the dishes, so Rae did as well.

"The two of us can work faster." Rae helped Evelyn finish up the dishes. Sometimes a mundane task would spark ideas as her brain continued to work.

And she got one.

After putting the few dishes away, Rae got back on her laptop and found the news story about Simon Astor's remains being discovered.

Air whooshed from her lungs.

Journalism 101. Check the facts. Then recheck them.

She reread the date. Forensic anthropologist Susan Geiger had assisted in identifying the remains and the cause of death. The date Simon's remains were identified, and Enzo would have been notified, happened *after* Zoey's abduction.

Rae hadn't considered this before.

Zoey had disappeared before the body was identified. Was her disappearance even related? It had to be. There weren't any coincidences. But this didn't make sense.

She pressed her head into her hands. Maybe she wasn't the person to figure this out.

Even though Dad was gone, she couldn't help but think about him—her Pulitzer Prize–winning, war zone–journalist father. Could she ever live up to his name?

Oh, Dad, I think I might just let you down.

CHAPTER FORTY-EIGHT

Liam stood on the porch in the cold, wishing he'd pulled on a coat. He didn't know what to make of those thriller novels, or for that matter, Pete's story that someone had stopped by the ranch and claimed they'd rented a cabin. Leroy had taken Evelyn out earlier today, so they hadn't been there. Pete had sent the potential clients away but questioned Leroy when he returned—and Leroy wasn't having it.

Liam's cell rang, interrupting his thoughts. Kelvin had needed to call him back, so Liam had waited on the porch. "Glad you didn't forget me."

"My apologies. I'll get right to it, then. Fox's lawyer got him out of prison."

A few heartbeats later, Liam still hadn't comprehended Kelvin's words. "What do you mean his lawyer got him out of prison?" Where Malcom had been waiting for his trial.

The prosecution had convinced the judge that the guy was a flight risk. All that money and those international connections, he could disappear for good. No bail for him.

"I mean what I said. He's free to walk the streets. The case was dismissed pre-trial. His defense attorney found some evidentiary problem."

Nausea erupted in Liam's gut. How could this happen? "Care to share the details? I don't want to hear that I spent two years working this case and now he's walking free. What happened?"

"I'm working on getting the details, Liam. I wanted to give you a heads-up."

All that work, months of working undercover. Liam was glad he had stepped outside. He didn't want Rae to overhear this conversation until he figured out how he would tell her.

"I can't believe this." Liam gripped the nearest lodgepole pine post.

"He'll be back in prison, don't you worry. He'll be back where he belongs."

Liam wasn't so sure. A sick feeling swirled inside and crept up his throat. He paced, his boots clomping on the porch. A horse's nicker echoed from the barn below. "Thanks, but I'm not sure what I can do with the information." Liar. He knew, oh, he knew—

"Watch your back, for one. We believe he wants payback."

Of course he did. But did he want it bad enough to seek Liam out? "You think he knows who I am or where I am?"

"In this day and age, it's getting harder to keep your identity a secret. You know that. Just keep your picture off social media. Out of the news. That sort of thing. But . . . I'm not even done yet."

"You're killing me here. Tell me."

Kelvin sighed long and hard. "We don't know where he is. He just . . . disappeared."

Great. "That it?"

"Isn't that enough?"

"What about Enzo Astor? Have you found out anything more since sending me that picture?"

"He's on my radar."

Liam wished he hadn't eaten the stew. It settled in his gut, along with fear and dread. He'd come here because he wanted to escape the ugliness. To get away from it. But it had been trailing him this whole time, and now it felt like he was coming full circle.

"You said he's on your radar. What can you tell me? It could help us to find Zoey Burke."

"This is DEA, McKade. You connect the dots."

Okay. Right. "I hope you've got someone in town watching him."

"I'll take that under advisement."

"You do that," Liam said. "Now, I have to go."

Drugs. Somehow. Some way. Every crime was connected to drugs. The big question—how did Zoey fit in with that scenario? Pieces were falling into place, but they seemed like the wrong pieces that were fitting into the same horrifying puzzle—and it wasn't the puzzle he'd started on.

CHAPTER FORTY-NINE

Rae had followed Liam to the resort in her rental vehicle. Piece by piece, they were uncovering the truth. This would be over soon. She felt that to her bones.

At the moment, she sat at a round table in the human resources office waiting to be given instructions on her new job. She would get to know the employees and "infiltrate," as Liam had termed it. He believed she would be safe at the resort with him, and he would monitor her location at all times through her cell. He was watching every shadowed corner of the place through cameras as well. For now they would continue their plan to look for anomalies.

While she waited, she typed out notes and created a mind map, bubbles, and everything.

Five years ago, Zoey was taken by a stalker but escaped. She married Rae's brother, Alan, and got rid of old thriller novels. Rae started investigating a human trafficking ring because of a comment Zoey had made—private, hold-her-secrets-close Zoey—and nearly died. Rae found and lost love as a result of that investigation. No. Delete that last bubble. It wasn't relevant.

274

Zoey disappeared again.

The new resort. The stalker's brother was an investor.

The books returned.

All these pieces went together somehow. If only she could find one or two more pieces.

Frustrated, she almost closed her laptop when she noticed a new email from Reggie. He said he'd gone through many layers of the shell corporation he believed were linked to E.S.A. Holdings and found an investor—Devon Winters. Rae wasn't familiar with the name and would run it by Liam when he surfaced.

Disappointment that Reggie's email hadn't been more helpful left her deflated.

Last year, she'd been at this same place mentally, when she'd inadvertently learned that important clue from Liam—the man, Malcom Fox—and she'd followed it to find Dina.

Life seemed to have come full circle for her and Liam, but they both knew to avoid the last half of that circle. It could mean injury or death. Except how did they avoid it, exactly?

Regardless, Rae was running on fumes.

To keep going, she needed one thing—inspiration. Encouragement that her mission wasn't impossible.

She grabbed her cell and found the last story Dad wrote before he died. Whenever she lost hope or needed to feel motivated about keeping her work going, she read his articles.

As she read this particular article he had written from a war zone, interviews of innocent civilians—those who bore the brunt of the battle between governments—all her work up to this point seemed frivolous in comparison.

Tears came to her eyes. She swiped at them. Great way to start a new job, a fake job. But the article motivated her, reminding her who she was and what she was about. She could do this. She *would* do this. Get to the bottom of Zoey's mysterious past and her disappearance and, with some digging, Rae would find dirt.

Liam being here at the resort as head of security put him in the best position to ferret out criminal activity. But Rae's "job" was a waste of her time and skills. She needed to get back with Sam and Ivan. Too many questions floated around about those books.

After reading Dad's article, she tugged the thriller novel from her handbag and skimmed the pages. Would she find the answer if she read the whole thing? She didn't have time for that. Then she felt it . . . a perceptible indention, an impression, inside the cover. Her pulse picked up. She ran her forefinger over the spot again. Several imprints could be felt, as though someone had left the impression of a word on the page. Had that been intentional?

She dug through her handbag for paper. But she needed a pencil. Rae rushed over to a desk and opened drawers until she found one. At the table, she placed the paper on top of the impression and rubbed the pencil over the paper as she pressed down—like every elementary school kid learned in art class using leaves gathered in the fall.

Success! She peered at the impression now made visible.

One word.

Ransom.

What could it mean?

Okay, that was it. She had to talk to Sam. Rae called her on her cell but got no answer.

Now she wished she'd grabbed more than one of these stupid novels.

Rae snapped a picture with her cell and forwarded the image to Reggie. She texted the details about the book. If she wasn't grasping at straws, he would figure it out.

Her cell rang. Sam.

"Sam, hi." Rae said the words as Natalie Ramirez stepped into the small office.

"Are you ready?" Natalie's smile was forced.

Um . . .

"I called because we had a cancellation," Sam said. "Ivan wanted me to ask if you'd like to go heli-skiing."

Natalie impatiently eyed Rae.

"I've learned something, Sam. Will you be there? It's important that we talk."

CHAPTER FIFTY

Dressed from head to toe in skiwear, Rae stood in the waiting area with a couple from France on their honeymoon. She'd read that people came from around the world for this. The adventure of a lifetime.

She had let Natalie know she would have to come back tomorrow. If she didn't have Brad behind her hiring, Rae surely would have been fired on the spot.

Then she'd driven out to the lodge where she had expected to meet with Sam, but Kelly had relayed the message that Sam was running late. Honestly, Rae had been surprised to hear from the woman, considering her condition yesterday. Rae was compelled to see this through, so she had waited until she got here to text Liam about her plans. She didn't need him standing in her way.

As the minutes ticked on, she grew concerned that Sam wouldn't show up. Ivan and another big guy—one of the other guides?—emerged from a hallway. The other guy headed outside, and Ivan angled for their group. His big shoulders appeared even broader in his ski jacket. He introduced himself to the couple and welcomed Rae. She wanted to ask about Sam, but he continued on to a well-rehearsed spiel that he'd probably given thousands of times but somehow made sound fresh and exciting. The thrill of anticipation filled the room as he spoke.

Had Zoey given this same spiel—back when she'd gone by Tawny? Rae tried to picture that as she listened to Ivan and, through the panoramic window, watched the other guy get into the helicopter. The pilot. If Rae were here in the area only to write her travel article, she had plenty of fascinating fodder from which to choose. But Rae was fact finding.

"Cowboy powder," Ivan continued. "It's all about the light, dry stuff. Fresh powder. You're privileged skiers since the government limits those who will ski the Snake River Range in Wyoming. Your tour today is exclusive and private."

Sam quietly stepped up behind Rae and whispered, "Sorry I'm late."

Rae urged her aside so they could talk without interrupting Ivan's pitch.

"I don't usually celebrate when someone cancels on us," Sam said, "but this was fortuitous. Now you can see what we do. What Tawny was involved in. You wanted to know her better. Maybe this will help."

Rae nodded. Seeing the men Zoey worked with in action could shed light too.

"You told me that she worked more on the business side and was into computers."

Sam nodded. "But she also knew how to take a group onto the slopes."

Sam's words sounded like she was holding out hope in the face of grief that threatened to overtake her.

Rae was too. She had a feeling in her gut that she would learn something substantial today. They would be together for hours, so

Rae would have the chance to ask Sam about those books. And if she snagged a few moments alone with Ivan, then she could possibly get information that he might not otherwise share in Sam's presence. She might learn something more from Ivan in this environment where he was most comfortable. She'd found that to be the case when she was searching for hidden truths. Secrets. People kept their guard up, but Rae had learned how to help them drop it, if only enough for her to see inside.

"I need to talk to you about the books."

Sam nodded, then eyed the couple. Ivan was wrapping up and urging them outside. "Okay. We'll make time today."

A text came through from Liam. She'd planned to text him before getting on the helicopter.

Are you okay?

She could sense his frustration even though it was only a text. She quickly replied.

I'm with Sam and Ivan and a couple of tourists. You work your end, I'll work mine. I'll be fine. I promise.

This wasn't our plan. I don't like it.

The sooner we find Zoey, the better. I have to go. I'll be safe with Sam and Ivan.

Relieved that she'd heard from Liam, Rae followed the group and fidgeted with her poles. A whole day spent in the mountains, away from civilization, sent a terrifying thrill through her.

Big snowflakes came down hard and fast and beautiful. Sometime in the next twenty-four hours, the weather would shift. A blizzard was coming. She imagined that people were crowding the slopes at the various ski resorts to get in as much ski time as possible before the storm shut them down.

Some people would head back home. Others would hunker down and stay in the resort. Once that blizzard hit, they would all be grounded for a while.

Together, Sam and Rae hiked out to the helipad. All skiers had already donned their helmets that included communications—a Mountain Valley Adventures requirement. A gust of wind slammed her cheeks. This would be nothing compared to the wind and snow on the mountain. Heart pounding, she waited for her turn to climb into the helicopter. Headset on, the pilot focused on his dashboard. Someone had taped a couple of photographs up near the controls.

"This is Wayne 'Powder Keg' Jaeger," Ivan said, his voice coming through loud and clear via the helmet. "He's piloted for us for fifteen years." He clapped him on the back.

The big man Rae had seen earlier tossed a small wave and a smile over his shoulder, then returned his attention to the dash.

Rae strapped into her seat.

The French couple sat across from her, Ivan next to her. "Where's Sam?"

Ivan pointed. Sam rushed away from the helicopter and toward the doors of the facilities.

The helicopter lifted.

"Wait. We're not going to leave without her, are we?" Rae tried to unbuckle.

Ivan pointed at his watch and turned his attention to the paying tourists eager to hit the cowboy powder, as Ivan had termed it. "She'll be fine. Something must have come up."

Rae wrestled with indecision, but the helicopter was lifting away, and she had no choice. This was better, actually, as far as questioning Ivan. If she could get him alone at some point, she could ask what he knew about Zoey. Then she could talk to Sam about the books when she got back. Relief settled in and she let herself hope. With Rae pursuing this side of their investigation and Liam working the resort, they would get answers sooner.

The photographs told the story—Ivan had been a big part of Sam's and Zoey's lives before Zoey disappeared. Why hadn't Ivan protected Zoey from her stalker? Rae had instinctively known that posing that question to him when she'd first met him at Sam's house would provide no answers. Now she might get a chance to ask him in his own comfortable environment on the cowboy powder.

Rae's heart rate soared. Her father had faced improvised explosive devices, direct bombs, bullets. He'd witnessed atrocities and suffered brutalities to expose the truth.

As for her—this helicopter ride. A day of skiing the slopes.

This wasn't suffering.

Even so, Rae had the feeling she would have to keep thinking about her father's endurance to make it through this day. Ivan, the ultimate tour guide, shared the names of the mountain peaks they flew over. The ridges and valleys. The pure, unadulterated wilderness. Snake River, whose path traversed from Wyoming through Idaho and then through Washington, where it joined the Columbia River and spilled into the Pacific.

The privileged few, Ivan continued to emphasize.

Finally, he turned his gaze on her. "And you, you're here with a 'press pass.'" He made invisible quotes with his fingers. "Since you're a journalist, I hope you'll write about this experience."

She stared out the window as Ivan droned on, and finally she was able to tune him out as her thoughts moved back to Liam. She could imagine him gripping her shoulders as he expressed hurt and frustration that she'd left the resort. But inflexibility, the inability to shift and change with the investigation, wouldn't help.

The helicopter swooped over the mountaintop, then dropped fast. Nausea rolled inside Rae like waves.

Liam. Think about Liam.

Those brown eyes she could get lost in. She *had* gotten lost in. His sunlit, wheat-colored hair that hung in waves to his collar. Broad shoulders. The moment she first met him—both of them following the same trail of traffickers but for different reasons. If she could go back in time, she would listen to him and back off. Instead, she'd hit the proverbial land mine and had blown both their careers to bits.

Ivan warned that the helicopter was fast approaching their drop-off. Her breathing kicked up a notch to keep up with her racing heartbeat. And now it was showtime.

The helicopter hovered near the top of a jagged-edged mountain, then slowly landed on a predominantly flat spot into fresh, white powder Rae had only seen in pictures. Breathtaking. No groomed slopes that ended at a resort with food and people. Only wilderness and adventure awaited her.

Then the rotor wash filled the air with white dust.

Zoey . . . Tawny . . . she had likely taken this same ski route hundreds of times. Heart pounding, Rae hopped out and landed in the cowboy powder, boots first.

She joined the others unloading the gear.

The helicopter lifted up and away, leaving them to tame the mountain. After gearing up, the French couple took off. Rae was alone with Ivan. She should ask him about Zoey.

He stared at her long and hard, then covered his dark eyes with reflective goggles. "Tawny skied here, Rae. This was her favorite place."

"Thank you for bringing me." Rae soaked in the sight of the snowcapped mountain.

"Let's go, then." Ivan pushed off with his poles and left her.

CHAPTER FIFTY-ONE

Liam gritted his teeth. He hadn't wanted Rae going on that heli-skiing tour alone. Though, if the intel he'd received was correct, she would be in more danger here at the resort than she would be with those who cared about Zoey.

Still, he struggled to relax. He needed to finish up and get to that heli-skiing place. His jaw worked involuntarily. He'd probably miss her, even if he left now.

Brad squeezed Liam's shoulder, then urged him forward. Memories of their times together flashed through his mind. But years stood between them now. Years and life experiences. Liam had taken the high road straight into dark places. Brad appeared to have walked a peaceful valley and was well on his way to success in Jackson Hole.

As Liam followed Brad to the exit doors in the lobby, he hoped Brad had remained aboveboard. Given Brad's knowledge of Liam's law enforcement experience, there could be no way Brad was involved in anything illegal, though one of his investors was loosely linked to Malcom Fox.

Liam would give Brad the benefit of the doubt. And at some point, he might find a way to share what he knew about the questionable investor with his friend.

He'd spent the morning reviewing the technical aspects of the security systems and meeting with his security crew, all while watching for suspicious activity. He would make sure they were all trained to watch for the warning signs as well, if they weren't already. If he wasn't here for Rae in her search for Zoey, Liam would still be here with Brad. This opportunity intrigued him. It would keep him *close* to home but not necessarily *at* home.

Still, the private investigating he was doing for Rae interested him, too, and Austin had invited him to join him as a private investigator. Maybe he would take Austin up on that. Whether he worked for Brad or with Austin, Liam had no idea how he would tell Heath that he didn't think guest ranching was going to work for him.

Brad popped his arm. "You're a million miles away, bro. What's up? Are you thinking about Rae? Or your investigation into the missing woman?"

"Yes to both questions." He jammed his hands into his pockets and gave Brad the grin he expected. *I need to get out of here.* "Don't worry, Brad. I'm on top of things here too."

Brad smiled as if reassured, but then he released a nervous laugh. That raised Liam's hackles.

"I met with the team today. Got a good look at the security and surveillance technology, but I need to meet up with Rae. You understand."

"I do. But, Liam, I need you here for a few more minutes."

Liam cringed. Before he could object, Brad continued. "I wouldn't ask, but one of the investors is here. Made a surprise trip. I only found out he was coming this morning."

Liam wasn't a fan of surprises. It couldn't be Astor, could it?

Brad lifted his chin high, confident. "I couldn't have come up with all the funding, all the permits required, or even connections to open another resort in this valley without his help."

"Who is he?" Liam crossed his arms.

"His name is Devon Winters."

Liam didn't know the man.

"We'll have to meet him in his vehicle. He doesn't like crowds. Kind of odd, but he's my father's longtime business partner, and now he's mine as well. I'm indebted to him."

"What are we waiting on?" Liam asked.

Brad glanced at his cell. "A text. That's him. They're here. Follow me."

Liam followed his friend out into the parking lot. He hadn't donned his coat. Brad hurried through the parked cars to a black SUV at the back. Brad climbed into the front passenger seat, and Liam got into the back, glad for the warm air.

Liam's vision tunneled in on the man sitting in the back seat next to him—his crisp business suit and red tie—then zoomed out again.

Devon Winters was Malcom Fox.

Liam's courage tried to flee, but he held on to it as he held on to the last breath he'd taken. Brad had known this man his entire life but didn't seem to be aware that he had recently been released from prison.

"Mr. Winters," Brad said, "this is our new head of security, Liam McKade."

He'd gone by Liam Mercer while working for Fox's organization.

Liam understood how difficult it could be to keep two or more identities—aliases—separate in this day and age, but with meticulous and careful planning, it could be done.

Liam had spent years playing along. Playing the game. His instincts kicked in, and without another thought, he thrust his hand forward. "Very pleased to meet you, Mr. Winters."

Recognition flashed in the man's eyes. Liam sported a different look now, but he'd met this man. He didn't think Malcom forgot a face.

Now they were together again. Face-to-face.

Accident? Deliberate? Nothing happened by coincidence.

All the pieces floating around in his mind started moving together. Making sense.

Malcom Fox, aka Devon Winters, had wanted to expand into trafficking via resorts and hotels. He'd long ago connected with the Astor brothers, who had resorts in the region. But five years ago in Denver, connections began to unravel when crazy-stalker Simon took Zoey. Zoey escaped, and Simon was murdered. Fox continued to work with Enzo, or perhaps blackmailed him, which was Fox's modus operandi for effective persuasion.

He'd been connected to this region long before Rae and Liam had exposed some of his operations last year. Only the feds hadn't linked him to his Devon Winters identity.

Fox didn't seem surprised to see Liam. Or maybe he was good at playing this game too.

"Brad spoke highly of you, and I told him, sure, why not. Let's see what this former DEA agent can do for us when it comes to security. But I think we've met before. You and I." He grinned. "Let's talk. Brad, do me a favor and grab us some coffees."

Brad hesitated, then said, "Sure. I'll be right back."

He exited the vehicle, slamming the door behind him.

Fox's grin grew. "I like the idea of you working for me."

"As head of security, I'll be sure that no one gets away with crimes like trafficking operations of any kind."

Revenge. Fox wanted revenge. But it appeared he would take his time to get it.

Liam's heart pounded. He should put a fist in the man's face right now. Liam had worked so long and hard to put Fox behind bars. How did Liam play this so Fox went back to prison and stayed there? This was an awkward position at best—the guy knew full well that Liam had been instrumental in taking him down. And yet he sat there, liking the idea that Liam would work for him?

Liam would *never* work for him.

Unless . . . Unless Fox had somehow found a way to extort Liam, like he'd done others.

Rae.

He wished he had a weapon on him. It suddenly seemed ridiculous that he had started a job as head of security and had no weapon. He forced his breathing to slow. He couldn't let this man know the fear he felt rising inside.

Fox placed his cell phone on the console separating the seats. A video played across the screen. The inside of Liam's home— Evelyn was fluffing pillows.

Acid burned in his gut. The person who'd come to the ranch and claimed to have booked a cabin. Pete must have stumbled on them, and that was their cover story. They must be responsible. "You lay a finger on her—"

Fox lifted his hand. He swept it across the screen to another image.

Rae at Jackson Hole Airport yesterday.

"You're going to work for me until I feel you've paid me back for what you cost me."

How long had Fox been planning this? The entire time he'd been in prison?

"Are you out of your mind?" That was never going to happen. Liam would get the police involved. Didn't Fox know this? Liam studied him, unsure what to say to someone this far gone. No one was invincible. Still, Liam had to think this through before he responded.

Fox held up his finger and swiped the screen again. Who else? Who else could he possibly target?

288

A beautiful redhead in a swimsuit laughed, sitting next to her husband. Heath.

Palm trees swayed in the breeze.

The image stunned Liam. Fox held all the cards.

The man leaned in. "You thought you could infiltrate my organization and bring me down. You thought wrong. And now you think you can save them. Have me arrested. You can try, but someone is going to die. My people are in place watching. If something happens to me, then someone dies. You can't save them all. And I'll simply disappear again. Worst case for me, I go back to prison—for a short time. But I conduct my operations from there as well. As you can see, I've been doing that all along. Someone you love is going to die this time, Mercer, excuse me, McKade. Can you risk that?"

Terror threatened to gut him, but he kept a stone face. "What do you want from me?"

"Nothing will change for you here. This is my new home of operation. My expansion. Work as head of security and keep silent about indiscretions you see. There could be times I need you to do more—like tonight. I'll assign you a task later, to seal the deal. Everyone stays safe as long as you play the game."

Play by your rules, you mean.

CHAPTER FIFTY-TWO

The cowboy powder was just as Ivan had described. Rae thought her heart might explode from the pure joy, the thrill of skiing across pristine deep powder, the glory of the mountains surrounding her, and a bright blue sky belying an approaching blizzard.

Ivan signaled, and everyone stopped as the hill flattened out. "We'll take the east slope, and at the bottom you'll see the flags marking the spot. Wait there. The helicopter will pick us up." He nodded and without another word took off again.

Rae's legs were beginning to shake. She wasn't in as good of shape as she'd thought, and this was more skiing than she'd done in years. She slowed down and skied long zigzags across the hills to pace herself.

By the time she got to the flagged area, the others, including Ivan, were already there. The French honeymooners had removed their skis. Ivan had removed his helmet but still wore his reflective goggles. The honeymooners tromped over to hold hands and take selfies with the magnificent landscape behind them.

Rae eyed Ivan. Now was the time. "Tell me about her stalker and why she left home."

He lifted his face to the sky for a few moments, then leveled it at her. "I'm sorry she felt like she had to leave us. I never would have encouraged her to do that, but her mother wanted her to be safe."

"And you couldn't protect her?"

"I tried. I beat the guy. I was charged with battery." She felt his penetrating gaze, though she couldn't see it. "The charges were dropped, but his unwanted attention toward Tawny continued."

He shook his head and gazed off as if remembering.

"I'm so sorry."

"Unless you've been through it, experienced it, you can't fully understand what it feels like to have someone obsess over you, and then the utter helplessness when there's nothing anyone can do to stop it. Not even the people who love and care about you. All that stuff about how to put an end to stalking didn't work for us."

Ivan sounded as if he'd suffered through it with Sam and Zoey.

"So, you and Sam, what's your relationship?"

"I was her husband's partner in this business. I promised him I would look out for Tawny and Sam, especially take care of them if anything ever happened. So far, so good, except I failed his little girl. If she returns, like she did in college—Sam shared with me what you told her—things will be different." He pursed his lips.

Rae had hoped her conversation with Ivan would confirm what she already believed, and it did. Ivan was a good guy. "As for Sam. I'm protective of her, of them both. Like a big brother. I watch over Sam like a hawk."

"But she's a grown woman."

"Big brothers always watch out for their sisters."

"But it's obvious you feel something much different for her."

"Now you overstep." He grinned—a charmer. Someone accustomed to making people feel comfortable no matter the circumstances.

The honeymooners approached, and Rae couldn't ask more questions. She hadn't learned anything that would help. No new clues. She hoped Liam was making more progress.

The *whop whop whop* of the helicopter drew their attention. In the distance, storm clouds gathered.

"Just in time," Ivan said. "We'll get back in time for everyone to get home and grab a warm bowl of chili before the weather turns."

Rae's stomach rumbled at the mention of food. Ivan chuckled and tossed her a protein bar from his pack. She glanced out over the mountains. "Thank you for bringing me to the same place where Zoey skied."

Ivan had stepped up next to her. "Yes. She loved it here. I hope you got a better sense of the person she is by coming today."

Rae nodded. This was too much to absorb in one afternoon. "I'm getting there. Have you talked to her since she left?"

But the helicopter and rotor wash drowned out her words.

When it landed, everyone loaded their gear and climbed in. Rae downed the protein bar while she watched the scenery below as the helicopter flew them over rivers and valleys and majestic mountains. Ivan sat up front laughing and making small talk with Wayne. She coughed a few times, and Wayne tossed a bottled water to Ivan, who then tossed it to her.

"Thanks!" She took note of the photographs pinned to the dash. Rae leaned closer, hoping to identify the people. Ivan and Sam. Wayne and Ivan and two other men she didn't recognize standing in front of . . . of . . . a Hummer.

A Hummer?

Her pulse jumped and her hands shook.

How many people around here drove Hummers that looked exactly like the one that had forced them off the road? Good thing she'd already finished the protein bar, because she lost her appetite.

She was with a group. She wouldn't panic. Nor could she let anyone see fear in her eyes. It was a coincidence. Nothing more.

She would tell herself that until she got off this helicopter and was back with Liam. They could share the information with the sheriff and find out if the driver who tried to kill them was someone related to the heli-skiing group.

Exhaustion crept in, and the beating rhythm of the blades lulled her. She could hardly keep her eyes open. Ivan glanced over his shoulders to look at her, his sunglasses removed.

The helicopter landed. By rote she climbed from the helicopter along with everyone else and gathered all the equipment. Rae headed for the facility while the honeymooners hung back, talking to Wayne and Ivan. She wanted to ask Ivan more questions, but panic had taken hold. He couldn't be the one who'd tried to kill her. He couldn't be the one behind Zoey's disappearance. But Sam had conveniently missed their flight today. Rae's thoughts jumbled together.

What about the books? What did they mean?

What about the Hummer?

Where was Liam? Why wasn't he with her? She couldn't remember.

Inside the facility, Rae found the sofa in the waiting area and plopped down. She rested her head, hoping to dodge a full-blown headache.

She would have grabbed some ibuprofen from her bag, but she couldn't lift her arms. For that matter, her legs.

Rae couldn't move. Her lids closed on her.

I have to move.

I have to get out of here.

Someone sat next to her on the sofa.

"Are you okay?"

Ivan.

CHAPTER FIFTY-THREE

Stone-cold fear drove him up the rocky mountain trail.

Rae wasn't answering her cell. Nor could he get a signal to track her with the app he'd installed on her phone. She hadn't returned to the ranch. Had Fox taken her for good measure, despite his reassurance that Liam's family and friends would be safe as long as Liam did as he was told? Liam wanted to find the man and make him talk. Make him pay. Make him call off his people. But he couldn't risk the lives of those most dear to him.

He feared using his cell or any of the house phones to warn them. He didn't know where the bugs were, but looking for them would tip Fox off. He needed time to think.

Liam had to initiate his own plan first.

He'd saddled his gelding, Duke, to save time on the trail, but at some point, he'd have to dismount and make his way along the snowy, icy trail to the old cabin. It would probably be dark by the time he headed back to Emerald M. Heath had stocked some supplies in the cabin. Just in case, he'd said. If a lost hiker stumbled on the cabin stocked with food, wood for a fire, a bed, and a solar-charged satellite phone, it could save their life. It made sense, and ranger stations throughout the national forests served the same purpose.

Liam had thought Heath had kept the cabin intact because it reminded him of Charlie, and Heath could be sentimental that way. Liam had wanted to tease him about it, but he'd stopped himself.

As he shined the light along the trail and urged Duke farther, he felt like he was that lost hiker. Someone who'd gotten caught in the wilderness without a way out.

Yep. That was Liam—and he was caught in the worst possible way. Nothing worse than being stuck and lost with a blizzard bearing down on you. A few hours remained before the storm was expected to blow in, but meteorologists were known to miss the mark.

Regardless, Liam had to save his people before it was too late.

Fox would be contacting him with his "assignment" to seal the deal. He was expecting Liam to perform to keep his loved ones alive. Maybe there'd been a reason all those years ago that he'd left home and not looked back for months that had turned into years. If no one ever held his heart, then he'd never have his chest ripped open and his heart pulled out and cut to pieces. That's what had happened the night his mother left them, and then again when she came back and he dared to hope she would stay—only to lose her in that house fire.

Liam had allowed his heart to turn to stone. Again and again. In the Middle East while in the marines, and then again while he was working for the DEA. The agency loved loners. People like Liam.

But then he'd made the mistake of working with Rae, who had a special way of making him open up just enough to let the light into his cold heart and crack it wide open. He'd let himself fall right before she betrayed him.

He understood the situation now and didn't blame her for doing what needed doing to find Dina and the trafficked women. But here he was in the exact position he never wanted to be in again. Trying to save Rae but helpless to do so. Only this time he was attempting to save not only Rae but everyone he cared about.

Malcom Fox had used the same fear tactics he used to coerce people, including trafficked victims, to force Liam into cooperating. Admittedly, Liam was scared for the lives of those he loved. One wrong move on his part could get someone killed. And Rae—he loved her. He cared about her too much not to be in love with the woman.

He couldn't call Heath or Austin or Rae or even Evelyn. Fox had someone watching them all. How much did he know?

Liam pushed beyond the feeling that he was skiing from a mountain peak and approaching a ledge with no way to stop himself from flying over the edge to certain death. Regardless, there was absolutely no way he was going to work for Fox, and the sooner he made contact to let someone know what was going on, the better.

Duke nickered and nearly stumbled. Liam tightened the reins and got off. "You wait here. I'll be right back. I promise."

Maybe there was an easier way to make contact without Fox being the wiser, but at the moment Liam couldn't think of it, and he didn't have time to brainstorm. He couldn't let Fox win. Liam couldn't risk using his own phone and had left it at the house in case Fox was tracking him. Fox couldn't be everywhere. And there was no one shadowing him in these woods out in this cold.

He hiked up the trail, shining the light as he went. Had he gone too far? He directed the beam through the trees. There.

The cabin. Dark and cold and lonely. He didn't think anyone was actually staying there, but he knocked on the door. "Liam McKade. Just making a supplies check."

When no one responded, he opened the door and shined the light around. The cabin was cold inside. He shut the door behind him and in five strides was at the counter on the opposite wall. The satellite phone. He had no idea if these things got too cold to work.

Please, God, please . . .

Liam took off his gloves and rubbed his hands together. He opened up the phone. He'd need to go outside, and maybe move out of the trees. In ways, satellite phones were as much of a pain as trying to catch a signal on a cell out here.

He powered it up and the red light came on. Yes! He would give Heath a big hug for thinking to keep a phone out here. Yes, a big hug—but first, Liam had to warn him.

Liam walked outside to the trail, away from the tree canopy until he saw stars. He dialed Kelvin's number and it went to voice-mail. He left a short but detailed message that he wouldn't be calling again from this number and that it was urgent. "Do not call my cell. It could be compromised."

He couldn't know for certain that Fox had gained access to Liam's cell, but if he had, then Fox knew much about what was going on. Far too much.

He waited a few moments, then tried again.

Kelvin answered. "McKade?"

Liam shared every sordid detail. "Get my family out. Get them to safety."

"All right, just calm down. That's going to take some time. You're talking Hawaii. We have to find them first. Seattle for Austin and Willow. Evelyn isn't so hard. And Rae . . ."

"I don't know where she is." Molten anger built up in his chest. How could he end up in the same situation that had sent him home? How could he be here again, trying to save Rae? To get to her before someone killed her?

I love her. God, I love her!

The line remained silent. Liam thought he'd lost his friend. "Kelvin?"

"I'm here. I was going to call you tomorrow with this news. Jack Anders is one of ours."

"The bodyguard?"

"Yeah."

"DEA?"

"No. He's FBI. On a task force. It wasn't easy to get this intel because he's deep undercover. My telling you could get him killed. Enzo Astor hired him because he's afraid for his life. He's in business with Fox. Maybe been coerced into a money laundering scheme and, as we suspected, some trafficking because of his deceased brother, Simon. It was Enzo's job to get some stolen money back, but the woman escaped."

"Wait. A woman escaped? What woman?" Zoey?

"We don't know."

"How can any of this help me at this moment?"

"I'm saying that we can all work together and bring Fox down."

"Okay. Whatever. Please get someone in to get my family out of harm's way. Once I know they're safe, then we can go after Fox. I'll find Rae, but I could need help extracting her."

"Anything else?" Kelvin's tone let Liam know he was taking him seriously. That Kelvin was in this with him as if he was still officially DEA.

"I don't know who else's cell phones have been compromised, so I won't trust anyone's. Please send a message to Heath and Austin to let them know the danger. That a hit has been put out on them—that should scare them. They can take cover. They have skills enough to protect their wives. I'll need you to get Evelyn out of the house. Leroy and Pete can take her away and protect her. But Fox will be watching me closely. I'll focus my efforts on finding Rae. And . . . " Liam's legs shook.

"And?"

"A blizzard is headed this way. If you're going to send reinforcements or backup, you'd better do it now."

The logistics were a nightmare. In other circumstances, he would bide his time until players were in place, but with Rae missing, Liam couldn't wait.

He should contact Sheriff Taggart. But he couldn't be seen with the man at the moment. It was too risky.

"How do you want me to get in touch with you?"

"I'll get a burner phone. I just didn't want to rush out of my meeting with Fox to buy a new phone. He's supposedly monitoring me, and until I find out exactly how and also know my people are safe, I have to appear like I'm cooperating. In the meantime, I'll text you. No calls. I'll ask how the fishing is. If it's good—that means they're safe."

"Will do. Hang in there." Kelvin ended the call.

Liam started a small fire in the cabin to take some of the chill out. This might be his base of operation or a hiding place or safe house, if needed. He didn't know what the future held.

CHAPTER FIFTY-FOUR

Liam floored it along the mountain road, the snow driving hard into his headlights.

The satellite phone had run out of power or else he would have tried to contact Reggie. Liam had memorized the man's number when he'd had the chance. Then Alan's. Until he got his hands on a cell phone he trusted, he wouldn't make that call.

If he couldn't find Rae with Samara Davidson, he would assume that Malcom had her, was holding her. That hadn't been the deal he'd made with Liam.

He knew Rae wouldn't deliberately go silent.

Worst case—the absolute worst case—Liam would find Rae with Malcom Fox and face off with him. Liam steered Heath's truck, speeding forward into the Mountain Valley Adventures empty lot, then he parked and jumped from the truck. Liam rushed to the front doors, kicking snow as he went. Locked. He pounded on the doors, anguish gripping him.

Where are you?

He would try Samara Davidson's home next. Back in the truck, he yanked the steering wheel and spun out as he drove from the parking lot, then floored it over the slick roads to her home. He parked behind a Jeep. Not Rae's rental. His heart sank.

He ran up the front porch, rang the bell, and pounded on the door.

A woman opened it, a deep frown carving her face. "Can I help you?"

"My name is Liam McKade. I'm a private investigator working with Rae Burke. Right now, I'm looking for her. The last I knew she was at your place of business. I can't find her—"

She opened the door wide. "Come in out of the cold."

He stepped inside, panic continuing to rise. This was on him. All on him.

"I'm Samara Davidson, by the way."

"You're Zoey's mom."

"Tawny's mom, yes." She led him deeper into the home. "We're sitting in front of the fireplace dozing. Going to wait the blizzard out here. Please have a seat."

"I don't have time. Rae's missing. Please tell me what you know. When did you see her last?"

A beefy man rose from the sofa. He could have been the man in the mask. He thrust his hand out. "I'm Ivan. I was with Rae today. Took her out on the slopes, along with a couple from France on their honeymoon." He appeared concerned.

But was he lying? Liam fought the need to grab him by the collar and demand to know where she was. He reined in his fear and anger.

"Well, what happened? Did you see her leave?"

He ran his hand over his mouth. "She seemed to have fun. Asked me a few questions. When we got back, she grabbed her gear and went inside. I was with the others getting stuff from the helicopter. When I got inside, I saw her sitting on a sofa in the foyer looking more exhausted than I'd expected. I asked if she was feeling well. She told me that she was okay. Then I got distracted with the French couple. When I turned back, she was gone. I assumed she had left."

"Her vehicle wasn't in the parking lot," Samara said. "So she clearly left. What do you think happened to her?"

"I'm trying to get to the bottom of this." Were they lying to him? If they truly knew nothing about her, then where had she gone? This had to be Malcom Fox or Enzo Astor. Those two were working together. Rae's disappearance had to do with Malcom and his using her as leverage over Liam . . . Or it had to do with Rae's search for Zoey. Liam should have asked Malcom about Zoey, but he didn't want to get into a conversation with him without leverage of his own.

"I need a minute to think." He paced the room. *Get it together, Liam. One mistake could cost Rae's life.* "Tell me about the books."

Samara's eyes widened. "Books?"

He moved to the bookshelf and ran a finger down the shelves until he spotted the spines of the novels by Zane Williams and tugged one out. "Rae pulled one of these from your bookshelf when she was here. She 'borrowed' it, she said. She'd discovered you were sending these to Zoey. So you were in contact with her, after all. Tell me what they mean. They could help me discover the whereabouts of both women. Zoey and Rae."

The woman gasped and shared a look with Ivan, who appeared stunned at the news.

"I . . . She sent those to me years ago. Made me promise to keep them. She told me they were important. I could never let on that we were in contact, I knew that. Then a month ago, out of the blue, I heard from her. She wanted me to send her a book. One per week so it wouldn't draw attention."

"What was so important about the books? They could hold the answer." He'd told Rae they meant nothing. He was grasping at straws now.

Sam stared, her mouth hanging open, then she bit her lip. "I honestly don't know. Tawny, in her new life as Zoey, was secretive. I think she was terrified that if he got her again, he would kill her. She told me the less I knew, the better. I wanted to keep what little contact I had with her, so I didn't ask more. I don't know anything about the books, but there is something I *do* know."

CHAPTER FIFTY-FIVE

Callie slept fitfully in her bedroom.

In his own bed, Alan lay on his side and stared at the way the moonlight streamed through the window and hit the sage green walls—a color Zoey loved.

Come home to me, baby. Come back to us.

His silent pleas wouldn't bring her back. Sleepless nights as he tried to figure this out hadn't brought the answers he sought.

The police had her laptop or else he would have spent the lonely hours of the night scouring it for answers. Zoey was a master at her part-time job for a cybersecurity firm where she was paid to hack her way into businesses—mainly financial institutions—and government entities to show them it could be done. On the flip side of that coin, she knew how to keep her laptop safe from prying eyes.

That's why he kept thinking about those books. He'd thought they'd been sent by a stalker, but Zoey's mother had a stash of them in Wyoming. So it stood to reason that Zoey's mother had sent Zoey the books.

Why?

Had Zoey hidden something in those books? And if she had, why would she hide something in old novels that she could just as easily hide in cyberspace?

He would have called Rae and talked it out, but he didn't want to wake Callie. And Mom had to go home for a couple of days, so she wasn't around to run interference. Her boss wanted her at his side during his presentation to the board. What a wasted trip. He'd decided to let himself depend on her, and now she was gone.

Even amid his crisis, the lives of others continued around him as if his own life hadn't been turned upside down. As if Zoey hadn't disappeared. Mom assured him that she would return next week if Zoey's disappearance wasn't resolved. So much for her wanting to be here for Callie.

He'd seen the look of sympathy and grief for her son's loss in his mother's eyes. She didn't believe Zoey was coming back, despite the hope he clung to because she'd returned before.

This was different. Yes. He'd admit that much. This time was different. Of course it was. Why had he continued to hold on to the hope that it would be the same as the last time she disappeared?

Hope was all he had.

In the meantime, Callie needed Alan full-time, and he didn't want to talk to Rae or upset Callie. He so easily used his little girl as an excuse when he could have texted Rae. He'd asked her to do this for him, after all. But the simple act of texting her left him feeling hollowed out.

Callie could sense that, and she was already on edge. For her, Alan wouldn't allow himself to step over that line and become a nonbeliever like his mother. Maybe even the detective and the rest of the police.

Callie counted on Alan, and maybe even Zoey counted on him to keep believing she was alive.

Come back to me, Zoey.

Alan had never been a violent man. But if given the chance, he would kill. He knew that now to his marrow. His gut boiled with anger. If given the chance—*God, please give me the chance*—he would look the man who took Zoey away from him in the eyes right before he exacted vengeance.

For now, he would do his best to protect his daughter. His handgun remained tucked under his pillow, within his reach.

If only he could escape this living hell and torture—reporters watching and waiting to catch him every time he left. The detective's endless questions. If he could take Callie from here, he would.

But he had to stay here and stay strong for Zoey. He had to be home when she came back.

A tear leaked out the corner of his eye.

Scritch, scritch. Scritch, scritch.

He stiffened.

Callie? The dread crawling over his body told him no.

Slowly, he sat up in bed and placed his shaking hands on his weapon. He started to call out to see if Callie was sleepwalking, but his gut told him to remain quiet.

Someone was creeping down the hallway. He got out of bed and backed into a dark corner and waited.

The figure crept slowly into his room until he hovered near the bed.

Alan aimed his weapon but kept his distance. He hadn't trained for hand-to-hand combat like so many others. He was a geek like Zoey.

The figure froze near the bed. He must have realized Alan wasn't in the bed but was behind him instead, because the stranger turned and whispered, "Alan?"

CHAPTER FIFTY-SIX

A lan." Again, the woman he loved whispered his name—the sound blowing unspeakable emotions through him.

He dropped the gun as his wife rushed forward and wrapped her arms around him, then buried her face in his chest.

Zoey sobbed.

Was Alan dreaming? No. Zoey was here in their home. In their bedroom. In the flesh. He held her in his arms and could have sobbed with her.

Thank you, God. All he'd wanted was to have her back safe and sound. He hadn't cared if she was having an affair—though he'd refused to believe it. He'd tried not to care that she'd simply walked away with that stranger. He hadn't cared about her secrets. The mysteries of her past. Only prayed she would come back to him.

He loved her too much.

He wanted to stay in this place—her in his arms forever. He wanted to keep her here where she belonged. But suddenly . . . now that she was back—he cared about all of it.

A chill crawled over him. Anger kindled in a place he hadn't known existed until this moment.

Zoey must have sensed the change in him—even before he recognized and accepted it himself. She slowly dropped her arms and stepped back. "I'm so sorry."

Alan remained silent. He wasn't sure what to say, what his first words should be. But that wasn't true. "Zoey, I . . . I feared the worst but wouldn't allow myself to think you were dead. I've been so worried about you. I was dying inside. Callie needs you. Where have you *been*?"

"I can explain later. We need to get out of here. You're in danger. There's no time."

"I'm not going anywhere with you until you give me at least some reasonable explanation. Who was the man you met with? Where have you *been*? I want answers." *You could have called or texted if you were free enough to find your way here!*

Zoey's eyes widened.

She appeared surprised that Alan would demand answers. He never had before.

Zoey frowned and nodded. She crept to the door and shut it. "I don't want to wake Callie. Is she . . . is she all right?" Her eyes shimmered with tears in the moonlit room.

"She misses you." He loved her so much. But unless she had a good explanation, she was going to break his heart. "I'm waiting."

Zoey sat on the edge of the bed and shoved her hair out of her face. She took a slow, shaky breath.

"This all started years ago when I was abducted. Before I moved to Denver and went to college, I had a stalker. His name was Simon Astor. I couldn't shake him no matter what. So I left and changed my name. Started a new life and left behind the old one. But Simon found me again and that time, he abducted me."

Alan's chest ached as he listened to her story, the past he hadn't asked her to share before and wished she didn't have to now. He heard the deep pain that remained. He pulled a chair from the corner to sit closer so she could keep her voice low.

"He found me by accident, actually. He'd come to Denver for business." She glanced up at him. "Illegal business. With all his partying and gambling and drugs, he was sucked in deep and was the middleman for a trafficking ring that continued to grow exponentially."

"You mean drugs."

"Yes. And human. It was all part of a diversified ring that's still going. I guess being part of that business made him bold enough to take me off the street."

Zoey sniffled, and Alan could tell she fought to hold back her sobs. "But I got him, Alan. I got him good."

"You killed him."

"What? No! No. I could never kill someone. If I could escape without committing murder, even in self-defense, then I would."

"Then what do you mean that you got him good?"

"He beat me. Abused me in every way. Had his fun."

His chest tightened as he held her gaze. "Is this . . . is this man . . ."

She squeezed her eyes shut. Lips quivering, she nodded, then opened her eyes. "I can't think of him as her father or having to do with any part of her. Never bring that up again. You're her father, Alan."

Alan felt her pain to his bones. He shouldn't have mentioned it. "You're right. I'm sorry . . . Please, tell me what happened next."

She cleared the thick emotion from her throat. "I let him think I was unconscious, and then when he was passed out drunk, I got on his laptop. He was stupid enough to open it and use it while I was there. Even before I graduated, I knew what I was doing. I hacked all his files. I learned about his business and his partners. Found what I needed about his interactions on the dark web—the names of real people behind dark web identities. Simon . . . I think he was going to use the information for his own leverage to free himself from the man he worked for. I needed that same leverage to protect myself so he would never come for me again. I memorized as much as I could. Didn't want to leave a digital trail for Simon or anyone else to follow to know what I was up to."

Alan's shoulders sagged. "Zoey, why didn't you just go to the police?"

She bolted from the bed. "Because!" She shrank back. She'd spoken too loudly. Her eyes shot to the door, then she lowered her voice. "Because I had already been to the police multiple times. What had they ever done for me? They could *not* stop him. I could only trust myself. I got leverage, Alan. He would never bother me again."

"Okay. Okay," Alan said. "But . . . wait. Simon is dead. What does any of this have to do with your disappearance now?"

"I'm getting to that." Zoey covered her face. "I don't want you to hate me."

"Please, Zoey, just tell me."

"I moved money."

"Moved? You mean you *stole* money?"

"To help others, Alan. I moved money from the organization Simon worked for. Small amounts at a time so it wasn't too noticeable, and I shared it with organizations that help trafficked women. They needed more funds to make a difference."

"That's right. You talked to Rae about trafficking."

"My mistake. I didn't know she would spend months investigating trafficking in Denver so she could write a story. I already knew where it would lead her." Zoey grabbed her hair and fisted it. "I hadn't meant to send her down that road. To dig so deep. She was going to get hurt. So I sent a message to threaten him."

Alan stood and gently gripped her shoulders. "Him . . . who are you talking about?"

Zoey shut her eyes and exhaled as if working up the nerve to keep going, then she opened them. "The man who would lose the most if she exposed him. The head of the trafficking ring in

Denver. He has many aliases. Malcom Fox. Devon Winters. William Granger. I threatened to expose him."

"But he didn't listen."

She shook her head. "Rae was taken anyway, then saved by that undercover DEA agent. But my threat had drawn Fox's attention, and I'd tipped my hand. He might have landed in prison, but he sent people to search for me just the same. Possibly because of what I knew about him, but probably because of the money."

She hung her head.

Alan lifted her chin so she would look at him. "Because of the money you diverted to helped trafficked women."

"Not that money. Different money."

Alan dropped his hands and fisted them. "My head is spinning here, Zoey."

She frowned. "At first, after I escaped Simon back in college, I was scared, so scared. I took money to help organizations, yes, but there's more. I took a chunk of *his* money."

Alan stared at her as he tried to comprehend her words.

"Only, it turned out it wasn't Simon's money. It belonged to Malcom Fox. I think Malcom thought Simon had stolen the money. I think he killed Simon. But he finally figured out that I was the one who stole his money."

This whole time Zoey was sitting on money belonging to this criminal. Alan swallowed hard. "And what did you do with the money?"

"I used it to buy cryptocurrency."

That surprised him. "What? You mean like Bitcoin?"

She nodded. "I was half out of my mind after Simon abducted me. Scared he would come for me again. I feared the leverage of knowledge wasn't enough. When I was in that room with Simon going through his laptop, there was a Zane Williams thriller novel sitting on the desk. It seemed out of place and caught my attention. Sure enough, Simon had written something inside. I don't know—he couldn't find paper? Didn't want to text or type the information into his computer, leaving a digital trail? But I took that idea and ran with it.

"I took the money and bought cryptocurrency. That week after I escaped Simon, I visited a used bookstore and grabbed Zane Williams's Benedict Jaynes adventure series—the first twelve books. I used those novels to hide passwords. Maybe I went a little crazy, but I was terrified. Don't you see? No one could ever find the money without those passwords."

"I'm not sure I understand. Why twelve?"

"Oh. Well, the cryptocurrency wallet has a thirteen-word passphrase—or seed. When you create it, the software instructs you to never store the seed electronically or on a website. In other words, you don't want it in digital form. So I wrote down twelve of the words in the Zane Williams novels in series order, which I sent to Mom, instructing her to keep them hidden in plain sight and to never get rid of them. To keep them for me until I needed them."

"It seems like overkill."

"I hacked into a huge illicit organization, Alan. I had to take every precaution. That last word—the thirteenth word—I kept in my head. In the unlikely event that someone got their hands on the other twelve words of the passphrase, they would need that last word to open up the cryptocurrency. They couldn't kill me if they wanted the money back. At the time, they didn't even know who I was. Bitcoins aren't linked to real identities. That's the beauty. It was just another tier of protection in case Simon came for me again."

"But that would only make him angry and come for you."

"If he ever found out who stole the money."

"And someone did."

"Yes. Malcom Fox did. I wanted to protect Rae, and I wasn't careful enough when I threatened to expose him."

"While that all sounds noble on the surface, you've committed crimes."

"The worst crime of all is that I've put you and Callie in danger. Malcom's people took me to find out the passwords. To get to the money. They couldn't kill me, but they could use others. I escaped before they could learn anything from me. I had hoped they would think I had died so they would give up looking for the money. Without me, they could never get it."

Alan released a long sigh. This was getting complicated. It wasn't over yet. "Why would they think you're dead?"

"When I was abducted this time, a man I knew from Wyoming contacted me. He said it was about my mother, so I left Callie to meet him. I thought I could trust him." She stared at Alan but looked right through him. "But he took me. He would never have done that if Malcom Fox wasn't holding something horrible over his head.

"I was held in a cabin in the wilderness surrounded by snow and a frozen lake. I knew I had to escape to get to you and protect you because of my mistake. I fell through the ice and would have died. But I'd heard a snowmobile earlier in the day. Some rifle fire. I knew that someone else was out there, and I just kept hoping I would find help. I hung on when I fell through and cried out for help. He made it to me before I succumbed to the frigid water. The snowmobiler pulled me from the ice. His name was Chuck. He took me to his home and let me recover enough. I told him my story. All of it."

She covered her face and shuddered, then she dropped her hands. "I had to tell someone. And once I recovered, Chuck helped me get back here. I rode along with one of his trusted long-haul trucker friends to Denver."

She exhaled. "It's imperative that no one else knows I'm alive. Not yet. Too much is at stake. I'm so sorry, Alan. I know you were worried, but I had to wait to contact you. I had to wait until I could sneak into the house without a reporter or one of the officers spotting me."

Alan struggled to comprehend all that she had told him.

"Chuck told me he had suspected something was going on at that cabin, so he would check it out when he saw smoke coming from the chimney. I wasn't the first woman he'd helped. He said that the other woman had been afraid to go to the police. Afraid for her life."

Alan took her hands and urged her to sit on the edge of the bed. He sat next to her and wrapped his arms around her. If only he could calm her trembling body—she was strong, so strong, to have survived. "You're here, Zoey." He wished that was all that mattered. "Why have you kept all of this from me for so long? Why have you kept silent about it?"

He wanted to understand. He needed to understand, because somehow he needed to restore the peace, security, and trust that had been taken from him and his precious family. Could they ever be the same again?

When Zoey disappeared, his world shattered. Now she was back, and the ground beneath him shook violently. He feared he wasn't strong enough to hold everything together.

Zoey abruptly stood and swiped at her eyes. She tugged something from a pocket. "I wrote this note for you in case I died out there, so when someone found my body, they would know who I was and could give it to you."

Zoey was the strongest person he'd ever met. Alan took the note. Instead of turning on the bedside lamp, he stood and moved closer to the window where the moonlight could illuminate the paper. Learning Zoey's secrets in the dark somehow seemed appropriate.

Had we never met, you and I, then you never would have loved me. I never would have returned your love.

And now look at us. I've caused you trouble. Brought you pain. All I wanted to do was protect you. Please forgive me.

Please know that I love you.

Loved you.

Pain squeezed his heart until he was breathless. Unable to speak. Eventually, he found the words. "You survived to give me this." He drew her into his arms. That had to mean something. She could have died. Should have died. But she survived. "You made it back to us."

That meant everything. He wouldn't let her go again. He would stand by her through the trials to come. No matter what. Love meant nothing if it didn't remain through the worst possible struggles. Love meant nothing if it wasn't unconditional. Then it wasn't love at all.

"Now, we have to get out of here," she said. "You and Callie aren't safe because of what I've done. I'm so sorry."

"Don't talk like that." He gripped her arms and looked at her face. She lifted her eyes to him. Beautiful eyes. More haunted now than he'd ever seen. But there was something else. Joy. She loved him. She'd come back because she loved him and Callie. He knew that, and that was all he needed. "We're going to survive this, Zoey. I love you. Don't ever forget it."

"I know. Your love is what kept me going. That, and an ounce of hope. But promise me that you'll love me enough to let me go in order to protect Callie, if it comes to that."

A sound drew his attention. The door creaked open.

"Momma?" Callie's small voice resounded.

"Oh, my baby!" She rushed to Callie, dropped to her knees, and pulled her daughter into her arms.

Alan joined his girls, wrapping them both in his arms. Tears blurred his vision. Maybe their world had been shattered, but they were together again now, and that was all that mattered.

CHAPTER FIFTY-SEVEN

BRIDGER-TETON NATIONAL FOREST

Rae woke up to complete darkness. Her head pounded.

What happened? Where am I?

She felt a mattress beneath her. She swept her hand across the top—a quilt. She was in someone's home?

Rae pushed herself up. Her temples hammered, catching her off guard. She gently rested back on the pillow and forced her mind to remember. She'd been on the heli-ski tour. She'd been exhausted and made her way to the waiting area to find a seat. Once settled, she hadn't been able to move.

Ivan had approached and asked if she was all right. Then she'd woken up here.

Abducted.

This wouldn't be her first time. And Liam had been there the last time. He'd untied her and then dove in front of her when the bullets started flying.

She squeezed her eyes shut and tamped down the whimper that wanted to escape. That had been one of the most terrifying experiences of her life. But she'd survived then. She could survive now.

Rae wouldn't give up hope. She would fight until the end. She tried to think . . . Ivan had given her the protein bar. Had he drugged it? He was in a photograph with a Hummer. Was he the one who had pushed them from the road? The man in the black mask behind the attacks?

She could figure that out later. Knowing who was behind her abduction wasn't as important as getting out of here alive. But right now she couldn't escape as long as she stayed in bed. Ignoring the pain in her head, she swung her legs over the edge of the bed and sat forward. Rae hung her head to catch her breath as nausea swirled inside.

The wind buffeted the cabin, howling at times. But there was another sound. A familiar, thrumming that her fuzzy mind couldn't identify.

Light suddenly burst into the dark room. Moonlight through the clouds? She glanced out the window. A flashlight beam shone from a few yards away and revealed deep snow and dense forest getting inundated with heavy snowfall.

The blizzard would soon be on them in full force.

Liam would track her phone. Did he already know where she was? She hoped he was on his way. Rae glanced around the room to get her bearings.

The burst of light disappeared, but she'd learned enough about the room. There was one door. Sure, there was a window, but she doubted it would be easy to open. Probably nailed shut. Even if it wasn't, this place could be in the middle of nowhere in the mountains. She could climb out, but where would she go? She needed to explore and find out as much as she could, then she could figure out her escape.

The room was sparse, and although she'd only caught a clear glimpse of it with the flashlight beam, it seemed like her abductor had already removed potential weapons. Rae found the bedroom door. To her surprise, it wasn't locked. Hearing a voice, she crept down a short hallway and into a massive living room where a fire blazed in the fireplace. The front door swung open. Cold air and snow swirled into the room. She stepped back into the shadows.

The man in the black mask. Her pulse roared in her ears, joining the wind and helicopter rotors. Snow covered his head and fell from his shoulders. He tugged off the mask.

Wayne?

The pilot.

The breath whooshed from her.

He'd given her the water—tossed it to Ivan, who'd handed it over. She hadn't seen a watch on him then.

Rae struggled to wrap her mind around the fact that this man—Ivan and Sam's friend and employee—had abducted her. Wayne had been the one who had stolen her laptop. He had needed to learn how much she knew about Zoey. And he'd shoved her on the slopes and was the man who drove the Hummer.

He quickly tried to get on his cell, cursing that he couldn't get a signal. Then he moved around until he found one. She kept her back pressed against the wall in the shadows.

"She's here. I brought her to Morning Glory like you asked. I don't care what you do with her. I'm not a coldhearted murderer. I've hauled human cargo around enough. I'm done. I want everything you have on me erased. Destroyed. Do you hear me? And another thing—I have to leave now or else I won't get out of here. I had to hide her vehicle and keep low until it was safe to get her into a helicopter and bring her here. Now the blizzard is starting to move in. She'll be stuck here, so I wouldn't worry about an escape. When she wakes up, she can throw another log on the fire. Do with her what you want, but just know that she's my last job for you. I made a mistake. One. I'm done paying for it."

The door slammed.

Rae's heart jumped around inside. She ran out into the empty living room. She gasped for breath. *No . . . No, no, no.*

318

Rae flung the front door open. Snow blew past her into the room. "Don't leave me here!"

For the person on the other end of that call to come for her and . . . do what he wanted with her.

The helicopter lifted off.

CHAPTER FIFTY-EIGHT

Samara opened her laptop and, while waiting for it to boot up, glanced out the window. "Not a good time to be searching for someone." Then her striking eyes found and held Liam's. "You care deeply for her."

"You've got that wrong. I'm working with her to find Zoey."

Her smile told him she didn't believe him. Her attention returned to the laptop. "Wayne has been embezzling from the company."

Ivan gasped. "What? That can't be. Here, let me see." He whipped the laptop around and stared at it. "This is all gibberish to me. How do you know?"

Seriously? "And how is that going to help me find Rae?"

"Patience." Her tone was firm. She tapped on the keyboard again. "I've been compiling a file on him. I wasn't sure about any of it, but if you remember, Ivan, he was the one who initially brought Simon and Enzo in for those helicopter rides."

She scrolled through images of Wayne with Simon and Enzo,

and then of Wayne with only Enzo over the last few years since Simon went missing.

"You've been following him?"

"I've wanted to find a way to help Zoey. To save her. To bring her home. In the meantime, life has passed us all by and she has built another life away from me. Like the old saying, 'Life is what happens while you're busy making other plans.' But your friend"— she directed her words to Ivan—"Wayne is still friends with the man whose brother stalked her and chased her away. And he's been embezzling from me."

Did her tone border on accusing Ivan?

"Why didn't you say anything?" Ivan appeared hurt, and his voice rose. "You could have told me, Sam."

Tears filled her eyes. "I was waiting, hoping for a way to bring her back. I didn't know her stalker was dead. I thought he was still out there."

Samara didn't suspect Ivan was involved with Wayne, then. Liam cleared his throat. "Enzo and a big player in the trafficking business are working together. Drugs and human trafficking. I believe he's trafficking women—let's call it an exclusive high-mountain club—and laundering money through the new resort he's heavily invested in. This pilot, Wayne, he could be working for either of them and could also have been blackmailed to commit heinous crimes. It wouldn't be the first time Fox has used those techniques. Someone even tried to kill us. Does Wayne drive a Hummer?"

Samara and Ivan shared a look. Ivan slowly nodded.

"Where would Wayne take Rae? What would he do with her?"

Samara's cell rang. She glanced at the screen and snatched the cell. Hands shaking, she eyed both of them to keep quiet as she whispered, "Yes?"

She broke out in a laughing sob. "Oh, baby. You're alive. Are you okay? Where are you?"

Samara put the phone on speaker.

"Mom, listen. I'm safe. I'm with Alan and Callie. We're safe. But you could be in danger because of what I've done. Please get out of the house. Go somewhere. I'm going to go to the police, but I have to make sure everyone I love is out of harm's way first."

Liam understood that strategy.

"Mom?"

Liam spoke up. "Rae is missing, Zoey. I need your help. Where would she be taken?"

The irony wasn't lost on him. He'd started this with Rae to search for a missing Zoey. Now he needed Zoey to find his missing Rae.

"I think I know where she is," Zoey said. "I . . . I was there too, briefly. But let me check." Zoey's fingers clacked on a keyboard. "Someone has checked in to the Morning Glory cabin tonight."

"Wait. How do you know this?" Liam asked.

"It's a long story. Me and this trafficking ring go way back. I hacked into their system a long time ago. They're branching out in this area."

Liam couldn't wait to hear that story but only after Rae was home and safe. "Okay, then. Who checked in?"

"A man checked in under the name 'Powder Keg.' And I know who Powder Keg is. Mom knows. Ivan knows him."

"Powder Keg is Wayne," Samara said. "Tawny, he's embezzled from us. We were thinking he could be the one who took Rae. But how can you be sure she's there?"

"I can't be 100 percent sure. But if he's checked in and Rae's missing, that could mean he took her. That's how this operation works. Men can spend a weekend at a private cabin with a beautiful woman of their choice. Come to the Saddleback Mountain Ski Resort for skiing and then an unforgettable tryst in an exotic cabin. You can pick your cabin on the website—one that can only be accessed on the dark web.

"Runaways and young women are the easiest—they fear for their lives and the lives of their families. But people like me or Rae, if we get in the way, which probably isn't that often, we're used . . . then disposed of. There's nothing you can do tonight until the blizzard blows through. Maybe even tomorrow."

He'd given Kelvin a similar warning about the blizzard, that he should send backup before it was too late.

Was it too late for Liam to help Rae?

"I brought this on her," Zoey said. "So I'm going to do what I can. I'm going to try to persuade the man behind all of this to let her go. Mom, the rest of the books. There should be eight of them. You sent me four already. I have those now. Pull them from the shelves. Do exactly as I say. Look at the book's number in the series."

Samara pulled the Zane Williams books from the bookshelf and laid them out in order. "Now what?"

"Using paper and pencil, rub over the impression inside the covers. Remember to keep the words in order as you retrieve them. That's crucial."

Ivan opened a drawer under the counter and pulled out a pad and a pencil, then set them on the counter.

Samara ran her fingers along the inside of the first book cover and nodded. "I understand now."

After ripping a page from the pad, she pressed the paper over the inside of the cover. Then she turned the pencil sideways and rubbed until letters appeared.

"What do these novels have to do with anything?" Samara asked. "What do they mean?"

"Each of the twelve paperbacks holds one word of a thirteen-word passcode to open cryptocurrency holding money I took from one of Simon's operations—the money actually belonged to Malcom Fox. I think that's why Simon was killed."

That made sense. Zoey hadn't killed him, at least directly.

Samara finished getting the impressions and ordering the words based on the order of the books in the Benedict Jaynes adventure series. She read them off. "Jackhammer, battle, guardian, use, stormy, grande, and ready."

"But that's only seven," Zoey said. "I need one more."

Oh no. "Rae took one of them."

"Not good. We'll have to get our hands on that book for the password. I hold the last one in my head. I'll give them the passwords, all except for the last one, if they will release her. I'm going to make contact now." And she hung up.

He wasn't in on all this cryptocurrency stuff and hoped Zoey knew what she was doing.

"Don't worry," Samara said. "She's always been weirdly brilliant."

He nodded. "So, she's making contact and going to offer leverage to free Rae. We don't even know who has her." And if this wasn't Malcom's doing, then Liam could very well have signed Zoey's death certificate. He fought that familiar nausea.

God, what path do I take? Which one was the right one? Only a few days ago he'd prayed for God to open doors. They'd all blown up.

But now he needed only one door. The right door to take him to Rae. Before he took the first step to fly in the face of Malcom's threats, he needed to call Kelvin to see if he'd made any progress securing his family's safety.

Just like he'd given the code to Kelvin, Heath and Austin would both know what his text meant when no one else would.

Liam had to know. "Ivan, can I use your cell phone?"

Ivan scrunched his face and handed it over. "Sure."

Liam didn't know if Ivan's phone was also compromised, given his proximity to the situation, but it was all he had, and Liam had to know if his family was safe. He'd trusted Kelvin to make things happen for him.

He texted his brothers in a group.

How's the fishing?

He hoped the message got out since the weather could mess with the cell signals.

Samara spread out a large map on the counter. Frowning, she shook her head. "In two hours, it's going to be a whiteout. It's dark. You can't do this. You're going to get lost or killed."

Ivan put his hand on Liam's shoulder. "If she's there, no one else is getting in or out until the storm has passed."

"What? You expect me to leave her there until the storm passes?" Liam's heart was already in his throat.

He thought back to their earlier phone conversation with Zoey. Her words would haunt him for the rest of his life. *"But people like me or Rae, if we get in the way, which probably isn't that often, we're used . . . then disposed of."*

"I have to go. I have to try. I grew up in this country. I've been out in blizzards before." Barefooted and running from an angry father. If Rae was even there, she might not be alone, and Liam couldn't bear to think what could be happening to her. Tomorrow could be too late.

His phone buzzed.

Heath had texted.

Fishing was bad, really bad, until we found ourselves a nice, quiet fishing hole.

Liam breathed a sigh of relief.

Austin replied shortly after with a similar message.

Next Liam texted Kelvin since he depended on him to protect Evelyn.

How's the fishing?

> The fishing is great. It's the best ice fishing I've
> done in a while.

They were all safe then.

All except Rae.

"I'm going with you," Ivan said. "I have a cousin who lives off-grid out there somewhere. He goes by Chuck. No one knows his real name or about his existence there, except for a few people, including me. He isn't that far from this place. We could stop there and maybe hike in. Snowmobiles are out back. I have the trailer to haul them."

Panic cinched tighter around Liam's chest. What if she wasn't there, and he wasted all this time to get there? This endeavor could take him much too long as it was, and the blizzard didn't help.

"What about a helicopter? Don't you fly them?"

"Nah. That's Wayne's job. We have other pilots. No one is going to take a helicopter out in this weather. But I know this country too. Together we can do this."

Samara stepped in front of him. "Ivan, are you sure?"

The big man softened. He leaned in and kissed her, then he held her arms and looked into her eyes. "I love you."

"Don't say that as if you're not coming back." She hung her head, then lifted it again, her eyes glistening. "I . . . Yes, to the question you asked earlier."

"It takes a crisis for you to answer me?" He chuckled. "All these years and finally I can make you my wife."

"I said yes because Tawny is okay. She's going to be okay. I couldn't think of anything else until I knew that for sure."

Liam didn't want to poke holes in Samara's belief, but if Zoey held the last piece of that code in her head, she was still very much in danger.

CHAPTER FIFTY-NINE

BRIDGER-TETON NATIONAL FOREST

Rae paced the living room. She'd thrown another log on the fire so she would be warm enough. After finding a flashlight, she'd looked through the place. It was elegant and cozy—like the Saddleback Resort. Same designer? A beautiful carving of a geothermal pool had been carved in the logs. There was nothing she could use for a weapon. Someone had been here before her though. Someone had torn something from the walls.

Maybe she could somehow set the whole place on fire and someone would see the fire and help would come.

Right. The blizzard stood in the way of help getting to her.

The wind had picked up and was howling eerily through the home. The fire flickered in the fireplace almost as though it might go out. She held her breath. That couldn't happen, could it?

She plopped on the sofa and thought about the words she'd heard Wayne say.

Awful words.

This cabin was one of the places used. Had Zoey been here?

Rae fought back tears. She had to find a way out of here. What could she do?

God, am I going to die here? Is this my war zone? Am I going to die on this battlefield?

The wind's howl twisted with another sound. Rae sat up and angled her head. What was that? A snowmobile?

Panic seized her. That couldn't be. No one was going to come out here during this storm.

She rushed to the window but couldn't make anything out. How was it possible someone was out there in this? Was this person coming to kill her?

Her knees shook—what would he do before he killed her? She had to act now. She glanced around the cabin. She rushed back into the bedroom and closed the door behind her. She tried to push the heavy pine bed over to block the door, but it barely budged. *The mattress.* She lifted the mattress and shouldered it over to the door.

Then while this person tried to get in, she would climb out the window and take his vehicle.

Yes! That was it.

With her heart pounding, she rushed to the window and unlocked it. It was stuck. Either nailed or glued or maybe it wasn't even meant to open. She grabbed the quilt and wrapped it around her elbow, then shoved it against the glass. Again and again.

The front door shut. Someone was in the house.

Fear threatened to weaken her limbs. She wouldn't succumb to that. Rae kept working on the window. There was no other way. Finally a crack. Then it shattered.

Using the quilt to protect her from the broken glass, Rae climbed through the window and landed in snow that went up to her waist.

Inside, someone pounded on her bedroom door. "Rae Burke, let me in. I'm here to help you!"

The voice was vaguely familiar, but she couldn't risk it. She pushed through the deep snow without her coat—that had been taken from her to prevent her from going far.

Even if she got on that snowmobile, how would she survive?

Still, she pushed on—walking around the house, huffing as she pushed through the snow. Her legs and feet were already growing numb. She made it to the front of the cabin and there . . .

A snowmobile.

She had to get away from here. Staying wasn't an option. She would die and be tortured first if she stayed. Rae sucked cold air deep into her lungs and pushed forward, her heart hammering against her ribs. She made her way to the snowmobile, keeping her bearings only because of the dim light spilling from the cabin. The snow was coming down hard all around her, making it difficult to see.

A pelt, as if hail had struck the machine, drew her attention. Gas spilled from a hole in the tank.

A bullet? Had someone intended to shoot the tank? Or had she been their intended target and they missed?

CHAPTER SIXTY

"Get down!"

Rae was thrown into the snow, rock-solid muscle covering her. "Stay down."

The voice was the same one who'd shouted through the bedroom door that he'd come to help her. Who was he?

"What now?"

"Keep low, crawl if you have to, and go back into the cabin. I'll cover you. Now, go!" Gunfire rang out, muted by the blizzard.

Rae crawled quickly and scrambled into the living room. The man rushed in behind her, and crouching, he kicked the door shut. Bullets sprayed the door.

He shoved her down and urged her over to the other side of the sofa. She glanced up at him to get a better look.

At the sight of his face, she gasped. "You're Enzo Astor's bodyguard."

Great. She was no safer here than she'd been out there.

He held a weapon at high ready—close to his head, aiming upward. "I'm his bodyguard, yes, but I'm undercover FBI."

"Undercover?"

"When Enzo learned that Wayne had brought you here instead of to him as requested, he was furious."

"Did he send you to get me?"

"Yes, but I'm not taking you back to him. I'm here to get you out of this before something happens to you."

"So, you're blowing your cover?"

"Maybe. It depends on what happens next."

What was it with her and causing agents to blow their covers? She was grateful, but she was worried about Liam and why he hadn't come for her. Obviously, Wayne had disposed of her cell, so she couldn't be followed.

"What happens next?" she asked.

"I had planned to wait out the storm, at least until it died down a bit and then we would leave, but with an active shooter closing in, everything has changed. We had planned to wait for the storm to pass, and then—" He rubbed his chin as if he reconsidered sharing more.

"We? Wait a minute . . . the FBI is going to raid his home."

"Yes. I tried to protect the girls. To get them out. But someone got to one of them and killed her." Thick emotion edged his tone.

"Who? The girl whose body was recently found?"

He nodded. "But now we have to wait to raid—the timing has to work so no one escapes. The blizzard interfered with our plans."

"Maybe I can finally find Zoey."

"Your sister-in-law. Astor kept her here in this cabin for his boss, Malcom Fox, a few days ago. I wanted to get out here to help her escape, but then I heard she had already gone."

"She was here?"

He nodded. "Yes. She stole a large sum of money from Fox and has a lot to answer for to the feds."

"Are you crazy? I don't believe it."

"I shouldn't have told you any of this, but in case the worst happens, I wanted you to know some of it. Someone's out there—it could be Astor or it could be Fox, the man I was protecting him from. Astor is in deep trouble now because he lost Zoey before he could extract the cryptocurrency passwords he needed to get the money back. I suspect Astor was going to double-cross Fox, though, and wanted the money to use against Fox as leverage.

"When you showed up, Astor blackmailed Wayne to take you out because you are so closely connected to Zoey. I think Wayne tried to scare you off at first. Wayne isn't a murderer, but he assisted in trafficking girls." Jack kept to the shadows with Rae. "All that to say, I can't be sure who took that shot at you. I'm going to try to put out the fire so there's less light, and you stay down and low. Go into the bathroom at the back bedroom and lock the door. Get down in the bathtub."

She nodded. No way would she argue with that.

As she moved, he pushed the logs and embers around with a poker. Darkness fell on the house.

Then she saw the light beams through the window.

Someone was coming to kill them.

CHAPTER SIXTY-ONE

Wind buffeted Liam as he steered the snowmobile close enough to Ivan that he could still see the lights. This was some kind of crazy. Ivan had provided helmets with radio communication as an added precaution.

The lights ahead of him dimmed. "Dude, where'd you go?" Red lights brightened, then shut off completely.

"I'm here. Stopping."

Liam veered to the left to keep from rear-ending Ivan.

Ivan gestured ahead of them. "Chuck's cabin is through the woods. Shut off your lights."

Liam did as requested. "Now what? I can't see my hand in front of my face."

If he sat here too long, the snow would bury him.

When Ivan didn't answer, Liam tried again. "What are we doing?"

"Something's wrong."

"Because?"

"There are no lights," Ivan said.

"Okay, maybe he went to town to wait out the blizzard."

"Not likely." Ivan sounded worried.

"Let's get inside and find out if something's wrong." Liam got

333

off the snowmobile. "We need to get to the other cabin to see if Rae is even there. We stay here too long, we'll be digging the snowmobiles out."

Ivan flipped on a flashlight. Liam did as well, and they hiked toward the cabin. Not even the glow of a fire. They kept their helmets on for warmth and communication as they hiked. Ivan knocked on the door. After no answer, he found it unlocked and entered. He shined the light around. "Looks like he was here today, but he's gone now. Chuck would leave his fire going, if anything, since that's his sole source of heat out here."

The big man clomped down a hallway, his flashlight casting eerie shadows, while Liam remained in place. His nerves prickled.

Close inspection let Liam know that a few embers remained. "Looks like he buried the fire with ash. Why would he do that?"

"*He* didn't." Ivan gasped over the comm. "He's in here. A shot to the head."

Liam could just bet who was responsible. Chuck's cabin was much too close to the Morning Glory cabin that Malcom and his trafficking ring used for their operation. He could cause problems. If he was off-grid and no one would miss him anytime soon, then whoever shot him hadn't had to think twice. Liam joined Ivan in the bedroom.

"Looks like he was shot in his sleep this morning," Ivan said.

"I'm sorry this happened." He squeezed Ivan's shoulder.

Ivan's loud exhale came through the comm.

"We'll call it in, Ivan—but after we get to Rae. Whoever shot your cousin could be the same person with her now." Wayne, Enzo . . . or Malcom?

He wanted to get his hands on all of them.

"We should take the snowmobiles instead of hiking in. The snow's getting deep, and as you say, this is taking too long. The snowmobiles will let them know someone's coming though."

"We'll take them until we see lights from the cabin," he said.

Minutes later, they were crossing the frozen lake on snowmobiles. Liam hoped Ivan knew where he was going, because Liam was lost. The man made his living guiding people over the mountains. Could Liam trust Ivan?

"I'm sorry, Liam. Looks like the lights are out in that cabin too." Ivan's tone was grim.

CHAPTER SIXTY-TWO

Multiple gunshots echoed through the cabin and jarred Rae as she hid in the bathroom. She covered her ears and tried to hunker deeper in the tub. She had to resist the screams threatening to erupt or she'd give away her hiding place. Rae imagined her father crouched down behind rubble, waiting on gunfire from opposing forces to stop. He'd been so strong.

And she would be too.

When the gunfire ceased, the resulting silence amplified the sound of her desperate gasps. She feared the deafening pounding of her heart would filter through the walls. Was Jack hiding and waiting for the right moment to ambush their attacker? She refused to think he had been shot and killed.

She would wait for him. If he was okay, then he would come for her.

Or he could be dead, and the shooter would be the one to find her.

Bile rose in her throat. She was trapped. Liam had been right about her all along. She always pushed too hard and dug too deep, endangering herself. But she couldn't do less than her father had done. She wouldn't give up either. Maybe here in the darkness she would remain hidden from the assailant. If Jack was down,

Rae's only choice was to outsmart whoever was out there. Could she overcome someone who had a gun and was willing to kill? What's more, she couldn't tell if others had joined the shooter in the house.

Jack had risked his cover to get her out of there. She owed him her life. She'd hoped that Liam would find her, but if he had been the one to come for her, he might have paid with his life this time.

A beam of light shined beneath the bathroom door.

The door slowly opened, and light shined bright in her face, blinding her to whomever she faced now. Rae shielded her eyes and braced herself as she imagined the feeling of a bullet slamming into her body. Or would she simply die without feeling the pain?

Every neuron in her body shook with fear. She didn't want to die. But one thing she knew, the fear would paralyze her if she didn't do something before it was too late.

Rae stood. "Who are you and what do you want?"

The beam lowered and the figure behind it became clear.

Malcom Fox?

But . . . where was Jack? *Oh no . . .*

"You? I—"

"You weren't expecting me. When I learned that Enzo had requested Wayne snatch you—against my wishes, I might add—I redirected Wayne to bring you to this cabin. I wanted to see who would come for you here. I suspected another undercover agent—like Liam Mercer, I mean, McKade. Turns out it was Astor's bodyguard. Enzo is as sloppy as Simon was. And now, here we are."

Fox waved her out of the bathroom but remained in the doorway. Heart pounding, she tried to make herself small so she wouldn't brush him as she passed. Could she sucker punch him? Elbow him in the nose?

He held a gun, so she had no chance unless she got it away from him. Guns were the great equalizer. Fox urged her down the short hallway and into the living area.

"What are you going to do with me?"

"I had everything where I wanted it when Astor interfered."

"Enzo?"

"No. Simon." Pointing his gun at her, he urged her to sit.

She eased onto the sofa, her mind racing with possible escapes, but she could think of no way out. The wind howled outside, and a cold draft curled around her. What if she asked to get the fire going again? Maybe she could hit him with a log.

"And now, I've been asked to deliver you in exchange for my five million dollars."

"Five million dollars? What are you talking about? I don't know anyone who has that kind of ransom money." Nor did she believe for one minute that Malcom Fox would simply hand her over, even for five million dollars.

"Oh, but you do."

Rae hated the tears that chose this moment to surge. "Who?"

"Simon had become a part of my circle of friends. Then he ran into an old friend—a woman he'd wanted. His obsession got the best of him and he took her, during which time she gained enough information on my operations to take me down. But she didn't." He leaned in, his face inches from Rae's. "Do you know why?"

He had to be talking about Zoey, but Rae didn't understand. She shook her head.

"She was too scared—at least until you were abducted last year as a way to bait the mole in our operation. A stinking undercover cop. Your friend tried to use her leverage to free you, but McKade was there to save the day. I intended to take him down. Even though I went to prison for a time, I made plans to get to McKade and worked to find the woman who'd stolen from me five years ago. I had thought it was Simon, so I killed him. He'd been sloppy and needed to die anyway."

"*You* killed him?"

"He was a liability."

"Why are you telling me all this?" *Because I'm now a liability.* She shivered with fear as well as cold.

He chuckled. "You're a reporter, aren't you? You wanted the story when you started digging around in my trafficking operations. Now you're getting it."

He offered a sinister smirk that left no doubt about his plans for Rae. That was a story she would never be allowed to run with. To share with the world, even if he successfully traded her to Zoey for that money. Zoey had taken five million dollars . . . Rae struggled to comprehend what he was telling her.

Oh, Zoey. Rae squeezed her eyes shut. *Please, please don't give him what he wants. He's not going to let either of us live.*

Zoey had to know that. If what Fox said about her was true, she had tried to save Rae last year when she'd gotten herself in trouble searching for Dina, but Zoey had showed her hand, revealed too much in that risky game she'd played, and Malcom had found her.

"If we're staying here, do you mind if I get the fire going again?" Rae asked. "It's getting cold."

"We're leaving."

"But this storm—"

"It's the best time to leave. Nobody is going to track me or follow me in this. It's the perfect storm. Now, give me the password you got for the cryptocurrency. Then we'll meet your sister-in-law, who has the last code."

The image of that moment she'd discovered the impression inside the cover of the Zane Williams novel flashed in her mind. She'd texted that word to Reggie.

Ransom.

"What? I don't know what you're talking about."

CHAPTER SIXTY-THREE

Liam waited in the kitchen and listened to Malcom Fox share with Rae far more information than he would share with someone he would allow to live.

With the howling wind battering the structure, Liam had easily slipped into the dark cabin undetected. The door had been ajar, so Liam's entry hadn't drawn attention, even when he shut it to cut off the cold and snow that swirled inside. Liam pressed against a wall. Waited. Listened. Sensing if someone else was in the room with him. He heard someone breathing . . . a ragged breath here and there.

A light switched on in the hallway, and Liam held his weapon ready. Then he saw the body on the floor behind the sofa. The man was still alive. What had happened here? Liam had almost rushed forward to assist him, but he froze when a voice echoed against the walls from farther down. The light dimmed.

Rae!

Then a second voice . . . Fox?

And Fox emerged from the hallway, holding Rae at gunpoint.

Anger threatened to erupt. Liam's instinct was to rush in and protect her. But he'd done that before. He'd been shot and left for dead. She'd escaped unscathed, and Malcom Fox had been put away because of Liam's undercover work.

Now they were back in this never-ending nightmare.

Liam struggled with the fact that Fox was here now with Rae. A man of his word, Fox was not. Liam had let Fox believe that he had Liam under his thumb with the threat of harming Liam's loved ones. Was abducting Rae Fox's way of showing Liam he meant business? Whatever the reason, Liam couldn't let what happened last year happen again tonight.

God, you opened doors for me. Now I'm here. What do I do? How do I save her?

Liam let his protective instincts kick in and rule him. He'd save Rae at all costs.

He hadn't known where he belonged before, but maybe, just maybe, he was here at this moment in time because in the end, he was supposed to save Rae again. That was his sole purpose in life.

He had no purpose after that.

His chest grew tight, squeezing his heart.

Ivan was waiting outside. Upon Liam's signal, Ivan would create a distraction.

With Fox making plans to take Rae with him—it was game time.

"*Now.*" Liam whispered the word into his helmet and hoped Ivan heard the call to action despite the storm raging outside.

A snowmobile started up. Lights shined brightly into the house, blinding them.

While Malcom backed away from the window, Liam rushed to stand between the man and Rae, tugging off his helmet so she would know it was him. "Go!" Liam pointed to the front door. "Ivan is waiting for you."

"Liam!"

"Go!" he shouted with all the command he could muster as he

lifted his gun, aiming it at Malcolm, even as the man aimed his gun at Liam.

She fled through the door and into the storm. The opened door allowed more light in . . . Light that shined on Malcom Fox—a dark, evil man who destroyed lives. Liam never took his eyes off the man. Every minute he'd spent working his way up in the man's organization, Liam had dreamed of this moment but never imagined it would happen.

Malcom laughed. "You can't survive this stalemate."

"I don't have to survive. And neither do you." But Rae had to live.

Liam heard the snowmobile zoom away. He had instructed Ivan to leave him behind and whisk Rae to safety.

"You might not care if you live or die, but I have a business to run." Malcom's eyes gave him away. He would shoot.

A gunshot blasted through the cabin, startling Liam.

Fox stared at Liam in shock, then dropped to his knees. He fell forward, the gun tumbling from his hand and clattering onto the floor. His eyes were lifeless.

Who had fired the shot? The other man in the cabin? Liam turned around and spotted him on the other side of the sofa, holding a gun. Liam scrambled over to him.

His lips twisted into a weak grin, and his hand went limp, dropping the gun.

Liam recognized him—Enzo Astor's bodyguard. Jack Anders. Kelvin said he was an undercover agent. "Stay with me!"

Liam found the gunshot wound at the agent's side and put pressure on it to stop the bleeding. Jack's hands were covered in blood too. He must have been trying to stop the bleeding. Maybe his efforts would be enough to save his life. With one hand pressing the wound, Liam tried with his other to call for help on his cell, but he couldn't get a signal.

Even if he could, out here in the middle of nowhere during this raging blizzard, he worried the response would be delayed too long to save the agent's life. Liam put away his cell and used the comm in the helmet to contact Ivan. "He's gone. Malcom Fox is dead. But we still need emergency services here. An agent is down too. Please get help!"

"I'm turning around," Ivan said.

"No. You get Rae back to safety."

"I can help whoever has been shot. My pack has a medical kit. Gunshot wound powder too. I'm coming back."

Liam wanted Rae safe, but he also needed to save Jack Anders's life. "You're going to make it," he said to the man as he kept pressure on his wound. "You saved me. I'm going to guess that you were trying to save Rae too. So you're not going to die on me."

Anders squeezed Liam's hand. "I'm too stubborn to die."

The snowmobile returned. Light blazed into the cabin, illuminating the room. The door swung open as Ivan ran in and dropped next to Liam with his pack. Rae ran in behind him, shutting the door, and began building a fire in the fireplace.

"The power's out or I'd turn on the lights for you," she said.

Probably had a generator, but he wasn't going out in that storm to get it started.

When Ivan had dressed Anders's wound, he looked at Liam. "With all the backcountry wilderness stuff, you never know what's going to happen, so I have all the certifications. I have a medical emergency kit on me at all times."

"That includes gunshot wound powder?"

He grinned. "We have hunters around here. People like that. I'm always prepared."

"I can't thank you enough for what you did tonight, Ivan."

"No thanks required. Now, I think it's okay to move him. Let's get him onto a bed, and I'll start an IV. He needs fluid."

They moved Anders into one of the rooms. Ivan pulled more supplies from his ample kit and started an IV.

"You really do have everything," Liam said.

"I'm glad I am able to help him." He crossed his arms, satisfied with his work.

Anders grinned up at Ivan. "Thanks, man."

Liam stood on the opposite side of the bed. "We owe you. You came here to protect Rae, didn't you?"

He nodded but appeared too weak to elaborate.

"Rest now," Ivan said. "Save your strength. I have no idea how long we'll have to wait out this storm."

Rae stood in the doorway hugging herself.

"At first, I thought you were the one who drugged me," she said to Ivan. "When I woke up here, I remembered that you'd given me a protein bar, which I ate right before I started feeling funny. But then I found Wayne in the cabin, and I remembered that he'd given me a bottled water. He brought me here. I heard him telling someone on the phone that he was done moving cargo and doing the man's dirty work. It sounded like he'd been blackmailed."

"We figured some of it out," Liam said.

"Ivan told me that Zoey is safe." But the fear in her eyes remained.

Liam slowly approached and took her in his arms. "It's going to be okay. It's over, Rae. This time it's over, once and for all." Liam would never have to save Rae from Malcom Fox's grip again.

As he held her, relief infused him. Rae had survived and was no longer in danger. Zoey was safe now too. Nothing else mattered.

But Liam couldn't help himself. A new fear rose up in him.

Realization dawned—without Rae, Liam was lost.

He feared that Rae would go back to her world and leave him here alone in his.

CHAPTER SIXTY-FOUR

Maybe I can live up to your reputation, after all, Dad.

Rae sat at a small desk in a room at the same resort she'd checked in to when she'd first arrived in Jackson Hole and documented the events as she remembered them. Now that she was no longer in danger of someone breaking into her room, she had no good reason to remain at the ranch. Staying in town seemed like the right move.

After the debacle of the break-in and the resulting ransacked room, the manager had been only too happy to offer her a room at no cost. A deputy had dropped Rae off here after another visit to the Bridger County Sheriff's Office to give her statement and answer questions asked by multiple agencies involved in the task force to unravel Malcom's intricate trafficking scheme.

Fortunately for Liam, Brad had already been cleared. He hadn't been connected with the plans his main investors—Enzo Astor and Devon Winters, aka Malcom Fox—had made to take advantage of the new ski resort. Those plans included using the shell company

345

that Enzo Astor had created for another protective layer to launder money earned from their exclusive sex trafficking scheme.

Rae debated whether to write the travel article, but she couldn't even attempt it until she'd poured every ounce of her sordid experiences onto the page. This story could land her a coveted position or open more freelance doors. Except finding Zoey hadn't been about a story. She couldn't do that to Zoey or her brother. Still, parts of it could be extrapolated for an article about Malcom Fox and Enzo and Simon Astor, and she hoped it would lead to freeing those already caught in the trafficking net. Fox's dark web operations were being dismantled, thanks to Zoey's extensive knowledge about his organization. Enzo Astor's properties had been raided, and he'd been taken into custody.

Zoey remained at the heart of this story.

She was in deep water with the government, though the extenuating circumstances regarding Simon Astor's stalking were being considered. Alan told Rae the feds would likely work with Zoey and use her skills for their own purposes. Rae hoped that was true—for Alan's and Callie's sakes as well.

At least they were all out of harm's way.

Rae continued typing her thoughts until she finally came to the man who had never been far from her mind. She'd been avoiding this moment when she had to face Liam McKade. Face him on this page as she typed, face him in her heart and mind.

Their relationship had ended in the worst possible way before, and it could have ended tragically this time. What else could she think but that her presence in Liam's life was dangerous to him?

That would no longer be an issue though. Her flight left tomorrow morning, and she honestly wasn't sure she wanted to see him again, even if only to say goodbye. She didn't want to hurt him again. The irony was that *she* would be hurt if he didn't try to see her before she left. He was the reason for her crazy, foolish heart.

Relationships were painful. Could end in tragedy. Even Zoey and Alan's relationship teetered on a precarious ledge—but Rae had no doubt their love would weather the coming storms. Their relationship was an example to her, though the commitment Zoey and Alan shared was rare indeed.

Rae closed her eyes and thought about her parents' relationship. She had idolized her father, but for all his brilliance, he had his flaws. Her father had told her it was his responsibility to speak up. *"Don't keep silent,"* he'd said. But his family paid the price for his efforts. Missed birthdays and anniversaries. Fear and worry that his endeavors would get him killed. Mom had planned to divorce him before his death. If he had known that he was about to lose his family, would he have left that dangerous war-zone journalism to someone else?

As for Rae, in the past, she'd given Liam up for her story. True, she'd saved Dina's life, and she wouldn't change that. But she'd suffered the emptiness, the loneliness, when she'd lost Liam. It scared her to death to consider how much she loved him. She couldn't take that heartbreak again and might prefer to suffer through being alone.

A knock came at the door, startling her. Her pulse jumped. "Who is it?"

"It's me."

Liam.

Moisture bloomed on her palms as she walked to the door and opened it. Liam, in a Stetson, filled her vision. She'd never seen him in a cowboy hat, and for that she was glad, because the sight made her entirely too unsteady on her legs. Rae leaned against the door for support. Longing twisted his features as her heart skated around inside, searching for an escape. Liam's brown eyes took her in, and that one simple look left her breathless.

"Well, aren't you going to ask me in?" His husky voice held hope and fear all tangled up together.

If I can find my breath. "Sure." Still clinging to the sturdy frame, she opened the door wider.

He stepped inside, his subtle cologne, mixed with evergreens and mountain air, wrapped around her. She shut the door and expected him to take a seat, but he remained where he stood, inches from her.

"You did it again, Liam. You stood between me and a bullet. But this time . . ."

"It all turned out differently."

Could that mean that this time—for Liam and Rae—things could turn out differently as well?

"Because things happen for a reason," he said, taking a step closer. "What's next for us?"

Powerful emotions swirled in his eyes.

Rae fought to breathe. She struggled to find her voice. "Is there an 'us,' Liam?"

He lifted a strand of her hair. "I'm going to be honest. Your response kind of hurts. After everything we've been through, I thought there was definitely an us."

Rae had thought the same thing the last time, but back then he didn't want anything to do with her. He thought she'd used him. He took yet another bold step forward, close enough to gently catch her waist. "Before you showed up, I struggled to know where I belonged. I didn't think I fit in anywhere. Not the DEA. Not at Emerald M, maybe not even in this valley. This wasn't my home."

His words weren't what she'd expected to hear. "What are you saying?"

A half grin hitched his cheeks, along with those dimples.

He inched forward, his face drawing near as he offered that same invitation he'd offered under the stars on that cold night when he'd blocked her path. And now, just like then, Rae was powerless to resist. She closed the distance and pressed her lips against his. All her fears melted away, and this time, she wrapped her arms around him fully. She allowed him to kiss her thoroughly, and she kissed him back. Rae let the raw emotions she'd held back for so long finally flow from her. She let her heart dance with his until they were both breathless. He eased away enough to whisper against her lips.

"I finally found my home, Rae. It's with you. You're my home. Let's make a home together. Be husband and wife."

She backed away and pressed against the wall. She loved him, but this? A proposal? "I'm dangerous for you, Liam. I'd be dangerous to your heart too. I have to go after the stories." *I don't want to hurt you again. I don't want to be hurt again.*

"I know you want that Pulitzer Prize like your father, Rae." He pinned her with his intense, dark gaze. "I wouldn't deny you that. Tell me now that you don't love me and you don't want me, and I'll go. You'll never have to see me again."

Heart pounding, Rae closed her eyes. Tears spilled out the corners, then she opened them. "I love you, Liam. I'm just scared."

He laughed. "You go into dangerous places, Rae, and you're scared of *me*?"

"I'm scared of the pain that loving someone can bring." Rae let herself smile a little.

"I know that pain, and I'm scared of it too, but I also know that I couldn't bear to lose you again. I finally realized what was causing this ache inside, this feeling that I don't belong anywhere—I missed being with you. I guess the question is, do you feel the same way? I hope so, because I don't want to lose you."

Liam had somehow known the exact words to tug at her heartstrings and reel her in. She could never walk away from him. Not this time. "Then don't lose me. Always keep me close." Rae smiled and kissed him, feeling deep in her heart for the first time that if Dad were still alive, she might have finally made him proud.

ACKNOWLEDGMENTS

I owe so many amazing people a debt of gratitude for helping me get this book on the page.

As with every book, it seems I owe you, Jeff and Tina Moyers, my brother and sister-in-law, for your encouragement through the years. For your help with the unusual scenes.

Susan Sleeman—I couldn't do this without your encouragement and your wealth of knowledge.

Crime scene writers' group—to the many technical voices within the group for always stepping up to answer my countless questions.

J. Gary Vineyard—thanks for your patience with all my questions regarding the DEA!

Sharon Hinck—you're a treasure and one of the deepest people I know.

Lisa Harris—you're always there for me.

Proofreader (and my amazing daughter) Rachel Goddard—you're awesome. I know you didn't have much time on this, but you work well under pressure.

The Revell team—Lonnie Hull DuPont, I'm so glad you got to read this one too! Rachel McRae, I hope we get to make many more books together! Amy Ballor, I'm so grateful for your keen eyes! Michele Misiak and Karen Steele—you guys rock. To the art department—LOVE the covers.

My agent, Steve Laube—I wouldn't be here if you hadn't taken me on.

My husband and children—thank you for giving me the freedom, the inspiration, and the encouragement to write novels!

To my Lord—it's all for YOU. You are my All in All.

CHAPTER ONE

hance Carter should have known this last delivery wouldn't go down without a hitch.

A monstrous thunderhead had popped up in a clear morning sky and now loomed directly in his path as if forbidding, or at least challenging, his approach to his destination—a lone airstrip in Nowhere, Montana. As an experienced pilot and courier for an airfreight company, he wasn't concerned with inclement weather as much as the troubled feeling in his chest, which he'd been trying to ignore since takeoff.

Given the cold, hard stone of unease that had settled in his gut, he'd failed miserably.

Earlier this morning, back at the FBO—fixed-based operator—the rhythm of his flight prep had seemed off. Excitement hadn't pumped through his every movement, and the usual bounce to his step hadn't accompanied him while he worked through his pre-flight checks. If that hadn't been enough, dread had replaced the anticipation that always filled him as he readied to climb into the cockpit of his Piper Cherokee 235, which he affectionately called Ole Blue.

Now, as he neared the airstrip, he shook off the apprehension and grabbed on to the assurance from years of experience and thousands of hours spent piloting.

A good, strong headwind, which was preferred for landing, buffeted the plane. He took comfort in the familiar deafening roar of the Piper breaking through his headset and droning in his ears. He wanted to focus on nothing but landing, delivering, and escaping. But this trip carried him back, and the evergreens, the winding rivers, the meadows, the crops, and the majestic mountains captivated him, reminding him of all he'd left behind.

Gripping the yoke, he sat taller and shoved beyond the melancholy.

At seven miles from his destination, he switched tanks . . .

The noisy engine sputtered and then stalled.

Nothing he didn't know how to handle. Chance would quickly remedy the situation. He trusted that forward movement and lift would propel Ole Blue along like an eagle riding in the wind long enough to give him ample time to restart the engine.

Only the engine failed to respond to his efforts. The fuel gauge indicated a fourth of a tank of fuel remained. He switched to the other tank and confirmed it was empty.

As if emphasizing his earlier presentiment, Ole Blue's propeller slowed to a stop.

Silence filled the cockpit. Moments passed before the slow cadence of his heartbeat ramped up and roared to life in his ears. He'd rather hear the engine and propeller.

The plane remained in the air, gliding on the current. But not for long. Creating a controlled descent was up to Chance and the tools at his disposal. Sweat beading at his temples, his instincts took over as he maneuvered the rudder, flaps, and ailerons, steering the plane through the air currents to maintain lift as long as possible.

Chance had to face the truth. Ole Blue wouldn't make it to the airstrip.

And those evergreens he'd admired moments before rushed at him now as the ground rose toward him, much faster than was safe.

He was going down.

Chance pressed the button on the yoke and squawked to a local frequency. "Mayday. Mayday. Mayday!" He detailed what he knew of the expected crash location, which wasn't a lot.

He got no response. Nobody monitoring the frequency today in Nowhere, Montana. Just his luck.

Between evergreen-topped mountains, Ole Blue surfed along a ravine. Not a good place to land. He hoped for a clearing. Something.

Come on, come on, come on . . .

There. Between the trees, he caught sight of a forest road and aimed for it. It would be close. The trees were dense in places. Worst case, the wheels on his fixed-gear plane would catch the treetops and flip him forward. Dead or alive, he'd be stuck in the tops.

Come on, baby, you can do this.

Palms sweating, he squeezed the yoke. Continuing the mantra in his head, he willed Ole Blue to stay in the air just a little longer. When he'd proclaimed today was his last delivery, he hadn't meant that to be a literal prophecy.

He mentally shook his fist at God. *You hear that? I didn't mean I wanted to die today. I just meant I'm done doing what I do.*

A thousand thoughts blew through his mind at once, not the least of which was that if he made it, if he survived, he'd have to file a crash report with the FAA. He was only supposed to take his flight bag from the crash site, but he'd have to make an exception this time and remove the package he was supposed to deliver.

The treetops reached up for Ole Blue, their lofty trunks and branches growing taller as if they would stretch to catch the plane's wheels. The Piper shuddered and vibrated. Chance held his breath, working the yoke until, finally, he maneuvered above the narrow road.

Lower, lower, lower . . .

The wheels touched the road, and the plane bounced hard.

Trees closed in on the narrowing road. Chance braced himself. The wingtips caught the trees. The sound of metal twisting and ripping vibrated through him as the tin can protecting him shook and rattled. The impact shattered the window and catapulted what was left of his plane, and Chance's body was flung like a rag doll despite the shoulder harness. Ole Blue slammed against a tree on the passenger side, crumpling the only door. Chance's head hit the yoke handle. Thunder ignited in his temples as pain throbbed across his chest.

But the plane had stopped. Finally . . .

Seconds ticked by. He drew in a few shuddering, painful breaths. Allowed his heart rate to slow.

Chance assessed his injuries. He could move his legs and arms. Maybe he had a few broken ribs. He touched his forehead and felt the warm, sticky fluid. Blood covered his fingertips. He stared at the tree branch protruding through the shattered window, caught a whiff of pine from the needles, and tried to grasp the near miss. He could have been skewered. That was only one of many possible fatal injuries that could have occurred. How . . . How had he survived?

He wouldn't waste time questioning Providence. For the moment, he was alive. But for how much longer?

And trusty Ole Blue was gone for good. Myriad emotions—anger, fear, grief—seized him all at once. His pulse raced again as dizziness swept over him.

He fought the darkness edging his vision.

Why had he harbored an ounce of hope that he would be able to walk away from this unscathed? He wished he hadn't broken his one rule and looked at the contents of that package.

If he wasn't able to deliver it, he was as good as dead anyway.

Elizabeth Goddard has sold over one million books and is the award-winning author of more than forty romance novels and counting, including the romantic mystery *The Camera Never Lies*—a 2011 Carol Award winner. She is a Daphne du Maurier Award for Excellence in Mystery and Suspense finalist for her Mountain Cove series—*Buried*, *Backfire*, and *Deception*—and a Carol Award finalist for *Submerged*. When she's not writing, she loves spending time with her family, traveling to find inspiration for her next book, and serving with her husband in ministry. For more information about her books, visit her website at www.ElizabethGoddard.com.

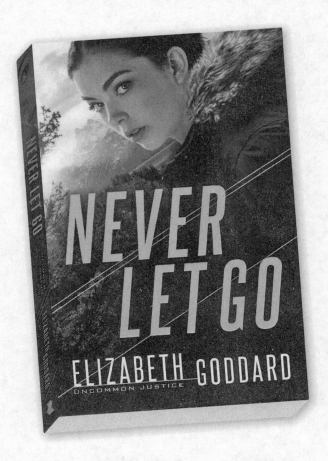

JUSTICE LIES JUST ON
THE OTHER SIDE OF FEAR

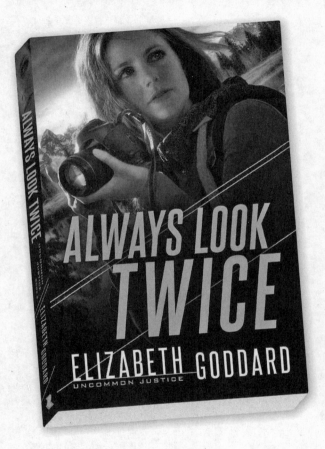

While photographing the Grand Tetons, Harper Reynolds unwittingly captures a murder on film. But when she loses the camera fleeing the scene, can she and rancher Heath McKade find the camera and solve the murder before the killer makes her his next victim?

MEET ELIZABETH

at **ElizabethGoddard.com**